THE PROTECTOR

BOOK 2

SHIFT

M.R. Merrick

The Protector - Book 2 - Shift

By M.R.Merrick

© 2012 M.R. Merrick

Paperback Edition

ISBN: 978-0-9877262-4-7

For Peyton,

I owe this entire journey to you. You reminded me what it was like to be a child: having an imagination without limits, always looking under the bed, and to never stop reaching for the stars.

Acknowledgments

There were more than a few people that took part in making this book happen. My wife Cherry, you were there to support me through the entire process. You always have been. When it came down to deadlines, you were there to pick up the slack, whether it meant putting the kids to bed, cooking dinner, mailing out books, or giving me space and time to work. You've been my anchor from the beginning, and without you, I could never have achieved any of this. For that, I am more thankful than words can say. Angeline Kace, Sarah Spann, TL Jeffcoat, and Heather Hildenbrand, you helped me turn this story into something more. Having such talented writers working beside me was an honor. Your critiques and input made Shift what it is today - a story I'm proud to share with the world. To my editor Kara Malinczak; you are amazing. Your talent and knowledge brought this story to the next level. Your ability to meet my sometimes crazy deadlines took away loads of my stress, and working with you was a pleasure. Amanda Shofner at Language Management, you put a polish on this manuscript I could have never managed on my own. With your help, I'm able to release this story with a new confidence. To Julija Lichman, thank you for all your hard work and dedication. Because of you, The Protector Series now has two incredible covers. You took my idea and made it into something that jumps off the page in ways I never imagined. You've given my story a face, and without you, this book would never be truly complete. A special thank you to Marni Mann. I am forever in your debt. You worked beside me to smooth out all the issues, you wrote the back cover copy with me, and you helped take Chase, Rayna, and the entire story exactly where it needed to go. Whenever I struggled, you were there to push me in all the right ways, and you rekindled my passion to tell this story. Without your talent as a writer and support as a friend, I'm not sure where Shift would be today. For all of that, I am grateful.

Thank you to everyone who contributed to this story and has supported me on this incredible journey. I've learned so much from each of you and in different ways, you each made this story better than it ever could've been. It thrills me to know I have so many wonderful people in my life, who love and support me as both a writer, and a person. I could never have done this without each and every one of you.

Chapter 1

My eyes tore open to the sound of screaming. The drywall rattled and Rayna's voice raged through the wall. My pulse jumped as panic set in and I leapt from my bed moving straight for the door.

I ran through the archway, pants tangling on my legs as I tried to pull them up. Marcus, Willy, and Tiki were halfway down the hall, their faces owned by fear.

Marcus reached the door before me, turned the silver handle, and pushed through. The door creaked and the smell of blood, sweat, and something else seeped from the darkness. Marcus flicked on the light and I saw what I already feared.

Rayna was on her hands and knees. Sweat ran down her face in streams, and her eyes moved to us. A deep growl that belonged to something far more ferocious snarled from her lips.

Marcus and I moved to either side of her, leaving Willy and Tiki to guard the door. This was her beast's third attempt at a shift this week. I wasn't chasing a half-naked Rayna down the street. Not again.

The hardwood floor was cold and stuck to my bare feet, and bright green cat eyes followed as I sidestepped around her. Another growl rumbled deep in her throat. A warning.

Rayna bent at the elbows and lowered herself to the ground. Her back end lifted in the air and her body moved with unnatural grace, her eyes consuming my every move. The muscles in her arms flexed as she prepared to pounce. She leaned forward, but her body bucked and twisted at an awkward angle. She collapsed to the ground and Rayna's voice cried out, but even that didn't override the sound of bones crunching.

Alien muscles moved beneath her skin as her body distorted from one angle to another. Something was pushing from the inside. A monster trying to claw its way out. Clear fluid burst as her skin split, and the hint of something primal spilled out over her arms. Her green feline gaze flashed back to me, but it wasn't the beast looking through; it was Rayna. Her eyes pleaded with me to make it stop, but we both knew I couldn't.

"Calm yourself, Rayna. You need to take control of the shift," Marcus said. His massive midnight torso was bare, revealing a smooth and muscled chest that disappeared into baggy, gray sweats. The light reflected off his shaven head, and a small patch of neatly trimmed hair grew under his lower lip. His dark brown eyes were calm but I could see the worry behind them.

Rayna whimpered and her eyes rolled back in her head, revealing nothing but thick bloodshot veins. More blood and fluid burst from her stomach, flying through the air and raining over us. Black fur pushed through the slits in her arms and stomach, and stood on edge. Veins pushed against her skin, changing from blue to black. Her vibrant, pale flesh glistened with sweat as thick, black veins creased around her eyes and spread across her face.

Rayna gasped as her fingers snapped and shifted. Her nails bled as claws tried to break through her human shell. Bones ground against one another until she screamed, and long, black talons burst through her fingertips. The beast reclaimed her eyes. I knew Rayna well enough to know when it was her looking at me. Right now, it wasn't.

Her skin stretched and rippled. The demon inside was pushing her body into another impossible position and Rayna screamed. She started panting heavily and her teeth shattered as fangs tore through her gums.

"Fight it, Rayna. You can do this," Marcus said.

Her limbs snapped and twisted, the sound alone making me wince with anticipated pain. Tears fell from Rayna's eyes as she fought the beast. She stared up at me as she tried to reclaim her body, but the monster inside was too strong.

I wanted to speak. I wanted to encourage her, but I couldn't find the words. I stepped forward and reached towards her, but with unparalleled speed, black claws tore across my arm and blood spurted from the wound. I screamed through gritted teeth and pulled my arm back, grasping it with my free hand and trying to stop the gush of blood.

Rayna stretched her back and rolled onto all fours. Her eyes flickered and the beast stared at me, pulling back its lips to reveal long fangs that took over both the top and bottom jaw. She paced from side to side and Rayna's bra strap hung on for dear life. Black pajama pants split down the sides as new muscles bulged from her legs. Dark fur and fierce claws owned her still human shaped feet, and tapped along the floor as she moved. Rayna arched her back and black fur exploded from her spine. Blood and fluid soared across the room, and made a splat as it hit Tiki, Willy, and the walls around them.

Rayna's near human hands crept onto the bed. Long, black claws ripped into the blankets as she pulled herself up. With each pull forward, feathers and cotton spilled into the air, talons tearing into the bedding with ease.

I tried to step back, but I hit the wall, unable to move as the beast closed in.

"Be calm, Chase. The beast can smell your fear. It will only make it more aggressive," Marcus said.

"Really? Thanks for the update," I said sarcastically. Blood rolled off my wrist in thick streams and a burning sensation covered my arm. I closed my eyes, reached inside, and pulled the magic up from that place in my soul.

The elemental power rose to the surface in a gentle wash. I imagined a cool rain falling over me, drops of water that would wash away the pain rushing through my arm. I pictured the bleeding coming to a stop and new skin pulling itself over the wounds.

I used that same power to help push away my fear. The water battled the storm of emotions roaring through me and brought with it the calm. Fear faded beneath the imagery of cold drops against my skin, and my muscles relaxed. My breathing steadied and my eyelids lifted, only to gaze into the green cat eyes before me. Rayna was on the edge of the bed and only an arm's length away.

The skin of my arm pulled itself shut and the final drop of blood hit the floor. My water element closed the wounds, but I didn't have enough control to pull it back and it spilled out into the room.

"Chase..." Marcus started, but it was too late.

My element emanated off of me, pushing against the monster like an invisible hand. The magic rolled over Rayna's skin and moved through the beast's fur, reaching down into her soul.

Rayna regained her composure as the magic coaxed the monster back, allowing her to regain control of her body. The beast in her eyes faded and I had a moment's hope, but in a jerk of awkward movements, her body shuddered and she was gone.

Bones crunched and Rayna's arms snapped, reversing which way they bent. She tumbled off the bed and clawed at the floor near my feet. Muscles flexed and strained, scarring the hardwood. Splinters slid underneath her nails, causing her fingers to bleed.

"Please..." Rayna gasped. She slurred her words as fangs jutted from red gums raw with pain. She winced in agony and her eyes pleaded, letting a single tear trickle down her cheek.

"How do we stop it, Marcus?"

Marcus shook his head. "We can't. *She* has to fight it."

"We have to do something. It's killing her."

"This is the only way I know..."

I looked at Tiki and worry owned his face. White, triangular pupils expanded over solid, orange eyes, and he flinched at the sound of Rayna's bones grinding together. His frame filled the doorway, muscles flexing beneath the caramel flesh of his shirtless body. Messy, black hair hung in his eyes and he continually brushed it away.

Willy's face was pale for an instant, quickly changing to match the bright red paint on Rayna's walls. His chameleon skin flickered back and forth between colors as panic filled his eyes. Blood and clear fluid dripped from his face, but he didn't seem to notice. He was frozen in fear, watching his friend's body break

4

and change before him. This was the first shift Willy had been here for. I didn't think he was quite ready for it.

Frustration won me over and I dropped to the floor, hoping the claws didn't strike me again. I laid my hands over Rayna's body and called my magic back.

"Chase, don't. You could do more damage than good," Marcus said.

I shot dark blue eyes to Marcus. "You know as well as I do, nothing I can do is worse than this, so back off!" I didn't expect for it to come across so harsh, but I didn't have time to worry about his feelings. I wasn't about to lose someone else.

The invisible hand inside me wrapped around the cool rush of my element and tugged it back to the surface. I pulled the wash of water from my soul and let it fill my body. The magic shuddered and the liquid moved under my skin as power prickled through me, making the hairs on the back of my neck stand on end.

"Chase, don't," Marcus said.

"I'm trying!" I yelled, quickly reeling my anger back and letting the element calm me. "It's a lot more than any of us have done for her so far."

Water was a healing and calming element, but it could be as deadly as any other. Marcus was right to be worried; my control was weak at best, but I couldn't watch this. Not again.

Magic ran up my body, into my shoulders, and down my arms in a wave of power. My fingertips tingled as it left me and flowed into Rayna's body.

I focused on calming Rayna. I didn't want to hurt her, and I wasn't sure healing the wounds would help. I focused my energy and hoped if I put enough power into sedating the beast, Rayna could regain control.

The moment my magic filled her, Rayna's earth element pushed back against me, trying to intertwine with mine. It was Rayna's way of reaching out to me.

Our elements met and wrapped themselves in each other, coursing from her body to mine in a circuit of power. Our bodies were one in that moment, our elements just an extension of ourselves. My magic moved through her, dancing beneath her skin as it fed off her power.

I imagined a small creek moving over stones, wearing the rough edges down until they were smooth. That gentle flow of water would push the beast back and carry Rayna to shore.

The beast retreated as the magic splashed through. Feeling the monster's resistance, I forced it back, letting the energy thrust it into a corner until it surrendered. I waited until I was sure it was gone before I turned my focus to her injuries.

I pictured Rayna's bones reforming, the claws and fangs receding, and the cool trickle of water filling her senses to mask the pain.

Rayna gasped as the cold element rushed into her body. She tensed at first, unnatural muscles flexing beneath her flesh, before she collapsed in a wave of exhaustion. She hit the floor and I pushed harder. I had kept the beast back for the moment, but now I needed to make sure it stayed away, at least for tonight.

Her breathing slowed and Rayna's eyes glossed over. Her bones cracked and shifted back into place, and soft cries whispered through her lips. Long talons slid back beneath her pale skin, and the fangs withdrew into her gums. The tears that filled her eyes leaked down the sides of her face. They merged with the blood that covered her skin and caused a pink liquid to disappear into her hair. The red highlights in her black hair stuck to her face, and the moonlight that shone through the windows reflected off her body, revealing a layer of sweat.

It took all I had to pull the magic back. It receded slowly and I tucked it away inside of me. Rayna stared up from the torn hardwood floor. Her tearing eyes showed the pain she'd been in. I brought my hand to her forehead and ran it down her cheek, trying to reassure her she was safe. She released a breath and her eyes fluttered closed.

Her skin was cool to the touch, which was good. When her body tried to shift, her temperature spiked to incredible heights. Heights the human body shouldn't have been able to withstand, but Rayna wasn't human. She was a demon and a hunter. A witch, yet…something more. The temperature drop meant she'd beat the change this time, but I was more concerned about next time.

I pulled my hand away and her eyes didn't open. Her chest rose and fell with deep breaths, her body giving into its demand for rest. I slipped one arm under her neck and the other under her legs, scooping her into my arms. Her body fell limp as I lifted her from the damaged floor, blood and sweat still dripping from her skin.

I moved past the others. Marcus looked sad. Rayna was practically his daughter and watching her go through this was painful for all of us, but I think it struck another chord with him.

I walked to the only spare bedroom we had left. Willy and Tiki were always here now and we were quickly running out of rooms. I laid Rayna in the bed as gently as I could and pulled the covers up over her. Her clothes were in tattered shreds and she was covered in blood and goo, but she finally looked at peace.

Nobody had gotten much sleep the last three nights, but it had been the hardest on Rayna. None of us knew much about shifters, except how to kill them. After watching what she was going though, I think we'd all gathered a new respect and a desire to learn more.

I closed the door and saw the last glimpse of Tiki before he slipped into his room. For reasons I didn't understand, Tiki had sworn an oath to me. He guided me through Drakar, and without him, I would never have been able to save Rayna. I might not have understood his loyalty, but I was grateful for it.

Willy had disappeared. For a demon, he didn't have much of a stomach for stuff like this, but then again, Willy wasn't like most demons.

Marcus stood in the hallway, his dark brown eyes unmoving, and as usual I couldn't read his expression.

My eyes fell to the floor. "Look, I'm sorry I—"

Marcus' hand came up. "What you did in there was quick thinking."

I looked up in surprise.

"This was the worst change she's ever gone through." Marcus ran a large hand over his cleanly shaven head. "She's never shifted that far before. You might've just saved her life."

I looked back to the floor and guilt tugged at me. I shouldn't have spoken to him like I did, but I'd lost my temper. Again. That was something that happened more often lately.

"Are you sure she can't shift? It looked like she was going all the way this time."

"I was...I'm not so sure anymore. For now, as always, we're treating this like she's a hunter and the shift will kill her. Whether or not that's the case, I don't know, but we don't have the liberty of experimenting."

"I'm not suggesting we risk her life and see what happens. I'm saying maybe we should look into it. No hunter could've made it that far into the change. They'd be dead. Something's different here."

Marcus sighed. "I know...I'll look into it." He turned and walked down the hall. His massive black form disappeared into the shadows and the white door closed, leaving the latch to click into place.

The cold hardwood felt strange against my feet as silence engulfed the condo. The moon outside shone faintly and shadows wrapped themselves around me. I went to my bedroom and flicked on the lamp.

This room was nicer than my previous one. The wood floors glistened and the walls were a warm mocha color. The dark brown dresser was clean, smooth wood. Not scarred and faded like my old one. My bed was a mattress, on a box spring, on a frame. Not a weathered sponge on a stained carpet. I even had a night table with a lamp. Compared to my old room, I might as well be at the Hilton.

I fell on the bed and stared up at the perfect ceiling. It was missing the cracks and nicotine stains of the apartment, and I still hadn't gotten used to it.

The silence followed and I felt its presence linger against me. It was nights like these that I missed my neighbors. They swore, they screamed, and they smashed things against the walls, but after three years it had become my lullaby. I'd give anything to have that apartment back, and the life that belonged there. The life I had with Mom.

I opened up the wooden case that sat on my nightstand and stared at the two daggers inside. Beneath the blades lay the folded up note that came with them, and just looking at the polished silver made me sad. It was the last gift and the last note my mother would ever give me.

Chills shuddered through me at the thought of her and goose bumps rode up my body. Rai fluttered in through the door and found her way to my shoulder. She puffed out her chest and white feathers ruffled themselves. The gold that lined her spine and tail sparkled under the lamp, and lightning crackled in her eyes. Rai stretched and her white feathers were soft as she moved both pairs of wings against my face.

"Hey girl," I said.

Rai tweeted softly in my ear, nipping at it before flying to the open cage on the dresser.

I lay back down, and as my eyelids fell, I could see Mom's face. There she was, smiling at me. Warm hazel eyes swallowed me and instantly I felt better. Soft brown hair fluttered in front of her face, bending to the will of the wind that moved around us, and still she smiled.

It warmed me from the inside out and tears welled beneath my eyelids, but I didn't dare open them. I wouldn't lose this image just to release the tears that fought to be free. But as quickly as it came, Mom's expression changed, and the warmth was stolen from me.

The gentle smile that held me so often disappeared, and fear took over. Her skin turned a sickly green, and a bright orange light reflected off her eyes before flames engulfed her.

My eyes shot open and I jerked myself upwards. The tears I desperately fought to keep back broke free and fell over my face. Her voice rang in my ears, screaming my name and begging for me not to leave her.

I shook my head to escape the sound and it shattered around me.

Silence rushed back into the room and I took a deep breath, trying to clear my head. That image sent waves of panic and fear through my body, jolting awake any part of me that wanted to sleep. I wasn't going back to bed. Not tonight.

Chapter 2

"I'm no–, not, coming!" Willy stammered.

"This isn't up for debate. The elders said we all have to be there, so we're all going," I said.

"Well, you can *all go* without me. I've got no–, nothing to say to them."

"Willy, you don't understand what the Circle is or what the elders are capable of–"

"And I don't care. I do–, don't want to go." Willy crossed his arms, trying to look defiant.

"I don't care what you want or don't want. Having to meet with the elders is bad enough. I'm not going to have your death on my conscience because I let you stay home. This isn't a discussion. Now go upstairs and get ready."

"But–"

"Now!" I commanded.

Willy's face paled. He cowered down from his want-to-be-defiant stance and looked hurt. I felt guilty for yelling at him, but I pushed it away beneath all the other emotions I didn't have time for. I didn't need to feel guilty right now and Willy would thank me later, when he was alive.

I looked out the wall of windows that lined the condo. The sun was setting earlier as the seasons changed. It was seven o'clock and the sun was gone. Darkness beat down on the city, but the lights and traffic made it look very much alive.

Life had changed so much in the past few weeks. I'd lost my mom. I was living with people I hardly knew, and I no longer had a job. I should've known I couldn't miss that many days without repercussions. I'd tried to get another, but Marcus had stressed that it was for the best. I needed to lie low until we knew what had become of Riley. My father. The man I was trying to stop from raising a demon god. The man who had killed my mother.

The strangest adjustment of all was the lack of Underworld attacks. Since we'd gotten back from Drakar, there hadn't been any. I'd never gone more than a few days, let alone weeks, without a demon coming after me. It should've been comforting, but all it did was make me nervous.

I flicked the TV on, stretched, and flopped onto the couch. I tried to fight it as a yawn crept up on me, but I was unsuccessful. It was early and last night's lack of sleep was already getting to me. My eyelids were starting to get heavy, but the sound of wings and footsteps snapped them back awake.

Rayna came down the stairs with Rai not far behind her.

Two sets of white wings flapped rapidly, landing on the iron railing that separated the third floor library from the main floor living room. Her golden feathers gleamed as flickers of light flashed in her eyes.

"Hey!" Rayna stepped into the living room with an unusual bounce in her step. She had showered away the filth, and her skin was glowing. You'd never guess that less than twenty-four hours ago she'd nearly turned into a werecat.

A yellow halter top hugged her small frame and dark blue jeans hung low on her hips, covering long, toned legs. Her hair hung down over her shoulders, red strands mingling with the black, decorating the thick locks.

"Hey..." I said, clicking the television off. "Feeling better?"

"I'm starving, but otherwise, great."

"Well you'd better hurry. We're leaving soon."

"Leaving..." Rayna brought a hand up to her forehead. "We have a meeting at the Circle tonight. I totally forgot."

"Are you going to be up for it?"

Rayna pulled out a huge sandwich from the refrigerator and took a bite. "Well, I don't want to go explain myself to a bunch of old guys who think they're better than me, but yeah, I'll be fine. Why?" she asked, watching me out of the corner of her eye.

"I don't know, maybe because you nearly became a giant cat last night?"

"It's just like before. It's not a big deal, especially now that we know how to handle it."

"Rayna, it's far from fine, and from where I was standing, it wasn't like before. That monster inside you keeps trying to rip itself out, and last night was the worst. How do you figure we know how to *handle it*?"

Rayna winced as I said *monster*, and I realized I was almost yelling. I hadn't meant to get angry, but how could she act like this was no big deal?

Rayna closed her eyes and took a breath. "Your element stopped the beast in its tracks last night. If it happens again, we know that works."

"For all we know it was a fluke. The beast inside you is getting stronger each time. We need to find a way to subdue it. Permanently."

"The full moon has passed. We don't even have to worry about it for another month."

"Well, I'm worried now. I'm not going to lose..." I cut myself off. "We're not waiting 'til next time. We need to figure this out before it happens again, or *next time* you might not be so lucky."

"Will you relax? Nothing is going to happen to me. Besides, as long as you stick around, we have nothing to worry about. Wait...you're not planning on leaving are you?" Rayna smirked.

"Really, you're joking about this? With everything that's happened during the past few weeks, we need to find out how to fix this, not deal with it."

Rayna's smile faded. "Look, I know it's been hard with everything that's...happened. With Riley still alive—"

"We don't know that for sure," I snapped.

"All I'm saying is we've had a lot going on. If you need someone...you know...if you need to talk..."

"You too? Really?" I asked. I wasn't ready to talk about *it* yet. I wasn't sure I'd ever be.

"Me too, what? What are you talking about?"

"Forget it."

Silence filled the air around us and I thanked the gods when the buzzer rang.

"I'll get it," I said.

I moved to the stainless steel box in the wall and pushed the talk button down. "Hello?"

"If you expect me to join you on this ridiculous escapade, I suggest you let me in." Vincent's voice rattled through the intercom carrying an accent I recognized, but couldn't quite place.

I pressed the buzzer and the thought of him being near me sent chills down my spine. What was he even doing here? Before I could answer my own thought, Vincent's fingers tapped along the door in an annoying, chipper melody.

I grabbed the silver handle and pulled the giant oak slab towards me. Vincent's golden orbs looked up at me and an amused expression played at his lips. Black hair was styled in perfect spikes, decorating his head and contrasting the pale skin that covered his body. His shirt was a shiny yellow silk, mostly unbuttoned and revealing a smooth chest. His shirt matched his shoes in an odd collaboration, and black pants fit snug against his legs.

"Could you have left me out there much longer?" Vincent pushed past me. This was one of those moments where I wished vampires actually had to be *invited* in. "Gods know what kind of monsters are running amok. This town is full of them, you know." Vincent walked into the room and twirled around in an overdramatic maneuver. The smile that accompanied his words managed to be both suave and unsettling.

"You don't say," I replied, closing the door.

The awkward silence I thought I'd avoided settled over us. Vincent's golden gaze flickered between Rayna and me, his smile changing to one of pure satisfaction. "Have I interrupted?"

"No," I said.

Vincent's hand came to his mouth, idly tapping a finger over his lips. "A lover's quarrel perhaps?"

"Who's a quarrel?" Willy asked, jumping down the last step with Tiki behind him.

Willy's flannel shirt was missing buttons, flaring out over acid washed jeans with a hole in the knee. The beard he was still trying to grow stuck out in awkward patches on his chin, never growing past stubble.

"Wonderful, the *help* is here." Vincent rolled his eyes.

Willy jumped back into Tiki, nearly knocking them both down. He regained his balance and stumbled against the wall, his skin turning a dark brown to match the paint.

"Wha–, wha–, what's he doing here?" His stutter thickened as his brown eyes found Vincent.

"He's coming to the meeting. I already told you that."

"Yeah, we–, well, I thought he'd me–, meet us there. You know, like you do at meetings."

I shook my head. "Tiki, I told you, you have to wear clothes today."

Tiki stood in the same rags he'd come here in. Baggy white pants were stained with dirt and hung from his waist with a frayed rope. His shirt was missing, revealing smooth caramel skin that covered an overly muscular body. His eyes were solid orange with the exception of large, white triangular pupils in the center, and the look on his face was not happy.

"Chase Williams, I do not like the clothing here. It is tight and uncomfortable. Especially when it bunches around my–"

"Okay, that's more than I need to hear. Come on, we'll try to find you something...less restricting," Rayna said, leading Tiki upstairs.

"My, you do like to associate yourself with pathetic creatures, my dear hunter," Vincent said.

The door opened before I could respond and the large body of Marcus walked in. Marcus' dark gaze fell over the room, and he frowned when he saw Vincent. "I thought you were going to meet us there."

"See?" Willy chipped in.

"Please. You think I'd go there alone? The only reason I'm even coming is to appease your associates. My family doesn't need any more unwanted attention from *your* kind."

"I told you, the Circle has sworn an oath of safe passage for all of you tonight," Marcus said.

Vincent laughed. "I've not survived five centuries by believing in the oaths of hunters. I'll come with you, but you will see to it that the Circle keeps their word, or my family and I will retaliate. Although we'd prefer to avoid the attention, if provoked, we will respond with a force you hunters can't imagine." Vincent's voice was calm, but his eyes showed how serious he was.

"Why must you make everything difficult?" Marcus asked.

Vincent shrugged. "You call it difficult, I call it self-preservation."

"A hunter's oath is his bond. How can you even suggest otherwise?" Marcus asked. The frustration was clear in his voice, and it caught me off guard. Marcus never showed emotion.

"Anyone who dedicates their existence to hunting my kind is far from trustworthy," Vincent said. "Why do we even have to attend this meeting? I don't know about you, but I don't owe the Circle. If anything, they owe *me* for the lives they've stolen from my family."

"They want to discuss Riley. He has so far been successful in evading the Circle. Although I would prefer not to share any information until we know who all is involved, it is best not to oppose the elders."

"Says the rogue hunter." Vincent smirked. "Either way, if you want me to go, I'm coming with you."

"Fine," Marcus said. "Chase, where is everyone?"

"We're here," Rayna came down the steps. "But we really need to take him shopping."

Tiki stepped into the kitchen and looked as uncomfortable as I'd ever seen him. Long brown dress pants fit his waist loosely, and a tight white t-shirt stretched over his body. Tiki wasn't a large man, but he was bigger than me, and his body was as fit as any I'd ever seen. I supposed living in a demonic dimension as an unwanted half-demon would keep you in excellent shape, but between Marcus, Willy, and me, it wasn't easy to find clothes that fit him.

"I'm ready," Tiki said through gritted teeth.

"Good," Marcus said. "Rayna, how are–"

"I'm great." Rayna cut him off. She stepped into her knee high boots, pulled them up the last few inches, and started walking out the door. "Let's go before we're late."

****

The Circle's facility was a few miles outside of town. I rode in the front, but with Vincent, it made for a cramped ride in Marcus' car. I made it until the highway before I couldn't take the bickering anymore.

"Will you guys shut up? We're going to meet with elders. Do you get what that means? We need a united front, not a group of babies."

"Well, it would be easier if we weren't all cramped in this tiny car. You know, *my* people could have escorted us and we would have ridden with class," Vincent replied.

I turned around and let my blue eyes pierce through him. "First, the only reason you're cramped in the back is because you were too scared to meet us there. Second, I wouldn't trust you or your people, to escort us anywhere. So deal with it, or get out and walk."

I waited for Vincent's anger, but he just smiled, which only infuriated me even more. "My, a little on edge, are we?"

"I'm about to be interrogated by the people who exiled and disowned me based on the advice of my father. Forgive me if I seem *on edge.*"

"I'd think you'd be happy to return. After all, that's where all your brooding comes from, doesn't it? Being exiled and not feeling like you have a place to belong? Isn't that confusion why you associate yourself with all these...*things*?" Vincent looked to Willy.

I started to reach back in my seat, but Marcus' arm shot out and stopped me. "Enough," he said. "No more bickering. The elders asked us to come, but make no mistake, it was merely out of common pleasantries. Had we refused, they would have collected us and forced the meeting."

17

"Are you suggesting we have no choice but to attend?" Vincent asked.

"You don't understand the Circle. You only understand what you've seen. The Circle began millennia ago, when—"

"We all know how it started and how Rayna was the chosen one born of both worlds to open the portal and raise Ithreal. Blah, blah, blah. Thank you for the history lesson, Marcus. I know how my own kind came to be. Perhaps you can share something we don't know?"

Marcus eyed Vincent in the mirror and shook his head. "The council has full control over everything the Circle does. They know more than anyone, and they filter everything a hunter knows to match their will. The council stated that Riley disappeared weeks before the…situation, but that doesn't mean they're not involved. Riley isn't capable of orchestrating everything unbeknownst to the elders, which means we have a bigger problem."

"And what might that be?" Vincent sighed.

"It means Riley has an air or earth elemental on the inside. And a powerful one at that," I said.

"Wh—, why those elements?" Willy asked.

"My god you should have that…condition looked at. Just hearing your voice makes me want to rip off my own ears…or your throat." Vincent's tone matched the hungry look on his face.

Willy sunk as low in the chair as possible. His pale skin darkened to match the black leather.

"Hey!" Rayna thrust an elbow into Vincent's side. "Be nice."

"Enough," Marcus said. "One power that can develop from those elements is psychic ability. If an elder were powerful enough—which they are—they could make it possible for Riley to do whatever he wanted. Had anyone on the council become aware of Riley's plans, a strong enough air or earth elemental could change another elder's thoughts…even their memories."

"I'd like to meet a hunter capable of controlling a demon's mind." Vincent laughed and the look that filled his eyes was far too curious.

"Don't do anything stupid tonight," I said, turning to face Vincent. "It's bad enough we have to go there at all. Worse we have to be there with *you*. I'm not babysitting tonight, so keep yourself in check."

"Watch your tone with me, hunter. If I remember correctly, you weren't much of a match against me." Vincent's eyes lit up and devoured me, daring me to push him.

"That's enough," Marcus said.

"And if I *remember correctly*, you're flammable." I didn't unleash the fire, but I let it rise and surge against him in an ember of power.

"Don't threaten me with your parlor tricks. I've survived your kind too long to fear a child with a match."

"Enough," Marcus said again.

"Stop the car and let him out. He's going to get us all killed. He's not coming."

"Fine by me," Vincent said, and the smug look on his face made my blood boil.

"I said enough!" Marcus shouted, and his element exploded.

The air was sucked from the car, and there was nothing but silence. I couldn't speak, and my chest tightened with fear. I could hear the squeak of leather as everyone struggled and shifted in their seats. I reached out and grabbed Marcus' shoulder.

His eyes were a solid white as his magic poured out. He was breathing heavily and a look I'd never seen owned his features. I squeezed his shoulder, tightening my grip to gain his attention, and as quick as it came, the power was gone.

"What the hell's your problem?" I asked, panting between each word.

"When I say enough, it means enough." The dark brown color seeped back into Marcus' eyes. He took a few breaths and turned to face me. "Chase, you of all people know what we're up against. The rest of you need to understand how serious this is, too. The elders are the strongest and the most experienced of the hunters. They have access to books, rituals, and magic that most of you couldn't dream of. To take this in any way but serious is foolish." His thick, dark lips moved quickly and enunciated each word with force. Marcus took another deep breath and recomposed himself, his calm expression reclaiming his face.

"Do keep yourself under control. Not all of them hold the gift of immortality quite like I." Vincent looked annoyed, rubbing at his throat.

Vincent was a vampire, but he wasn't exactly dead. Vampires drank blood to keep their body alive, and besides the demon inside them, functioned just as any human. But when they slept, their life faded. Their bodies died, decayed, and turned to rotting corpses until their next awakening, when they were reformed anew.

Nobody spoke, and an awkward silence fell over us. I rested my head against the chair and stared out the window. The shadows moved and stood still all at once. In that moment, I wished I could disappear into them and forget this meeting, forget Riley, the Dark Brothers, and everything that had happened, but I couldn't.

I knew the elders wanted to know about the portal. Now that it was open, any pureblood demon from the other dimensions had access to Earth, but I wondered how they knew we had anything to do with it. There was something more to their motives, and the thought of what it might be made my stomach clench. There were those in the Circle that could've felt the shift in power when the wall between our dimension and the others collapsed, but that didn't explain how they knew I was involved, or that Marcus was alive. Maybe one of the rogue hunters collaborated with the Circle, or one of the elders had a vision. Either way, we couldn't hide anymore.

Marcus took the exit ramp off the freeway and turned down a secondary road. The pavement disappeared beneath us and gravel shot up around the vehicle. Dust swallowed the car and the headlights' reflection off of it was bright. My stomach tightened again and sweat gathered on my palms. We were getting close to the Circle.

A chill tingled down my spine. I closed my eyes and tried using my water element to calm myself, but between the rough road and my nerves, I couldn't stay focused. Silence filled the car and the shadows outside were closing in. I silently begged them to take me away. To be able to vanish in that moment would suit my needs perfectly.

The darkness seemed to shift and move as we drove, and as a chill moved through me again, I narrowed my gaze on the shadows outside. I thought I could see a figure moving through the shadows alongside the car, but it was too dark to make anything out.

Marcus slowed the car and it bumped onto a new section of paved road. I did a double take as the light reflected off a strange figure. The brief glare of cat eyes flickered through the darkness. They flashed again into the eyes of a snake, and the chill shot through me again. "Did you see that?" I asked.

"See what?" Marcus asked.

I searched the edge of the road, but there were only shadows and forest. "Nothing..." I whispered, shaking my head.

We turned down the tree lined driveway, the scent of my past coming through the vents. As the dust settled, street lamps lit our way, skimming through the vehicle one by one until we reached the bright spotlights that covered every inch of the property.

The building we approached towered above us, and I could feel the glamour pouring off of it. It was a large warehouse made of worn metal siding and dirt stained windows. Bright lights sat above the garage's overhead doors, and spotlights swept the grounds from side to side.

I pulled my magic up from within, fighting to keep my concentration as the muscles in my stomach pulled and released, tightening with each contraction. As the glamour fell around it, the facility's true form came into view.

Dark red bricks built the building from the ground up until tinted glass windows took over the last three floors. The massive garage doors were clean white panels, and I knew what hid behind them: assault vehicles, buses, sports cars, SUVs, and bikes. They had a vehicle for every possible need.

Bright flood lights covered the exterior of the building, revealing the clean, landscaped grounds, and all the doors were windowless steel, laced with silver.

Large trees, well-manicured bushes, and flowers sprouted from the earth. Dirt walking paths led into the forests, taking you to training areas, greenhouses, and herb gardens. Seeing the outside of the compound brought back memories of a life that was no longer mine.

Marcus slowed the vehicle and we coasted beneath the lights lining the driveway. Only half the lights were turned on, confirming the Circle planned to let the demons in safely. Had they all been on, Vincent wouldn't have been able to get out of the car without catching fire. Wherever there was a street lamp, a floodlight, or anything electrical, UV lights sat above them, bright enough to fry a vampire to dust in seconds.

The car gave a soft jerk as it came to a stop. Marcus shifted into park and turned the keys. As the engine died, the silence that pushed against us was thick. I wiped my palms on my pants and took a breath. "Here we go," I whispered to myself.

Everyone opened their doors at once and stepped out. The ground beneath my shoes felt both foreign and familiar. Memories of my childhood flooded back. The sound and smell of the woods, the sight of the building, even the paths that led into the forest brought back memories. This was the place I once called home.

One of the large bay doors creaked as its motor roared to life and pulled the door upward. Dim light filled the garage and we all stood waiting. As the last few panels of the door folded into the building, a man came out dressed in a standard hunter's uniform.

Black clothing covered almost all of him: pants, a long sleeve shirt, combat boots, and gloves. His lightly tanned skin shone over his face as the only exposed skin on his body. He had a medium build and walked with arrogance only a hunter could manage.

"Welcome," he said, his masculine voice firm and confident. Dark brown sideburns ran down his face and his thick brown hair was styled neatly. He had large, round eyes staring with a hazel glare that looked angry under thick, unkempt eyebrows.

Nobody responded. We all stood near our respective car doors waiting, and I silently hoped for a quick escape.

"I'm Jameson. The council has asked me to escort you. If you'll please follow me, I'll take you to them."

I watched him carefully as he turned and started walking back towards the building. Marcus was the first to follow and we all fell in stride behind him.

The air was warm for October, and the smell of the forest was thick and cleansing. The bark that hung on the trees gave off a cedar aroma that moved with the cool breeze. Multicolored leaves tumbled across the ground, and the glisten of forming dew danced under the moonlight. I took it all in and it helped calm my nerves, if only for a moment.

Four hunters walked out of the open garage and my stomach tensed again. They stared as they walked past us, all of them wearing the same black attire as Jameson. The hunters split into pairs, taking separate paths into the forest. I knew they were walking the grounds, but I couldn't help but watch over my shoulder. I was expecting a fight tonight. Whether physical, magical, or mental, I didn't think this would end well.

Jameson led us through the garage and as I remembered, it was full of vehicles. The walls were lined with weapons: swords, knives, shields, and heavy artillery. The back of the garage had a caged off area full of guns, bulletproof vests, and ammo. That was new to me. I'd never seen a hunter use a gun. They weren't very effective when it came to the Underworld.

We came to a stop in front of two steel elevator doors and Jameson pushed the button. It wasn't a standard elevator you'd see in a mall or office building. It was longer and wider, meant for industrial use. As a hunter, you never knew what you might have to fit in one.

Jameson pushed the number four on the panel and the steel doors closed. The elevator jerked as it started upwards and the silence from the car seemed to be following us.

As the elevator slowed and jolted, the doors slid open again. Jameson slipped to the front of the pack and led us down the hallway. The calming smells of the forest were gone, and the sweat on my palms thickened. Stale air filled the hallway and flashes of my fifteenth birthday swallowed me.

I could feel the rough hands of the two hunters that had dragged me kicking and screaming down this hall. The fear that had raced through me was like a freight train driving through my veins. All I could do was wonder what was going to happen. Why didn't I get an element?

"Are you okay?" Rayna asked.

"I'm fine." I took a deep breath and wiped my hands on the back of my pants. I didn't meet her gaze, but I could feel Rayna's eyes staring at me. The soft skin of her fingers reached out and slid down my arm. A wave of goose bumps followed her touch and a chill shuddered through me.

"Now you two, save it for the honeymoon." I could hear the smile playing on Vincent's lips.

I pulled away from Rayna and my pulse jumped as Jameson reached for the handles on two large, wooden doors. He turned the brass levers and the doors gave a heavy sigh as he pushed inwards.

As the room was revealed, the memories came rushing back. A room full of hunters had watched the council, and I could see my mom standing at one of the chairs, yelling at the elders. A younger form of me collapsed to the floor as they had announced my exile. I remembered Riley standing in the middle of the room, a smug grin on his face. The head elder had banged his gavel as the room broke out in whispers, and Riley's cold blue eyes had met mine.

I stepped back and shook my head before the vision vanished, but my hands were already shaking. The piercing gaze of Riley, even in memory, was enough to crawl under my skin.

"Come now, hunter, don't tell me you can kill demons and you can't face your tiresome past," Vincent said.

His hands pushed me forward with restrained violence and I stumbled into the room. Anger flooded into me and I turned in stride. I grabbed Vincent's shirt and pulled him towards me, letting my blue eyes look down into his.

"Careful, hunter. We don't need you losing control and sending us all up in flames." He wrapped his cold pale hands around mine and broke my grip on his shirt. "There we are. Good boy. That was just what you needed." He let his shoulder hit me as he walked past.

Fresh anger coursed through my veins. I swallowed what fear lingered inside me and turned to face the room. Anger propelled me forward and with each step, it pulsed.

There was a large bench at the far end that overlooked the room, but instead of one, there were five tall chairs sitting behind it. It was higher than everything else in the room, letting the elders look down upon us. Rows of chairs lined each side like a courtroom, leaving a space between them as an aisle. Two long tables sat in front that looked up to the elder's bench, where the *defendants* would take their place.

Jameson escorted us to the tables and we each picked our spots. Rayna, Willy, and I sat at one table, with Marcus, Vincent, and Tiki at the other. I looked up at the elder's bench and took in each of their faces. Although more weathered than I remembered, they all looked the same.

Lawrence Blackwell was the head elder. He sat in the middle of the bench, his chair raised higher than the rest. His hair was combed over to one side and the black had grayed, giving it a salt and pepper look. His matching mustache was thick and trimmed neatly above thin lips, and though his face was wrinkling, he still looked youthful. His pale gray eyes were serious and watched us over small wire rimmed glasses.

Once we'd settled in our chairs, Jameson bowed to the council. Blackwell nodded and waved him away without a word. As the doors latched behind him, the sound echoed through the room, signaling the meeting had begun, and reassuring me that I wasn't ready for it.

Chapter 3

Laurence Blackwell sat on his lofty perch, welcoming everyone into the room and introducing the council. On his right were Tom Bradmoore and Riddley Peterson, with George Carlyle and Jeremiah Clay on his left. They all looked exactly as I remembered.

When he'd finished, his eyes moved over each of our faces. Besides Marcus and me, I knew he didn't recognize anyone, and he expected an introduction in return.

Marcus nodded and stood from his chair. "Here we have—"

"Please state *your* name first...for the record," Blackwell interrupted. Marcus' eyes met Blackwell's and they stared at each other for a long moment. "For procedure's sake...of course," Blackwell added.

Marcus cleared his throat, and for a moment, I thought I saw anger flash in his eyes. "Of course. I am Marcus Starkraven."

The elders rustled in their seats, with the exception of Blackwell, who stood strong and motionless. He nodded and began writing something down.

"Next," Blackwell said.

"I am Tiki-mi-char-ni-kato of the Suriattas Clan." Tiki bowed softly and sat back down.

"Well, that's a mouthful, isn't it? And you are not from...here?"

"No. I am born of the Lavinos dimension."

"And where is this dimension?"

Tiki looked at him strangely. Confusion washed over his face and he leaned forward. "Lavinos...it is where I am from..."

"Okay...Moving on then. And you are?" Blackwell eyed Vincent over the top of his glasses.

Nerves clenched in my stomach as Vincent stood. I had warned Vincent to behave, but for that reason alone he might act out to spite me.

"I am Vincent Taryk, of the Taryk family," he said.

Blackwell didn't hesitate and moved his gaze to Willy. I felt a tension leave my shoulders the moment Willy's stutter hit my ears.

"I–, I'm Willy Morrow." Beads of sweat dripped from his brow and his skin faded in and out from its natural white to the dirty brown of the chair.

The elders watched him a moment before turning and discussing amongst themselves. They whispered briefly before all their eyes were on Rayna.

"And the female demon?" Blackwell asked.

Rayna's feline eyes lit up. She stood and leaned over the desk. "*The female demon* is Rayna Lansing. I'm also half hunter. You probably don't remember, but you murdered my mother." Her words were quick and sharp.

She caught me off guard and I instantly felt horrible. I'd spent so much time worrying about her shifting and my own fears of having to face the council that I hadn't thought about what this might be like for her. She stood in front of the very people who had ordered her mother's death.

The other elders passed whispers back and forth, but Blackwell remained calm and watched her ferocity. "Yes, yes of course," he said, waving her away and scribbling in his notebook.

Rayna's knuckles turned white as she gripped the edge of the table, and she remained standing. Blackwell finished his scribbling and looked back to Rayna.

"And lastly," he said, turning to me.

"Come on Blackwell, you know who I am," I said.

"Please, you of all people know how important procedure is," he said, turning his gaze back to Rayna. "And you, young lady, can sit down."

"No," Rayna snapped.

"Excuse me?"

"I said no. I didn't realize you were deaf too. I thought you were just heartless killers."

Blackwell took his glasses off and set them down. "Young lady, you will show respect in—"

"Respect?" Power flashed through the room as Rayna's element moved around her. "Don't talk to me about respect you—" Rayna cut Blackwell off, but before she could finish, Marcus was there. His dark hands gripped her wrist and his lips moved quickly against her ear.

Anger filled Rayna's eyes and her magic emanated off her skin.

"May we proceed?" Blackwell tapped his pencil against the desk.

Marcus said a few final words before stepping back, and Rayna turned her angry gaze to look at him. She stared for a long moment before sitting back in her chair, a deep breath huffing from her lips. Her magic that begged to be released disappeared back inside her, but the anger never left her eyes.

Blackwell cleared his throat. "I said, may we proceed?"

"Of course." Marcus nodded.

"Thank you. Now please, if you will." Blackwell looked back to me.

"Chase Williams," I said through gritted teeth.

"That wasn't so hard, now was it? Why don't we begin with how you, Mr. Williams, got involved with all this? If I remember correctly, you were specifically told to stay away from the affairs of the Circle and the Underworld."

"I wasn't given much of a choice, considering the Underworld has spent the last three years hunting me."

Blackwell put his glasses back on and eyed me over the top. "Well, then why don't you tell us how you managed to get so *deeply* involved?"

I explained how I had stopped the hunters from beating Willy. That was when I had first learned some of the hunters were working for a different cause. They had been looking for the demon whose blood could open the portal. They had been looking for Rayna.

"And what inspired you to show heroics to save a filthy demon?" Blackwell asked.

"He–, Hey!" Willy said.

"Silence!" Power flashed through the room and Blackwell's deep voice bellowed at Willy.

Willy's skin turned back to the dirty brown of the chair and he slouched back down in his seat.

"Chase?" Blackwell tapped his pencil against the desk again.

I sat up in my chair and glared at him. "I took an oath as a hunter to protect the innocent. Last time I checked, torturing a helpless demon didn't qualify."

"That's preposterous. First and foremost, you are *not* a hunter. Second, no demon is innocent and we all know they are far from helpless."

"Well, if you ever spent any time in the field, you might realize it's not that black and white, especially when it comes to Willy."

"Ch–, Chase!" Willy stammered, but was silenced again, this time by Blackwell's gaze alone.

"Must I remind you of your place, Mr. Williams? I can make an example of you if you wish. To show your peers how the elders are to be treated?"

"I know my place, thanks to you, and it isn't here."

"I don't care if you think your place is amongst the scum of the Underworld. How you choose to live your life is up to you, as long as it doesn't interfere with the Circle's operation. It seems, however, your life *has* interfered with us, and as such, you will show us respect." Blackwell's voice was quiet, but the force behind each word was acute and strong.

I didn't respond. I'd lectured everyone on respecting the elders and ending this as quickly as possible. So far, I'd not only overlooked how all this would affect Rayna, but I was the one causing this process to be slow and painful.

I checked my attitude and sat up straight in my chair. "I didn't feel it was right to torture him. I thought if they were going to kill him, they should kill him, but there was no need to cause him unnecessary pain."

"Interesting." Blackwell wrote in his notebook. "And how did you become involved with this...Rayna creature, and come to know Marcus Starkraven was alive?"

"They both helped me when I was attacked by vampires."

"And you didn't feel the need to contact the Circle once you realized who Marcus was?"

"I considered it, but I was told not to contact anyone involved with the Circle. As you so pointedly just reminded me."

Blackwell nodded and continued writing. "Rayna, how was it you became involved with Mr. Starkraven?"

Rayna sat with her arms crossed, the anger still pouring off her. "He saved me after your people finished off my mother." She spat the words at him. Her eyes were glossy now and I wasn't sure if it was because she was angry, or because she had to talk about her mother's murder so plainly.

"If I remember correctly, the house was searched quite thoroughly. How exactly did you manage to stay hidden?"

"They didn't check thoroughly enough."

"I see...and when did you discover you were the key to unlocking the portal?"

"Brock and Lena tried to kill me in the basement of my old house. When my blood dripped on a symbol they'd painted on the floor, something happened to it."

"You said that you are both a hunter and a demon. What is it that makes you think you're a hunter?"

"I am an earth elemental."

"And how do you know your abilities don't stem from your demonic magic? You are a witch, correct?"

"I am, but my father was a hunter."

"Okay, who is your father then?"

"He's...I don't know. I've never met him."

Blackwell laughed. "Then how can you make this ridiculous claim that you're one of us?"

"I..." Rayna's anger faded and she was starting to get flustered. She looked to Marcus, but he only nodded. "Marcus told me he was a hunter."

"Ahh, back to Mr. Starkraven again," Blackwell said, turning his gaze to Marcus. "Mr. Starkraven, how do you know her father was a hunter?"

Marcus' dark gaze didn't flinch. He was calm and collected, like he expected it. "I knew Rayna's father well. He and Rayna's mother had been involved for some time."

"Her mother was a demon, correct?"

"Yes, a witch."

"Given her heritage isn't it possible that someone else fathered this child?"

"No."

"Are you suggesting the demon was monogamous with this unnamed hunter?"

"Yes, they were in love. And he is not without a name. His name—"

"Preposterous." Blackwell interrupted. "How can you suggest that such a creature is capable of monogamy, or love for that matter? She was a demon. A witch. Nothing more than a whore of the Underworld."

Rayna jumped out of her chair. "Don't you talk about her that way!"

"Sit down," Blackwell commanded.

"How dare you talk about my mother!" Power stormed through the room and the ground began to shake. Unoccupied chairs began to rattle and slide across the marble floor.

Blackwell sighed and the pale gray of his eyes expanded until no white remained. The room filled with magic and Rayna's body jerked back into the chair. The shaking stopped and her magic vanished.

"I will not tell you again!" Blackwell's voice boomed through the room, echoing off the walls.

"Release her." Marcus stood from his chair and his element came to life. My stomach clenched, and my nerves confirmed what I'd feared all along. There would be a fight.

"She will learn her place, or she will die."

Rayna's veins turned black and pushed against her skin. The pale flesh that shone under the bright lights of the room turned gray as the air was crushed from her body, and the witch came to the surface. Her magic prickled along my skin, and her eyes filled with black.

I jumped to my feet and called to my magic, adrenaline overpowering all other emotions.

Tiki's skin moved on its own like something else lived beneath it. I'd never seen his demon before, and it caught me off guard. His skin stretched and something primal threatened to burst out. At first I thought he might be a shifter, but he held his demon back as solid orange covered his pupils.

Vincent's white skin faded into a transparent film, revealing the moving muscles beneath. His fangs dropped from his gums and his jaws clenched through clear skin, muscles tensing and flexing as black took over his eyes. Vincent opened his mouth and a horrifying roar escaped his lips. He'd released his demon in a way I'd never witnessed before and it scared even me.

The elders pushed their chairs back and stood in unison. Elements filled the room, riding the air like an electric force. Power made the air thick and a tingling sensation danced along my skin. Earth, Fire, Air, and Water pulsed as the elders flexed their power.

"Enough." Blackwell held his hands up. The elder's magic faded, responding immediately to his command. Rayna coughed as air flooded back into her lungs, and she keeled over, gasping for air.

Blackwell made a small gesture with his hands and the elders all sat down. Marcus stayed standing, anger flooding his dark cheeks like I'd never seen before.

"Marcus, let us have this discussion calmly. There's no need for it to turn violent. I simply ask your people to respect the rules of this court."

"You will not touch her again. Not physically, or magically. And you will give her mother, gods rest her soul, the respect she deserves, or gods help me I will end you."

Blackwell laughed and the salt and pepper hair from his mustache wavered as the air escaped his lips. "Soul? Respect?

Where do you get such ideas?" The other elders chimed in and laughter filled the room.

"We see the world in a different manner than you. You will show us that respect, or this meeting is over." Marcus' voice was low and fierce.

Blackwell's smile faded and he raised his hand; the other elders' laughter ceased. He leaned over and spoke to the elder on his left that I recognized as George Carlyle. They whispered to each other before he turned to his right and continued with Tom Bradmoore. When they finished, Blackwell looked back to Marcus and nodded.

"Your request is granted. The elders will do their best to abide."

Marcus looked back to Rayna and nodded, as though the simple action could help.

Rayna caught her breath, but her eyes carried a silent battle. Sadness and anger flickered back and forth between them until sadness finally won. She adjusted herself in her seat, her hands rubbing the sides of her throat.

"Is there a problem, Mr. Williams?" Blackwell asked.

Vincent and Tiki had returned to their seats. Their demons had been pulled back and neutral expressions owned their faces, leaving me the only one left.

"Yes."

"Oh?"

"We're here to cooperate and try to help with your...investigation, or whatever you want to call it. So far, you've disrespected everyone in this room, and some who aren't alive to defend themselves. If this meeting is going to continue, it won't be an interrogation, it'll be a meeting of equals."

Blackwell smirked, his mustache wrinkling with the movement. "Is that not what we just agreed to? Please tell me you have further reason for delaying this meeting."

"I want to know what you know. We've shared information, now it's your turn. What happened to Riley? He's the one who orchestrated everything. The rest of us were just caught in the crosshairs. I want to know what happened."

"We are not here to exchange information. Your father..." Blackwell stopped and cleared his throat. "Riley Williams will be located and dealt with accordingly on terms decided by this council." I shook my head and started to speak, but Blackwell's voice shot out before I could begin. "That answer is final."

Blackwell's eyes flickered, and I laughed. "You've no idea."

"I beg your pardon?"

"That's why we're here. You don't have a clue what happened. You're hoping we can answer that question for you."

"Your foolish accusations are not welcome here, Mr. Williams. Now sit down."

"Why are you so against working with us? Riley is stronger now than ever. If we work together, we might be able to stop him."

Riddley Peterson stood up from his chair. Dark black hair hung loosely around his shoulders and matched his thick beard. "Come now Lawrence, this isn't working. These are outcasts. They're not going to cooperate. I say enough with this. We put them in the containment room and I take the answers from them." His voice was hoarse and his dark green eyes stared at me with a hatred I didn't understand.

"No," Blackwell commanded, and turned his angry gaze to Riddley. "We will continue this meeting in an orderly fashion."

Riddley shook his head and took his seat, but I could feel his anger pulsing towards me.

"Mr. Williams, please take your seat so that we may continue."

I wanted to argue, but things were getting tenser than I wanted. I sat back in my chair, but Riddley's eyes were fixed on me.

"Before we get to the others, Mr. Williams, it has been brought to our attention that you made contact with Serephina, the goddess herself. Is this true?"

The question caught me off guard. "How do you know that?"

"Answer the question."

"Yes, it's true."

"Where did this happen?"

"The south woods of Stonewall."

"And you were given something there...a scroll and a ring. Where are they now?"

"I'm wearing the ring. Vincent has the scroll."

Blackwell's eyes shot open. "You gave the goddess' scroll to a vampire? Why on earth would you do that?"

"I needed to, in exchange for the safe return of Willy."

"You gave a powerful scroll to the head of a vampire family to save a demon?"

"The magic of the scroll was gone. I was told it was of no use to him unless the portals were open. At that time, I didn't know it was possible to open the portals, so yes, I gave it to him."

"What do you mean the magic was gone?"

"It was gone. I already had it."

The elders shuffled in their seats and began whispering.

"Order," Blackwell said, tapping his gavel against the table. The elders quieted.

"Would you explain exactly how you were able to find and enter a sacred sanctuary, obtain an ancient scroll, and extract its power?"

"I hitched a ride into the sanctuary on Rayna's earth element. After we defeated a trio of pureblood demons, the spirit gave it to me. Then—"

"Stop right there. You said a spirit gave it to you?"

"Yes. A piece of Serephina's spirit occupies the soul piece and protects it."

Blackwell wrote furiously in his notebook. When he was finished, his eyes watched me with renewed excitement. "And you extracted the power how?"

"The spirit told me to read the scroll. Once I did, the power just sort of...came into me."

"And this is how you developed your powers? From what I understand, you've obtained the ability to create and control both the water and fire elements."

I shook my head. "No, those came before."

"Then what exactly has the scroll's power done for you?" Blackwell sounded flustered.

"Nothing."

"You expect me to believe that you absorbed the magic of an ancient scroll and have nothing to show for it?"

"I don't know what else to tell you. It's the truth."

Blackwell watched me for a moment before looking back to Riddley. "Then you won't mind if Riddley takes a look? Just a peek to confirm this?"

Marcus stood up from his table and walked towards me. "I don't think that will be necessary."

"I can assure you, it will be simple and painless. It will do nothing more than verify his story."

Marcus looked to me, but he seemed as lost as I was.

"Mr. Starkraven, surely you don't have anything to hide?"

Marcus sighed. "The court must agree to take an oath of honesty and intention. Chase isn't to be harmed and Riddley does nothing more than confirm Chase's story."

My eyes opened wide. "Marcus…" I whispered, but he didn't respond.

"Of course," Blackwell said. "Riddley, if you please."

Riddley walked behind the other bench and down the stairs. His black dress shoes echoed and his round belly filled out his white council robes fully. He stopped before Marcus and without so much as a smile, took the oath.

Marcus nodded and stepped to the side.

Riddley's dark blue eyes lit up with anticipation and then the color faded. Ready?" he asked, solid white eyes staring out at me.

I nodded, but before the action was finished, a strange vibration moved through my head. His air element came to life, and a cool breeze washed through my skull. I winced at first, and a bright light filled my vision. I started to lose my balance and I felt as though I was falling from my chair. I braced for impact with the floor, but it never came. Riddley's power moved over my soul and through my mind. The discomfort faded and the sensation of power was gone.

"He speaks the truth," Riddley said. "I can confirm his story." He turned back to the bench, his golden sash bobbing with each step.

Blackwell scribbled something in his notebook. "Give us a moment to deliberate please."

The elders turned in their chairs and began discussing amongst themselves. I sat in discomfort and the bright lights twinkled in my vision. I readjusted in my seat and shook them away. The pain faded, but enough remained for it to be irritating. I tried to ignore the discomfort and strained to hear the elders' rapid whispers, but their words were muffled at best.

After an eternity, Blackwell turned in his chair with a serious expression on his face. "Mr. Williams, please remove the ring. We'll need some time to review and examine the artifact."

My stomach tightened as he spoke each word.

"Don't give it to him," Rayna whispered.

"I'm sorry Lawrence, but that isn't going to happen," Marcus said.

"I beg your pardon?"

"You heard him," I said. "I'm not taking it off."

"That ring is an essential piece of evidence for our investigation. It is an ancient artifact crafted by the goddess herself, creator of the hunters. Therefore, it is the rightful property of the Circle."

"This ring was crafted for the Protector. For the hunter who passed the goddess' test and proved himself worthy. Those were the words from the spirit herself," I said.

Blackwell snorted. "This is not a request. I don't care if the goddess herself handed you that ring, you will give it to the council."

"You made it very clear I'm not part of the Circle, so you don't get to demand anything from me anymore. This ring isn't coming off my finger."

"Must we continue down this road?" Blackwell pulled the glasses from his face again and set them down on the paper in front of him.

I knew what was coming and I tried to brace myself. The gray of Blackwell's eyes washed over the whites and his magic came to life.

"You will deliver that ring to us or we will remove it from your finger. Whether or not your finger is still attached to your hand is completely up to you."

"You'll have to pry it off my cold, dead fingers." I stood from my seat and started to pull the magic up from my soul when Blackwell's element hit me. The air around me became heavy, and the oxygen in my lungs vanished. There was no chance for me to gain my focus; the air was gone and I felt the color drain from my face. I hit the floor, catching myself with my hands as the force of his magic shoved me down. A thin gloss filled my eyes and Marcus' power broke into the room to strike back.

Air rushed back into my lungs and Blackwell soared through the air. His small body crashed against the far wall of the room and collapsed to the floor. The other elders sprang into action, bringing their magic with them. I climbed to my feet and called my element. I pulled the fire towards my hand and a dark blue flame ignited in my palm. I fed it more power, watching the flame flicker and grow.

"Don't do this, Blackwell. This is not the way," Marcus said.

Blackwell was crumpled on the floor and using a chair to help himself to his feet. Marcus' magic hung around him, and his wrinkled features grew pale.

"Stand down," Marcus commanded the other elders.

The elders' magic receded, but didn't vanish.

"You're a powerful elemental, Blackwell. You all are, but there is no need for lives to be lost tonight."

Blackwell finished pulling himself up and looked to Marcus, gasping for air. "You've grown stronger, Starkraven."

"I have. And so has Riley. With his new powers he bested both me and Tessa Williams at once. We have a common enemy Lawrence; let us not make war amongst ourselves."

Blackwell looked up to the council. The elders watched, unsure of what to do. Their magic roamed beneath the surface and their combined power was impressive. I prayed Marcus' diplomatic skills could get us out of this alive.

"We need that ring, Marcus."

"You cannot have it, and you will not get it until every one of us is dead."

"That can be arranged if you so wish it."

"As can the fate of you and your brothers. You won't all make it out of this alive."

"You speak with such confidence. You're a lone hunter Marcus. Your element is strong, but it cannot save them all."

"You forget the company I'm in. Chase's magic is here, and stronger than you know. Rayna's power is unique, with unseen boundaries. Vincent is one of the most powerful of his kind, and behind him stands an entire family whose lineage is so ancient, it can't be fully traced. That in itself is a war you don't want at your doorstep. Tiki is a half-breed unlike any that we've seen. An entirely new breed you're not prepared to face. And Willy…Willy has an extraordinarily powerful grandmother." Marcus looked to the council who stood strong and united, each waiting to unleash a fury of magic upon us.

"We will have that ring, sooner or later."

"That has yet to be seen."

Blackwell and Marcus stared at each other for a long moment.

"Stand down," Marcus repeated.

Blackwell looked to the other elders and nodded. "Do as he says."

One by one, each elder let their magic fade. Marcus released his elemental grip on Blackwell, and although the others had withdrawn, I could still feel Rayna's and my elements boiling at the surface.

"Jameson!" Blackwell shouted.

After a few moments, the large doors creaked open and Jameson walked into the room.

"Escort these people off the property immediately!"

"Yes, sir."

Jameson walked into the room and ushered each of us out. Nerves hammered around inside me, battling each other like iron against steel. I followed Jameson, but continued to look over my shoulder. When the elevator door slid shut, I finally let my magic recede.

The elevator dinged and the doors opened, revealing the dimly lit garage we'd entered through. Jameson led us out into the open space of the facility and I let the fresh, cold air rush into my lungs. A strange tingle moved down my spine and my eyes darted to each corner of the grounds.

"What is it?" Rayna asked.

I knew that feeling. It was the feeling that a demon was near. It caught me off guard at first. I'd gotten so used to having them around me that I hardly noticed it anymore, but this was different. This was new.

"Keep it moving, Williams," Jameson said.

I glanced back over the grounds and nothing but darkness stared back at me. I shook the feeling away and started walking.

"You okay?" Rayna slowed her pace to match my own.

"I'm fine. It's...nothing."

"You sure?"

I looked back over my shoulder. "Yeah."

Jameson escorted us to the car, and I didn't have the energy to argue with Willy as he claimed the shotgun seat. I reached for the handle, and my pulse jumped as the sound of feet brushing gravel scattered behind us. I moved for the daggers strapped to my back and wrapped scarred fingers around them. Two hunters walked out of the forest, and I released the breath I held.

"We need to get out of here," I said.

"Agreed," Marcus replied.

I took a breath and opened the door to the backseat when the voice came.

"There he is," a man growled.

Startled, I jumped back from the car. A chill shot through me again and I'd wished we had left moments earlier. A group of people were walking out of the trees. Nearly a dozen pushed through the brush and stepped into the clearing. Men and women stood side by side and made their way towards us in a wall of power and grace.

"That's the hunter who killed Jack." A man leading the pack pointed at Jameson. He was tall, with a large build and bulging muscles I didn't know existed in the human body. Then again, he wasn't human.

Brown hair hung down around his shoulders with natural waves rolling through them. Dark eyes gleamed under a thick, furrowed brow. His shirtless body glistened with sweat as he stepped into the light. Baggy sweats barely hung onto his waist and were torn in multiple places.

"We're going to need backup. We've got shifters on the grounds." One of the hunters spoke into his radio.

"Did you think we wouldn't find you? You killed one of ours, and tonight you're going to suffer the repercussions of the Shadowpack," he said.

I dropped to the ground at the sound of gunshots. All the hunters fell to their knees and aimed at the pack. We were caught in the crossfire of the shifters' suicide mission.

One of the pack members screamed as a bullet hit him. His eyes lit up with fear as he reached for his shoulder. Silver liquid poured from the wound, spreading through dark red streams of blood that ran down his body.

The entire pack reacted with rage and roared into the midnight sky. The injured member collapsed, and the feeling in my gut told me things were about to get a whole lot worse. The pack moved as a single unit and dropped on all fours to the ground. Before their hands hit the earth, they were replaced by massive paws. Clear fluid exploded into the air, mixing with blood as their skins split seamlessly. Fur pushed its way over their bodies as blood and fluid dripped from their skins.

Their faces cracked and deformed as long snouts filled them. Human teeth grew and shifted with their bodies, letting ferocious fangs fall from their gums. Their muscles swelled and tore at their skins, while bones broke and dislocated themselves, moving into more agile positions. Their bodies grew longer and taller as the bones restructured. In seconds, there were eleven angry wolves with teeth bared, standing on all fours. Some were small, while others stood taller than me.

The one who'd been shot was on the ground in human form, trying not to get hit as more bullets fired towards them. His torso was covered in red blood with silver lines sizzling through it. The hole where the bullet entered was steaming. The skin around the wound was already a dark purple and looked infected.

The pack split into two parts. One went left and the other right, dodging the spray of bullets coming at them. The Circle's facility came to life as the garage lights came on and alarms sounded. More of the bay doors opened. The trampling of feet on concrete and the clanking of metal echoed in the air as soldiers rushed into the field.

Tiki pulled me to my feet. I didn't know what to do. On one hand, I wanted to watch the events unfold; on the other, I was still a hunter.

My mind was made up for me as a wolf leapt over the car. It stopped and turned, bright blue eyes aimed at us. Its jaws opened and lips curled back, baring teeth in a fierce snarl.

I called my element, but before it came, there were two more wolves on either side of us. Howling filled the air as more wolves rushed from the bushes. This wasn't a suicide mission; it was a full-blown assault.

Dozens of werewolves jumped through the brush and came from all angles. Wolves growled and jaws snapped, the sound of flesh tearing beneath their teeth. More hunters joined the fight and the battle quickly balanced itself. Gunshots fired and echoed through the compound. The hunters weren't even using their elements now; they were resorting strictly to weapons.

Three wolves surrounded us and we had no choice but to react. I pulled the fire up and unleashed it on the wolf closest to me. It yelped in pain and scurried off as singed hair smoked, leaving nothing but the horrible scent behind.

Another wolf pounced towards me, and it took all my strength to keep its jaws from my throat. The wolf was easily seven feet tall on all four legs, and its strength was immense. Its gray and white coat was thick and coarse. I pushed at its neck to hold it back.

Earth exploded from the ground as Rayna called her magic. Rocks burst through the grass protecting her and hitting the approaching wolves.

Bursts of wind crashed through the trees, knocking wolves off balance. More wolves soared through the air in pairs as Marcus pushed the onslaught of reinforcements back. His element moved with ease, leaving the air around us thick with power.

Tiki picked up wolves by the neck and threw them effortlessly. Long supernatural talons jutted from his hands, cutting deep into leaping werewolves. His muscles flexed as he pushed the shifters back. He was a fierce warrior. Strange fangs dropped from his mouth and razor-sharp bones burst out of his forearms. White plates split through his skin, revealing solid bone that protected his arms, shoulders, and part of his torso.

Vincent was on the ground draining the blood from a small brown wolf. Furry bodies lay motionless around him, torn in multiple pieces. His skin was translucent, black veins pushing against it as though they could split his flesh at any moment. Solid black filled his eyes and they glowed with a primal need. His long razor claws had fur and skin stuck on them.

Drool fell over my face as the wolf fought my resistance. Thick and sticky, his saliva slid down my cheeks. I focused my power and called to my water element. I ripped the cool rush up from my soul and let it crash into the demon.

The wolf tried to pull back as water flooded into its lungs. I gripped its white fur with everything I had, but it jerked back and tore itself from my grasp.

I jumped to my feet and kept the magic flowing. I wasn't touching it anymore, but my magic still poured into it. I didn't stop to question the power. I kept pushing. The power moved in a fluid motion from my hands and into the wolf, filling the air between us.

Two more moved in around me and I let the energy surround me. All three wolves yelped and tried to step back from my elemental grasp, but it was too strong. Their thick legs pushed at the earth, unable to move. I didn't know how, or why, but I didn't care. Nobody was going to bite me without my say so.

Power crashed through me and water drizzled out of the wolves. Their ears, eyes, mouths, and noses released waves of water until their bodies gave in and collapsed. I waited until their forms went limp before I pulled my magic back and turned back to face the battle.

Everyone kept the shifters at bay, but I could see another half dozen trying to creep up behind Tiki and Marcus. I moved in front of them and pushed the magic out. A glowing ball of power grew between my palms and the wolves sprinted towards me.

Drops of liquid formed idly in the air, shaking as my power drew them in. Streams of water slid towards me, like rain riding the windshield of a moving car. As each bead of water came together, the power built and grew in my hand, creating a wall of water. The wall hovered in front of me as the power expanded until I couldn't hold it anymore.

A wave of dark blue water burst forward, rolling over the ground and crushing the Underworlders back with liquid force. The water pushed their limp, furry bodies across the earth.

Adrenaline pounded in my veins and the battle filled me with a rush of excitement that I hadn't realized I'd been missing.

I was disappointed as I heard the howls. Several of them called into the sky and turned to retreat into the woods. The other shifters followed, and in moments, the grounds were vacant of any breathing wolves.

Half a dozen lay dead in a deep puddle of my own making near the driveway, and single bodies were scattered everywhere. Injured hunters called for help, while others lay motionless in the moist grass, painted red with injuries. Those still standing and fully able radioed for more backup and began collecting their wounded.

"Chase–" Marcus started.

"I don't know what happened," I said in a rush. "I've never been able to do that."

"Your power is growing more rapidly than usual."

Tiki, Vincent, and Rayna came to stand beside Marcus, and before anyone could say anything, I realized someone was missing. "Where's Willy?"

"He–, Here…" Willy gasped. "Ov–, over here."

I ran around to the other side of the car to find Willy sitting against it. Huge teeth marks marred his scrawny, pale flesh and blood poured from his shoulder, covering his body.

"It's okay, Willy. I'm here buddy," I said. I fell down beside him and called my magic back. I pushed a calming wave up from my soul and let it fill him.

He gasped at first as the cold magic leaked into him. His skin changed from its natural white to the shiny black of the car behind him. I opened his shirt and panic filled me. Huge teeth marks had sunk deep into his flesh. Chunks of skin hung from the wounds, only threads of flesh keeping them attached. Blood leaked from each hole, and they hadn't even started to heal.

I could feel myself wavering on the brink of exhaustion. My elements were still taking a lot out of me, but I tried again. I pushed the magic harder this time, black dots spotting my vision, but the bleeding didn't slow.

"Why isn't it working?" My anger came out in my words, but I was talking mostly to myself.

"Water is an unusual element, Chase. It can't magically heal everything," Marcus said.

"It's worked every time I've tried."

"The magic is unpredictable. It could be that the werewolf's bite has something to do with it, or it could be based on what kind of demon Willy is."

Marcus popped his trunk and pulled out a first-aid kit. He reached over and cut the shoulder off of Willy's shirt, pulling it with ease from the wound. He tore open packages of gauze and bandages, but by the time he'd covered the wounds, they were blood-soaked. He unrolled a long roll of gauze, wrapping it around Willy's shoulder. Marcus folded a thick blanket over top and used another strip of bandaging to hold it in place.

"He's a demon. This bite isn't going to keep him down," Marcus said.

"Are you sure? Can't it infect him or something?"

"No," Vincent said. "He's already a demon. The shifter virus only transfers to humans."

Willy was sweating now. Thick drops fell from his messy hair and ran down through the patchy stubble on his face. I reached up and touched his forehead, but it was too hot to keep my hand there. He was burning up.

"Hang in there, Willy."

Willy tried for a smile but winced in pain. The thought of having yelled at him for wanting to stay home entered my mind. I couldn't keep the guilt away as it seeped in and threatened me with sadness.

Marcus put the first-aid kit back and pushed the trunk closed. "Let's go."

"Don't we need to stay or something?" Rayna asked.

He shook his head. "This is their mess. Let them clean it up." He slipped into his seat and slammed the door shut.

I was surprised by Marcus' reaction, but for the first time, I agreed with him.

Tiki and I lifted Willy into the front seat of the car and the rest of us squeezed into the back. I had never wanted to be this close to Vincent, but after everything that had just happened, I could suck it up. I definitely wasn't fighting for shotgun now.

Chapter 4

Once we got back to the condo, everyone dispersed. Tiki took Willy upstairs, hoping to bandage the wounds better. Vincent left, and after the fight we just had, Rayna wasn't up for much but sleeping. I was exhausted and tried to follow her upstairs, but I didn't get away so easily.

"Chase, I'd like a word please," Marcus said, his voice its usual unemotional tone, leaving me no idea what I was in for.

He led me into the training room and turned, shooing Rai off my shoulder before closing the door.

"Is it so bad the bird had to go?"

"We need to talk...without any distractions."

"Umm, alright..."

"How are you?" he asked.

"I'm good. How are you?" I smirked.

"That's not what I mean."

I sighed. "I know."

"I want to know how you're really doing. I need to know where your head's at."

I shrugged. "I'm fine."

Marcus crossed his arms and his gaze stayed locked on me. "What?"

"Tonight was...difficult. This past month has been tough on everyone, but it's been more personal for you. I want you to know you can talk to me. You shouldn't feel like you have to deal with this alone."

"Yeah, I get it, but I'm fine," I said. "Thanks for the pep talk."

"I mean it, Chase." Marcus' voice was soft but commanding. "Your magic is getting stronger, you've been ignoring your training, and you've been dodging all of us. You've hardly spoken to anyone since—"

"What did you expect, Marcus? I'm living in a strange house with people I've only known for a few months. My mother–the only person who mattered to me–is dead, murdered at the hands of my father, the same father who had me exiled from the Circle, and tried to kill me. What do you want me to say? I'm dealing with it."

Marcus sighed. "I know this is a lot to deal with, but we have to stick together. Emotions fuel our elements. If we lose control of them, we can't properly manage our magic. At the rate your power is growing, you need that control, and we need to be open and able to trust each other. Talking about–"

"I don't want to talk. I want to be left alone and I want to kill the son of a bitch who murdered my mother!" My blood started to boil with anger. I wasn't angry with Marcus, but he was pushing this, so he got to be on the receiving end.

"I know you haven't known us for very long, but I knew your mother my entire life. She trusted me, and you need to know you can too. I understand you're hesitant, and that's okay, but I know what you're feeling."

"You do? Did your dad kill your mom right after he stuck a knife in your stomach?"

"No..."

"I didn't think so. You lost a friend. I lost the only person who ever gave a damn about me. So don't pretend you understand what it's like. You don't. Which means you can't relate or help me."

"But Rayna does. If you don't want to talk to me, talk to her. Talk to someone."

"Did you not hear me? I don't want to talk. Why are you pushing so damn hard?"

"This meeting with the Circle was just the beginning. If the Circle wants the ring, you can be sure the Underworld will too."

"You're warning me about the Underworld? Thanks, but they've been after me since I got exiled, so what else is new?"

"Once they realize you have it, the last three years are going to seem like a holiday for you. Whatever the ring does, it's wanted by many. That paints an even bigger target on you. We need to deal with this before that happens, and in order to do that, I need you to have a clear head."

"I appreciate what you're trying to do, but in all honesty, I don't give a damn what you or anybody else wants. I want a normal life. I want my mom back. I don't want to be looking over my shoulder for the next person trying to kill me. If it's not the Circle, it's Riley, and if it's neither of them, it's a demon who thinks I'm a trophy. But I don't get what I want, so I don't give a shit what anyone else wants!"

Blood pushed through my veins in hot waves and hurt my skin. It was going to burn me from the inside out. Magic throbbed at my fingertips and the fire grew in my palms.

"Don't do this, Chase. Calm yourself."

I threw my arms in the air and started pacing. "You want to talk? Let's talk. I've lost everything. What have you lost? A friend? A fellow soldier? Your freedom, now that the Circle knows you're alive?"

"It's not like that."

Fire exploded inside me and I keeled over. Pain shot through my head as the magic threatened to explode. Without thinking, I brought my hands up to my face. The burning was instant, and the smell of singed hair stung my nostrils. I screamed as the heat scalded my skin. My palms were pulsing with a bright, red glow and instinct tore my hands away. Raw flesh blistered and ripped from my cheeks. Screams echoed from my lips and I fell to my knees.

The lights flickered on and off. Random fluorescent bulbs exploded from the ceiling, raining glass until the room went black. All the candles that lined the wall burst into flame. Flames shot high off their wicks in a rainbow of colors. Blues and greens flickered over the room, mixing with reds and oranges as the temperature spiked.

"Chase, you need to take a breath and calm yourself."

"Don't move," I commanded, pointing a glowing hand towards Marcus as his shadow crept closer.

Marcus froze and I took a few breaths. The scent of burnt hair moved to the back of my throat and stuck to my tongue.

I fought the fire and called my water element. I could hear the babbling brook, trickling over the same stones it had for centuries. The cooling sensation filled my body and the change in temperature stung, causing my muscles to tense. The remaining lights flickered and came back on, but the candlelight didn't fade. Smoke drifted up from my fingertips, disappearing into the air as water washed my self-inflictions away.

I looked down at the floor and Marcus' shadow hovered over me.

"I'm sorry. I just…"

"I shouldn't have pushed. I just don't want anything to happen to you too."

"What is happening to me?" I asked, staring down at my hands. The bright red glow had faded, and now a soft blue magic rippled beneath my skin. "I've never been able to do what I did tonight: the shifters, the candles, the lights."

"Your power is progressing at an unnatural rate. It could be the ring, the mark, maybe neither, maybe both. It's growing faster than you can control, and without full control of your emotions...you're a danger to yourself."

"And everyone else around me," I whispered.

The fluorescent lights flickering above us were dimmer than before. Several had burnt out, and others were empty from shattered bulbs. I looked up at Marcus, towering above me, yet somehow managed to look small in this moment.

"Whatever it is, we'll figure it out together." Marcus' brown eyes were calm and sincere, his welcoming aura pulsing around us.

I nodded. I should've thanked him for saving me in Drakar, and for taking me in. For everything he'd done. I had never thanked him for any of it because I was always too busy trying to deal with my own problems. Before I could organize a thought and try to share my appreciation, the phone rang. The ring was loud and blared through the room.

Marcus moved with the grace of a man half his size and picked it up. The image I had of him being small vanished as he clutched the tiny receiver in his massive black hand.

"Hello?" His voice was as deep and masculine as ever. "Are you sure?"

I ignored the next part and let the last of my element cycle through me. The water grounded me. I didn't know how to handle the fire. It was destructive, painful, and unpredictable. I couldn't imagine being without its rival.

My body ached, but the water coursing through me gave me the energy to stand. Marcus was right—when I lost control, my magic had a power all its own. One I didn't care to see again, not unless it was on my terms.

"Bad news I'm afraid," Marcus said.

I cleared my throat and turned to face him. "What's up?"

"The rogue hunters have had an incident a few states over, in southern Maine. He's alive, Chase. Riley and the Dark Brothers..."

"Are you sure?" I asked, panic surging through my veins.

Marcus' dark eyes looked to the floor. "I'm sure. They tried to stop him...they didn't all make it. I'm going to have to leave for a few days. Unless you need me to stay." He looked up, and although he tried to hide it, I could see the sadness brewing inside. With him here, it'd make things easier, especially if what he said about the ring was true, but he'd just lost another friend, maybe more. I couldn't keep him here with my problems.

"We'll be fine."

"Are you sure? I can stay Chase, really."

"I promise. You go. I'll clear my head."

Marcus tried for a smile. "I need to speak with Rayna before I leave. Please call me if something happens, or if you need anything."

I nodded and gave him the most sincere smile I could manage. "I will."

I waited until the door closed behind him and looked across the room. The candles flickered in the air, still burning in their multicolored warmth. Their energy called to me, as though their own magic moved through the wax.

The blood in my veins pumped faster. Fear and adrenaline danced beside each other, and as my pulse sped, the heat of the candles increased, their flames stretching off the wick. I closed my eyes and focused my mind, trying to calm my element.

Riley was alive. I should've been excited to know I would get my revenge, but I wasn't. I was worried. More than that, I was scared. If Riley was alive, he could be anywhere, and he had powerful warlocks on either side of him. That meant everyone was in danger. If he was alive...our problems had just begun.

Chapter 5

"Let's go, sleepyhead. Wake up." Rayna's voice rang through my ears.

I twisted under the blankets and my eyes winced open. The sun was already high in the sky and sunlight poured into my room.

"No," I murmured, and turned away from her.

"Come on," she said, tugging gently at the sheets.

"Careful, you don't know what I might, or might not, be wearing."

The covers fell against the side of my bed and I smiled. I could practically feel the color rushing to her face.

"I gave you 'til eleven. Now get up. We have things to do."

"Marcus has only been gone a few hours and already you're pushing?"

"Trust me; when I push, you'll know it. It'll feel a lot like when I punch." Rayna walked back towards the hall, grasping the door frame and turning around. Her dark hair was pinned on the top of her head, red strands falling down over the back of her neck. "You've got five minutes."

"Fine," I said.

Rayna smirked and watched me for a moment before pushing off the frame and disappearing down the hallway.

I groaned and pulled the pillow over my head. It was after eleven, but I wasn't ready to get up. I didn't know when the last time I'd slept this late was or when it'd happen again, but one thing I'd learned since staying here was not to keep Rayna waiting.

I rolled out of bed and pulled on one of the few pairs of jeans that littered the floor. I took a gray t-shirt from the dresser and started pulling it over my head when I caught my refection in the mirror.

Dark ink still covered my back, the Mark of the Gods—or so Elyas had told me. A long sword started at my neck and ran down my spine, the tip barely hidden by the waist of my pants. Two glyphs were drawn on the blade: one representing fire, and the other water. Shaded wings covered the rest of my back, spreading out from my shoulders and running down to my hips. I'd never forget this mark. It was—what I believed to be—the turning point that led to my mother's murder. If I hadn't gone after Vincent, I wouldn't have this stupid mark, or the ring. If I had listened and waited for her and Marcus, she'd still be alive.

"Chase!" Rayna's voice bounced off the walls and found its way into my room.

I shook the thoughts away and pulled the shirt down the rest of the way. The shirt fit tight against my body. I wasn't huge, but between fighting demons and Marcus' training sessions, I'd managed to stay in excellent shape for my 6'1" size.

I looked myself over in the mirror. A circle of light gray on the outside contrasted the dark blue of my eyes. The dark circles beneath them, however, didn't do much for me. I ran my hands through thick, messy blond hair a few times and called myself ready. I didn't know what Rayna had in store for us today, but whatever it was, this would have to do.

Rai had her claws clamped gently to my shoulder as I came downstairs. There were crumbs of pancakes and a few pieces of leftover fruit in a bowl. The smell of hash browns and bacon filled the room and Rai jumped from my shoulder and flew into the kitchen.

"You made breakfast?" I asked with surprise.

Rayna shook her head. "Breakfast? I've been up for hours. This was just a snack."

"Were you feeding a small village?"

Rayna turned and glared at me. "Don't start with me. Get your shoes on. Let's go." She threw the last few dishes into the dishwasher. "Tiki, we're ready!"

"Be right down." Tiki sounded excited, matching his expression as he leaned over the iron railing from the library above.

"I thought we were training?"

"Later. Marcus wants us to take Tiki shopping first."

"You woke me up for shopping? I really hope you're kidding."

"Well, I for one don't want to take him anywhere in what he's wearing."

"What's wrong with what I'm wearing?" Tiki stepped into the kitchen.

He kept his baggy, sand stained, white pants on, and the same frayed rope holding them up. I'd offered on countless occasions to give him a belt, but he'd refused, stating the belt was a confusing and useless contraption.

"Nothing, it's umm...Chase?"

"It's just..." I eyed Rayna. "You can't walk around in that all the time. You need to try and fit in a little better and not look like you're from another world."

"I am from another world."

"That's not what I...never mind, let's just go."

"Great!" Rayna smiled and took the keys off the hook. "I'll drive."

****

"This is perfect!" Rayna's eyes lit up as she held a blue and white plaid shirt beneath my chin.

"She's right. It does bring out your eyes." Tiki smiled and searched a rack of clothes.

I raised my eyebrows. "No."

"Why not?"

"We're shopping for Tiki, not me. I don't need new clothes." I pushed the shirt away. "Besides, this isn't my style."

Rayna laughed. "Have you seen your clothes? You wouldn't know style if it bit you in the–"

"How about this?" Tiki's voice came from behind. "I could wear it when you take me to Revelations tonight."

Tiki held a sheer leopard print shirt against his chest and the smile on his face was wide. Bright white triangular pupils expanded with excitement.

"Revelations?"

"Yes. You said I would meet more people like me."

"And you have. You've met Rayna, Willy, and unfortunately, Vincent."

Tiki eyed me over the coat rack. I looked to Rayna who had a matching glare and sighed.

"Fine. We'll take you."

Tiki smiled. "So, you like?" He held the shirt up again.

Rayna arched a brow, trying to find a way to let him down gently.

I smirked at Rayna before she could reply. "That's perfect."

Tiki's smile grew wider. "I'm going to see if they have pants like this." He turned and disappeared behind another rack of clothing.

"Chase!" Rayna's fist slammed into my shoulder. "Why would you say that?"

"He likes it. Let him have it."

"That's worse than what he's wearing."

I shrugged. "Maybe you should've taken him shopping by yourself."

"Back to being an ass as usual, I see." Rayna eyes were fierce. "That's fine. We're training later, so I have an excuse to hit you."

"Great! I'll gladly beat some of that attitude out of you."

"Go try this on." Rayna shoved the shirt back against me and rushed away. "Tiki...put that down."

I held the shirt out in front of me and looked at it. "Yep, that's definitely not going to happen." I stuck the shirt on a circular rack between some heavy fur coats and ruffled dress shirts. She'll never look here.

I shuddered as a chill trickled down the back of my neck. I had the strange feeling someone was watching me, and it wasn't human.

My eyes moved around the store. People were bustling around racks of clothing. Rayna was trying to pry the leopard print shirt away from Tiki, who was firmly refusing while eyeing the zebra print dress shirt on the rack next to him. I weaved through racks to the front of the shop. Large bay windows let streams of sunlight in, and as I peered through the panes, my nerves clenched.

The tingle moved back through my spine and I lifted a hand above my eyes, blocking the onslaught of sunlight pouring in.

My eyes struggled to focus, but as my hand blocked the sun, my eyes opened wide. Riley stood across the street, with the Dark Brothers and a man I didn't recognize on either side of him. They all peered at me through the rush of traffic driving on the road between us. Panic, anger, and a rush of emotions I couldn't separate from the rest scorched through me.

The door slammed open against the front of the building as I pushed through it. I came to an abrupt stop on the edge of the road as more vehicles rushed by.

A devilish smile played on Riley's lips as I was stranded on the other side. Our eyes locked for only a moment before a string of large trucks and buses passed between us. As the vehicles disappeared, so did they, but the sensation that danced along my skin was still there.

I searched the sidewalk up and down, scanning each face. Shoulders and elbows shoved into me as I fought through the busy crowd. A blur of black moved and caught my eye. As the shoulders of people pushed past me, a sharp pain cut through my back. I winced, and my back arched in reaction, absorbing the pain. The blur moved again; this time the pain ripped over my stomach. I keeled over in agony. My eyes darted left and right, looking to each face as it passed me.

Warmth hit my hands as I held my stomach, and blood seeped through my shirt. Panicked breaths were quick and sharp at the sight of it, and my pulse exploded in my throat.

Another shoulder bumped me and knocked me to the ground with an inhuman force. I curled up, holding my hands over my stomach as the blood flowed beneath my palms.

Screaming started as a passing lady pointed and shouted at me. Blood had soaked through my shirt and pooled on the sidewalk beneath me. I ignored the pain and struggled to my feet as the crowd started rushing around me. Panic ensued as more people began to scream.

"Chase!" A voice yelled, faded behind the screams.

Every face turned into a cloudy haze. All of them were moving at a speed I knew couldn't be possible. I turned in circles, desperately searching for Riley.

"Chase," the voice yelled again.

The world around me swirled in a haze and faded to darkness. I shook my head, as though that could stop it, and a flash of light blinded me.

The air from moving vehicles rushed past me and I was back on the sidewalk. The crowd was gone, and the screaming disappeared with them. I was closer to the edge of the road now, and car horns honked as they drove by in an angry rush.

"Chase!" Rayna said.

The pain was gone and my hands searched my body. My stomach and back were untouched, and the blood had disappeared.

I looked out across the road where Riley had stood, but no one was there. The chill that ran down my spine had faded, Riley was gone, and the Brothers were nowhere to be seen. No one was here.

"Chase, I know you can hear me," Rayna's voice called out.

I turned around and the expression on her face was angry. She held the blue plaid shirt halfway out the door.

"Don't think for a second you're getting away without trying this on."

Chapter 6

My stomach tightened as I walked into the training room. I didn't want to be here. Last night was strange enough, but after this afternoon, I wasn't sure I wanted to be working with any kind of magic right now.

"Let's start with a simple warm up and call your elements," Rayna said.

"I'm not sure this is a good idea today."

"Training and practice are the only way things are going to get better."

"Rayna, I really don't..." I stopped. Unhappy glare aside—she was right. I couldn't let any of this stop me. I'd been ignoring my training for long enough. "I'm ready."

Rayna nodded. "Let's work with fire first."

I walked toward the center of the room and took my position. I spread my legs shoulder-width apart and closed my eyes. The blue exercise mats beneath my feet were cold, squishing against my skin as my weight settled into them. I put both hands out, palms up, and called to my element.

"Pull your magic to the surface and push it to your hands."

I fed off her calm demeanor and drew the fire upwards. It warmed me as it coursed through my body, the heat bubbling beneath my skin. The magic spilled into my palm, and the flames shifting seamlessly in both of my hands.

"Keep your breathing steady and pull the power away from your left hand, but keep it burning in your right."

The dual flames flickered in my palms as my hands trembled. I tried to pull the magic back, while maintaining focus. The left flame flickered as it began to dwindle, shrinking to a small spark before fading from sight. Excitement danced along my skin as the flame responded to my command, but my focus began to drift.

I tried to stay focused. But Riley was alive, and here. He'd told me his ultimate goal was to invoke the power of the demon god, Ithreal, but I still didn't know how he planned on doing that, or why. He said it was to bring power back to the hunters, but I wasn't convinced. There was something more going on. I just hadn't figured it out yet.

"Chase, be careful..." Rayna said.

I snapped out of my daze, and the remaining flame in my right hand was growing.

I tried to pull back, but the element kept flowing. The flame reached higher into the air and my pulse sped. Beads of sweat ran down my face as I tried to rein in the power. I could feel the burning sensation growing in my palm. The blue flame began to lose color, fading to white and biting at my skin.

"Don't panic. Take control of the moment."

"I'm trying," I said through a clenched jaw, and I tried to cut the magic off, but it wouldn't waver. There was a flow moving through me now that I couldn't stop. The white flame burned and my palm grew raw.

Rayna stepped forward and her element trickled through the room. When she pushed her magic, my pulse slowed. The world stilled, and for a brief moment, all I could hear were my own breaths and the beating of my heart.

As the world came rushing back, the training room was bright with the white flame. The walls blurred in the blazing heat, and a vision washed over me as Rayna's element coursed through my body.

The life of a forest blessed my ears: the rustling of wet leaves, the padding of wildlife that walked the forest floor. A bird's melody was faint in the distance, and the scent of fresh rain on bark trickled over me.

My panicked breaths paced themselves and the pain in my hand ceased. I was standing in the middle of a forest, my own magic gone, and Rayna's swirling around me.

"Think of something positive. Something that makes you happy and calm." Rayna's voice came from everywhere, carrying softly in the air, moving up from the ground, and echoing off the trees.

I closed my eyes and thought of the only thing that made me happy. I pictured my mom's youthful face in all its beauty. Her warm hazel eyes gazed at me, and did what they always did: they made everything okay.

I opened my eyes and took a deep breath, using that calm to focus on my element. I pulled the magic back, redirecting the excess power into my soul. The flame didn't shrink, but I stopped it from getting bigger.

"Excellent," Rayna said. "Now keep that focus."

I smiled as I managed the flame. It didn't regain its dark blue color, but I kept the bright white fire in my control. I closed my eyes again and recreated the forest in my mind, using it as a calming center to harness my power.

My mother's hazel eyes watched me as she neared. I was tempted to reach out to her, but something held me back. I wanted to talk to her and ask her if she was okay, but before I could form any words her hand came up and stopped me.

Shoulder-length brown hair hung around her shoulders, covering the straps of a white summer dress. A light tan warmed her skin all the way down to the bare feet that stepped over crinkled leaves. Moist dirt collected around her toes as each step pressed deep into the soil. Her eyes wavered for a moment, almost unnoticeably, but when they looked back to me, they were different.

"Mom?" I asked.

She turned away and I followed the sway of her hair as the wind picked up. The blue sky above us darkened and gray clouds rolled over the canopy of the forest. With the clouds came a booming thunder so loud it startled me, and the trees shook in response.

"Mom?"

She stopped with her back to me and her hands hung loosely at her sides. My stomach tensed and I tried to pull myself out of the vision. Something was holding me there, something more powerful than me.

"Mom?"

I tried to step away, but I had no control over my body. Something urged me forward and I reached towards her, placing a hand on her shoulder. Her skin was icy and the moment I touched her, her body jerked back around.

"Not anymore," said a dark, demonic voice.

I jumped back as the demon inside her unleashed a primal snarl that stung my ears. The fiercest fangs I'd ever seen replaced her teeth, and the black tongue of a snake shot between them, hissing towards me.

Black filled her eyes and her tanned skin turned to an ashy white. Small cracks broke over her body and face. Blood seeped from the freshly made breaks. It was red at first, but turned black as her skin paled. Her black tongue slipped from her mouth, sliding over her lips and they changed from a light pink to a deep purple. Her breaths began to come in heavy pants, and she stepped towards me.

I tried to move back, but my legs were frozen in place. Her steps quickened as she rushed towards me, and I held a hand out to brace myself for the impact. Her body stopped against my touch, and her purple lips curled into a disturbing smile.

Bright orange light flashed through the cracks in her body. The life was gone from her eyes and a soft breeze blew past us, pushing flakes of her skin into the air. Her body lit up in a stream of orange and red and began to collapse.

"Mom!" I screamed.

She fell towards me and I reached out to catch her. My hands plunged into her chest and ash exploded everywhere, scattering her remains in a swirl of powder. I pulled my hands back and they were covered in a black, viscous fluid. Loose pieces of gray and white ash stuck to the liquid, feeling like hot tar that reeked of sulfur.

"It's your fault you know." The voice that spoke made me shutter.

I turned around and Riley was standing behind me. My pulse burst in my throat and pain shot through my arm. I could feel the emotions tugging at my heart. I'd lost her. Again.

"If you hadn't come after me, she wouldn't be dead, Chase. You did this. You took her from us."

"That's not what happened," I said.

"It is, and you know it. You murdered her."

Pain moved up from my elbow and over my shoulder, creeping up towards my neck. Riley lifted his empty palms and I felt his power. My hands trembled. I pulled at my magic, searching that place deep inside my soul. It wasn't there. The stirring of the untamed power that lived within me was gone, stolen by the fear that consumed my veins.

I winced in pain and turned to run. Leaves slapped against my face and branches scraped my skin. I tried dodging them, but another obstacle was in my way. I skipped over large rocks and dead brush, but when I tried to jump a fallen log, a force hit me from behind. Something sharp stabbed my back and I flailed to the ground, landing in a mud hole.

It was thick and cold, and a grim force that lived inside the hole pulled me deeper. I grasped at the wet dirt around me, digging my fingers into the thick flesh of the earth, but it crumbled in my grasp and stuck to my skin. Thick claws of mud wrapped around my ankles. I tried pulling at the bank of the mud hole, but I only succeeded in pulling in more dirt.

A huge orange tiger sat at the edge of the hole. Its massive form had an air of strength, and its eyes shifted from cat eyes to snake eyes and then back again.

Riley laughed and stepped onto the fallen log, his black dress shoes shiny and untouched from the earth. His black pants were held up with a bright golden belt buckle, and the tight black t-shirt that hugged his muscular frame was out of place. The man I knew was a collared shirt type of guy. This wasn't the man I knew.

Riley's blue eyes glared down at me. His face was smooth and unblemished. Sandy blonde hair was cut short and neat around his ears, but the look painted on his face was fierce. It was the look I remembered from my days with the Circle. The look he got right before a hunt.

"I see you've met my new pet." Riley smiled, and I could feel the heat of his power moving around me. "All of this is your fault,

Chase," he said, and his hands reached towards me. "Your mother's death is on your shoulders, and if you don't cooperate, her life won't be the only one taken from you."

Red flames exploded over my arm and I tried to defend with magic. I pulled at my elements, but they weren't there to be summoned. The fire crackled against my skin and I screamed. I waved my arm in the air trying to extinguish it, but it only swayed with me.

I dipped my arm into the mud hole, suffocating the fire in thick, liquid dirt, but as I brought it back up, the mud acted like an accelerant and it moved up my arm.

The fire ate away at my flesh, forcing it to blister and burst all at once. I used my other hand to try and push myself up, but thick mud covered hands had wrapped around my waist and pulled me deeper. Pain seared through my arm as blisters popped. I screamed and cried out as the flame caught my shoulder, the skin splitting and curling back at the fire's command.

The wind picked up and the trees swayed. More thunder boomed, but this time, I could feel the magic. It wasn't my magic, but Rayna's, coming back and pulling me to safety.

"Chase! Snap out of it. Come on!" Rayna's voice echoed around me. The leaves shot up from the ground at the sound of her voice, flailing in the wind. Her element surrounded me, forcing its way inside and tearing the forest away.

I shook my head and my vision blurred. Bright dots encircled me, leaving a fuzzy sensation to cover my body. The training room came back into view and Rayna was standing in front of me, trying to protect herself from the flame.

The fuzzy feeling faded and pain seared through me as bright white fire coursed up from my hand, covered my arm, and started to blister my neck. My pulse raced and I muffled a scream through gritted teeth. The skin on my neck split and peeled back as the flames caught the skin. Hot, clear fluid burst from the blisters and ran over my body, unseen beneath the flames.

"Use your water element!" Rayna screamed, holding her arms up in front of her eyes.

I ripped the water up from my soul and the cold rush responded. Water shot through my body and over my arm, smoothing the flames. Smoke barreled up from my injured flesh, but the water didn't stop.

Power rushed down my arms and filled my palms, exploding forward. I tried to draw it back, but I couldn't. Water burst from my hand and pushed me back across the mat, like someone had opened a fire hydrant. The eruption sent Rayna across the room and pinned her to the wall. I heard a cry of pain as she made contact, breaking the drywall and falling through, but the magic still didn't let up.

The water moved in a rapid assault and wedged her between two wooden studs, a solid display of strength and power. My pain faded as the ice water numbed the wound. I took that moment of relief and pulled the water back with my mind, cutting the element off. I pictured that invisible hand reaching out and tearing the element back, forcing it into my soul. The water slowed and came to a stop as though someone had tightened a leaky faucet. It dripped from my palm and as the room grew silent, all I could hear were the panicked breaths that raced from my lips.

"What's going on?" Tiki burst into the room, looking between Rayna and me.

"Help her." I winced, unable to move or push myself to my feet.

Tiki ran straight for Rayna, reached inside the wall, and pulled her back into the room.

My deep breaths didn't slow as I watched. I couldn't move; all I could do was stare in disbelief. I wasn't controlling this power, it was controlling me.

Rayna collapsed to the floor. She was drenched, her lips were blue from the icy water, and she was gasping for air.

Tiki smashed his hand into her back repeatedly until Rayna choked against the force. A downpour of water fell from her lips and spilled onto the padded floor. She gagged and coughed before another mouthful came up, finally allowing a rush of air into her lungs.

Rayna coughed and wheezed as she got the oxygen her body craved. Black and red hair stuck to her face, and the streams of liquid that ran off her slowed to a steady drip. Tiki pulled her to her feet and once she'd caught her breath and gained her footing, she rushed towards me.

"Chase, oh my God, are you okay?"

"What did I just do?" I couldn't take my eyes off of her, but I was speaking more to myself.

"It's not your fault…" She trembled, the blue color not fading from her lips.

"Yes, it is. It's all my fault. He's right."

"Who's right?" she asked.

"What is going on?" Tiki asked. He opened one of the cabinets that lined the wall and came back with a blanket to wrap around Rayna. "Your arm…"

Rayna pulled the blanket tightly around her and covered her mouth as she followed Tiki's gaze.

From my shoulder to my hand, all the skin was gone, leaving nothing but raw flesh. It oozed clear fluids, glowing bright red near my shoulder. As it moved down my arm, the burn got worse. Strings of dead, black flesh swirled in the creases of marred skin.

My eyes opened wide. My entire body began to quake and I couldn't speak.

"Chase, you need to heal this, now." Rayna shivered.

I tried to move my hand and there was nothing but pain. A chill set in through my body and the tremble turned into violent shaking. Rayna's element covered me and reached inside, searching for something to cling to.

"Come on, Chase, give me your element," she said.

I could hear her voice, but I couldn't comprehend what she was saying. All I could see was the damage to my arm flashing through my mind.

"Please."

"What's happening to him?" Tiki asked.

"He's going into shock," Rayna replied. "Chase, come on, come back to me."

"Can't you do some witchy stuff?" Tiki asked.

"I can't. My witchcraft is…undeveloped. I can only do minor spells. It takes a powerful witch to heal, and even then it's usually in the form of a potion."

I could feel Rayna's hands moving over my neck, checking for a pulse.

"Come on, Chase, work with me!"

I pushed through the fear and met Rayna's eyes. She stared down at me, assuring me that I'd be okay. I realized then, that besides my mother, I'd never completely trusted anyone. Not like I did Rayna. It should've worried me that I had such faith in her. Worried that one day she might leave, too. I should've been scared, but I wasn't.

Drops of water bubbled inside me as her element latched to mine. The power grounded me and gave me the push I needed to come back to reality.

"Just focus and let my magic guide you." Rayna's voice was strong. Her slit pupils grew as I stared into them, and they didn't bother me; they made me feel safe. They weren't the eyes of a demon anymore. They were the eyes of someone I cared about. They were Rayna's.

As the water filled me, I focused on the magic healing my arm. It wasn't like all the other times. It wasn't smooth and calming. It was painful, and it took all my strength not to cry out and lose focus.

I felt the skin growing, moving, and tearing over battered flesh. Skin grew down from my neck, and a million needles plunged through my arm at once. The water raged under my skin, but I didn't lose control. I clung to Rayna's magic and let it steer the element down to my hand until I felt the warmth of fresh skin wrap around my fingers.

When Rayna's element unraveled from mine, I opened my eyes. She still kneeled above me, but the worry had faded, and relief painted her face. Parts of my arm were fully healed, but most of my skin was red, sore, and scarred. I tried to move my fingers, and although it hurt, I had full function of my hand. I silently thanked the gods and collapsed back onto the mat.

"How does it feel?" Rayna asked.

I shook my head at first, fighting the exhaustion. Sleep pulled at my eyes. I was fading fast.

"Sore. Are you..."

Her skin was a shade of gray with dark blue veins beneath it, but as the minutes passed, the pale color came back, pushing the veins beneath her naturally milky white skin. The blue of her lips washed away and a soft pink hue came back into her pouty smile. The glossy film that covered her eyes was gone, and aside from wet hair that clung to her face, she looked normal again.

"I'll be fine," Rayna said, still wheezing.

I tried for a smile, but it came across as more of a wince.

"What happened? It's like you went to another place," Rayna said.

I knew she could handle it. I knew I could trust her more than anyone else, but I couldn't tell her. She had enough going on with the shift; she didn't need my insecurities dragging her down further.

"Nothing. I...I just lost control."

Rayna's lips fell into a pout and she pulled her eyes away.

"I think that's probably enough fun for one day."

"I'd say so," Rayna said.

"Fun? You Earth people have a strange idea of fun." Tiki shook his head.

"That's not what...never mind."

I moved to my feet and black dots flooded my vision. Tiki reached out and helped me regain my balance.

"Are you sure you're both okay?" He eyed us carefully.

Rayna and I nodded.

"Good." He smiled. "So we're still going to Revelations?"

"Maybe later. I need to lie down," I said.

I took a few steps forward, but the darkness took over more of my vision and I stumbled to the ground. I caught myself on my knee and brought myself down to the mats. The cold fabric squished and molded against my face.

"Chase, what's wrong?" Rayna's voice echoed in my head.

"I'm fine...I just need to rest." I heard Rayna start to speak, but the words were lost. I couldn't fight it anymore and I let myself fall into darkness.

Chapter 7

I opened my eyes to a soft chirping. I was in my bed, and Rai's bright white feathers were gleaming on the bedpost from the incoming moonlight.

"Hey, girl."

Rai chirped, flapping her wings idly. Light flickered in her blue eyes, and she leapt from the bed, flying out of the room.

I tried to roll over, but winced as my arm touched the mattress. The skin was red and purple, bruises and blisters spotting the half healed flesh. A strip of white skin that had fully healed left a long scar that spiraled up my arm and disappeared under my shirt. I made a fist and clenched my teeth through the pain, trying to call my element.

The water came up in a surge of smooth, calm power. I envisioned the pain vanishing and the pale tones returning to my skin. Nothing happened. The magic coursed back and forth under my arm like a tide rolling in, before falling back to my soul.

I unclenched my fist and cursed under my breath, swinging my feet over the bed. The pain in my arm faded to a simmer, but it hummed along with an annoying consistency. I pulled my neck from side to side, letting the bones crack down my spine. Aside from the pain of my arm, I felt great.

I heard the soft tap of footsteps coming down the hall and Rayna appeared. My eyes opened wide as she leaned in the doorway, my breath catching in my throat.

A tight black dress wrapped around her small frame with thin straps that crossed in the back. The dress was short, stopping just above her mid-thigh, revealing long, toned legs. A low v-neck showed more than I was comfortable with, but voicing my opinion wouldn't change anything. Then again, I wasn't sure why it bothered me at all. It was just Rayna.

"Hi…" I said, my voice raspy and hoarse.

Rayna smirked and rested her head against the doorway, red and black ringlets curling down to frame her features. "Feeling better?"

"I'm good." I nodded. "Look, about earlier, I…"

"I know," she said, lips curling into a half smile. "The magic is really starting to take its toll, huh?"

"You could say that." I looked down at my battered arm.

"We're getting ready to leave. I wasn't sure if you'd still be up for coming with us."

"I'll come. Just let me grab Willy."

"He's not coming…" Her eyes fell to the floor.

"What is it?"

"He doesn't look so great."

"But it's been twenty four hours. He should be fine by now."

"He should be."

I sighed and ran a hand through my hair. I told Rayna I'd be down in a few minutes. First I wanted to check on Willy.

I pulled on a pair of jeans, a long-sleeved white shirt, and put my black cap on backwards. This was as dressed up as I got.

I knocked on the door to the spare room until I heard a rough cough and a gravelly voice. "Co–, come in."

The door was silent as I pushed it, and I cringed as the smell of sweat and body odor hit me. Willy was under the covers. His discolored face was a greenish-gray, and a thick layer of sweat gleamed off the surface.

"God, Willy, are you okay?"

Willy's brown eyes watched me as I inched closer. They were glassy.

"I'll b–, be fi–, fine…My bo–, body is just fighting the infec–, infection."

"You don't look so great. Maybe I should call Grams…"

"No!" Willy said. "I'll be fi–, fine, Chase."

"You sure?"

"I'm su–, sure. I'm ju–, just going to re–, rest," he said, but it wasn't his usual stutter. He was trembling. "I'll be good in a da–, day, or two. Promise."

I eyed Willy; his glossy brown eyes seemed to look right through me.

"Re–, really. I'll be o–, okay."

"We're taking Tiki to Revelations for a while. I'll be back soon to check on you. Okay?"

"Tha–, thanks Ch–, Chase."

I nodded and closed the door. I knew demons couldn't get sick and they didn't get infections, but something wasn't right, and the feeling in my stomach told me it was my fault.

I started down the stairs and decided if he wasn't better by tomorrow, I would call Grams. I shuddered at the thought. For a decrepit old lady, she was scary, and that was before you considered she was a powerful witch. But he had gotten hurt because of me, and if I couldn't fix it, I wouldn't avoid her and risk something worse happening to him.

"What do you think?" Tiki asked as I came into the kitchen. He was wearing the tight, sheer leopard print shirt he'd bought. It looked flashy against his caramel skin, but oddly, it didn't look horrible. Light gray dress pants, however, seemed out of place below the glossy fabric.

"It's...nice." I tried for a smile.

Rayna laughed and a smile broke over her freshly glossed lips.

"And me?" Rayna twirled, black and red ringlets bouncing as she moved.

"Judging by your outfit, it looks like you shop in the little girl's section, but you look good." I smirked.

"Good?" She sounded disappointed. "What do you think Tiki?"

"You look incredible." He grinned.

"Thank you." She tilted her head, lips curling into a smile.

"I said you looked good, is that bad?"

Rayna shrugged. "It's fine. Let's go."

****

Stonewall, New York wasn't different from any other city now, but at one time it had been a thriving mom and pop community. That world died sometime in the sixties when it became more of a business center than a family run town. The rundown buildings and burnt out neon signs still littered the streets in the seedier part of downtown, showing what once lived here.

Revelations was at the end of an unlit alley, and as we neared the entrance, we had to break the glamour. As it peeled away, the red and blue neon signs flashed Open and Revelations, casting a glow over the entrance. The front door was at the bottom of a concrete stairway, a solid steel slab covered with dents. It was the only thing that separated us from the half-demon world behind it.

Rayna went first, pulling the door open with ease, and the aura of Revelations overloaded my senses. The smell of sweat, blood, and something more filled my nostrils while rock music blared into my ears. The tingling sensation that all hunters got around demons shot through my body, leaving goose bumps spiraling up my arms.

The doorman was well over seven feet tall, with a messy beard that covered his face. Tribal tattoos covered his body and metal rings hung off his ears, eyebrows, lips, and nose. His thick body swelled as we approached, the ink moving with his flesh as his muscles bulged. Solid black eyes stared down at us and the expression on his face was blank, yet somehow managed to be intimidating.

"Weapons," he demanded, and the voice suited him perfectly: deep, dark, and scratchy.

Rayna reached out and handed him two small blades and the bouncer raised a brow.

"Where does she hide weapons in that tiny…dress?" Tiki asked.

Rayna turned around and eyed us both. "You'd be surprised." She winked.

I pulled both daggers out of the sheath on my lower back and the bouncer grunted, holding out an enormous hand. I placed both blades in it and tried not to make eye contact. I'd never encountered any problems here before, but I wasn't exactly a welcomed patron at establishments like this.

Revelations was packed and we weaved our way through rows of full tables. Underworlders occupied the pool tables, dart boards, and the dance floor. There was even a line in front of the jukebox.

We followed Rayna as she navigated through the crowds until she stopped at a small, empty table with four stools. Chills rode up my arms, and I was happy to see Vincent's usual booth was vacant.

"What do you want?" The waitress glared at me.

Her jet black hair was pulled back in a tight pony tail. Dark makeup was painted on her face, and a barbed wire tattoo that started at her neck disappeared under a tight pink tank top that read Get It Yourself in glitter.

"I'll have a Coke," I said.

"Me too," added Rayna.

The waitress looked to Tiki who shrugged. "I will have this Coke they speak of."

The waitress stared blankly at him and Tiki's lips curled into a sheepish grin. She rolled her eyes and mumbled under her breath before walking away, hips swaying in her short red and black plaid skirt.

Tiki's orange eyes floated around the room and a smile crept over his lips. "I've never seen so many of them."

"Well, if you're going to stay here you better get used to it," I said.

An awkward expression fell over Tiki's face as two pretty girls stalked towards our table. Seductive glares swallowed him as they moved in on their prey.

They both had knee high leather boots, matching black dresses, and white as milk skin. Long, blonde hair hung down their backs, and the only difference between them was their eyes. One had blue, while the other girl's eyes were green.

They closed the gap between us, their eyes devouring Tiki. "You have to dance with me," one girl said.

"With us," the other added.

Tiki's eyes turned away from them quickly, but his smile grew.

"Aww, he's shy," said the first girl.

"Maybe he just needs a little push," the second added, a moist pink tongue slipping out over her lips and flicking the long ivory fangs that dropped from her gums.

Both girls giggled and reached out their hands.

The sight of the fangs kicked my instincts into gear and I reached around for my blades. I sighed in disappointment as the sheath was empty, and Rayna grabbed my arm.

"Chase, relax."

I looked back to the girls who were paying no attention to me, and they each slipped a pale hand decorated in fake nails and an array of bracelets around Tiki's. Tiki looked to me with a goofy smile and let the girls lead him to the dance floor. It only took a moment before they threw their bodies around him.

Rayna arched a brow. "Wow. He makes friends fast."

"I'll say."

The waitress came and dropped our drinks at the table. Pop splashed over the edge of each glass as she set them down and walked away without a word.

Rayna and I sat quietly across from one another. Her nails tapped idly on her glass and her eyes wandered around the club.

"You sure you're okay? I know you said you were, but what happened in the training room...it was pretty intense," I said.

Rayna played with the straw between her lips, letting feline eyes move over my face. She seemed lost in thought for a moment before she pulled the straw from her mouth. "I'm fine. I shouldn't have pushed you when you didn't feel ready. But we really need to get control of this before someone gets killed."

"It's not that easy..."

"Look at it like this. Why is it when we're in a fight your control is impeccable, but when you try to call your elements in a controlled environment your magic goes everywhere?"

"When we're fighting, things are different. I'm calling my element and unleashing it on an enemy. I don't care how it happens and I'm not trying to control it. I turn it on, let it out, and turn it off. When we're training, I'm trying to bend it to my will. It's easier to start a fire than it is to contain one."

"We need to try something different. Find something that works for you. Your elements are different than Marcus' and mine. Maybe we need to train them differently."

"Well, whatever it is, I hope we figure it out soon. Something bad is going to happen. I can feel it."

"With Riley?" Rayna's eyes locked with mine and I turned away, searching for Tiki in the mesh of people rubbing up on the dance floor. "Chase, talk to me."

I sighed. "I saw him."

Rayna perked up in her seat and pushed her drink to the side. "What? When?"

"In the street when we went shopping, and again when we were training."

"When we were training?"

"I had a vision, or I went somewhere else. I don't know. But he was there...with my mom."

"Your mom?" Rayna asked.

I explained the visions as vaguely as I could. I had no desire to relive it in detail again. Rayna's expression turned from surprise to sadness, and I turned back to the dance floor. Tiki was in the middle of the two girls, not really moving, but he was grinning as they danced against him. Tiki waved eagerly and his excitement forced a smile to my face.

"I don't really think he needed us to be here."

Rayna smirked, but didn't look at Tiki; her eyes were all for me in that moment. "You know I'm here, right? If you want to talk about...I mean, I've been where you are. I know what you're going through."

I watched the ice clank against the side of my glass, and I stirred it around the dark liquid with my straw. I didn't want to talk about it, but as the tension crept up between us, I realized I'd rather be open with her than have things be uncomfortable.

"I just don't know what to say. Does it hurt? Yeah, of course it does. But talking about how much it sucks that she's gone won't bring her back. My father killed her, but it's my fault."

"It's not your fault! How can you even think that?"

"I'm the reason it all happened. If I hadn't pushed you to go to Vincent's, we wouldn't have had to get the scroll. If I would've waited for Marcus to go to your old house, they'd never have found out you were the key. Everything that happened was because of me, and my mom had to come save my ass, all because I didn't listen. I was too stupid to see the dangers."

"First off, that's a lot of ifs. Second, you saved my life. Riley and the Dark Brothers would've found me one way or another. If it wasn't for you, I wouldn't be here."

"Maybe..."

"No maybe. You saved me, and if you hadn't gotten the scroll, Vincent would've found another way to get it. Then he'd have the scroll, the Mark, and the ring too."

"The mark that does nothing, a ring that just sits here and looks fancy, and powers I can't control."

"This place is fantastic." Tiki ran up to the table. He took a drink of his soda and spit it across the table and all over my face. "What is this? Poison?"

I grabbed a napkin and wiped the spit and soda that now dripped from my face. "It's a soda," I said through gritted teeth.

"How can you enjoy drinking this?" He pushed the glass away and Rayna laughed.

"Yeah, this is hilarious," I said.

Tiki looked between a giggling Rayna and me, but he didn't seem the least bit phased by anything that had just happened.

"It's strange here. At home, I was nothing. I didn't belong among the purebloods, and I had nowhere to go. I've rarely met any others like me, but here, I am an equal. And these women...they are everywhere, and they won't stop touching me." Tiki was practically glowing, his caramel skin flashing under the club lights.

"Hey, you didn't think you could hide from us, did you?" The two girls who had claimed him were back, licking the tips of their fangs.

I shuddered at the imagery, and if it was possible, I think Tiki's smile grew wider. Rayna rolled her eyes as more girls started to crowd around, all of them trying to touch him.

"It looks like you're doing just fine on your own, Tiki," I said. "I'm going to head home. I want to keep an eye on Willy."

"Me too," Rayna said.

"You don't want to stay? Come dance," Tiki said.

Rayna's smile faded and her eyes met mine.

I laughed. "No, I'm good. Are you going to be okay on your own?"

Rayna's eyes fell to the floor and then back to Tiki.

"Oh, yes," he said.

The women pawed at him and before I could say goodbye, he was being dragged back to the dance floor.

Rayna left some cash on the table and led the way out. We stepped outside and I slipped my daggers back into their sheaths. The air was brisk and the scent of fall was thick.

"It's nice out tonight, want to walk?" Rayna asked.

I took in a breath of fresh October air and nodded.

Things were quiet at first, only the sound of Rayna's boots tapping along the sidewalk. The awkward tension from Revelations was gone, but I felt like there was something else. Just as I was about to break the silence, Rayna spoke.

"My mother was a good person you know. The Circle made her sound...dirty. She wasn't like that."

I turned to Rayna, but her eyes were staring at the pavement.

"The Circle has a way of making even the smallest thing seem terrible. I'm sure she was really great."

Rayna half-laughed and shook her head. "You don't have to say that. We both know you don't believe it. She was a demon after all."

The comment forced me to do a double take. "You don't really think that do you? Maybe a few weeks ago you would've been right, but I don't look at the Underworld like that anymore. You of all people should know that."

Rayna shrugged.

"You have to understand where I grew up. The Circle isn't a warm and fuzzy group of people doing magic tricks. It's a boot camp. What the elders say goes. There is no difference of opinion. You do what you're told to do, and you believe what you're taught to believe."

"If it's that bad, I'd think you would've been happy to get away."

"Until I was exiled, it was all I knew. I was angry. I'd never be a hunter, never have my father's approval, and never have an elemental power. But once the Underworld got wind of what happened, I became a trophy waiting to be claimed."

"I guess you weren't given much of a chance to decide things for yourself."

"Not until I met you and Marcus. I never thought a half-demon would punch me in the face and turn around to save my life, that's for sure."

Rayna laughed. "You were being an ass that night."

"I think we've established that." I laughed.

The laughter faded and Rayna looked up at me. "Do you ever miss being part of the Circle?"

"Not since I realized what I missed didn't truly exist. Everything I thought the Circle stood for was a lie. The only thing I miss now is Mom and the life we had. At the time it seemed hard and I was angry about everything. But I'd give anything to have that back."

"I'm sorry...Tessa was really great."

"It's not your fault."

"I know, but...I know how much it hurts to lose a mother."

I didn't know what to say. I couldn't believe I was talking about my mother, but I realized then that Rayna really did know how I was feeling.

"They didn't let up, you know? They tortured her for hours, but she wouldn't tell them where I was," Rayna said.

"You watched the whole thing?"

"I didn't have a choice. When the hunters came, we didn't have time to escape. She shoved me into a cubby in the wall and masked it with a spell. I couldn't get out, and no one could get in. I watched them peel her skin off, one strip at a time, until there was nothing left. They tore…" Rayna stopped and covered her mouth. She closed her eyes, took a deep breath, and looked up at me. Tears built up on the edge of her eyes and spilled down her cheeks.

"You don't have to…"

"They tore her hair out by the handful. When she couldn't scream anymore, they set her on fire."

"That's…horrific." I dropped my gaze. I couldn't put into words how terrible that must have been.

Rayna sniffed and wiped the tears off her cheeks. "My mom was a powerful witch. After she died, the spell didn't fade right away. Even Marcus couldn't find me at first. I sat there, screaming, forced to stare at her lifeless body for an eternity."

Rayna's tears fell in streams and she lost her breath in a rush of sobs. Streaks of dark makeup slid down her white cheeks, and the reflecting moonlight made them paler than I knew they were. I stepped towards her and did the only thing I thought mattered in that moment. I wrapped my arms around her.

When I pulled her against me, her sobs became heavier. Her nails dug into my shoulders as she pulled herself into me. I winced at the strength in her grip, having forgotten in that moment that she was more than just a girl.

"Sometimes I hate her. I hate what she did. If she'd just given me to them…" She gasped through trembling breaths.

"Then you'd be dead too."

"But it might've gone quicker for her." Rayna sniffled and tried to draw back the tears.

"Your mother spent her last moments alive, keeping you safe. She left this world a hero."

"And now yours is gone because of me too."

"No," I said. I grabbed Rayna's shoulders and pulled her back from me, forcing her to look me in the eyes. "Don't think that for a second."

"She did, Chase, and you know it. I'm surprised you don't hate me." Rayna pulled away from my grip and turned her back to me.

"If it wasn't for our mothers, we wouldn't be here, and I wouldn't have you right now," I said. The words surprised me and I wanted to backtrack, but I couldn't.

We were outside the condo, and the building was a silent tower of dark glass. Rayna's tears stopped. She sniffled and glossy green cat eyes stared up at me. Streaks of makeup ran down her face, black drops of liquid hanging along her jaw.

"They're heroes, Rayna. We owe it to them to remember that."

Rayna was silent for a long moment. "You're right, it's just sometimes..."

"I know," I said. "It's easier to think about if you blame yourself."

Rayna nodded. "Thank you."

"For what?"

"For being here." She brought both her hands up and tried to wipe the smears of black from her face. "I've never talked to anyone about this before. Not even Marcus."

"I'm honored you would share that with me."

"I needed to. You need to know you're not alone." Rayna stepped into me and wrapped her arms around my neck. She squeezed her body against mine and I held her tight in my arms. The embrace lasted longer than I expected, and I felt Rayna's head tilt up towards me. I looked down into her eyes and I felt a closeness with her I'd never had before. I couldn't pull my gaze away from hers, and a smile came over her lips.

She pulled back slightly so her body was barely touching mine and only pushing against it with each breath. My stomach tightened as her warm breath rolled over my skin and a chill ran through me. Her lips parted the slightest bit and she tilted her chin up. My pulse exploded and adrenaline surged as she rose on her tiptoes, her lips coming closer to mine. I brought my hands up to rest on her arms, and the urge to pull her against me tore through my body. I resisted the impulse and leaned towards her.

When a sound crashed above us, we both jumped back. I gripped Rayna's arms, pulled her down, and covered her body. As shards of glass shattered around us, I could feel them raining over me, small pieces biting at the exposed skin on my neck.

As the last few bits of glass littered the sidewalk, a light flashed from the top floor, followed by a crash of thunder. It was coming from our condo.

I tore through the lobby, Rayna running at my heels. I smashed my fingers into the button on the elevator, hitting it repeatedly.

I couldn't wait and we moved for the stairwell. We put floor after floor beneath us in supernatural speed and broke through the stairwell door, slamming it against the wall. I drew both my blades and pushed the condo door open, taking caution with each step. Shards of glass crunched beneath my feet and I squeezed the blades in my hands.

Thick claw marks had been torn into the walls, decorating the floor with bits of drywall dust. Bursts of blood speckled the walls, and clear fluid ran down in fresh, thick streams. The hardwood was scarred with scratches, and the leather couch was ripped to pieces, clumps of white fluff covering the floor.

A body lay motionless in the center of the living room. Smoke billowed up from it and brought the smell of burnt hair and charred flesh, giving me an instant headache.

Amongst the fluff were white and gold feathers, some still floating down from the ceiling. Rai's four wings were extended, flapping about in one corner of the room. Her feathers were ruffled and falling to the floor. Loud, rapid squawking echoed through the condo, sounding fiercer than the small creature it came from.

Once Rai saw me, she dove from the ceiling, landing hard on my shoulder. Her small claws gripped me and pierced my skin. I could feel bubbles of blood from the punctures seeping through and clinging to my t-shirt.

"Easy, girl." I brought a hand up to pet her. She calmed as my fingers sifted through soft, white feathers. The squawking became a quiet tweet, and the grip of her claws lightened.

I stepped down into the living room, watching the creature lying face down on the floor. The stench was thick as we neared, and most of its skin was dark, charred, and still smoldering. I lifted my foot and used it to turn the limp body, but as soon as my sneaker touched it, the clean pieces of skin flashed and changed, matching the dark blue of my shoe.

"Willy?" I gasped.

His chest smoked, revealing a black burn that covered most of his torso. Long claws drooped from paw-like hands, and a strange snout took over most of his face. Vicious teeth hung from the jowls of his half-snout, and colorless, white wolf eyes stared lifelessly towards the ceiling.

His body twitched and began to shift. Bones cracked and the hair that covered the paw-like hands disappeared. Long black claws retreated into his fingertips and his face shifted and reformed. As the human counterpart came through, the dirty brown came back to color his eyes. His body took in a deep breath and I jumped back. The burns covering his flesh started to fade and the wounds closed.

"Okay, this night just took a very strange turn."

Chapter 8

Willy coughed and pushed himself up with his hands. Thick red mucus shot out of his mouth and he gasped for air.

"Ch–, Chase?" he asked.

"What the hell happened?"

Willy groaned as he propped himself up on his elbows. "I ha–, had an accident." His eyes shot around the room, confusion on his face.

"Yeah, I'll say."

Willy shook his head and looked down at himself. "My sh–, shoulder...it's healed." The bloody bandage lay on the floor by a torn shirt, his wound healed, not leaving a scar.

"But he's a demon. I didn't think he could contract the virus," Rayna said.

"I don't know what's happening, but it's not even a full moon," I said.

"What happened to your chest?" Rayna asked, watching new skin crawl over and cover the burn.

"When the beast took over and I st–, started to shift, I wa–, was starving..." His eyes flickered to Rai who squawked and started flapping her wings.

"You tried to eat my bird?"

Willy's eyes quickly pulled away from me and diverted to the floor.

I reached up and petted Rai, soothing her with my touch. She chirped and nuzzled her head against my cheek.

We all jumped when the condo's buzzer rang and the movement made Willy wince in pain.

"Hello?" I asked, my thumb on the button.

"Let me in." The hoarse and elder voice of Grams crackled through the speaker.

The voice sent a chill down my spine. I hesitated for a minute with my finger over the button before pushing it.

"I cal–, called her," Willy said. "I didn't want her to kn–, know, but then the pain was too much. I didn't know wh–, what else to do." Willy tried to stand up and fell back to the ground.

"I know it hurts," Rayna said. "Just try to relax."

"What the hell is going on?" Grams stormed into the room, leaving the door open behind her. A long cream dress that looked more like a nightgown covered her to her knees, but revealed frail, veiny legs. Her features were gray, making her look decrepit, but they contrasted with her bright blue eyes in an odd way. Her white hair was frayed, as though it hadn't been brushed in days. Bright purple high heels tapped along the floor towards us, and over her shoulder was a giant purse. A smoking cigarette hung from her lips and she took a long pull, letting the smoke seep out of her thin nostrils.

"Gr–, Grams," Willy gasped.

"What'd he do to you?" Grams turned and exhaled the smoke in my face.

"No–, nothing. It was the bi–, bite," Willy said, touching his healed shoulder.

Grams eyed me from head to toe and sighed. "Dammit." She waddled towards Willy, pushing past me with her shoulder. "When'd it happen?"

"A couple da–, days ago."

Grams dropped her purse to the floor and kneeled with surprising ease. She put a hand against Willy's face and pulled his lids up, examining his eyes. She reached an ancient hand into her bag and removed a small dagger. "Give me your hand."

Willy lifted his hand up and winced, turning away before she'd even touched him. Grams dragged the blade across his hand violently and Willy cried out.

"Don't be such a baby; it's just a scratch." Grams put the bloody blade back into her purse and dug around until she retrieved a small bottle of yellow powder. She yanked the cork out with her teeth and sprinkled the dust onto his hand.

Willy bit back a cry of pain as the powder bubbled and steamed in his palm. Grams used her long fingernail to stir the blood and powder together. Her lips moved quickly, but her voice was below a whisper. The dark red blood lightened as it mixed with the powder and began to swirl on its own.

"What are you doing?" I asked.

Grams looked up at me and licked the blood off her fingernail. A chill ran straight through me.

"This will tell me how soon we can expect a full shift."

"Why does that matter?" Rayna asked.

"Because the shift can be deadly. I need to know how much time I have to get him help."

"You can cure him?" Rayna sounded hopeful.

"Of course not," Grams said. "He can't very well do this on his own, now can he?"

Grams mumbled a few more words and the mixture bubbled before turning a bright purple. She grunted and pushed herself back to her feet. "Well, that didn't take long now did it?"

"What does that mean?" I asked.

"It'll only be a day or two now before he'll be a full werewolf."

"How is this possible?"

"He got bit, didn't he? What'd you expect to happen, puppies?"

"I just...I thought demons couldn't get turned."

"Well you thought wrong. It's rare, but it happens."

Willy looked up at her with fear in his eyes, and Grams reached down and ruffled his hair. "Ah, don't worry, William, we'll get you some help. Besides, I always wanted a puppy." She laughed and snorted, patting him on the head.

Willy's face paled and sadness pulled at his eyes.

"Oh, relax boy, I'm just messing with you," she said. "You're going to be fine."

"Fi–, fine? I'm a werewolf! How is that fine?" Willy yawned, and it stole his anger. He lay back down on the floor and closed his eyes. "I'm so tired."

"It takes a lot out of you," Rayna said. "You need to rest."

Before Willy could reply, his jaw fell open and a loud snore escaped. He was instantly in a deep sleep, enough so that he was the only one who didn't startle when foreign voices came into the room.

"We'll take it from here." A voice came from behind us, and it sounded far too deep for the man it belonged to.

The man was shorter but more muscular than me. His eyes were nearly black, and brown stubble littered his shaved head. Camouflage pants were tucked into black combat boots, and a tight brown shirt hugged his dark olive-colored frame. He stood at attention with his hands crossed behind his back and a blank determination on his face.

"Who the hell are you?" I demanded.

"I'm Jax Turner, beta-alpha to Radek Lawson, of the Shadowpack. That, there, is our pup," he said.

"I don't know what makes you think you can just walk in here and–"

"That pup is part of our pack now. It's our duty to train him, with, or without, your permission."

"You don't have my permission," I said, stepping in front of Jax.

Rayna stepped up beside me and Jax smirked.

"I've got no time for a demanding child and his girlfriend. Stand down."

"Does this look like the army? This is my house, not your backyard, so don't try marking your territory here."

"Oh, cut it out," Grams snapped.

Two more shifters walked into the condo, taking a stand behind Jax. But Jax and I didn't break eye contact.

"Chase!" Grams voice cackled again. "I told you he'd need help. Willy's better off with them for now. They can help him."

"But–"

"I'm his family, and I say what's best," she said. "Go on, take him."

Jax nodded and one of the other shifters moved in, picked Willy up with ease, and threw him over his shoulder. Grams stepped between Jax and me and took a full drag of her cigarette.

The bright red embers burst with light as she sucked the smoke into her mouth.

"Don't think I don't know what goes on in the Shadowpack," Grams said. "I know exactly what things are like there. So you take him, and you help him, but if you so much as step on his tail, you'll be answering to me."

"He will learn the way of the Shadowpack, starting at the bottom, like all of us did," Jax stated, locking eyes with her.

Grams grunted and Jax nodded, his eyes scanning each of us, before he turned and walked out of the room. With a snap of his fingers, the other shifters moved and followed him.

"Are you sure he'll be okay?" I asked.

"He'll be fine. They can teach him to control the beast. It'll be easier for him that way."

"You're not worried they'll hurt him?"

"He's a demon, even more now than ever. It'll be good if they toughen him up a bit…" Grams said, but her voice trailed off and she didn't seem her confident, witty self.

"I'll keep an eye on him," I said.

Grams snorted and laughed, but quickly stopped, eyeing me with a look that wasn't full of hate. She took a drag off her cigarette. Ashes fell off the tip as the embers burnt up to the filter. She dropped the yellow butt on the floor and squished it beneath a shiny purple heel.

I grimaced, eyeing the cigarette butt.

"You should consider checking this one in, too," Grams said pointing to Rayna. The concern for Willy was pushed back beneath her frail exterior.

"Rayna? Why?" I asked.

Grams reached into her purse and pulled out another cigarette, lighting it up and taking in a deep drag. "Look at her— she's practically shedding."

"Excuse me?" Rayna snapped.

"Neither of you knows a damn thing about shifters. Believe me, dear, you're better off in the hands of an experienced shifter than an ignorant hunter." Grams blew smoke from thin, pasty lips.

Silence surrounded us and Grams cackled, waddling to the front door, leaving a cloud of smoke behind.

"Who does that bitch think she is?" Rayna snarled.

"I don't know, but maybe she's not entirely wrong."

Rayna turned her icy gaze on me. Her emerald eyes glared like a lion on the hunt.

"I'm just saying maybe we should consider it. Marcus and I don't know the first thing about shifters, except how to kill them. An experienced shifter could be helpful."

"I don't want to be a shifter, and I definitely don't want to be part of some pack. I'm not going to be anyone's property. I can't believe you'd even suggest that." Rayna stormed towards the stairs.

"Rayna, wait..." But her heels clicked up the stairs and she disappeared around the corner. "What the hell is happening?" I sighed.

Rai chirped into my ear and startled me. She leaned against my head, her black beak rubbing on my cheek.

"I can't believe Willy tried to eat you," I said, rubbing my finger beneath her chin.

I took a deep breath and looked around the room. White fluff was everywhere, and the walls were torn from floor to ceiling. Unless Willy was scaling them, I didn't even know how he'd managed that. I frowned at the burn mark Gram's cigarette had made on the hardwood and kicked the butt across the floor. I didn't bother cleaning up. The mess would still be there tomorrow. Instead, I made my way upstairs in hopes I could sleep this strange night off. Maybe I'd wake up and discover it was all just a dream.

Chapter 9

Rayna was on all fours in front of me, but everything around us was a blur. Her green cat eyes were shining, as though someone held a flashlight behind an emerald.

She stared up at me, head moving from side to side. I tried to look around, but each time I focused on an object, it would blur and shift. The world turned around in a slow haze and when I came back to Rayna, she had changed.

Thick black paws took over her hands and black hair covered her arms. Blood ran down her chin as fierce teeth filled her mouth, lips pulled back in a snarl.

"Why do you want to send me away? I'm not a monster." Her voice was deeper, speaking awkwardly through her new teeth.

"I don't think you're a monster," I said, lowering myself to her level, but when she snapped her jaws, I backed up.

Rayna released a low growl and turned away. Her bones cracked as her limbs shifted into thick, black, muscular legs. Her torso stayed human as she crouched and leapt forward, letting four black legs break into a run.

"Rayna..." I shouted, but her figure faded into a blur.

I waited, hoping she'd return, but instead the voice of my father came from all around me.

"Difficult creatures, those women," Riley said.

Everything suddenly became clear. I was standing in the street outside Revelations. The October air was cool and streetlamps flickered around me. A bright half-moon hung in the sky, raining light onto the shadow-stricken street.

Riley's voice engulfed me and came from everywhere. His laughter leapt from the darkness and I turned in a circle trying to find him.

Like fog fading, the shadows split and he walked into my reality. Large black wings drifted like smoke behind him, and dark blue eyes mocked me as he stepped onto the pavement. He moved closer to me, and a streak of black swirled throughout the blue of his eyes.

"Chase, my son, I've missed you. How have you been?" he asked, giving me his sincerest smile. His voice was strange. His demeanor, calm. Everything about him was different than I remembered.

I was frozen. I wanted to move, but my stomach tightened like an iron fist that weighted me against the earth. My father, Riley Williams, stood before me. The man who murdered my mother had just smiled and asked how I was. I should've been angry. I should've tried to kill him, but all I could do was stare.

"Would it be too cliché if I said cat got your tongue?" He stepped around me in long smooth strides; the black wings, an extension of his body, wavered from side-to-side as they drifted behind him.

When I didn't react, he let out a laugh that was whole and deep.

"Relax son, it happens to the best of us. Sooner or later a girl comes along, takes our breath away, and leads us on a wild goose chase. Or in your case, a game of cat and mouse, I suppose." He laughed again. "Let her go, it's fine. You're better than her anyways. You shouldn't be slumming in the Underworld, Chase. You should be sitting on a throne, next to me, with ultimate power at your fingertips."

I took a breath and stepped away from Riley, keeping him in front of me. "You've got a lot of nerve coming here."

"It's a dream. What harm can come from us meeting here?"

I looked around. Everything seemed strange and different, but it felt so real. I called fire and the blue flame came with surprising ease. "I don't know how much harm a dream can cause, but I can cause plenty."

Riley's black wings blurred in and out of focus and snapped at the fire. The blue and silver flame sparked and extinguished itself, an unseen force pushing the magic back into my soul.

"Don't do that." His face turned serious, the black in his eyes still swirling throughout the blue. "Fire is my element Chase. I have more power and control than you could dream of. In fact, I have more control over your power than you do."

"You may control fire, but I have more than just flames at my disposal." I called my water, but I didn't draw its power out in the open. I pushed the magic against him and let him feel it.

"I think it's safe to say I know more about your abilities than you do."

"How's that?"

Riley chuckled and the black wings expanded. "All in good time, son."

I shook my head and let my magic fade. I knew I should be boiling with anger, but I wasn't. Riley's presence vibrated through the street, and power shuddered around me. All I could feel was fear.

"What do you want?"

"I just wanted to see my son. Is that too much to ask?"

"You're a murderer. And I'll kill—"

"Don't throw idle threats at me. We both know you're not capable of that. Especially not now." Riley's wings grew larger, the smoky black growing until it stretched over the entire street. I stepped back and cowered.

"You criticize me about the people I keep around me, but you've got plans to turn yourself into a demon? Look at you, you're nearly there," I said.

Riley's perfect white teeth disappeared under his lips. The black swirls flickering in his eyes grew thicker. "How dare you? Ithreal is a god. The creatures you associate yourself with are cockroaches in comparison."

"Ithreal may be a god, but that doesn't make you one."

"This is but a sample. Once I've completed the invocation, I'll be invincible. Not with a demon's blood, but a god's. You'll bow to my power, son, or you can choose to be a part of it. You can stand beside me, Chase. We can rule together and be a family again."

"You killed the only family I had."

A strange sensation warmed my soul and burned along my spine. A new magic surged, expanding like a balloon inside me. The fear Riley forced over me collapsed, and I reached for my element.

Like an addition of my body, a wave of water burst from my hands and crashed over Riley in a tidal wave. I pulled back to find him still standing in front of me, black wings surrounding him in protection. Disappointment filled me as the wings unfurled, revealing a calm, dry Riley.

"Your mother stood in the face of my greatness and dared to challenge it. She was expendable, as is anyone who stands in my way."

"You bastard," I said.

I called my magic again, but Riley's power came to life and pushed it away, leaving it simmering inside my soul.

"Enough! In this dream, I control things. I'm going to make this world a better place, son. With Ithreal's essence inside me, I'll bring power back to the hunters. I will do this with or without you. I was simply offering you another chance to correct your...bad judgments."

"I won't join you, and I won't let you do this."

"You can't stop me. Nobody can. You can't even conjure your own elements in my presence. Make the right choice. I will not extend this offer to you again."

"Good, I'm tired of hearing it."

Riley sighed. "Well then, now that we have that out of the way...you have something that belongs to me. The ring, give it to me." His tone turned icy and serious, dark eyes moving over me with a transformed determination.

"Forget it."

"You've met my new pet; do not make me unleash him on you, son. He will change your world in a way you cannot imagine. I am only asking out of courtesy. You do not actually have a choice."

"We always have a choice, and I'm choosing not to let you have it. I'd sooner give it to the Circle."

Black smoke blurred my vision, and in an instant, Riley's hand gripped my throat. His element was at his fingertips and heat nipped at my skin.

"Don't test me, boy." His voice was dark, the black swirls in his eyes expanded and merged with his pupils until his eyes were claimed by darkness.

I struggled against his magic and pushed past it, managing to call my elements up with ease. The water came and neutralized the burning around my neck, but that wasn't all. Surprise overwhelmed me when my fire element came up alongside it, working with the water to fight against his power. My elements were strong, but I'd never known the ability to call both at once.

Riley's magic wavered as I tested it against mine, and I could tell by his face that it caught him off guard. I took the opportunity and broke his hold on my neck. Black wings swung down and hit me, smashing me to the ground.

Riley's body was lifted into the air and the wings flapped, forcing him back in a single hovering motion. His feet returned to the asphalt and the strange magic I'd felt was back, tasting thick in the air.

"Give me the ring!" A demonic tone took over his voice and angry black eyes peered down at me.

"No." I challenged, jumping to my feet.

Riley growled and his black wings moved at an unnatural speed. They changed shape as they neared and shadowed claws ripped across my chest. I hit the ground, rough pavement rubbing along my back. The front of my shirt had been torn, and blood seeped through where the claws had broken the skin. Sharp pains came as the wound turned red, then black blisters formed around the raw, open flesh.

"That was a warning," Riley said, the black smoke coiling around him.

I jumped to my feet and pulled my magic to the surface. It moved with control I'd never known. Both fire and water came at once and I didn't hesitate.

Water burst from one hand and flame from the other, moving towards Riley in two separate beams of crushing magic. His wings

SHIFT

folded around him, but as the force hit him, he stumbled back. The shadowed wings broke briefly, and he grunted as my magic skimmed around him. I thought the elements would break his power, but the wings held strong. Fire and water blew past him, his wings absorbing what they couldn't deflect.

Smoke rose from his protective shell and took the form of an arrow, shooting towards me with mystic authority. I took my newfound control and pulled my elements back, switching to defense. A thick wall of icy water shot up from the pavement, but before I could do anything more, the arrow broke through and struck me to the ground. My focus broke and the elements retreated inside me. The arrow stuck from my chest, digging into the wounds from the previous attack. Tendrils of magic shifted and separated from the arrow, pushing against my body and holding me down like a massive hand.

Riley's black loafers clicked against the scarred asphalt as he neared. More tendrils of power shot out from his wings, merging with the arrow and pressing against me with renewed force.

"Last chance," he said, and the amusement I'd expected to see on his face wasn't there. A vacant expression owned his golden features, and his demonic black eyes contrasted the angel-like figure above me.

"No," I said.

The black smoke shifted and the wings vanished, becoming giant strands of dark power. They moved as a cohesive unit and all came down at once. They crushed the air from my lungs and broke through my skin, one tendril at a time.

"It doesn't have to be like this, Chase, just give me the ring."

The pain was too much. I couldn't respond. I gritted my teeth as tendrils pushed through my skin, forcing it to split. Branches of his power moved inside me, grinding against my muscles and biting into the raw flesh beneath.

"You can end this now, just give it to me."

I couldn't bear it any longer. My mouth opened and I released a scream. The black wisps tore themselves from my body and I cried out in pain.

I rolled to my side and coughed. Thick blood filled my mouth and poured onto the pavement. Thin lines of black ran through the blood, and more dripped from my mouth as I panted for air.

"Why do you need it? What does it do?" I asked, huffing between words.

"That is not your concern." Riley extended his hand.

I stared at his empty palm and shook my head. "I won't give it to you."

Riley sighed. "You're just like your mother. Defiant until the end." He growled, and the power hammered back into me. Black claws reentered the wounds and went deeper, pushing against the tendons beneath my skin. "This is just a dream, Chase, but I can still kill you."

I screamed in pain, Riley's words ringing through my ears. You're just like your mother. Anger roared through me, bringing with it a rush of adrenaline. I fought against his magic, my emotions masking the pain in a surge of relief.

"This...is... my...dream." I tried to bring my magic back and this time something was different. The fire and water came together, but something else rose with them: new power. The alien magic shot through my body, and it should've broken my focus, but I didn't let it stop me.

In a collision of pain, magic, and adrenaline, blue flame exploded and engulfed my body. It turned white as soon as it hit the air, and a heat I'd never managed shattered around me. The black tendrils screamed and ripped away from my body. White flames bit back against the black magic, forcing the streams to retreat to their maker.

I coughed and pushed myself to my feet. The fire was blinding and covered my body, but it didn't burn. Water steamed as it exploded around me. I sent it forward, and even as the black shadows engulfed him, it pushed Riley to the ground.

The black shell kept him protected, but my magic still crashed into his body and spun him across the road. I withdrew the fire and water, calling it back to my soul. As my two elements vanished, the new power came forward in a burst of energy.

The shadows came to life and pulled themselves towards me. Darkness leaked out of every crevice, moving like liquid over the pavement. Shadows draped themselves over everything. The magic blanketed me, shutting out the flickering streetlamps and the bright moon above.

I didn't know what was happening, but the magic was strong and it revitalized me. I moved forward through the darkness and although everything was black, I somehow managed to see perfectly.

Riley struggled to his feet, eyes scanning the shadows. I tried to slow my footing to a silent crawl, but I realized I wasn't walking on the street. I moved on the shadows above the ground, hovering on the air.

As I neared Riley, I swung my fist forward. My hand hit the side of his cheek and a loud crack echoed between us. Smoky tendrils broke free of his wings in the form of claws and swung around him, but shadows and air pushed me back.

As the branches of power missed me, they crashed into the ground. The pavement cracked and chunks of the road shot into the sky, trickling down around us. The stems wavered, transforming from long, smoky claws, to blades that cut through the darkness, desperate to find their opponent.

I walked on the shadows, calling my flame as I neared Riley. The fire stayed masked in the darkness and I let my flaming fist smash into him again. Black wisps moved to protect him, and the tendrils snapped towards me, but shadows moved with physical force and blocked their attack.

Riley's wings unfurled and his head peeked out. I swung my fist towards him again, but he predicted my attack and caught my hand. His huge grasp covered my fist, crushing my bones with something more than a hunter's strength. The pain broke my focus and the shadows around me paled. Riley came to his feet and reached for the ring. His scarred fingers pulled my finger back and tried to tear the ring from my hand, but it wouldn't budge. A blast of white magic exploded and he pulled his hand back. Riley growled in frustration and black wings took the shape of a hammer. The black weapon hit me and I soared through the air, rolling across the pavement.

I came to my feet as quickly as I could, and found it hard to breathe. With each breath, a piercing pain shot through my chest. Riley stood across from me, black eyes locked with mine, and the look on his face was one of pure anger. Black wings opened and with a single leap, they shot him into the sky, pushing the air beneath him.

"Give me the ring!" His demonic voice flared through the street, echoing off the abandoned buildings.

"No!"

His wings beat into the air, keeping him high above me. He screamed in anger and a dark growl shot from his mouth. "This isn't over!"

The wings folded and arched behind him, his body diving toward the ground. Just as he was about to hit the street, the road blurred, reality tore, and the ground opened, his body disappearing as the portal swallowed him.

The world around me shook and all its clarity vanished. The shadows peeled away and the flames faded, leaving not a mark on my body. The streetlamps and moon came back to life, and I was left alone, standing in the abandoned street. Everything around me shifted, merging together in a hazy portrait. The street vanished, the lights faded, and consciousness sucked me from the false reality.

Chapter 10

Beads of sweat ran down my face. The sheets were wet and cold against my skin. My pulse raced through my body and when the bedroom door opened, I panicked. I moved to grab the dagger from under my pillow, but I regretted the move as pain shot through my body.

"You know, I thought if I slept on it, I'd feel better, but I still can't believe..." Rayna stopped and covered her mouth. "What the hell happened?"

I followed her gaze to find myself, and the bed, covered in blood. The cuts on my torso were closed, but the flesh around them was raw and sore. Blood had run down my sides and soaked the bedding.

"I...I don't know, it was just a dream," I said. My voice sounded distant, even to me.

Rayna walked towards me and placed a hand on my shoulder, lowering herself to examine the wounds.

"I don't know what happened," I said. "It was Riley...."

"He's getting inside your head. I don't know how, but I can feel it. I can feel the magic around you." She shuddered. "What does he want?"

"The ring."

"The ring? Why?"

"Why does the Circle want it? It seems to me, that's our only lead to getting answers about any of this."

"He's getting stronger. It's like whatever power he invoked is growing. And so are you."

I ran my hands through my hair and sighed. "You're right. Something is going on with me. I just don't know what it is yet."

"You don't have to keep it all to yourself. You can trust me."

My body felt foreign to me, like it wasn't mine anymore. There was something else inside and I couldn't control it. But Rayna was right. I could trust her, and she of all people would understand. There was a giant cat that kept trying to tear itself out of her body. The problem was, I didn't know what was going on with me.

"I don't want you to think I don't care, because I do. It just seems like anytime my life gets on level ground, everything shifts and I'm stuck climbing back up the same hill."

"Maybe we should just call Marcus," Rayna said.

"No. Marcus is dealing with his own problems right now. I need to handle this on my own."

"You're not doing anything on your own. Remember what happened the last time we handled things?"

"I'm not saying let's go on a crusade. I'm saying let's figure it out as best we can. When Marcus gets back, we'll go from there."

"Maybe we could try Elyas?"

"We already went back to the tree. There's nothing there," I snapped.

Rayna lowered her gaze. I hadn't meant to sound harsh, but the backlash of the dream was running through my veins. I tried to think of another option, but I couldn't.

"You're right. Let's go to the tree. It's worth a try," I said.

Rayna smiled and her eyes held a look I remembered all too well. One I wished I could find again: hope.

****

The trees and brush of the south forest thickened the deeper we went in. Long branches threatened to mar our skin, while roots and decrepit trees tried to tangle our feet. I came prepared, wearing a long-sleeved shirt and pants, but it didn't keep the wooden limbs from scratching against my face and neck.

"I wish Tiki would've come. I think he'd enjoy this place," Rayna said.

"I didn't hear him come in last night, and after five minutes of shaking him, I gave up trying to wake him."

"Last night?" Rayna laughed. "I'm pretty sure he didn't come home until this morning."

The scratches on my face started to burn as we stepped into the clearing, and I was relieved to be free of the forest's grasp.

The sun was high in the sky, but the natural blue light that hung in the air was still there, floating around the largest tree I'd ever seen. It stood in the center of the field and the rest of the forest grew up around it. Multicolored flowers covered the tree and stood in full blossom. Soft, thick green leaves covered the branches, rejecting autumn's grasp. The other trees, however, had been clutched by fall, shaking every leaf from their branches. The open area was littered with crisp browns, reds, oranges, and yellows.

"I can feel it—the magic's still here," Rayna said.

We both moved to the tree and placed one hand against the bark, interlocking our free hands with one another. Rayna channeled her element through my hand and into the tree. Her breeze of energy made me smile, but the magic of the tree didn't ignite like it had before.

Rayna sighed, closed her eyes, and tried again. This time her Earth magic engulfed us. A breeze broke through the forest and into the clearing, lifting the dead leaves and blowing them into the air. Encircling us was a multitude of colorful, crisp, dead life.

The trees around us swayed and their roots stretched deep into the wet earth, but no other magic came.

"It's not working," Rayna said.

I pointed to the ring. "It's because she's in here. This is the soul piece."

Rayna took my hand in hers and stared into the ring. The silver band wrapped around my scarred finger and the unmarked red gem that was embedded inside.

Her magic throbbed under my skin as she channeled her power into the ring. Power encircled it, and spurts of her magic shot out of the gem and vanished up my arm. Goose bumps rolled through me. A power exploded and a bright light flashed between us until an invisible force blew us apart. We both tumbled to the ground in a shockwave of power.

I brought my hand up to inspect the ring, but it sat on my finger untouched. The band gleamed with an unblemished shine, and the red gem looked unscathed by whatever had happened.

"Sorry," Rayna said, wincing as she sat up.

"Don't be." I extended a hand and pulled her to her feet. "It was worth a shot."

A chill shuddered down my neck and the sound of feet shuffling caught my attention. Demons.

A man and a woman stepped out of the forest, leaves crunching beneath their feet. The man was tall and slender, with tanned skin. The sunshine reflected off his shaved head, and mud and pieces of dead leaves stuck to his clothes. He looked calm and comfortable, despite the white scratches the branches had left behind.

The woman was short, with chocolate brown hair in a pixie cut. A tank top and blue jeans covered her slender build, and she carried herself with poise and confidence. Her hazel eyes were large, round, and serious, but there was something about them—something familiar.

When they walked towards us, the sensation moved through my body again. I reached for both daggers and the man froze. He put his hands up as if to calm me, and stepped back.

"We are only here to speak with Rayna. We mean you no harm," he said, his voice warm and gentle.

"Who are you?" Rayna asked.

"I'm Garrett Bronson, proud member of the Hollowlight Pride, and this is Karissa Johnson."

Garrett spoke directly to Rayna and Karissa's eyes were locked on mine. Her gaze had a focus that narrowed in on me, but playfulness pulled at the edges.

"What do you want with me?" Rayna asked.

"We've been asked here by Charlie Tanamay, leader of the Hollowlight pride. He would like to request a meeting with you."

"Who is Charlie and why didn't he come himself?" I asked.

Karissa stepped forward, looked at Rayna, and spoke in a soft voice. "He didn't want to impose. He hopes by giving you a respectful and formal request, you'll be more willing to hear him out."

"Willing to hear what?"

"He wishes to help with your current...*situation*," Karissa said.

"I assure you his intentions, however cryptic, are honorable. He only wants to help," Garrett said.

"Well, you can tell your leader I'm not interested," Rayna said.

Garrett looked disappointed, but nodded kindly. "Of course. Sorry to intrude."

"We can help her." Karissa stared at me, her voice pleading yet confident, all at once. "We really can."

"Come, Karissa," Garrett said. "She said no, let's go."

Karissa sighed and the pair started to push back through the brush, branches cracking beneath their feet.

"Wait!" I shouted.

They stopped and turned to face us, but didn't attempt to get closer again.

"The Hollowlights are werecats, right?" I asked.

Garrett nodded curtly.

"Rayna, we should think about this."

"Don't start this again, I already..." she started, and a sudden realization came over her face. "You put them up to this didn't you? I can't believe you."

"I didn't do this, but I think we should talk about it."

"There's nothing to talk about."

"Something is happening to you and Marcus and I don't know how to help. Grams was right, you're better off working with an experienced shifter."

"We can figure it out without them."

"The night Willy shifted the wolves knew exactly where he was and what they could do for him. You may not like it, but whoever this Charlie guy is, maybe he really can help."

Rayna fought a silent battle in her eyes and stared at me with defiance.

"It's just a meeting," I said. "Please?"

"Fine." Rayna rolled her eyes and turned to Garrett. "But he comes too."

Garrett nodded. "Agreed."

When we broke through the last of the forest, there was a black SUV parked along the side of the road. Rayna and I hopped in the back, and as all the doors shut, Garrett turned around and sniffed at the air. "I smell dog..." he said, sounding confused.

Rayna and I exchanged glares and Garrett shrugged. He turned the key and the SUV roared to life.

"Where are we going?" Rayna asked.

Garrett dropped the vehicle into gear and it jerked forward. "Charlie owns a club on the north side of town. He'll meet us there."

"I don't remember there being a club on the north side. What's it called?" I asked.

"Shift."

Chapter 11

Shift was a club on the other side of Stonewall. By the time we got there, the sun was already starting its descent. Streaks of pink, hues of red, and blends of orange littered the sky, casting a warm shadow over the old, worn warehouse.

The windows that weren't smashed or boarded up were covered with years of dust. The grout between the bricks was sporadically missing, causing some to crack and fall from their respective places.

A small group of people gathered around the entrance of the building. Looking abandoned, like so many things in the Underworld, the club was covered in glamour. As I broke the glamour down, the red bricks turned to metal panels—clean gray sheets that covered the building. All the windows were whole, each tinted black so you couldn't see past the setting sun's glare. A purple neon sign flashed, *SHIFT*, and hung above two glass doors, with a large man standing in front of each of them.

The two bouncers stared down at us and sniffed the air simultaneously as we approached, disgust taking control of their features.

"Forget it, Garrett. They smell like mutts," one of them said.

Garrett turned and looked at both of us.

"They're here on request of Charlie," he said politely.

"If I let them in, there will be a riot. I can't do it."

Garrett stared up at the man twice his size and locked eyes with him. The bouncer struggled at first, trying to claim dominance before tearing his gaze away. He sighed and reached into his back pocket, pulling out a small unlabeled glass bottle.

"They have to put this on. I don't need everyone inside getting worked up." The bouncer tossed the bottle towards me and I grabbed it out of the air.

"Cologne? Really?" I asked.

"Pheromones. If you want in, that's the deal, hunter. Besides, I'm doing *you* a favor. You don't want to go in smelling like a wolf. It tends to get the kitties all worked up."

"If you say so."

I pushed the cap down and sprayed it a few times. I expected an overpowering scent to take over my senses, but there was nothing. Just a clear, odorless mist that sprayed over my body. Rayna rolled her eyes when I passed her the bottle and gave it a few sprays. She grimaced immediately and coughed. "That's horrible," she said, tossing it to the bouncer.

"Oh no, that's what heaven smells like, sweet cheeks." The bouncer grinned and took in the scent. His dark eyes turned back to me and his smile faded. "Don't cause any trouble, hunter, or you'll be dealing with me."

Past the first set of glass doors were two solid steel ones. Garrett pulled the handle and the bass poured from the darkness, music rocking through the entrance. Flashing neon lights exploded and the beat picked up speed. The crowd of demons, who covered the dance floor, screamed and machines poured smoke over the room, making it hard to see and even harder to breathe.

Karissa weaved through the crowd of people, past a row of booths lining the wall, and around the dance floor. When we reached the DJ booth, she moved up the steps and pulled open a door that read, *VIP ONLY.*

As the door shut behind us, the techno music stopped and softer music started. Leather couches and dark tables lined the walls. There were men in suits holding clear glasses full of dark liquor in one part of the room, and on the other side, guys in torn blue jeans and stained white t-shirts. Beautiful women wearing skimpy, tight dresses swarmed from group to group, giving off fake laughter and empty promises. Everybody seemed to be enjoying themselves.

At the end of the room was another door marked, *Employees Only.* It was made of heavy wood and Karissa pulled it open with unnatural ease. This room was quiet, with people sprawled out over the furniture. The dress code varied from dress shirts and ties to completely nude. Strangely, the ones wandering around naked seemed to be the most comfortable.

We stopped in the center of the room in front of two vacant leather couches with a small, wooden table in between.

"Make yourselves comfortable," Karissa said, and disappeared through another door.

My nerves clenched as all eyes turned to us, but when Garrett took up post behind us, everyone diverted their attention.

"What's going on?" Rayna whispered as we settled onto the couch.

"I don't have a clue."

Karissa returned, followed by a smaller native man. He was short, with long black hair that hung to the middle of his back. He wore blue jeans, a white t-shirt, and a red and black flannel jacket that was open and drifting around him. His steps were silent on the tile floor and he moved with grace, giving off a vibe of calming energy. His thick lips curled into a smile as he approached, extending an oddly large hand for his size.

"Welcome, my friends," he said, and his voice was deep but gentle.

"Thanks...I guess," Rayna said.

"What exactly are we being welcomed into?" I asked, shaking his hand. His skin was hot to the touch and extremely soft.

"To Shift!" He smiled and sat across from us. "I hope Garrett and Karissa were welcoming."

"They were," I said.

"I'm glad. My name is Charlie Tanamay, but everyone here calls me Chief. I'm the leader of Stonewall's Hollowlight pride, and a proud were-tiger."

"And why are we here?" Rayna asked.

"We'll get to that, but first, I'd like to tell you a little about our pride. We're not like most, after all."

"Okay..." Rayna said.

"Unlike most, we are a conglomeration of many shifters. Mostly cats, of course, but we do have a few more unique types."

His smile grew, revealing less than perfect teeth. Some crooked, some straight, and most of them stained yellow.

"Other breeds? Do you take werewolves?" I asked.

Charlie's smile disappeared. "I'm afraid not. The Shadowpack would never allow such a thing. Werewolves' blood in general runs a little hotter than most, but especially so when it comes to the Shadowpack."

"They won't allow it?" I asked.

"They're an organization that relies on its hierarchy. They rule with a heavy hand and force their members to live in fear. As such, they would never allow a wolf in Stonewall to be free of their pack. This is simply not our way."

Fear for Willy ran through my veins, but as Rayna spoke, I pushed it aside. This was an opportunity to get help for Rayna; I didn't want to muddle it with anything else.

"What exactly is *your* way?" Rayna asked.

"Werecats are a peaceful creature, but our strain of the virus is highly selective. Our kind is fading from the world, and as our numbers drop, we need now more than ever to come together. Our goal is to unite all the werecats under one banner."

"If it's so hard to transfer the virus, how did I become so lucky?"

"I'm afraid we have yet to find any rhyme or reason for why the transfer occurs in some and not others."

"Wonderful." Rayna rolled her eyes.

Charlie didn't seem bothered by Rayna's reluctance. He managed to keep the smile on his face even as the uncomfortable tension set in around us. "You're here because I can help you."

"With what?"

"There is no need to play coy. I can help you bring out your beast," he said.

"I don't need help with that. I don't want it out."

"Rayna..." I started.

"Don't, okay? Everybody is so keen on helping me control this. I don't want to control it; I want to be rid of it."

"Whether you wish to have the gift or not is not of importance. It is yours to have. You should feel proud, Rayna. The werecat is a strong and independent creature. The other animals respect it."

"Gift? More like a curse."

"Oh, but it is, child. With my help, we can move past the pain it causes you. I can teach you to control it so it comes only when you call it. As you learn control, the shift becomes less painful."

"I already told you I don't want to control it, so unless you can help me get rid of it, we're done here." Rayna stood up and looked at me. "Let's go."

I didn't move. I didn't trust random strangers, but I also wasn't about to blow off the only help we'd been offered. I knew Rayna was scared, but I wouldn't let her fear stop us from hearing our options.

"There is more for you to know. Please sit." Chief gestured back to the couch.

"And if I refuse?"

"You are not a prisoner. I simply want to help you. This can be a revealing and positive experience if you let it, but if you fight it, there is a high probability it will be the last experience you ever have."

"Are you threatening me?"

Chief shook his head. "The shift you're experiencing is deadly, even to a pureblood if not properly handled. You are a born shifter, yet you are not a pureblood. As such, your beast is wild, and requires even more attention than most."

I waited for Rayna's quick remark, but she stayed silent, the defiance in her eyes fading slightly.

"You've helped others?" I asked.

Chief nodded.

"Other half-demons with hunter's blood?"

"To my knowledge, there is no other exactly like Rayna, but there are hunters who've been granted this gift whom I've been able to help."

"And they survived?"

"It isn't easy, but it's not impossible. The shifter *virus* does not blend well with hunter DNA. With training, however, we can increase the chances of a successful change."

"So you can help her?" I smiled.

"How is that great news?" Rayna snapped. Her eyes were fierce and her tone, frosty.

"What do you mean?"

"I'd think you of all people would have my back on this. I don't want to shift. Can't you understand that?"

"Yes, I can, but you don't have a choice. If you don't get help, you're going to die. Do *you* understand that? I don't want to lose anyone else. I won't..." I let my voice trail off and diverted my eyes. "The shift will kill you."

I could feel Rayna watching me, and although she wasn't pleased, she sat back down. "What can you do for me exactly?"

"We need to bring the beast out slowly. You must learn to call it to the surface, and push it back down. Once you've mastered that technique, we can move into the specifics about shifting."

"That's it?" Rayna sounded unimpressed.

"It sounds simpler than it is. A painless shift is about being centered in your world, and understanding the beast. In order to accomplish this, you must connect with it, and be able to command it. I can teach you, and help keep your beast controlled."

"What makes you think I can't do that alone?"

"It's dangerous. If you don't know how to work with your beast, it will tear itself out and rip you in half in the process. These violent transformations are what take so many young lives. Plus, you shouldn't have to be alone. The first shift is painful. As you become more experienced, it gets easier. As a shifter, we don't rely on the cycle of the moon, but we do run on a monthly cycle. Once per month, from the date of your first full shift, you must release your inner animal. Some of the older shifters can change at will without suffering the side effects; the younger ones aren't that lucky.

"What side effects?"

"A young shifter needs hours of sleep after a shift. It's an exhausting process. When they finally wake, their appetite is tremendous and they're oversensitive to smell and noise. It doesn't happen to everyone, but there is an adjustment period."

"That's not so bad," I said, but those words earned me a glare from a still unhappy Rayna.

"This is a big change, Rayna. I understand that. Nobody is here to force anything on you. I simply want to extend the invitation. Our pride is leaving in a few days for a retreat. It's a perfect opportunity for a young shifter to get in touch with their beast in a safe environment."

"How exactly do you even know about me?" Rayna asked.

"Shifters are always aware of their own kind. Especially when they are of the same pride," Chief said.

"You said yourself you've never dealt with anyone like me. What makes you think you can even help?"

"I have helped many through this. Some were purebloods, others were hunters, and the rest were bitten."

"That doesn't answer my question."

"Your situation is different because you were never bitten. Without knowing when the first major shift is coming, we don't know how much time we have to work with."

"I've just met you and you're telling me you have a *feeling* you can help me. Not to mention, you haven't said what you want in return. Forgive me if I seem a little unsure." Rayna's sarcasm was thick, but the confidence she tried for wasn't there. She sounded confused.

"I understand. I am a stranger to you and I'm asking you to trust me. All I can do is tell you I wish to help, not harm you. And I want nothing in return. You are a shifter in need, and as such, I wish to help. I cannot promise any more than that."

"I need to leave," Rayna said.

"It may seem strange to you, but the werecats are peaceful people who take care of their own. Please consider my offer."

"I said I want to go."

Chief nodded, looking disappointed. "Garrett will take you."

I reached out and shook Chief's hand, thanking him for his time. Although Rayna wasn't happy about it, I felt relieved

knowing there might be a chance we could help her. Now I
needed her to see it that way.

****

The SUV hummed over the pitted road and an odd silence
hung around us. It was thick and uncomfortable, and I was happy
when Garrett spoke.

"He's a good man," he said, brown eyes watching me
through the rearview mirror. "Chief, I mean. You can trust him. I
was where you are once. I hated what I was. I didn't want
anything to do with anyone, especially not the Hollowlights."

"What changed?"

"Chief came into my life. He came into all of ours."

"It sounds kind of strange that one man changed all your
lives," I said.

Karissa turned around. Her hazel eyes held the most serious
expression. "If you'd ever met Arian—our old leader—it wouldn't."

"What made him so bad?"

Karissa released a sarcastic laugh.

"Arian was not a nice man," Garrett said. "He thrived on
torturing shifters, and if a werecat refused to join his pride, he
killed them. Plain and simple. Things were not ideal for us."

"That's putting it lightly," Karissa added.

"When Chief came to Stonewall, he saw the fear and pain
Arian inflicted. He taught us what Arian refused to: how to control
our beasts. As more and more shifters went to Chief for help,
Arian started to notice a change in his pride. When he discovered
what was happening, he kidnapped and tortured Chief,
threatening to kill him if he didn't fall under his command."

"So how did he get to be the leader?" Rayna's mind seemed
distracted by the story. Her feline eyes looked eager to learn what
happened next.

"Chief challenged him."

"To what?" I asked.

"All shifters follow a code. When a challenge is made, a shifter must either step down from their rank and leave the pack, or accept. If he accepts, the challenge is to the death."

"So Chief won," I said.

"Had there not been other shifters present, he would have surely killed Chief on the wall he was chained to, but even Arian wouldn't attempt that in front of the pride. It wasn't an easy battle, but even after weeks of torture, Chief defeated him, making him our new leader."

"Wow."

"Like I told you, he's a good man. He is honest, and most importantly, he shows compassion."

"Is that so?" Rayna's sarcasm came back with a vengeance.

"Chief didn't kill Arian. He gave him the opportunity to choose: death or exile. Arian chose exile and left the pride. With Arian gone, Chief has built this pride into something amazing. Other shifters like bears, foxes, coyotes, and all the birds, have always been on the bottom of the food chain. They are even rarer than the werecats, and because of that, they have no families. No pack. Chief has opened the door to them. Given them a home and somewhere they can belong. He cares not just for his people, but all people."

Garrett brought the vehicle to a stop in front of the condo and turned in his seat. "You don't have to love what you're becoming, Rayna, but you should love who you are. Love the life you have and the people who are in it. If you try to do this on your own, you won't have it for much longer."

Rayna stared at Garrett, but I couldn't read the expression on her face. She shook her head, jumped out of the vehicle, and didn't look back.

"Try to talk to her, Chase. It's in her best interest."

"I'll see what I can do."

Rayna was in the elevator and as I raced to beat the doors, our eyes locked and it started to close. She leaned back against the wall and crossed her arms. I was too late. The doors closed and the elevator sprang to life.

I moved up the stairs with a hunter's speed. I let the concrete steps vanish beneath me and I gripped the railing as I turned around the corner of each flight of stairs. "Rayna, wait." I came through the front door of the condo, but Rayna didn't stop. She took the last few steps and disappeared to the second floor. I followed her up and used my hand to stop her bedroom door from closing. "What, am I invisible?"

"Out!" Rayna pointed to the door.

"No, not until we talk about this."

"There's nothing to talk about. Now leave."

"Well, I'm telling you there is."

"What do you want to talk about? How much easier things will be for me if I go? That I need to gain control of this *monster* inside me?"

"Why are you making this so difficult?"

"Because I don't want to go."

"What's so bad about learning to control it? Or are you happy to let it kill you?"

"Don't stand there and nobly tell me it's for my own good because you don't have a clue what's best for me."

"I know it's killing you. You're trying to shrug this off like it's nothing, and it's not. I was there. I saw what it did. You need Chief's help."

"I don't need anything. Not from him, and not from you. Now get out of my room!"

"Too many people have died to keep us alive. I won't let you throw that away," I said, and my stomach tightened. I knew that was a low blow, but it needed to be said. I didn't know how else I could get through to her.

"Don't you dare throw that in my face!"

"It's true, or have you forgotten the sacrifices that were made for us?"

"Screw you, Chase!"

"Dammit Rayna, why are you so afraid of this?"

"Because you'll think I'm even more of a monster!" Rayna screamed, and silence fell over us.

I was frozen. "What?"

"Forget it. Just leave me alone."

"That's what this is all about? What I might *think*?" Rayna turned and stood with her back to me. "I don't know how many times I have to tell you, but I'm not that person anymore."

"Oh please, I see the way you look at me. At Tiki, Vincent, even Willy. You pity us."

"I do not."

"You feel sorry for what we are. You think you're better than us." Rayna's voice was quiet, but I could hear the anger in it.

"You have no idea what I think. If you did, you'd know the reason is so I can keep you in my life. I don't want to lose you, Rayna. Not Willy, not Tiki...I'd be okay with losing Vincent, but that's beside the point. All of you and Marcus are all I have left." Rayna turned around and met my eyes, but while her face showed anger, her eyes showed sadness. "But since you can read minds, you don't need me to tell you that, do you?" I turned and walked out of the room, slamming the door behind me.

I felt the fire burning within me. Anger and fear vibrated in my soul, rising to my fingertips and threatening to explode. "Not now." I spoke to myself through gritted teeth, closing my eyes and concentrating on the element. I tried to push the power back, not focusing on water to neutralize it, but reaching down and shoving the flame into my soul.

The memory of my dream came back. I had perfect control then and I needed that now. I couldn't afford to let this power own me. Not anymore. That confidence calmed me and allowed me to hold the fire back. The element churned, and with an invisible hand, I pushed it back beneath the surface.

The magic faded, as did my anger, and I released the breath I was holding. My pulse was racing in my throat and I took deep breaths, slowing it to a steady pace. I stood in the hallway, surrounded by silence, when Rayna's voice came from the other side of the door.

"I'll think about it."

Chapter 12

"Chase, come on, get up." Rayna's voice echoed around me. The world was fuzzy and I rubbed the sleep from my eyes. "What time is it?"

"It's late. Come on, we've got to go."

I pushed myself up and leaned against the headboard. "Forget it. I'm not coming shopping with you again."

"We're going to Vincent's."

That name pushed away the sleep that had clung to my body. "You woke me up to take me to Vincent? No thanks."

"He's got information about the ring."

"I'm sure he does. And I bet it comes with a pretty little bow and price tag attached. Not interested." I slid back down onto the bed and rolled over.

"He's offering it to us for free."

"Now that doesn't sound like there's an ulterior motive at work."

"Look, I don't buy it either, but if the Circle and Riley both want it, it's worth checking out. Get dressed," she said and walked from the room.

I pulled the pillow over my head to block out the sunlight. Rayna wasn't wrong. Riley and the Circle wanted it, and that painted an even bigger target on me than usual. But this was Vincent and he operated on hidden motives. He was the reason I had the ring and the Mark in the first place. I wanted nothing to do with him, but he did have a talent for finding answers.

I cursed myself and rolled out of bed, getting ready for what I could only imagine would be a day full of lies and deceit. Maybe once we'd sifted through all that, we'd get lucky and find some answers.

I didn't want to bring up Chief and his offer to help Rayna again. I knew the discussion wasn't over, but the last thing I wanted was another fight. She hadn't said a word about it on our trip to Vincent's, but the tension was there, floating between us.

Vincent's warehouse looked dull. The chain link fence was sagging in most places and the gate that was usually chained and locked was open and inviting. The boarded up windows and broken brick walls were in their true form. No glamour to be taken down. I still couldn't wrap my head around why the head of a powerful vampire family lived in a place like this. It just didn't seem right.

A blonde woman met us at the gate and led us inside. She pushed open one of the dented steel doors and smiled. "Welcome. I'm Veronica and I'll be taking you to Vincent."

She was one of the many vamplings Vincent had working for him. They watched over the vampires during the day and did whatever was needed on command. I knew they were just emergency food, but the vamplings thought they were a key piece to the vampires' survival; they all hoped to serve their master until he sought to turn them.

Veronica led us to the elevator and we got off at the mezzanine above. There was a single door with a handle and a deadbolt. The lock clicked with a turn of her key and she pulled it open. Darkness spilled from the room and she flicked a switch. Fluorescent bulbs flickered and hummed as they came on. The room was long and narrow and filled with musky, stale air. Painted brown walls were solid and windowless, hiding the light from the coffins that filled the room.

It was noon already, and by the smell alone, I knew each of these boxes was filled with a lifeless, rotting corpse. The thought of being in this room full of vampires–even dead ones–wasn't my idea of a good time. The fact that Vincent was still awake in the middle of the day spoke volumes for how powerful he was.

She led us into another room and rather than switch on the light, she touched the wall and pushed open a secret passage. Carpeted floors and warm colored walls were a change of pace from the concrete and steel warehouse. Wooden doors lined the hallway, and I could hear Vincent's voice as we neared the end. Veronica opened the last door and ushered us in.

Vincent sat in a high backed leather chair behind an oak desk. Leather furniture sat around the room, creating a modern feel and making the old paintings that hung on the wall seem out of place.

"Yes, I know what's at stake here," Vincent said. He turned in his chair, hands clasped together, and a single black earpiece hung from one ear. He put a finger up and continued with his conversation. "I can assure you that you have nothing to worry about. The Taryk family appreciates your support, and as always, we promise to deliver. Talk soon." Vincent pushed a button on the headset, pulled the earpiece from his ear, and threw it across the desk. He gave us a strange smile. "Forgive me, you know how things are. The Taryk family is involved in so much it's hard to find a moment's peace." His eyes fell on Rayna, a seductive hunger filling them. "And might I say, you look stunning today."

"Uh-huh," Rayna said.

Vincent frowned before turning to me. "To be honest, I wasn't sure Rayna would be able to convince you to come."

"The last thing I expect from you is honesty, but we need answers, so we're here. What do you know?"

"Skip the pleasantries and straight to business. I like that. Now, where to begin..."

"You said you had information about the ring, so start there," Rayna said.

A look passed through his eyes, one that made my stomach clench, but his tone remained cool and even. "I've been looking into your little finger decoration, and it turns out it may be a thing of great importance. An item many have spent lifetimes searching for."

"I'm listening."

"After the Great War between the Circle and the Underworld, the gods made an oath, one that forbade them from returning to the dimensions they'd created. The oath physically bound them to the higher plains, however, they all feared that

Ithreal might one day break free of his prison, so they made a loophole of sorts." Vincent pointed to the ring.

"This allows the gods to return?"

"Not exactly. That ring was given to you by Serephina's spirit, so unless I'm mistaken, that is *Serephina's Ring* or better known as *The Ring of Contact.*"

"Which is?"

"It isn't a key as much as it is a doorway. It allows its wearer to communicate with the gods. Some historians suggest the ring transports its wearer to the Otherworld: the higher plain where the gods reside. A few eccentrics even believe it can summon the gods back to their dimension."

"Let's hope the eccentrics are wrong," Rayna said.

"And you're telling us this out of the goodness of your heart?" I asked, sarcasm hanging on every word.

"You said Riley and the Circle have already shown interest. It won't be long before everyone else knows, too. Don't be so naïve as to expect this to remain a secret. Even with my influence over the Underworld, I can't keep you safe from this, unless of course...you wish to no longer possess the ring?"

And there it was. The silver lining in the cloud of misery he painted for us.

"If you think I'm going to give it to you," I said, "you're about to be very disappointed."

"I'm simply offering my services to protect it. I may not be able to control the way the Underworld responds when they discover *you* have it, but I can guarantee its safety in my possession. I can't extend that same protection to a hunter and a demon who kills her own kind. That would be...unhealthy for my family."

"That's great, but that doesn't change the fact I'm still not giving it to you."

"I understand." Vincent smiled, and I imagined it showed every ounce of sincerity he wanted us to see. "Would you at least do me the courtesy of allowing me to see it?"

"The ring doesn't leave my finger."

"I didn't ask you to take it off. I only want to look at it. Surely it's the least you can do after I so willingly shared this information."

I sighed and placed my hand on the desk in front of him.

"Breathtaking," he said, taking my hand into his. His hand was cool, and the skin abnormally soft, like a silk grip that wrapped around my fingers. His smile grew and his grip tightened as he pulled himself closer to the ring.

"I think that's enough." I tried to pull my hand back, but Vincent's grip closed around my wrist. "Vincent, I said that's enough."

"Relax, hunter. I'm admiring a true work of art. That's not something that happens every day. It's an honor to be in the presence of something so ancient. An item crafted from the hands of the gods."

"And that item currently occupies my finger."

"That it does..." Vincent's expression changed and a disturbing smile took over. "You know, technically speaking, this ring belongs to me."

I laughed. "How exactly did you come to that conclusion?"

"We made a deal. In exchange for your friend's safe return, you were to go and gather the scroll for me."

"And we held up our end of the deal; you were given the scroll."

"But you took the essence that scroll contained, a power that was rightfully mine."

"The only power that came from the scroll was the Mark, and that was meant for a hunter, not a vampire."

Vincent made a motion that resembled a shrug. "Perhaps, but a power, nonetheless, and one I asked you to retrieve for me. So it seems you have an outstanding debt to the Taryk family."

"You're turning the tables on us? Like I didn't see that coming."

"I would be willing to clear you of this debt, however. Simply let me protect the ring. You must understand it's in the best interest of my family that the ring does not end up in the wrong hands."

"You can't be serious," Rayna said.

"The men are talking here, love. Why don't you leave the business to us, be a dear, and fetch me a pint of blood?"

"Excuse me?"

"Now, now, my sweet. Don't make this bigger than it is. I need a few moments to discuss this with your friend."

"For someone who's five hundred years old, you're an immature dick," Rayna said.

Vincent's finely plucked eyebrows raised and anger filled his eyes. Black veins moved under his skin and I tried to pull my hand back, but his grip was too tight. He snapped his gaze to me and his anger vanished. Black veins disappeared beneath pale flesh.

"Look, *Vince*, as far as you and I are concerned, we're even. As for your family, I don't owe them anything. Now let go of my hand."

"Then it seems we have ourselves in a bit of a predicament, doesn't it?"

"Not at all. In fact, I'd say we're about done here." I channeled my element and drew fire to the surface. The blue flame ignited in my palm and Vincent jerked back, yellow eyes opening wide.

"Mr. Williams, that's downright underhanded. You're not playing by the rules."

"We're playing by *my* rules," I said, pulling my hand to my side and letting the power fade. It had come and gone with such ease; it nearly caught me off guard.

"Are we now? And what might those rules be?"

"One: don't ever try a stunt like that again. I don't like or trust you, and I have no qualms about killing you. Two: we're even. You asked for the scroll, and I gave it to you. You never said anything about power. You're a vampire who talks in riddles. You of all people should know when you make a deal: Be. More. Specific." I stared down at him, but he looked unaffected. Thin lips curled upward and amusement pulled at his eyes.

"Excellent speech, Mr. Williams. Very commanding and masculine, but you overlooked one detail." Vincent's face turned dark and serious. "You're in *my* house, and while here, you play by *my* rules."

"This meeting is over."

"I couldn't agree more," Rayna said.

"Is that a problem?" I stared at Vincent, pushing my magic over him and daring him to challenge me.

He clamped his pale hands together and brought them up to his lips. His golden eyes stared at me with indecision before he shrugged. "Of course not. You are free to go."

"Good," I said.

"But one more thing, if I may?"

I turned back to face him.

In a blur of speed, he appeared in front of me. His gaze was fierce and he stared up at me with a primal anger. His white skin turned translucent, black veins pushing against the flesh. Long fangs hung from his gums and all the muscles moved beneath his skin. His eyes filled with darkness and the stench of coppery death came off of his breath.

"Do not ever talk down to me again. I, too, have no *qualms about killing you.*" His words were sharp and acute, and I made the mistake of meeting his black gaze.

His power was like a freight train, smashing through my shields and into my mind. I collapsed to the floor and in seconds his body was on top of me.

"Next time, speak to me with respect, or I'll rip your throat out and dance in your blood."

I tried to move, but he was inside my mind. I was his puppet. He could kill me right now, or enslave me, all because I had locked eyes with him and didn't have my shields up.

Rayna grabbed Vincent's shoulder and in unparalleled speed, he gripped her arm and threw her across the floor.

"My kindness has its limits, even for you, my sweet. You've rejected me for the last time, and I will not allow you, or your pet, to interfere with my affairs." His voice wasn't smooth or seductive anymore. It was a deep, demonic growl.

Rayna crawled back to my side, and Vincent's eyes followed her. I lay on the ground beneath his grip, waiting for his power to crush me. But it didn't. Vincent rose to his feet, the milky white of his flesh rushing to the surface. Black veins faded, the yellow returned to his eyes, and the long fangs slid back into his mouth.

He looked down at me and then at Rayna. His voice was still dark and unfriendly, but the demonic tone was gone. "Get out." Vincent's power collapsed and Rayna helped pull me to my feet. We both rushed out the door and down the hallway. Neither of us dared to look back.

Chapter 13

We put as much distance between Vincent and us as possible. I'd never felt a vampire's power like that before, and once again, I feared I had underestimated what he was capable of.

"I've never seen him like that," Rayna said. "Never felt that kind of...power. You know, you really need to start thinking before you talk or you're going to get us both killed."

"Me? What's his obsession with *you*?"

"I..." Rayna sounded like she was ready to argue, but she stopped herself. "I don't know."

Once we were a few blocks away from the warehouse, we slowed our pace. It was daytime and the sun was high in the sky. We were safe for now, but I still couldn't help looking over my shoulder.

"Do you buy what he said about the ring?" Rayna asked.

"I don't know what to believe. Seeing how he reacted, though, I'd say it can't be far from the truth. The Circle wants it, Riley wants it, and now Vincent wants it. I'm sure it won't be long before everyone else is after it too. We need to figure out how it works."

"You want to use it?"

"This could be the one thing that gives us the upper hand. If we can contact Serephina, she can tell us how to stop Riley."

"Maybe, but what are we going to do in the meantime? We've got the elders, an angry hunter with godlike powers, and one very pissed off vampire after it. Did I mention we don't have a clue where to start? Maybe we should call Marcus."

"Marcus is dealing with his own issues right now. In the meantime, we do our research to figure out how it works before anyone comes knocking on our door." I looked down at the ring.

SHIFT

Rayna stopped and grabbed my shirt, pulling me back. "Looks like our time's up. *They* just knocked."

Four men in hunter's uniforms stepped out of the alley and walked towards us. I recognized Jameson, who led the group, but I didn't know the other three.

You've got to be kidding me.

"Nice to see you again, Mr. Williams," Jameson said.

"I wish I could say the same."

"So you know why we're here?"

"The elders sent you for this." I held up my hand, the silver band and red gem gleaming in the sunlight.

"Smart boy. Now keep those smarts and hand it over, and we can avoid a whole mess of problems that way."

"I wasn't going to hand it directly to the elders, so what makes you think I'm going to give it to you?"

"The elders are giving you the opportunity to handle this peacefully. Certainly, you don't think you and your demon slut have a chance of surviving a fight with us?"

"We've survived a lot worse than anything you can dish out."

Jameson threw his magic forward, and a ball of yellow flame flew towards us.

I reacted with my own magic and it moved with ease. A wall of water shot up from the pavement and when the flame hit, nothing but steam broke through.

"It's not going to be that easy," I said.

"The hard way it is then."

Jameson signaled the others and they ran towards us.

Rayna's magic exploded over the street. The earth shook violently and two of them fell sideways to the ground, but as the quake faded, one stumbled through. He pulled out a blade and jumped into the air, bringing it down on Rayna. Rayna blocked his arm and used his momentum to throw him to the ground. The hunter hit the pavement and his element sprang to life. Air magic spiraled around us, picking Rayna up and flinging her across the street.

Rayna skidded across the pavement and crawled to her feet. Road rash covered both her arms, but she didn't let it faze her.

125

She unlatched her whip and snapped it against the ground, sparks flying around her as the metal claws hit the concrete.

The other two hunters jumped to their feet and moved in. One made it a few steps before Rayna cracked her whip, breaking it across his neck. He grunted as blood spewed from the wound and anger took over his eyes.

The other man came at me with a blade in each hand. I stepped back and dodged the first strike, pulling my daggers out. The hunter brought his magic to life, channeling it through his blade. Red flames engulfed the knife, sparks of yellow rippling through it.

I mimicked him, bringing water to the surface and pushing the magic into my daggers. I imagined the silver to be cold, frozen in a storm of ice water. The blades grew shiny, the silver coating faded, and a dark blue glow emanated around them. A white layer of frost grew thick on the blades as the water magic turned to ice.

Adrenaline rushed through me as flakes of frost formed on the blades. Controlling the direction of my elements was one thing, being able to manipulate the physical state was another.

Flames flew in front of my eyes as he launched towards me. I reacted with a hunter's reflexes and sparks of fire and ice exploded around us. His blade came down again and I blocked it, pushing him back. The hunter kicked my stomach, and with his supernatural strength, power exploded.

The force threw me against the ground and I skidded across the broken asphalt. My back throbbed and burned from the pavement, and when I got to my feet the hunter already had his blade mid-swing. I dropped both daggers and grabbed his wrists, trying to keep his blades away from me. But he had too much momentum.

The blades neared my chest and I used the adrenaline to call my magic. I didn't focus on either element, but something strangely familiar came. Magic burst between us and without so much as a push, his body flew over my head and crashed into a lamppost. It dented upon contact and the glass from the light shattered. His body collapsed to the ground as glass rained over him, and although his chest rose and fell, he didn't try to get up.

I turned my back on him to face Jameson. His power was alive and rushing towards me in streams of heat. I called my element to meet his, but instead of my own blue flames, I took control of his magic. The yellow flame stopped at my hand and I pushed it back. His magic moved from my fingertips and took aim for their creator.

Flames exploded over Jameson's body, scalding his skin and knocking him to the ground. He screamed as the fire wrapped around him, but it quickly faded as he pulled his magic back. He squirmed and I moved towards him, letting my power hum beneath the surface.

Rayna dropped her whip and tackled the other hunter to the ground. She threw her arms at him, a fury of fists cracking against his face.

Jameson got to his feet as I approached, jumping towards me with a spin kick. I dodged his kick with ease and came back to parry him, but he continued to spin and brought his elbow across my face. My body jerked to the side and in the same motion, his other fist hit me. I fell on all fours and rolled away, forcing some space between us.

I got to my feet and Jameson was already swinging a blade towards me. I caught his arm and hugged it against my body, turning with force until his shoulder cracked. The blade fell to the ground and he grunted in pain.

Jameson pulled away, his arm dislocated and hanging by his side. He winced as he lunged towards me, and I wrapped my hand around his throat. His head snapped back, his feet flew out from underneath him, and I slammed him into the ground.

He groaned and reached for another weapon, coming back with a nickel-plated .45. Surprise overwhelmed me as he drew the gun. I'd seen the cage at the compound full of ammunition, but I'd never known a hunter to use one regularly.

Jameson tried to take aim, but he was winded and hurt, his good arm holding up his dislocated one.

I ducked as the gun went off and then jumped on top of him, pinning his arms to the ground. The gun broke free. With my knee on his chest, I pushed the gun against his cheek.

"So this is what it's come to. The elders are going to try and kill me, and the hunters resort to guns to win their battles?"

Jameson grunted, struggling against me. "It doesn't matter what you do. They won't stop," he said through gritted teeth.

I cocked the hammer back and jammed the barrel against his face. "And what makes you think I will?"

"Please..." he pleaded, his brown eyes opening with fear as I pushed the cold steel against his face. "I have children..."

I stared down into his helpless eyes and anger roared inside me. I was tired of being hunted. It was bad enough with the demons; I didn't need the Circle after me too.

Jameson's eyes were welling with tears and full of fear. I should've used him as an example and sent him back in a body bag. But I wasn't a murderer.

I pulled the clip from the gun and threw them in separate directions across the street.

"Tell the elders if they come again, I won't be so generous. Next time, I'm taking this personally." I stared into Jameson's eyes, making sure he felt every ounce of anger that scorched inside me.

He nodded and I pushed myself off of him.

Jameson gagged and coughed as he struggled to his feet and ran down the road, leaving his fellow hunters behind. A few moments later, the squeal of tires sounded and a black SUV roared down the street. Jameson sat in the driver seat and represented exactly what the Circle had become. Cowards.

"This isn't going to stop, is it?" Rayna stepped up beside me, breathing heavily.

I turned the ring on my finger. "It's only going to get worse."

Chapter 14

Marcus was on the couch, surrounded by torn leather and white fluff when we got home. Tiki sat beside him, his head down and looking ashamed, like he'd just been scolded.

"What happened here?" Marcus stood, and he didn't sound impressed.

"Willy had an accident, of sorts," Rayna said.

"I'm never leaving you home alone again." Marcus' eyes narrowed as he saw the blood on our hands and face. "You two have some explaining to do."

We told Marcus everything. He was as surprised as we had been about Willy, but seemed to expect what we told him about Vincent and the Circle.

"I expected the Circle to react, but not with such immediacy. I thought we'd have more time...I shouldn't have left."

"You had to go," Rayna said.

"Did you have any luck tracking down Riley?" I asked.

Marcus shook his head. "He vanished after the fight with the rogues. He's the most skilled among the hunters; tracking him will be impossible."

"Is everyone else okay?" Rayna asked.

"Most will recover, but the hearts that mourn for the hunters who died, and their families, will take time to heal."

"I'm sorry..." Rayna said.

"It's to be expected in our line of work. The rogues tracked Riley as far as they could, but once they got to the edge of the state, his trail vanished. With the Brothers at his command, he could be anywhere by now."

"Well, he already came here...kind of," Rayna said.

"What? When?"

"Chase saw him when we took Tiki shopping. Then he was in Chase's dream and when he woke up...there was a lot of blood."

"We don't know exactly what happened—"

"Enough." Marcus sighed. "Offers from werecats, Riley astral projecting into your dreams, Tiki partying to all hours of the night. None of this is good."

Tiki looked up briefly, only to hang his head again.

"Astral what?" I asked.

"First," Marcus said, "Tiki needs to be with you two, or me. We've got too many enemies for anyone to be out alone, especially at a place like Revelations. Second, what's important is your safety, Rayna. I'm not saying you have to go, but it's an option we should consider. We can't do anything more for you here, you need to understand that."

"But—"

"No buts. An experienced shifter might be the best option. However, I would like to speak with Chief before we decide anything."

"I'll set up a meeting." Rayna stomped out of the room.

Marcus watched her leave before running a hand over his smoothly shaven head. "Is she okay?"

"She's really against this, but it's our only shot. If she doesn't get help soon... "

"I know." Marcus sighed. "And where's Willy now?"

"With the Wolves. Grams decided it was best for him; they could help him control his beast."

"Much like what the Chief is offering to do with Rayna."

"Exactly."

"It's done." Rayna came back into the room. "Tomorrow night."

****

The sun had already set when we got to Shift. The only positive to having Willy gone was we didn't smell like wolf, so we weren't forced to put on their pheromones again.

I hadn't heard from Willy yet and that made me nervous. It'd only been a few days, and I was worried, but I pushed the nerves away. I was here for Rayna.

We followed Garrett through the same rooms as before, and once we settled ourselves on the couch, Charlie came out.

"Marcus Starkraven, it's nice to finally meet you," Chief said.

Marcus looked slightly taken aback, but nodded. "You as well."

"I understand you have some questions."

Marcus nodded. "I'm interested in knowing exactly how you can help her."

"When we help someone bring out the beast, we like to do it in parts, with another shifter present to help control the beast. The first shift is painful, but once she's learned control, the process is not as lengthy, and over time becomes less painful."

"Why can't we do this on our own?"

"Shifters always respond better to their own kind. Rayna's beast doesn't understand her other magic; it understands other werecats. Having one present to help coax the beast out is the safest method."

"And you're confident you can do this?"

"There is no guarantee. Most I've worked with have made it just fine, but not everyone makes it through unscathed. It's a traumatic experience for both your mind and your body. Most come through the shift safely, but for some, only parts of them come back, and the rest...well, not everyone survives."

"So there's not only a risk I'm going to die, but if I don't, there's a chance I'll go crazy?"

"Even among born shifters we have our casualties. There are many risks involved, but none as high as attempting this on your own."

"You think I'm not strong enough to do it?" Rayna's green eyes challenged.

"I'm saying you shouldn't have to. There is more experience in this tribe than you have pride, my girl. The Hollowlights are a family, and whether you choose to join that family is up to you, but regardless, we want to help you through this."

131

"So you're saying once she shifts, she won't be forced to join the pride?" I asked.

"We don't force membership among our people. We may be animals, but we are not wolves."

"What do you think?" Marcus looked to Rayna.

"Do you really want to know?"

"Chief, is there somewhere the three of us can speak privately?"

"Of course. Garrett, will you please take them to one of the meeting rooms?"

Garrett nodded and led us through a doorway and into a small room with four chairs and a small round table.

"Take your time, and come back through here whenever you're ready," Garrett said.

"Let's sit," Marcus said and closed the door behind him. "Now, I want to hear what you really think." Marcus watched Rayna.

She avoided eye contact and stared at the table. "I don't know…"

"If you have something to say, now is the time."

Rayna shrugged. "I don't want to go."

"Why is that?"

"Because I don't want to, okay?"

"Rayna, you need to understand how important this is. This could—"

"I know how important it is, but it's nothing we can't handle."

"I'm honored you have that kind of faith in us, but we're not equipped to deal with this."

"I just…I don't want to leave," she whispered.

"Without Chief's help your life is in danger. I won't risk that."

Rayna was silent. Her gaze stayed locked on the table and confusion filled her eyes.

"What if I go too?" I asked.

"What?" Rayna asked, finally looking at me.

"What if I come?"

"I'm not sure you'd be welcome, Chase. Not to mention you'd be a little...out of place," Marcus said.

"We can't just ship her off. With Riley, the Circle, the Ring, and Willy, there's too much going on. I'll go with her. That way she's not alone."

"She's hardly going to be alone. There will be dozens of shifters there."

"Can I have a minute with Chase?" Rayna looked to Marcus.

Marcus lowered his gaze and after a moment, he nodded. "Of course. I'll be outside."

"What's up?" I said, trying to lighten the mood.

"Why are you really pushing me to go with them? You said yourself it's a *monster* inside of me. Why would you want it to come out?"

"I say a lot of things without thinking, but it doesn't mean that's what I believe. I think this is the best thing for you. I don't want to see you go through that again, not alone."

"You guys keep using that word. I haven't been alone. You guys have been there every time."

"That's not what I mean and you know it. Chief can help you, Rayna. So you don't have to go through this over and over again until it kills you. So you don't have to worry. So I don't have to worry..."

Rayna's green gaze lifted and met mine. "You'd really come?"

"Of course I would. Besides, I could use a few days away from this place." I smirked.

Rayna smiled.

"So we're going?"

Rayna shrugged. "Well, it can't get much worse, so I guess it couldn't hurt."

We walked out into the hallway and Marcus was leaning against the wall. His massive black hands were deep in his pockets and he looked lost in thought.

"I'll do it," Rayna said. "But only if Chase can come."

Marcus sighed. "I suppose that's a start. Let's see what Chief has to say about it."

Chief was on the couch, that same gentle smile covering his tan features.

"Have you come to a decision?" he asked.

"I have." Rayna looked to me and I gave her a reassuring nod. "I'll do it, but only if Chase comes too."

"Where we are going is sacred ground. Nobody outside our pack has ever been included. Rayna, it's in your best interest to come. It will spare you a lot of pain and probably save your life."

"It's in my best interest to be with people I trust."

Chief sighed. "I had a feeling you would say that. I've already spoken with a few of the higher ranked members. They are not pleased with it; however, they refuse to leave a fellow shifter on their own when they have the ability to help."

"That's great," Rayna said.

"I am happy you have decided to come, but please know, we are sacrificing a longstanding tradition to meet your request. There will be certain events that Chase will be unable to attend, but for the most part, he's free to be included. We're leaving tomorrow. You just worry about packing your things and we'll pick you up."

We all stood up from the couch and Marcus stepped towards Chief. "I trust you'll take care of them." Marcus stared down into Chief's eyes and his expression was as serious as ever.

"You have my word."

"Thank you," Marcus replied.

"Rayna," Chief said, "be sure to bring baggy clothes. Preferably something you won't miss when it's gone."

"Umm...okay."

"Trust me."

Garrett led us back into the VIP lounge. There were only a few people here now, but as we neared the door, it flung open and bass pounded through the room.

A tall man burst through with wavy brown hair and unnatural blue eyes. Warm skin was evenly tanned and thick stubble covered his face. He stormed into the room, and bumped into Marcus.

"Oh, excuse me," he said. His voice was full and masculine, and his smile vanished when he noticed Marcus.

Both their eyes lit up and the man stepped back.

"Marcus..." he said.

"Jonathan..." Marcus' voice sounded startled.

"You were told not to be here," Garrett sounded unimpressed.

"I just came back to..." he stopped the moment he saw Rayna.

Rayna shifted and looked uncomfortable as his blue eyes continued to stare at her. "Wow. You look just like your mother."

"Excuse me?" Rayna's defenses shot up and her cold gaze returned with ferocity. "What's going on?"

Marcus sighed and looked back towards us. His gaze locked on Rayna. "Rayna, I'd like you to meet your father. Jonathan Winter."

Chapter 15

"Have you decided if you're coming on the retreat?" Jonathan asked.

The air was thick with tension and Rayna's face drained of color. Her breaths came in heavy pants and she dropped to the floor, power emanating off of her.

"This is neither the time, nor the place for this," Garrett said.

"It had to happen sooner or later," Jonathan said.

"It didn't have to happen now." Garrett turned to Rayna. "Are you okay?"

"Get him out of here!" Chief burst through the door with a feline's grace and dropped down next to Rayna.

Garrett grabbed Jonathan by the neck and dragged him from the room. Jonathan fought against him, but Garrett was too strong. He submitted to his grip, looking over his shoulder at Rayna until the door closed behind him.

Chief crouched low to meet Rayna's gaze, but it wasn't Rayna looking out. The beast released a low rumble and locked eyes with Chief, but he didn't flinch. He raised himself up on his hands and knees and called to his own cat.

The power was incredible and Chief released an even deeper growl. Leaning forward, he pushed his nose against Rayna's.

Blood dripped from her mouth and her fangs lowered. Veins pushed against her skin in black streams, and clear fluid shot out of her fingertips as long, sharp talons came out.

Chief moved over top of her and the power of his beast filled the air. He pushed the energy against her and her beast briefly faded.

"Chase," Rayna cried out. "Chase, please." She whimpered, but the beast returned with an eardrum bursting screech.

I dropped to my knees beside her and searched for the cool rush of my element.

"No," Chief growled.

"I can help her!"

Chief turned to me and the brown of his eyes was gone, replaced by light purple cat eyes. "No."

I ignored him and drew my magic to the surface. I pushed it down my arms and reached for Rayna, but Chief's hand shot towards me. His palm hit my chest and I flew back to the floor, his own beast growling at me again.

"She needs help, not magic."

Marcus came to stand beside me, pulling me to my feet. Worry covered his dark features as he stood by while Chief's beast filled the room with power.

Rayna's beast growled before her body jerked and bones crunched, moving back into human form. When her last few joints snapped back into place, her body collapsed and she began to gag. Her body was jerking, forcing her to cough and then dry heave until blood spilled from her lungs. I tried to move towards her, but Chief's arm stopped me.

"Let her rest," he said.

"Whoa, take it easy man." I pushed his arm away but he sidestepped to block my way.

"Rayna needs to shift; she doesn't need magic pushing her beast back." The purple feline eyes faded and the brown returned.

"It was hurting her."

"It always does, and it will continue to, as long as you use magic to heal her. The first shift is painful, but it's a necessary evil if you ever want her to control it." His fierce gaze softened as he looked back down at Rayna.

Her hair was sticky with blood and it stuck to her face in strands of red and black. Blood ran from her ears and nose, and she dabbed at it with a napkin Chief handed to her.

"That's bull—"

"It's fine, Chase," Rayna said.

"I'm sorry for that." Chief turned to Rayna. "He...wasn't supposed to be here."

"You thought you could keep that from me? That's a great way to instill my trust in you."

"I wasn't trying to hide it. I wanted you to shift successfully before I said anything. As you can see, an untrained shifter is highly volatile. Strong emotions awaken the beast, but those emotions are the worst for a shifter who has yet to change."

"Maybe we should rethink this," Marcus said.

"I understand your caution, but after what I just saw, I think it's more important than ever. She's further along than I knew. We're running out of time to help her."

"Helping would have been telling us about Jonathan," Marcus said.

"Perhaps I owe you an explanation."

"I'd say that's a start." Marcus didn't sound impressed.

"Jonathan was my first. The first hunter I ever helped through the shift," he said.

"You've known about me for long enough; you could've told me." Rayna scowled.

"It wasn't for me to tell. That's his story and I have to respect that."

"Is he going to be a problem?" Marcus asked.

"When we deal with born shifters, it's always better to have a blood relative present. It helps coax the beast–"

"I don't want him anywhere near me!"

Chief cleared his throat. "As I was saying, it helps coax the beast out. *However*, given the current state of the relationship, I don't think it wise. He's been given strict instruction not to make contact with Rayna."

"Sounds like he listens well," Rayna snapped. "If he's going to be on the retreat, I'm not coming. I don't need your help badly enough to be anywhere near him."

"Rayna, we've made many exceptions to allow you to join us. Jonathan will not speak to you unless you wish it."

"You just told me he wasn't supposed to be here. Your plan to keep him away from me didn't work for one day. You expect me to believe you can keep him away from me for a whole week?"

Chief sighed. "Should you choose not to join us, I understand, but I will not refuse a member of my pride the honor of the retreat."

"Good, I'm not asking you to." Rayna turned away and stormed towards the door.

Marcus turned to Chief, but he looked angry. "I will talk to her," he said, following her back into the club.

****

We walked through the door to the condo after an awkward ride home. Rayna walked in without a word and disappeared to her bedroom.

"Wow," I said.

"I'm really never leaving you two alone again." Marcus sighed.

"So that's Rayna's dad, huh?"

"It is..." Marcus' dark eyes looked vacant in thought.

"What a dick," I said.

Marcus did a double take and looked at me.

"Come on, the guy's been alive this entire time and never came for Rayna? What a coward."

"I'm not sure coward's the right word. I knew him when he and Rayna's mother were together. He was a fine hunter and a good man. Now that we know for sure where Rayna's shifter genes come from, I'd be interested in hearing what happened to him. Given his circumstances, I can see why he went into hiding. If the Circle found out he—"

"Screw the Circle or what happened to him. He has a daughter. She's going to be eighteen in a month and she never knew he existed."

"You need to understand—"

A scream barreled through the ceiling, cutting Marcus off and we both ran for the stairs.

Tiki hovered near Rayna's room, hesitating with his hand by the handle. I went through Rayna's door first with Marcus right behind. Tiki sheepishly sidestepped to look in from the hall.

Music blared and all the pictures and posters had been torn off the walls. The mirror on her desk had been smashed to the floor and paper and debris littered the room.

"Get out!" Rayna screamed and threw a book towards us. We all ducked as it flew overhead and slammed into the wall behind us. The hard cover put a hole in the wall and pages ruffled as it fell to the ground. Rayna sat on the floor with her knees pulled tight to her chest. Streams of tears ran down her cheeks and she buried her face in her knees.

Marcus turned off the stereo and spoke in a voice softer and gentler than I'd ever heard from him. "Rayna, I understand what you must be feeling, but you need to know you're not alone in this." He lowered himself to the floor and tried to inch his way forward.

"Stay away from me."

Marcus stopped. Neither of us wanted to make her more upset. If she started to shift again, we might not be able to bring her back. We both stepped back into the hallway and shut the door. Silence surrounded us, each of us turning to the other for answers.

Even through the door, Rayna's sobs were heavy. They sounded forced through gasps and trembles. Sadness moved through me and I turned to Marcus. "Maybe I can talk to her," I said. "I can kind of relate to father issues."

Marcus sighed and looked lost for a moment. "Perhaps that would be best. I'll...be downstairs." He ran a hand over his smooth head and moved down the hall, his huge form disappearing down the stairs with heavy footsteps.

"Meeting didn't go well?" Tiki's caramel features were lost in confusion.

"That's an understatement," I said, pushing Rayna's door open.

"Rayna..." I said, walking carefully and trying to avoid the broken glass.

Rayna didn't reply, which was an improvement from screaming and throwing books.

I moved some of the shards of the broken mirror around and made a clear space on the floor. Rayna didn't move. Her sobbing faded, but the pace of her breathing was still quick. Silence danced around us for a few minutes and all I did was watch her. I didn't want to tell her everything would be okay. I didn't know that it would be. Instead, I started talking about my dad.

"When I was nine or ten, my dad took me on a holiday, just the two of us. We went to Florida and I remember being so excited. He told me he had a surprise for me, and I had myself convinced he was taking me to Disney World. Turns out, his idea of a holiday wasn't like the rest of the world. We went to visit the Circle in the southern district. They had a tournament going on and my dad had entered me. I had to compete against all the older kids with more training than I'd had. I didn't want to fight, but I wasn't given a choice. I stepped in the ring and got my ass kicked so badly, I was disqualified after the first day. Their elders stated I was unfit to properly defend myself. You should have seen him. Dad was so...angry with me. He cut the holiday short and didn't speak the entire drive home." I shook my head and spun the ring idly on my fingers.

"When he finally came around to talk to me, it was a week after we got home. Seven days later the swelling had gone down enough that I could finally open one of my eyes, and all he said was how disappointed he was. He'd pulled some strings to get me entered, and I'd embarrassed him. I get beat up and *he* looks like an idiot. Can you believe that?"

Rayna sniffled and lifted her head. "If your idea of cheering me up is telling me what a jerk your dad was, then you're horrible at this."

"At least now you know where I get it from." I smirked. Rayna let out a laugh between sniffles. "There's that smile."

Rayna wiped the tears off her face and rested her cheek on her knees, watching me behind a gloss of tears. "You probably think I'm such a girl. Always crying about my mom, now my dad..."

"You *are* a girl." I smiled.

"I can't believe he's alive. I've been here, alone, and he's been around the whole time?"

I nodded, but I didn't know what to say. Rayna was right; I was horrible at this. "Maybe he was scared."

"Scared of what?"

"Scared you'd hate him. Scared you wouldn't want to be part of his life. It could be anything. We men are fickle creatures."

"You guys are something."

We both laughed, but as it faded, the silence started to move back over us, so I asked the obvious. "Are you going to be okay?"

Rayna shrugged. "I don't want to go to the retreat now."

"You have to go. I'm going to be there with you, so you don't have to worry about it, okay?"

"It just makes things more complicated."

"More complicated? Since when are things ever uncomplicated?"

Rayna smiled and drew back another sniffle. She wiped the last tear that clung to her jawbone and shook her head. "I don't know..."

"I could try and get in touch with Willy if you want. Maybe he could help? He's only been with the shifters for a week, but it's a week more than either of us has."

Rayna nodded.

"I'll see if I can get a hold of him tomorrow. Can I get you anything else?"

"I'm just going to sleep. The shift back at the club...you know, it takes a lot out of me."

"I know." I stood up and made my way to the door.

"Thanks, Chase."

"Of course, that's what I'm here for."

"No...I mean it. For everything."

I smiled. "I know."

I pulled the door shut behind me and made my way back downstairs. Marcus sat on the leather couch, and although Tiki had tried to put all the white stuffing back, some still hung out of the gashes in the cushions.

Marcus stood up as soon as I came down the stairs. "How is she?"

"She's okay, or she will be. She's going to try and get some sleep."

Marcus nodded. "Thank you…"

"You okay?" I asked.

Marcus looked behind me at the empty stairwell and sighed. "Lately she hasn't been responding to me the way she used to…the two of you have developed a real bond though."

"We still fight, but sometimes things just click and we get each other."

"Well, I appreciate it." Marcus tried for a smile.

"She'll come around. It's just a tough time for her right now."

Marcus nodded. "I'm going to try and get some sleep too. It's…been a long night. Have a good sleep, son." Marcus squeezed my shoulder as he walked past.

I wanted to correct him, but I stopped myself. I wasn't his son, but I knew he didn't mean it like that and I didn't think he needed to hear that right now. Not after everything that had happened. I'd only known Marcus a few months, but in the last few days, I'd seen more emotions from him than ever before. Something was wrong. I just didn't know what.

Chapter 16

"You sure this is the right place?" Rayna asked.

"I have no idea. You know how Willy is with directions."

"What did he sound like when you called?"

"Okay, I guess. There was so much noise I could hardly hear what he was saying."

"There he is." Rayna pointed out my window. "Who's with him?"

Willy pushed through the bushes and a group of four guys walked around him. They took turns pushing him and giving him shots in the arm and back, but when they started throwing rocks, I'd seen enough.

I jumped out of the driver's seat and down into the ditch on the edge of the road. Tall grass rose up past my knees that led to the thick trees of the forest.

"Enough, you g–, guys. Come on, st–, stop it," Willy said.

"What the hell's your problem?" I asked, staring at one of the boys.

Willy lowered his eyes and shook his head. "It's fine, Chase."

"Who's this? Your guard dog?" One boy laughed and shoved Willy.

Willy tried to balance himself, but another boy stuck out his foot, sending Willy in a nosedive for the ground. I reached forward with a hunter's grace and caught the back of Willy's shirt.

"Ooh," one of them said.

"I don't know who you think you are, but lay off," I snapped. I pulled Willy to his feet and guided him behind me. The boys' laughter seized and seriousness fell over each of them.

"Chase, don't," Willy whispered.

"You got a problem?" The largest boy stepped forward.

"Yeah, I don't like seeing my friends get pushed around."

The boy was inches taller than me, but I didn't let his size intimidate me. I could feel his beast beneath the surface and I followed suit, pulling my magic up.

The boy's eyes lit up and he clenched his jaw. "I recognize you. You were with the hunters that killed our pack!" His eyes shifted into bright red wolf eyes and a growl rumbled in his throat. His hand shifted and a clawed paw swiped towards my face. I batted it away and shoved both hands into his chest. Power surged and a blast of blue flame burst between us, throwing him across the field.

The other boys reacted and growls filled the area, quickly silenced by a commanding voice.

"Jason, get back to camp."

I didn't know where it came from and I didn't care; I had only one focus in that moment.

"Now!" The voice boomed and it made me shudder.

"You're lucky." The boy huffed, crawling to his feet, two handprints burned into his shirt.

Jax stood at the edge of the forest, eyeing the boys as they passed him. He crossed his arms and a calm expression covered his face. He was a few steps behind a man I didn't recognize, whose light blue eyes caught my attention.

His thick build was barely clothed by a dark green muscle shirt. He reeked of power and commanded attention with each step. Dark stubble covered his scalp, but his face was as smooth as any blade could get it.

"You got a problem with my boys?" His voice was gruff and he enunciated each word perfectly.

"Not yet."

I could feel his beast and I should've been nervous, but as Willy hung his head and stared at the ground, my own anger rose.

"Well, it seems they have a problem with you. Were some of our pack's lives taken by your hand?" He spat the words at me through gritted teeth.

"We were caught in the middle of a fight we didn't belong in. Your wolves attacked us, not the other way around. I don't discriminate; I'll kill whatever I have to, to keep my people safe."

"*Your* people?

"That's right."

"So what about *my* people? What should I do about the ones I lost?"

"Did they attack on your order?"

"Not that it matters, but no."

"Then it seems to me *they're* your problem. Not me."

The man's gaze locked with mine and his eyes searched my face. Jax stood at attention behind him, both eyebrows raised as I spoke back to the man.

"So you're saying it's *my* fault?"

"I'm saying, had *my* people attacked and *your* wolves were trapped in the middle, you'd expect your men to protect themselves."

The man's intense gaze flickered over my features before a smile crossed his lips and he laughed a deep, rough laugh.

"I like your attitude, boy." He slapped me on the shoulder and I stumbled, nearly knocked to the ground by his strength. "You want me to bite you? You'd fit right in around here. Wouldn't he, Jax?"

"Yes sir, I believe he would."

"I'd rather you didn't," I said awkwardly.

"I'm Radek Lawson, Alpha to the Shadowpack." He extended a large, scarred hand.

Radek's handshake was solid, his muscles flexing as he gripped my hand. His skin was rough and calloused, cracks and scars blemishing it completely.

Jax stood strong behind him, but after taking in a few deep breaths through his nose, I felt his beast come to life. Radek reacted and stepped back. Both their faces changed in an instant and were ready to fight.

"What is it?"

Radek put his hand up to shush me and sniffed the air. "Werecats." His human eyes morphed into wolf eyes. He sniffed towards me and made a disgusted face. "You!" He growled.

Rayna had stepped out of the Jeep and stood above us at the side of the road. Jax and Radek growled at the sight of her.

"Rayna, back inside!" I ordered, and I was surprised when she listened.

"That's your cat?"

"It is."

"The werecats are sworn enemies of the Shadowpack. How dare you bring one of them here! My pup isn't going anywhere with that filth."

Radek reached around me for Willy and I caught his arm in my hand. His wolf eyes exploded with anger and looked down at my hand. "You have one second to release me."

I released my grip as Willy tried to step around me and I pushed him back behind me. "Get in the car."

"Chase, I can't. If he–"

"Get. In. The. Car." Willy's skin paled and he backed up, confusion painting his face. "Now!"

Willy turned and ran up the hill behind me. He pulled himself up into the Jeep and shut the door.

"Don't you dare challenge my authority, boy. I won't have my pack associate with such disgusting creatures. That pup is learning to control his beast. It's not safe for him to be with other shifters, especially *that*."

"Willy's free to make his own decisions," I said.

"We've been at war with the werecats for a decade. You think you can waltz in here, upset my pack, and take one of my pups to go hang with them?"

"Your wars are your own, but those two have been friends since before he was one of you. That's not going to change."

"He's one of us now so he falls under my command. That's all that matters. Trust me when I say you don't want us as an enemy."

"Do you know how often I hear that threat? It means nothing to me," I snapped, my eyes locked with his. "I have no problem with you, or your pack, but Willy comes first to me. I won't let him be treated like this. Not by you or your mutts."

Radek growled and his beast spilled out, long fangs dropping flawlessly from his gums.

"Around here, respect is earned. That pathetic excuse for a wolf hasn't earned shit since he's been here. He'll be an Omega before he knows it."

"He has my respect. That's enough to ensure that nobody touches him."

"Careful, son, talk like that will get you in a lot of trouble around here."

"I'm not your son. And this isn't a discussion."

Jax shifted his weight from one foot to the other, eyes flicking between Radek and me. Even trying to hold his neutral expression, I could see he was nervous.

I locked eyes with the half-wolf before me and the intensity rose. His beast roared beneath the surface and pushed against me, but I brought my power up and pressed back.

"You're a hunter?" Radek's eyes lit up. "What are you doing with Underworlders? We're your enemy."

"I decide who my enemies are. And those two aren't."

The intensity rose and I expected a fight, but Radek pulled back his beast and the power faded.

"Fine, but he'll be back and when he comes, I'll be waiting."

"And it better be to welcome him, because if anything happens to him, *I'll* be back."

"Is that a challenge?"

"It's a promise."

"You would risk your life for that pup? What is he to you?"

"He's family."

Radek stared at me and his wolf eyes faded, leaving the crystal blue orbs to replace them. "Don't be fooled, hunter; the rules are the rules. When he gets back to camp, things will be the same and he will earn his place."

"As long as nobody hurts him, then we don't have a problem."

"Associating with a werecat won't make things easier on him; I can tell you that much." Radek smirked and moved back towards the forest.

Jax looked surprised as Radek turned away. He nodded to me before following behind him and pushing back through the trees.

Releasing the breath I held, a nervous chill ran through me. There were dozens of wolf eyes peering out from the forest as I climbed the ditch. The image made me shudder and I pulled myself up into the Jeep.

"Well, that was fun," I said.

****

"Ch–, Chase, what have you done?" Willy asked.

"You mean standing up for you? A thank you would do just fine."

"You don't understand the pa–, pack."

"Then enlighten me."

"What you sa–, saw back there, that's how they operate. There's nothing you can do to make it st–, stop. I have to earn my place."

"No, you don't. You're a person, Willy, not a punching bag. You're better than that.

"Says who?"

"Says me."

"And me." Rayna turned in her seat. "Willy, you're a great guy. You don't have to take that crap from people."

"Yeah we–, well, it's not like I have a choice."

"You always have a choice," I said.

"You obviously don't know much about the Shadowpack."

I slowed the Jeep down and pulled up tight to the curb. The glamour collapsed as I stepped into the alley, and a bright neon sign flashed *Revelations*.

"I might not know anything about them, but I know you have a lot of people that care about you. If you wanted to leave, we'd stand behind you."

Checking our weapons at the door, we made our way past a few crowded tables before we found a spot near the back.

"It's not that simple," Willy said.

"You've spent this entire time telling me how hard it is there. What's so difficult about not going back?"

"I ca–, can't leave. It's against the rules. You can't stand behind me, Chase. There is an entire pack behind Radek. They're ter–, terrified of him, and they're loyal because of it. You can't protect me all the time."

"I'm sorry if I made things difficult, but I have a hard time watching people treat my friends like that."

"I appreciate you looking out fo–, for me, but don't."

"I didn't come here to argue. Rayna's leaving tonight with the Hollowlights, and I need you to give her some insight into pack life and shifting."

"*Maybe* leaving," Rayna said.

"You're joining their pa–, pack? You haven't even shifted yet, and as you both just discovered, the Hollowlights and the Shadowpack aren't exactly friends."

"This isn't about the wolves, Willy, it's–"

"Chase, let him talk," Rayna said.

I held back my urge to argue and sat back in my seat, arms crossed.

Rayna rolled her eyes and turned back to Willy. "They think they can help bring out my beast. Their leader, along with everyone else, is convinced if it doesn't come out soon..."

"If it doesn't come out soon, what?"

Silence fell over the table and Willy lowered his gaze. "Oh...Then it doesn't seem like a very dif–, difficult decision."

"Maybe not, but now that I've learned my father is alive and part of the pack, I'm not sure it's a good idea."

Willy's eyes opened wide. "I guess that comp–, complicates things. What ca–, can I do though?"

Rayna shrugged. "I hoped you could tell me about shifting and your pack, but after what I saw, I'm not sure I want to know."

"Do–, don't let that discourage you. The wo–, wolves are different from most. They don't have anything good to say about the werecats, but fr–, from what I've heard outside the pack, the Hollowlights are a peaceful pride."

"What's with that anyways? The war between the two?" I asked.

"I don't know the spec–, specifics. All I know is that it had something to do with the Hollowlight's old leader."

"But he's gone," Rayna said.

"Yeah, but Radek isn't the forgive and forget type."

"What about our friendship? Chase nearly got himself killed just bringing you here with me."

"It won't mat–, matter if you're a Hollowlight or not. You're a werecat. They'll hate you just for that. But that doesn't matter. If they can help, you sh–, should go."

"And have to *earn* my place? No thanks."

"Chief told you it was up to you if you wanted to join," I said.

Rayna shook her head and sighed.

"It's not as bad as it se–, seems," Willy said. "I'm doing alright."

"Are you kidding me? They treat you horribly!"

"The wolves may seem harsh–"

"*May* seem harsh? That's an understatement."

"They've still helped me. They taught me to shi–, shift, and they're teaching me to control the beast. I know the pa–, pain you go through, but it's already getting easier for me. If the werecats can help and it ke–, keeps you alive, I don't see any other choice."

Willy jerked as a loud noise came from his hip. He lifted up his shirt, giving us a glimpse of his hairy belly and a black pager.

"Since when do you have a pager?" I asked.

"Everyone has to have one." Willy struggled to unclip it from his belt and squinted to read the screen. "I've go–, got to go."

"We just got here," I said.

"I'm sorry. Emerg–, emergency meeting. I have to."

"You don't *have* to do anything. Just stay."

"I know it doesn't se–, seem like much to you, Chase, but this is important to me. I haven't earned my place yet, but I will, and when I do, they'll respect me."

I sighed. "Well...just wait and I'll drive you back."

"That's okay. They're already on their way to get me." Willy slid off his chair and turned to Rayna. "I'm so–, sorry if I wasn't much help, but if it's a choice between living and dying, you should go."

Rayna smiled. "Sorry if my smell gets you in trouble."

"I'll survive. See you gu–, guys later." Willy waved awkwardly and walked out of the club.

I watched him leave and shook my head. "I can't believe he lets them do that to him."

"You can't? Really?"

"Yes. He's better than that. He doesn't need them."

"You don't get it. This isn't about how he's treated or where he ranks. Willy's never belonged to anything. Never fit in. He's always been the goofy kid whose skin changes color and who can't talk right. They might not treat him great, but he's one of them. It's something he can belong to. That's a big deal for him."

"He's part of something here with us."

Rayna glared at me. "It's not the same."

"Whatever you say. So, what now? That wasn't much help."

"Actually it was just what I needed. Finding out my father is alive is...something I'm not ready to deal with, but it proves that Chief might be able to help. Hunters aren't supposed to be able to shift. It's supposed to kill them. If he can help a full-blooded hunter survive, then maybe he can help me. Willy's right; staying alive is what's most important right now."

"That's what I've been saying all along."

Rayna arched a brow.

"So you're going then?"

"No, we're going."

Chapter 17

I threw a duffle bag on the ground and opened the door. Karissa, Garrett, and Chief stood in the hallway, and Chief was wearing his usual warm smile.

"Rayna, time to go," I said.

"Be right down."

Rayna struggled down the steps dragging an enormous suitcase and two smaller ones clutched under each arm.

"You know we're coming back, right?"

"Don't start. There are two more upstairs." Rayna glared, but her eyes weren't angry; they were nervous.

I met her halfway up the stairwell and took the large suitcase. "What did you pack?" I asked, heaving the bag to the door.

"You've got superhuman strength; don't act like it's heavy."

"I don't think that allows me to carry suitcases full of concrete." I laughed.

Marcus came down the steps behind Rayna with two more bags. "Charlie, if I may, I'd like a word with you in private."

"Of course. Garrett, will you and Karissa take the...luggage down, please?"

Garrett nodded and he and Karissa both loaded themselves up with suitcases, while Chief followed Marcus into the training room.

"You ready for this?" I turned to Rayna.

"Is it too late to turn back?"

"Yes."

"I'm not sure I can do this." Worry painted Rayna's soft features.

"I'll be with you the entire time. You're ready."

"I don't feel ready."

153

"You are. Trust me."

The door opened and Chief slipped back into the hallway. "All set?"

"We are," I said, before Rayna could reply.

"Excellent. I'll wait for you downstairs."

Rai fluttered down the stairs, landed on my shoulder, and chirped into my ear.

"No; you've got to stay here with Marcus."

Rai chirped again, flapping her wings in a rush against my ear.

"Sorry girl, you can't come this time." Rai dug her claws into my shoulder before jumping off and disappearing. "Ouch!"

"You two take care," Marcus said. "I'll see you in a week."

"That long?" Rayna pouted.

Marcus smiled and stepped in front of her. He placed a massive hand on each of her shoulders and leaned down to look her in the eye. "You'll be fine. I know you can do this."

"We'll see." Rayna tried for a smile, but her nerves were showing.

"You made the right choice. I'm proud of you."

"Thanks," Rayna whispered.

"I love you," Marcus said awkwardly, leaning in and kissing Rayna on the forehead.

"I...love you too." Rayna sounded surprised.

"Wait!" Tiki came down the steps into the kitchen, a small bag hanging over his shoulder.

"Sorry, Tiki; you can't come either."

Tiki's orange eyes stared blankly at me. "I don't understand."

"I don't think we can convince them to let another non-shifter join in."

Tiki frowned and looked up at Marcus.

"He's right," Marcus said. "Plus, I'm going to need your help with a few things around here."

Tiki sighed and his caramel features showed his disappointment. "I should not have been spending time at Revelations. I'm supposed to help you on your journey, Chase. It's been seen. Do not punish me."

I laughed. "You have helped Tiki. Nobody is punishing you, but right now I need to go help Rayna. Trust me; there will be plenty left to do when we get back."

Tiki nodded.

Rayna and I made our way downstairs, picked one of the three black SUVs that lined the front of the condo, and climbed in. I didn't know where we were going or what to expect, but I tried to keep my nervousness to myself. The last thing Rayna needed was to know I was feeling uneasy too.

****

The drive took us several hours south of Stonewall and the majority of it was spent on gravel back roads. We turned off the gravel road and into the trees, riding over a dirt path that was too narrow for the large vehicle.

Branches and leaves hit the window and scraped the sides of the SUV. The road was bumpy and I spent most of my energy holding onto the door, trying not to hit my head on the roof. When the path finally smoothed, we pulled into an open space.

Tall, healthy trees towered into a sunless sky, moving back and forth against the wind. Heavy black clouds were rolling in from the east and the faint sound of thunder rumbled miles away.

Garrett drove through the clearing and under an archway made of two large wooden poles. Rusted hooks hung from the thick, square beam that connected them, but the sign that they were meant for was missing. We stopped in front of rows of cabins, and I was eager to get out and stretch. It didn't matter how big the vehicle, I wasn't built for backseats.

The fresh air tasted sweet. Birds chirped and leaves rustled together, filling the clearing with the melody of wildlife. The smell of the coming rain hung around us, and the air was thick with the static charge of the storm.

"It's beautiful," Rayna said.

A booming screech came from the sky above and I looked up to find Rai. She soared through the air, four small wings gliding against a bright blue backdrop.

Rayna laughed. "I think someone is tired of playing the pet."

"I think you're right."

"Welcome to our home away from home," Chief said. "Let me show you to your cabin!"

We followed him down the row of cabins and into the last one on the right. Wooden steps led up the front porch and I brushed away an outbreak of cobwebs. The boards creaked with each step and a large rocking chair sat off to one side. On the other side, a small swinging bench hung from the rafters. Chief opened the door, releasing an oaky musk of stale air desperate for a taste of the wilderness outside.

The cabin wasn't large, but it was more than adequate for the two of us. A small sitting room with an old couch and a single chair crowded a wood burning stove. In the opposite corner, a single counter made up most of the kitchen where a green fridge and a two burner stove sat. Passed the kitchen was a single room with two beds and a night table between them. The bathroom sat outside the bedroom made up of a small, green shower with dark rust stains throughout, a sink, and a toilet.

"And that's it! I'll let you two get settled and come check on you in a bit." Chief's excitement was clear in his voice and he smiled as he closed the door.

"Well, this is...cozy." I said.

"Is there even hot water?" Rayna asked.

The door swung open and Garrett strolled through, carrying a few pieces of Rayna's luggage. "There...you...go." He struggled and set the luggage down with a *thump*. Another man came in behind him, set down the last few pieces and left.

"Only a week, right?" Rayna whimpered and moved into the bedroom.

"I'm sure you can find something in one of these suitcases to help you through." I laughed.

"Funny." Rayna unzipped the main pouch on one of her suitcases and a few books spilled out. She grabbed a small one with yellow pages and a creased spine and came towards me. "I almost forgot; I've been looking through some of Marcus' books, and I think I found a lead on the ring and how it works."

"That's great…"

"What? What's wrong?"

"That's not important right now."

"What do you mean? It's the most important thing right now; you said so yourself."

"Not now it isn't. We're not here for me, or the ring. We're here to help you, and until that happens, nothing else matters."

Another knock came at the door and I used it as an opportunity to get away from the conversation.

"This isn't over!" Rayna yelled from the bedroom.

I was ready to respond, but when I opened the door, the words were stolen from my lips. The light blue eyes of Jonathan Winter stared at me.

"You're not supposed to be here."

"I need to speak with Rayna. It's important."

"No, it's not."

"Who is it?" Rayna stepped out of the bedroom and froze.

"Rayna…" Jonathan pushed past me and stepped into the cabin. He put his hands out in front of him and walked slowly towards her. "I know I'm not supposed to be here, and you have every right to want nothing to do with me, but–"

"You're damn right. I don't want you anywhere near me." Rayna stepped back.

"I just want a chance to explain."

"I have nothing to say to you."

"Please, I just need five minutes."

"I don't–" Rayna cut her words off with a scream and keeled over.

I pushed past Jonathan and dropped down next to her. "Rayna, are you okay?"

Rayna was breathing heavily. She lifted her head to look at me, but the eyes that looked out belonged to the beast.

"Shit…" I whispered.

Chief and Garrett came rushing through the doorway, and without a word, Garrett pulled Jonathan back, dragging him outside.

"I need to talk to her!" he said, fighting against Garrett's grip.

Garrett didn't reply with anything but an inhuman growl. Jonathan snarled back and met Garrett's gaze, but as a low, angry rumble came from Garrett's lips, Jonathan pulled his eyes away.

"Rayna, don't fight it; own this moment," Chief said. He was down on all fours staring into Rayna's eyes. The beast growled and swiped towards him, but Chief leapt backwards with reflexes no human could have. "You control this beast; it doesn't control you." His eyes were fixed on Rayna's, not daring to turn away and give up dominance.

Low rumbles vibrated from both of their throats until Rayna's body gave out. She collapsed to the ground, bones cracking and moving beneath her skin. Thick blue veins rushed with black and pushed below the surface, causing her skin to have a ripple effect. The skin on her arms split, black fur pushing its way through. The clear fluid didn't burst across the room this time; instead, it seeped out in a steady flow over her skin until there was no skin left on her arms. Bones broke, reformed, and in minutes her arms were gone, replaced by massive legs. Wide black paws held them up with fierce white claws protruding between them. Rayna's lower jaw cracked, her human teeth reforming into short, jagged points. Rayna screamed in pain through thick fangs.

"No, don't fight this!"

"It hurts!" Her words were muffled through feline jaws and a half snout that began pushing out from her face.

"You need to see past the pain. Push your beast to the surface on *your* terms."

Rayna stared at me for only a moment before the beast took over. The sound of bones rubbing together sent a shiver down my spine before her kneecaps buckled. They dislocated themselves and moved, bending her legs at opposite angles. Rayna's lips parted, but instead of a scream, a growl came from her mouth.

"Yes. Take control. This is *your* moment!" Chief said.

Her body flipped and pushed itself up on four paws. Rayna's shirt stretched, her skin rippling as something pushed from inside. Her spine cracked and arched in a way a human's couldn't, forcing her shirt to ride up her body. Clear fluid dripped from the fabric as black fur pushed itself out from her hips.

Rayna's body trembled and Chief brought his beast to the surface, slamming his power into Rayna. Her voice broke out in a scream and she collapsed to the floor, lying motionless on the ground, half-shifted and panting for air.

"What's happening?" I asked in a panic.

Chief sighed. "Nothing."

"Is she okay?"

Chief pushed himself to his feet. "She's fine. Unconscious, but fine." He adjusted the long black hair he'd tied into a ponytail. "I didn't think it'd be that easy, but she'd shifted so far I thought, *maybe*."

Rayna's body twitched a few times before it began changing. Bones cracked, moving back into place, and claws slid back into her fingertips. Blood dripped from her lips as the fangs receded, and the thick black hair that covered her body pulled itself back inside through the wide slits in her body. The skin closed itself shut and returned to its toned, human form.

Chief slipped his hands underneath her and scooped her up with ease. He carefully guided her body through the narrow, crooked doorway and laid her in one of the beds.

"Is she going to be okay?"

"She won't wake up for a while, but she'll be fine. Too bad. She'll miss out on some of the festivities tonight." Chief grew quiet, and dark brown eyes watched Rayna.

"What the hell was that about? I thought we had a deal; she comes, he leaves her alone."

"He was given strict instructions–"

"That's not good enough! Rayna trusted you. There's enough going on right now. We don't need him making things worse."

"I assure you he will be dealt with accordingly. For now, she needs her rest, but I must ask you to do something for me."

I sighed and shook my head. "What?"

"When Rayna wakes, she'll be in pain, but you must promise me you will keep your magic to yourself."

"Why?"

"Each time you heal her from the shift, her body reacts to the next one as though it's the first. It prolongs the process. I think you'll agree that we don't want that."

I looked to Rayna lying still on the bed and nodded.

"I know it's hard to stand by and watch when you have the ability to help, but with this, I need you to do just that."

"I understand."

"The pride will be going on a meditation tonight. If you–"

"I have to stay with Rayna."

Chief paused a moment before nodding. "I want you to know this retreat can be good for you as well. Marcus explained what has been happening to you. The power inside you is strong, but you are stronger. Perhaps some of what I have to teach Rayna may be of value to you as well." I looked at Chief, but I didn't respond. "Just think about it," he said, and his feet tapped quietly on the floor as he left.

Rayna was passed out, her chest rising and falling with deep, heavy breaths. Bloodstains covered her body, and her clothing was torn in random places.

I set up a chair by the bedroom window and watched as dozens of people walked through the clearing and disappeared through the brush. I hoped I'd made the right decision in making Rayna come here. Every time I pushed to get my way it never worked out. I hoped this time was different, for Rayna's sake. The last thing I wanted was to have anyone else die because of me.

Chapter 18

Everything was hazy and I rubbed my eyes. My back ached from sleeping in the chair, and my spine cracked as I stretched, giving me that *hurt so good* feeling.

Rayna was still asleep and in the same position I'd left her in. She'd been out all night and hadn't made a sound. She was still breathing; at least that was a good sign.

A fog so thick hung over the clearing outside you could barely see the forest. I watched as hues of pink, red, and orange exploded over the tree line, trying to push the fog back as warm rays dove into the clearing.

With the exception of Rayna's breathing, everything was quiet. The scenery surrounding us was beautiful, and for a brief moment I stared out the window and enjoyed the silence. An odd feeling overcame me then and in that moment, I felt at peace. I was in the middle of nowhere surrounded by nature. No phone, no TV, and most importantly, no one trying to kill me. For this one moment I was hidden from reality. I couldn't help but enjoy the feeling of calm, and the thought that Chief might be right crossed my mind. If I could gain control of my elements, I'd be one step closer to stopping Riley. Maybe this retreat could be beneficial for both of us. We were here for Rayna and that was the priority, but maybe there was more to Chief than just taming the beast.

The last few days I'd had more control over my elements than ever before. Something had clicked inside me and they were working, but there was something else there, too. It was unfamiliar. It stirred inside my soul, dancing among flames and rapids, but I couldn't explain it.

"Morning." Rayna stretched out over the bed.

Even with the blood and fluid from the shift covering her body, she looked better than yesterday. The bags that had started to swell under her eyes from stress, lack of sleep, and too many tears were gone. She almost looked refreshed.

"How are you feeling?"

"I hurt." She gave a pouty face.

"Chief said you would. He also said I can't help you with that."

"Why not?" Rayna swung her legs over the bed, wincing with every movement.

"He says healing you is making things worse. Every time your body tries to shift and I heal you, it makes the next one feel like the first time all over again."

Rayna groaned and fell back on the bed. "I tried this time. I really did, but I couldn't do it. It's too strong."

"You can't think like that. Chief said nobody does it the first try. It's going to take time and practice."

"This isn't the first try and it's not something I want to practice. Getting better at turning into an animal was not something on my bucket list."

"Bucket list?" I laughed. "I think you're a little young to have one of those."

"Well, considering how often someone tries to kill me, I should."

Silence fell over us and I watched her stretch again, her expression alone told me that she was in pain and I wished I could help.

"What time is it?" she asked.

"I don't know. There are no clocks here."

"We're so far from civilization that time doesn't exist here. Great." Rayna shuddered and looked up at me. "Did Jonathan come back?"

I shook my head. "He was told not to come at all. I don't know why he was here in the first place. Chief assured me he'd deal with it, but his way of handling it hasn't worked so far."

"I can't believe him. How can he just walk up after all this time and be like *"hey, let's chat."*

"I don't–"

"It's unbelievable to think he has the guts to try and strike up a conversation. It's been eighteen years, I'm my own person, and I don't even know him."

"Maybe—"

"I just don't know how to deal with him. How do you talk to the guy who was supposed to be your father, but vanished and let the world think he was dead? He could've stopped them."

"Them?"

Rayna looked up at me and although her voice was angry, her eyes were full of sadness. "The Circle. He knew they didn't approve of what he and my Mom were doing, but still, he just disappeared and left my mother to…" Rayna started breathing heavily and anger pushed itself over her last few words.

"Okay, you just woke up. Let's not do this now." I moved to the edge of her bed and crouched in front of her. "Look at me."

Rayna's breaths came faster and she started to shake. I took her hands in mine and heat poured off of them. I squeezed them tight in my grip and pulled her forward.

"Hey, look at me."

Rayna's eyes met mine. She was fighting a battle inside. The beast wanted out.

"I know you don't understand it. I don't either. But you can't think about that. There will be plenty of time for that once you're okay. I'll help you find the answers you want, but right now, we can't do this."

Rayna put her head on my shoulder and tried to calm herself. A low growl rumbled from her throat but she quickly took hold of it, swallowing it back down. She took long, deep breaths until the trembling stopped.

"It's so hard…"

"I know, but you're not alone. Together, we can do this."

The cabin door opened and Chief came strolling into the bedroom. "Good, you're awake." He smiled. "Everything okay?"

I looked at Rayna, waiting for her to respond. She took a few breaths and nodded.

"Everything's fine," I said. "What's up?"

"Hiking time. Get dressed."

163

МM.R. MERRICK

"Can I shower first?" Rayna asked.
"No time. We're already late."
"Late for what?"
"Come on!" Chief ignored the question and left whistling a tune I didn't recognize.
"I hate morning people," I said.

****

None of the shifters spoke to us when we gathered in the clearing. There were a few kids running around and a couple teenagers scattered throughout the crowd, but the majority of them were adults. Rai flew around me as I walked into the field and then she disappeared into the forest. She'd been cooped up in the condo for far too long. I guess she'd been longing for the chance to spread her wings.

I lost sight of Chief over the heads of the crowd, but his voice was loud enough that it filled the clearing.

"I want everyone to follow me. Today, we will stay in human form."

There were gasps and moans throughout the crowd, but Chief quickly quieted them.

"There will be plenty of time for doing things as a pride in animal form, but not for this. We're going as we are and you'll be put in pairs. Chase and Rayna, where are you?"

The crowd whispered among themselves and separated, leaving an aisle between Chief and us.

"There you are. Rayna, today, you're with Garrett. Chase, you are with Karissa."

"But–" Rayna said.

"For this exercise, everyone is being paired with someone that doesn't know them very well."

Rayna grumbled and walked down the aisle, meeting Garrett at the front. She looked back at me, nervousness painting her face before the crowd closed between us.

"Hey, walking buddy!"

I jumped as Karissa appeared beside me. Her large hazel eyes had a bright ring of gold circling them. Her tanned skin was clear, and her short brown hair shone as though freshly showered. She only came up to my shoulders, but looking up at me, she carried herself with a confidence I didn't understand.

"Walking buddy?" I raised a single brow.

"Yeah, that was kind of lame, wasn't it?" She smirked. Her voice was far too chipper for this early.

"A little bit." I gave a sheepish grin.

"Oh well, onward and upwards," she said, and everyone moved forward.

We walked through the clearing and into the thick brush. I dodged branches as they reached out to scrape against me, bending back their flexible limbs to protect my face. Thick dead logs rotted along the way, slowing our travels as we moved deeper into the woods. The forest air was heavy and even though the storm had missed us, the smell of fresh rain filled my senses. It was a smell I loved and I took it in with every other step.

We walked until the sun had risen above the tree line, but a heavy canopy of leaves and branches kept us shaded. Dew hung off the leaves and clung to me as I pushed past them. This many hours in, I should've been cursing the brush, but I wasn't. The landscape was similar to Stonewall, but everything else was different. Pride members stopped and helped each other. Hands came from the left, right, and center when there was an obstacle someone couldn't scale alone. There was laughter, friendly chatter, and the odd stick fight among the kids.

"You're kind of tense." Karissa pulled herself over a fallen tree with grace a human could never manage. She reached her hand to me, but I ignored it and pulled myself up.

"I'm not tense. I'm...focused."

Karissa laughed. "Whatever you say."

"Being here is just...different."

"It's different for us, too. We've never had an outsider here before."

"Outsider...yeah, I'm kind of used to that one."

"I don't mean that rudely. You should feel proud. No non-shifter has ever been on a retreat."

"Great, I feel honored." I didn't mean for it to sound as sarcastic as it did, but I couldn't take it back now.

We walked in silence for a while. Karissa and I were at the end of the line, and everyone had made some distance on us. The trees had separated and the ground became trampled.

"I guess I owe you a thank you," Karissa said.

"Okay, I'll bite, what for?"

"I was there."

I ducked an oncoming branch and climbed up over the next set of rocks that blocked our way. "I'm not following…"

"In the basement of that house. I was there."

I pulled myself up and stopped on the last boulder to look at her.

"I guess you wouldn't recognize me, being as I was in my animal form."

"At Rayna's house…you were one of the panthers?"

"Garrett was too."

Karissa pulled herself up the rest of the way. She looked up and a flash of emotion I couldn't recognize sparked through her eyes.

"I mean it. Thank you. I couldn't have gone another day in that cage. Without you, who knows what would've happened to us?"

"How long were you there?"

"All the time is sort of jumbled together. Chief said we'd been missing for weeks. What I do know is we're lucky to be alive, and it's all thanks to you."

"I don't know about that, but I'm sorry for what you went through. I wouldn't wish anyone to be at the mercy of Lena."

"Mercy?" Karissa looked offended. "Lena is a lot of things, but merciful isn't one of them."

"How did you guys even get there?"

"I remember Garrett and me shifting to go on a hunt, and then we woke up in cages."

"Hunters have a way of doing that—taking everything from you before you even know what's happening."

"They took our blood and tried it on that symbol, thinking one of us was the key. I don't know why they kept us alive after they realized we weren't who they were looking for. I thought they'd just kill us."

"Lena doesn't *just kill* anything."

"Yeah, we found that out the hard way. She kept injecting us with something to keep us in animal form. That girl is all sorts of crazy."

"Why?"

"Shifters don't work like other demons. We heal quickly in human form, but not like the rest. Our wounds heal best when we shift, and once we're in animal form, we can take more damage. She kept us that way so we'd stay alive while she tortured us."

"That's horrible."

"It was a nightmare...until you came."

"I'm no savior. That was just dumb luck, mixed with coincidence."

"Don't kid yourself; you were there for a reason. You didn't have to save us. You're a hunter. You could've killed us or left us to our own fate, but you didn't."

"I've kind of had a change of heart when it comes to the Underworld...most of it anyways."

"Well, I for one am grateful."

Voices called out to us through a wall of brush, and as we pushed through, we came out onto a stone platform.

The pride had spread out over the edge of a huge cliff. Rayna and Garrett were at the far end of the platform and Karissa led me to the opposite side. We stood at the edge, and the forest below went on farther than the eye could see.

The canopy of different colored leaves was amazing. Red, brown, yellow, green, and orange decorated the trees below. Colorful birds dove down through the canopy, making an explosion of leaves float up into the air and float away on the wind.

"Why are we here?" Chief asked, and his voice echoed around us all.

"Cause it's got a killer view!" someone answered, and laughter fell over the group.

"The view is amazing, but not quite what I was looking for. I don't mean why we are here in this exact spot. I mean, why are we here on the retreat? What is the point of all this?"

"To unify our pride," another voice said proudly.

"True, but let's go deeper. We come to this place year after year, not just to come together as a pride, but to discover ourselves. We are more than humans and more than animals. The power we hold in ourselves, whether it be beasts, witches, or elementals, is a gift, but we as individuals are more than that gift."

Chief walked along the edge of the cliff, not looking down to see how close he was to the edge. Instead, his eyes met with each person he passed. As he came to me, he gave me a curt nod before turning and moving back the other way.

"All those things are a small piece of who we are. Our actions and the way we treat others and the world around us is another small piece. There are a million little things we do, and each is another piece. We're here to reflect on our lives and find out who we are. We do this every year because it's too easy to get lost in rage, sadness, our own problems, and in life. We come here, together, to find ourselves as individuals. Only then, can we find ourselves as a pride."

"Amen," someone called out and the crowd giggled.

Chief smiled. "For today, I want you all to reflect on yourselves. Think of who you want to be and what you're doing to achieve that. Do not dwell on the times you were not that person, for they do not matter. They are stepping stones to get to where you want to be."

"If you want us finding ourselves, why are we in pairs?" One of the younger boys asked, looking up at Chief with bright, innocent eyes.

"Because," Chief said excitedly, kneeling down before the boy, "what better way to see yourself, than in the reflection of another?"

The small boy thought about it, smiled, and nodded as though he understood. I wasn't convinced he knew what Chief was saying; I sure didn't.

"Take your partner and do whatever you like today, but most importantly, talk. Get to know them. I mean *really* know them. You'll find as each of you share who you *think* you are, so shall you discover who you *truly* are."

Everyone chatted amongst themselves and drifted back into the woods. Karissa and I stayed on the cliff. Standing on the edge, the wind was strong. It blew around us, carrying the smell of trees and wildlife. We were together, but alone in the world in that moment. Witnessing one of the greatest things life had to offer: life.

The sun beat down in warm rays, balancing the cool air that washed over our skin. The forest below swayed in the wind, multicolored leaves blowing into the air and scattering for miles in the opposite direction. Eagles soared above the trees, waiting for the next small bird to pierce its way free of the canopy. Exposing itself to the world above the forest would either be its first or last major experience.

"It's beautiful," Karissa said.

I nodded but didn't reply. I had almost regained that peaceful feeling from the cabin and I didn't want to ruin the moment. I was caught up in the life of the forest, hearing and seeing it in a way I never had before. I could taste a sweet flavor on the tip of my tongue, while the air danced along my skin.

"Chief's never brought us to this place before. Arian used to use this getaway as a torture ground. Until the last few years, most of us were too nervous to go out and really explore."

"Arian, that was the old leader?"

"Yes. Nobody can hear your screams when you're this far out. That's what he used to say." Karissa dropped her eyes and shook her head. "Even now, when he's been gone for so long, people still fear him."

"I keep hearing that."

"Remember what I told you about Lena injecting us with that serum?"

"To keep you in animal form, right?"

"Arian had a gift, one that allowed him to force your beast out. I've never known another shifter who could do it. It's excruciating, and he used it as a means to keep us in line. He'd threaten us with it first, but if he ever committed to disciplining us, he'd do it—over and over again. We heal faster in animal form, but it's dangerous to stay that way and he knew it."

"Isn't it more natural for a shifter to be in their animal form?"

She shook her head. "Our human form exists inside the animal, just as the animal exists inside the human, but they both need to be released. In the case of the animal, it's monthly, but the human inside needs to be out more often. If we stay in animal form for too long, sometimes parts of us won't come back. Like your friend's eyes."

"But Rayna's never shifted."

"I think in her case, it has more to do with her other parts. She's a hunter, a shifter, and a witch, so her beast affects her differently. For a regular shifter, the result would be the same. It might not be their eyes; it could be anything, a tail maybe?" She smirked.

I pictured her with a panther tail and laughed.

"Sometimes, though, we don't come back at all."

"It kills you?"

Karissa shook her head. "I don't mean like that. I mean the human won't come back. We'll be stuck in animal form forever."

"Oh..."

"The human doesn't disappear when we shift. It stays trapped inside, watching through the beast's eyes. If it's unable to get out, well...you can imagine what that can do to a person's psyche."

"And you guys were stuck like that for weeks?"

Karissa nodded. "That's why we're lucky. The chances of a shifter coming back from that are slim-to-none. We were both blessed, but we have you to thank."

"I'm pretty sure I didn't do that."

"You're a water elemental, right?"

"Among other things, yes."

"It was your magic that healed us that night."

I thought back to that night in the basement and shook my head. "I don't remember using my water element."

Karissa smiled. "You think too literally. You don't have to use your magic for it to affect people. You were just learning about your abilities. When you don't know how to control yourself, whether it's your beast, or in your case, your element, it leaks out. It moves around you like an aura and spreads on its own free will. Most don't notice it, but shifters' senses are hyper-sensitive. "

"I think you're stretching it, but I'll take your word for it."

Karissa smiled. "You're doubtful and that's okay. I know why I'm here, and why Garrett and I are okay. It's because of you."

"You seem to know more about me than I do."

"No, I just see you for what you truly are."

"And what's that?"

"A hero."

I laughed. "Maybe all of you didn't come back after all. Sounds to me like you lost your mind a little. I'm no hero."

"You saved us. You protected us when no one else could."

I shook my head and looked back out over the forest.

"What do you see when you think of yourself?"

I shrugged.

"Don't be like that. This is an exercise for both of us. Whatever we say here doesn't go anywhere else; it stays between us. It might seem silly, but it helps. Just let it out; don't be shy." Karissa's smile was honest and genuine.

I looked out over the cliff and felt her eyes burning through me. I remembered what Chief had told me. This retreat could be good for me, too. In this moment, I wasn't able to help Rayna with her shift. She was in Garrett's hands.

I took a deep breath and turned to her. "Fine, what do I do?"

"Tell me what you see when you think about yourself."

"I don't know...a hunter that has a lot to learn I guess."

"That's way too vague. Dig deeper. Who do you want to be?"

I rolled my eyes and kicked some stones that broke free of the platform. "Right now, I just want everyone to be safe."

"But..."

I sighed. "But most days, I'm lost. I spend more time trying to keep myself in check and my elements under control that I forget about everyone around me. I let my emotions rule me, and more often than not, they get in my way."

"Tell me about your elements. They sound a lot like our beasts. They're ruled by our emotions too."

"Most days they control me, but for no rhyme or reason, the last few days it's gotten better. Nothing's different, it's just...easier."

"Don't spend time searching for answers because they aren't there to find. For us, one day shifting becomes easier. It's less painful, it happens quicker, and as time goes on it becomes an enjoyable experience. Maybe that's what's happening with your magic."

"Maybe..."

"What's it like? Being able to manipulate the elements?"

"I don't know." I shrugged. "I never really thought about it. I don't do it unless I have to."

"Why?" she asked.

"Using your elements comes at a price. In small amounts it's fine, but it uses energy just the same as anything physical. In large portions it's exhausting, not quite as extreme as after you shift, but similar."

"Strange."

"Look at it like this. If you're training for a race, over time, you strengthen your body. You can run farther and faster than before and it uses less energy."

"So you're learning to control your abilities. That's a long process among any of us; it doesn't come overnight. You let your emotions rule you; we all do, that's a part of growing up. It sounds to me like you're a lot harder on yourself than you should be."

"It's not that simple..."

"No?" Karissa got to her feet and moved towards me. "From the outside looking in, I'd say you spend too much energy worrying about everyone else. Nobody *expects* you to be their protector, Chase. You don't have to be the hero. You're a person like anyone else."

"If you only knew..."

I tried to turn away, but Karissa grabbed my shoulder with surprising speed, forcing me to look at her. "You have to take care of yourself first. You only think about others and keeping them safe, but you can't do that if you don't know who you are. You need to find peace within before you can truly help anyone else."

I looked down at my hands. I could feel the magic stirring inside me. Power vibrated beneath the surface of my body and it was more than I could handle. There was something new inside me. I didn't know what it was, but it was there, craving escape.

I wanted to tell her she was wrong. I did know who I was, and what I wanted out of life. But I couldn't. I'd never looked that far ahead. My goal since I'd been exiled was to survive. So far I'd done that. I should've been happy, but I wasn't. Someone hadn't survived, and that death took all the happiness I had left. Finding myself would have to wait. Right now, I needed to stop anyone else from dying. There'd be time to search my inner feelings when everyone was safe.

Silence fell between us again and we both noticed the sun getting low in the sky. The sound of leaves slapping together came from behind us, and Rai burst out of the forest. She chirped and landed on my shoulder, rubbing her head against my cheek. I couldn't help but smile. I let my hands rub down her back, caressing the soft, golden feathers.

"Oh my." Karissa jumped to her feet. "We better head back."

I didn't want to go back. It was quiet here. No hunters, no Riley, no Dark Brothers, and no demons trying to make a trophy out of my head, but most importantly, everyone was safe for the moment. Here was good.

"Come on. We're going to miss out on the festivities!" Karissa yelled from inside the thicket.

"Festivities?" I asked, looking at Rai. I didn't do *festivities*.

Chapter 19

The sun made its final descent when I stepped into the clearing, only to find it empty.

"Hurry, we're already late," Karissa said. At the other side of the field, Karissa ducked down under a few branches and disappeared into the trees.

"More forest?" I grumbled. I followed Karissa through an opening and was thankful to find a path. I couldn't handle anymore bushwhacking today.

It was dark and it took my eyes a moment to adjust. Karissa seemed to move through the shadows with ease, but by the time I got used to the darkness, a light flickered, signaling our destination.

Surrounded by more trees, the forest opened up to reveal a fire pit warming the area. Logs and stumps sat around the fire, and the smell of burning wood was thick.

"Last, but not least. I thought we'd lost you." Chief stood from his seat as we arrived. "I trust your day was wonderful and full of self-discovery."

"Of course it was!" Karissa said.

"Excellent. Why don't you take a seat and we can begin."

There was only a single log that remained unoccupied and we took our seats. Rayna sat a few stumps away and I smiled at her, but it only earned me a glare. I was guessing her day wasn't going well. Jonathan sat next to Chief. I imagined Chief arranged it that way to keep him close, but Jonathan's pale eyes were fixated on Rayna.

"Today, we searched our human-selves through others. Tonight, we come together as a pride and find ourselves through our beasts. You will stay in your pairs as previously indicated, but Karissa, you shall go with Garrett, and Rayna, you will stay with me. You may shift when you are ready and go discover the other side of yourselves beneath the moonlight."

Everyone cheered and jumped to their feet. Power ignited the air in a suffocating wave. The crunching of bones and dripping of fluid surrounded me as dozens of shifters changed into their animal counterparts.

Rai's claws bit into my shoulder and her chirps were panicked. She pushed off my shoulder and the bright white feathers faded into the dark sky.

Orange tigers with thick black stripes, lions with the largest of manes, cheetahs built for speed and agility, and a spread of cougars, lynx, jaguars, leopards, and panthers all came to form. Scattered throughout the cats were coyotes, foxes, a few bears, and abnormally large birds that disappeared into the sky. Some of them shifted flawlessly, the fluid and blood hardly noticeable. Others ripped their beast forward, spreading the liquid with an explosion of authority. I felt like I was stuck in a cage at the zoo, but the power was enticing and forced adrenaline to pump through me.

Watching the cats take shape sent chills down my spine. They roamed around me, hungry eyes devouring me. My pulse sped and my nerves tightened. Magic flexed inside me and I clenched my fists, as if that could help. My elements came to life and a new magic throbbed in my soul. It pushed inside me, begging to be set free.

Sweat ran down my face as the cats neared and I tried to hold the power back. Fire and water stormed inside me while a new magic roamed between them.

"Relax." Karissa's hand touched my arm and I could feel her beast vibrating beneath the surface. "They won't hurt you."

The warmth of her hand grounded me and the pulse in my throat slowed. "You sure about that?" I asked, rising from the log and stepping back.

"We still have our own minds when we shift. Things just become more primal."

Garrett stalked towards us and extended his hand to Karissa. "May I?" He looked at me.

"Uh, sure."

"I had a good day with you." Karissa smiled.

"Me, too."

"See you tomorrow?"

Before I could respond, they both changed. In a few bone crunching moments, two large panthers stood in front of me. Garrett was huge and came up to my hip, while Karissa stood just above my knee. She turned, and bright golden cat eyes stared up at me. Garrett rubbed his head against her neck and they both broke into a run, diving into the underbrush.

The rest of the pride cleared the area. Paw prints of all sizes littered the dirt around the fire pit, and as the last few animals broke into the woods, the only sound that remained was the crackling of the fire. Chief stayed seated on his stump, staring into the fire, while Rayna had her head down, her body throbbing with deep breaths.

"Hey." I walked towards her. "Everything okay?"

Rayna grunted and her breathing sped up.

"Okay, so you're mad. What'd I do?"

Rayna's head snapped up and heavy breaths escaped her lips. Blood stained her chin and fangs hung from her gums. Black veins moved beneath her skin and the bright light of the fire showed the thin layer of sweat on her face. Bright eyes reflected the flames as the beast inside of her stared at me, and it didn't look happy.

"Oh..." I said, taking a step back.

"It's the power of the other shifters. It calls our beast to the surface," Chief said calmly.

"You seem fine," I said, not taking my eyes off of Rayna.

"It mostly affects the younger shifters, those who cannot yet control their beast."

"Why'd you bring her here if you knew this would happen?"

"She needs to know what it feels like to be in the presence of her own kind. When the beast feels the power of a united pride, its natural instincts are to join it. Once it respects what we are, Rayna can force it to submit to her command in order to be a part of it."

Rayna fell onto all fours and her body quivered. Her hands shifted quickly into the thick black paws I'd seen all too often lately. Deep growls moved through her lips in a ferocious roar as the beast pushed outward. Her legs shifted, but as the beast began to fully break through, she collapsed.

Chief dropped and pulled his beast up from within.

"Don't let it go, Rayna."

His power filled the space like a dozen werecats and he threw all that power into Rayna. Her beast roared and I jumped back again. Its eyes found me and Rayna fought the beast back until she broke through.

"You're afraid of me..." she gasped. Her face was human, but her mouth had changed; it was full of long, sharp teeth.

"No—"

"Yes you are!" Rayna cut me off. "I'm a monster."

Rayna's power vanished and her body shifted back, but this time she didn't fall unconscious. Fangs receded and she cried out in pain. Tears fell in streams as her bones broke and morphed back into her human shape. Covered in torn clothing, she lay in her human form with sweat, fluid, and blood running over her skin.

"Are you okay?" I dropped down and tried to pull the hair away from her face.

"I'm fine," she said, pushing me away and crawling to her feet. She was still trying to catch her breath when she stood, but her knees gave out and she fell back onto one of the stumps.

"Rayna, I didn't mean—"

"It's too late. We're here. So I have to learn to control this, regardless of what you think of me."

"I don't think—"

"Just don't, okay? I saw you; you were afraid of me."

"Rayna..." Chief stepped forward. "Are you okay?"

"Why can't I do this?" Rayna kicked at the dirt, but the anger she tried for only displayed her pain.

"This will come," Chief said. "It takes time. You nearly shifted full circle yesterday. Tonight you went that far again, but much faster. A few more tries and I'm sure you'll get it. You must give yourself to the beast, while still controlling it."

"I'm trying. It's not working," she snapped.

"You are being impatient. You and Garrett worked on this today; we know how hard you're trying, but you are pushing too far, too fast. It must happen in stages."

"I want to try again." She looked up at Chief with renewed determination.

"Not tonight. Tomorrow is another day."

"No, I'm ready now."

Chief shook his head. "It isn't that simple. Forcing your beast into a shift again right now could cause irreparable damage to your psyche. I won't risk it."

"Then what do we do? Talk more about who I am and who I want to be? No thanks."

"You stay with me. Tonight we will work on a meditation to help you communicate with your beast. Just as you need to know yourself, you must learn the ways of your animal. Once you can call your beast without shifting, you will understand it and be able to feel what it feels. You will learn respect for one another."

"Getting to know the monster inside me in order to gain its respect? I'd rather just beat it into submission."

"Let's try my way first." Chief smiled.

Rayna nodded and her eyes fell to the ground.

"I'm afraid this is something you are unable to be a part of, Chase. Rayna must do this in the presence of another shifter only. Any other aura or power will cloud the process."

I looked down at Rayna but she wouldn't look at me. Her eyes stared into the crackling flames as red and orange arms leapt from the pit, snapping against the cedar logs and sending warm scents into the air.

"I understand. I'll just head back." I crouched to look Rayna in the eyes, but she turned away. "Are you going to be okay?"

"You don't have to worry about me. I'm a big girl. I can take care of myself."

"Okay," I said. "I guess I'll see you back at the cabin then."

"I guess so."

The silence of the night engulfed me as I walked down the path, but I couldn't help feeling that someone was watching me. I stopped and listened, trying to hear any hint of someone around me, but there was nothing.

A cool breeze rode the air, carrying on it the smell of nature, and there wasn't a cloud to be seen, leaving the stars and moon to hang above me. We were hours from civilization and with no lights to obstruct the view, they shone brighter than I'd ever seen.

I moved towards our cabin when a movement caught my eye. I turned to face it, but all I could see were the trees, swallowed by shadows. My pulse sped and my stomach clenched as I searched the darkness, desperately seeking whatever was lurking inside.

Silence swallowed me again and I continued my walk, trying to push away the uneasy feeling. I was nearly to the cabin when a tingle shot down my spine and something leapt from the bushes.

The black form moved towards me with the grace and speed of the shadows that masked it. By the time I'd pulled out my daggers, the panther was gone, having shifted back into human form. The shift was flawless and transpired in seconds. One minute the cat leapt towards me, the next it was a man standing naked in front of me. But not just any man: Jonathan Winter.

I stepped back and took a breath, regaining my composure. "You can't take a clue, can you? I nearly stuck this in your throat." I slid the daggers back into their respective sheaths.

"I need your help."

"Why would I want to help *you*?"

"Because you care about Rayna."

"That's right, I do. And that's exactly why I don't want anything to do with you."

"You may not agree with my decisions, but you don't understand the reasoning behind them. I need you to convince Rayna to speak with me. I deserve a chance to explain."

"You don't deserve anything. She owes you nothing, except maybe a swift beating." I spat the words at him.

"You don't know what you're talking about!" His voice turned into a low growl, and his eyes shone as his beast came forth.

"I know Rayna wants nothing to do with you, and unlike you, I respect her decision. I'm not about to be the messenger for the man who abandoned her and left her mother to die."

Jonathan growled, and in seconds, he'd already shifted. He roared and the screech blasted through the darkness, stinging my ears. Yellow eyes lunged towards me with strength and agility I'd never known, but I dove underneath him to avoid his claws.

His body hit the earth with a *thud*, landing on all fours. He turned and crept towards me, each paw crushing the grass with silent power. The moonlight reflected off his fur, revealing a sleek, black coat. His body swayed with each step, and I called my elements as his pace quickened. The panther pounced and my magic rushed upward, but the element that came out was foreign.

Power lashed out and the panther scowled as his back arched, an invisible force crushing him to the ground. He landed on his back and squirmed against the moist grass until I released the magic, letting him come back up on his paws.

He roared again and the ferocity sent chills down my spine. He lunged towards me. Thick black talons cut through the air, but the alien power returned and pushed him back. A blur of darkness shot towards him and he turned mid-jump, moving with the magic. He landed on his feet and took a few steps, regaining his footing.

The magic scared me. It was new and untamed, but I didn't hesitate. Just like Chief told Rayna to give into the beast, to touch it, learn it, and control it, I reached my hand towards Jonathan and brought the power out fearlessly. I focused on his throat and squeezed that invisible hand around him.

The beast fought against the power. His paw clawed at his throat, trying to brush the unseen force away, but it wouldn't waver. He gagged and coughed like he'd swallowed a giant hair ball and talons tore at his neck, leaving black hair to flutter in the air. He wheezed and fell to his side, pawing and tearing up the earth in a desperate attempt to breathe.

Watching him struggle forced a surge of panic through me and I released the magic. The strange power moved back down into my soul, adrenaline and fear coursing through my veins.

Jonathan lay on the ground breathless, gasping for air as the power released him. As he started to take full breaths again, he crawled up on all fours. His sleek black fur was messy and ragged, and bright yellow eyes stared up at me.

He scowled softly and turned his back on me. With elegance only a feline could carry, he broke into a run and bounded into the forest. The snapping of branches cut through the night as he hit the forest floor, and then there was nothing.

Darkness closed around me and all I could hear was the racing of my own heart. I ran to the cabin and I didn't stop until the door had latched shut. I hunched over with my hands on my knees, trying to catch my breath.

The strange magic that stirred within me was no longer strange. I knew what it was. It was the air element. It was one in a million odds for a hunter to get two elements, but no one ever got three. I caught my breath and calmed myself. This couldn't be happening. Could it?

Trying to understand what was happening to me, I paced the cabin floor. The only light came from the moon and the flame inside the stove, and I ran my hands through my hair.

I pulled deep at my magic and searched my elements. I called upon fire first and brought it to the surface. It came to my hand with ease. Blue and silver light cascaded over the room, and surprise overwhelmed me at the sight of it. It never came this easily.

Next, I called water and I was sure it wouldn't come. I couldn't have three elements. My power had to be changing. I knew it wasn't possible but it was the only explanation. With the same ease as the flame, the element rose to the surface. Small drops of water formed on the air and like a magnet, they came together in my palm. Streams of water coursed towards my hand until a small orb floated above my palm. I grew nervous at the sight of it and it grew bigger until my focus broke. The magic vanished and the orb collapsed. Water spilled into my hand, dripped to the floor, and seeped through the cracks in the floorboards.

"What's happening to me?"

I looked around the room, searching for something, anything small to move, but there was nothing to be found. I moved to the bedroom with the same result. Only two beds and the chair I'd brought in.

I reached towards the chair and moved that invisible hand deep within my body. I focused on the new power I felt stirring inside, and I tried pulling it to the surface. I imagined the wind on my face, standing on the stone platform that overlooked the forest. The smell of rain came on a soft breeze and took over my senses. I focused all my power towards the chair, on making the heavy wood a weightless object. The chair shook, inching its way across the floor before it stopped. Pushing harder the second time, adrenaline coursed through me and the chair lifted off the ground. Disbelief filled me as it floated above the bed and it broke my focus. The chair dropped, bouncing on the mattress and crashing to the floor.

I shook the disbelief away and pulled at the shadows on the wall. I didn't know if it would work, but I'd seen Marcus do it, and I'd done it in my dream.

I pictured a lightless room, just me and the pure darkness that only came on a moonless night. Shadows tore themselves off the wall and covered the room. The moonlight that shone through the window vanished and a thick black fog blocked its light. The room became pitch black and the silence was eerie, like I stood deep inside a cave.

I released the magic and the darkness receded, sliding back into shadows on the wall. The moonlight broke through and I fell on the bed. My pulse beat loud in my ears. There were too many thoughts swimming around my mind. I didn't believe what was happening. I couldn't. I didn't understand the magic that moved inside me. I was exiled. I wasn't supposed to be an elemental, yet here I was, lying on a bed with three elements throbbing inside me.

Was it the Mark, the ring, or something else? I had enough difficulty trying to control two powers. Adding a third to the equation wasn't on the list of things I wanted.

Sleep tugged at my eyes. The adrenaline had faded, and using this new power had drained me. All I could think was that I was dreaming. This was another nightmare I would soon wake up from, but as sleep pulled at my eyes, that hope vanished. My body drifted towards darkness, and silence engulfed me before I was thrust into the real dreamscape.

Chapter 20

"Where do the hunters come from, daddy?" I asked. My voice was young, undeveloped, and innocence clung to each word.

Riley laughed and patted the seat beside him. "Come here and I'll tell you."

I pushed up on the floor, my small and youthful legs wobbling towards the couch. I climbed up and threw a leg up over the edge, pulling myself up and rolling onto the soft cushions. Once I'd straightened myself, I took a few unsteady steps and flopped down next to him.

His arm wrapped around my shoulder, and I looked up at him with anticipation. His short blond hair and warm features gazed down at me with a gentle smile.

"The hunters were made thousands of years ago, and put here to protect the world."

"Wow," I said.

"The gods blessed our people with the ability to control the elements after demons of the Underworld came to take over."

"Demons?"

Riley chuckled. "They're evil creatures with all sorts of bad magic."

My eyes opened wide. I pictured the fiercest beast my imagination could create. I started to shake and tears welled up in my eyes.

"But you don't have to worry, son. Your daddy's a big, strong, demon hunter. I make sure the bad guys don't hurt anyone."

"You do?" I sniffled.

"Of course I do," he said, ruffling my hair with a smile.

I wiped the two tears that trickled down my cheeks. "How?"

"With magic."

"Whoa!" I jumped up onto my feet, the fear overrun with excitement. "You know magic?"

"Let me show you."

He picked me up and moved me to the other side of the couch. Riley sat back in his seat and held out his hand. I shivered as a strange feeling came over me. My eyes nearly popped out of my head as fire flickered to life and a bright red flame grew in his hand.

"Fire magic."

"Doesn't it hurt?" I crawled to my knees, leaning closer and not daring to take my eyes off the power in front of me.

Riley laughed. "No, it doesn't hurt, son. I can control it."

The funny sensation moved through my body again. The flame grew and shot higher in his hand.

"All hunters can do it. Some can use water, some air, and others use earth. Once, a long time ago, there were some who could even use lightning."

"Where'd the lightning go?"

The flames in Riley's palm shrunk and vanished, not leaving even a trail of smoke. "We're not sure. Hunters just stopped getting that magic."

"Maybe when I grow up, I'll be able to play with lightning." I giggled.

"No way!" Riley scooped me up in his arms. "You're going to be a fire elemental, just like your dad."

He laughed and spun me in the air. I couldn't keep the smile off my face. He was my dad. A hunter. How cool was that? He was a real-life hero with real magic. When I grew up, I was going to get to kill monsters, just like him!

Riley stopped and pulled me in his arms as my mother came into the room, clearing her throat and crossing her arms.

"Not telling him stories again, are we?"

Riley put me down and I ran to my mom, pulling at her dress.

"Mom, Mom, guess what? Dad has magic! He can make fire and it doesn't hurt and he told me about the demons he fights and keeps from hurting us, and guess what? When I grow up, I might get to play with lightning, but dad thinks I'll play with fire like him." I took a breath and smiled, my young blue eyes gleaming up at her.

Mom's hazel eyes looked at my father and I didn't understand the look. "Riley Adam Williams. He's too young for that!"

"Too young?" Riley walked over and grabbed my arm, holding it up. "Look at these arms. He's strong. He's nearly ready to start training."

"You know how the council feels about starting them early." Mom glared at Riley. "He's five, and he's not starting anything. He needs to be a kid first."

"Nonsense. I was three when my father started me."

"Three?" I asked, turning back to Mom. "Can I? Please, Mom? Dad started when he was three, and I'm five and three-quarters. I'm ready."

"Go get washed up for dinner."

"Come on, Mom..."

"Go." Mom chuckled and ran her hands through my hair.

I huffed and walked towards the bathroom. I made it through the living room and into the kitchen, but when I started down the hallway, my mind began to wander. A rustling sound diverted my attention and I followed it into my bedroom.

"How cute," a deep voice said.

A man stood in my bedroom holding a picture of Mom, Dad, and me. I remembered that day. It was the first time they took me to the zoo. As I stared up at his face, he slowly became more familiar, and like a forgotten memory had been revealed, I knew who he was. Darius Sellowind.

"What do you want?" I demanded. Anger swelled inside me and my young, innocent voice was gone, replaced by a deeper, more masculine tone that caught me off guard. My small hands grew before my eyes until they were full, thick, and covered in scars. The floor moved farther away from me, and I wasn't looking up to Darius anymore. I was at eye level, staring into deep black eyes.

He threw the picture to the ground and the glass broke. Cracks split over my parents faces, leaving mine untouched. When

I looked up, the room was gone. We were at the werecats' camp, standing on the stone platform. Wind blew and a colorful forest grew up and swayed around us.

Darius' long black dreadlocks hung down past his waist, and the dark color made his pale skin look paler. His eyes were a solid black with long, dark eyelashes curling up above them.

"I came to say hello. Is that so wrong?" he asked. His voice was strange. It wasn't local, but I couldn't place the accent. It sounded English, but with a touch of something...different. "After all, we have not been formally introduced. I'm Darius Sellowind." He extended a large hand. His flawless skin looked soft, but I knew the power that touch could carry.

I stepped away and jumped as birds flocked out of the forest canopy below.

"Fair enough." He shrugged and pulled his hand away.

"Get out of my head."

Darius smiled. "Make me."

Darius was a powerful warlock, and I knew my elements would be useless against him. Cutting off their heads and lightning elementals were the only way to kill them, or so I'd been taught. It'd been centuries since any hunter had the power of the lightning element, and since I'd learned how deceptive the Circle could be, I didn't know what was true anymore.

Magic was useless, so I did the next best thing. I reached for the daggers along my back, but panicked when I felt the spine sheath empty. Darius released a deep chuckle and smiled. I couldn't use magic and I didn't have a weapon. I was useless in this fight, so I did the only thing that was left for me to do. I ran.

I jumped into the thick brush and let the forest swallow me. Branches slapped against my face and cut my arms. I was wearing long pants, but my feet and body were bare and taking a thrashing from the landscape. I ducked under branches and leapt over the fallen trees in a single bound, clearing them with ease. My body moved with speed and grace, lunging over any obstacle that got in my way. My pulse raced and adrenaline pushed me farther and faster than I had ever run. I broke through the other side of the forest, the thick undergrowth biting at my flesh as I came into the clearing. The grass was longer than I knew it should be, growing up past my knees and slowing my pace. With each step, I lost momentum, losing my ability to run. Finally, my body slowed and I was frozen in place.

A ripple of air moved in front of me and Darius peeled back reality. He parted it like two sheets of paper and stepped out from a black split in the world. My stomach clenched and I gasped for air, trying to catch my breath. A stinging sensation covered my torso from the branches that had left their mark. Scrapes and cuts lightly bled, not closing as they should have.

Darius stood like a statue before me: pale, calm, and composed. "I control this dream," he said, and the portal rippled behind him. The black hole closed itself, leaving power thick in the air. "I can be anywhere, and everywhere."

I knew I shouldn't use magic, but I was out of options. I tried to conjure my elemental powers, but nothing came. The elements stirred in my soul but wouldn't move. They burned, swirling inside me, begging to be released.

"That won't work either. I won't allow it." He moved toward me with an eerie power, and goose bumps rode up my arms. "You can relax, Chase. I mean you no harm. I've simply come to discuss our current...situation."

I tried to turn but my body was paralyzed. His magic swam around me, keeping me in place. He stepped through the tall grass around me, and it separated for him without a touch. Each blade bent, creating a clear path until he came to stand in front of me. My stomach tightened and sweat gathered on my palms as he neared. I could feel his magic enveloping my body, ready to crush me at any moment.

"Do not fear me. I told you, I mean you no harm. I only need a small favor."

"Kill me if you want. I'm not helping you."

"Kill you...whatever do you mean? This is just a dream." Darius winked.

"I've seen what dreams can do."

"You've only experienced what can happen when I use my power to send someone else into your mind. Imagine what I can *do being here myself." His thin lips curled, showing perfect white teeth.*

"I already told you, I'm not doing anything for you."

"You don't have to. Just give me what I want."

"The ring stays with me."

Darius raised a finely plucked brow and began walking circles around me. I followed his movements, but my nerves pounded inside me like an iron hammer each time he vanished from my sight.

"Why must you children make things difficult? In all my thousands of years, I've always hated that: young, undeveloped minds, and your sense of entitlement. Your arrogance disgusts me."

"Thousands?"

"Oh, you didn't know?" Darius laughed. "All in due time, child."

"Riley wasn't able to get the ring from me, so what makes you think you've got a better chance?" I let the arrogance he hated hang on every word.

Darius stopped and a serious expression covered his face. Black eyes locked with mine and his power pulsated around me. "Don't taunt me," he said. "Your father is..." he stopped, looking both frustrated and amused at the same time.

"My father is what?"

Darius shrugged. "My brother says hello, by the way. He did wish to come, but he had other errands to tend to. So, here I am to retrieve the ring, all by my lonesome."

"You know I won't give it to you, so if you're so old and powerful, why don't you just take it?"

Darius shrugged.

"Or maybe you can't!"

Darius' dark eyes narrowed, but he didn't respond.

"That's it, isn't it? You can't take the ring. It was crafted by the gods and designed for the Protector, not a demon."

Darius sighed. "When it comes to the ring, there are certain...rules."

"Then listen closely. You. Can't. Have. It."

"I thought you'd say that."

"Then why are you here?"

"I'm here to help you see the light. We'll be meeting soon, outside of your dreamscape that is, and I want to spare you some pain. You've seen but a speck of our power. Should you refuse my offer, you'll be left to Ithreal's mercy. Trust me when I say he has none. We can take the ring, only then we'd have to kill you, and that isn't in the cards for you. Not yet. Give me the ring, work with us, and Ithreal will give you a throne of immortality. Everybody wins."

"Tell your god he can go to hell. Or in his case, stay there."

"You're such an ignorant creature," he said with a surprising calm.

Darius lifted his hand and with a flick of his wrist, two blades of power cut across my chest. The skin ripped with ease and the pain covered my torso. Blood spilled from my body and my jeans turned black as they absorbed the viscous fluid. Power exploded above my head and pushed me to my knees. It surged around me and my head snapped back, forcing me to look up at Darius.

"You will learn respect," he said, extending his hand.

I tried to pull away, but I couldn't. His magic held me firm against the earth. Pale, cold fingertips touched my forehead and as he pulled them away, my magic came to life. I gagged and choked as a rush of water tore itself from my lungs. I spit the water out and tried to bring in a breath, but more water filled me.

Smoke drifted up from my hands. Thick waves of steam poured off of them before a bright blue flame ignited in my palms. I tried to scream as it scalded my skin, and the scent of burning flesh filled my nostrils, but only more water spilled from my lips.

Darius tilted his head, watching as I screamed silently, begging for death to stop the pain. "Don't you see? I have the power, Chase. This power was given to me by Ithreal and you will bow to him, as will all your gods." He raised his hand and the light vanished from the sky.

Thick shadows filled the air and my body rose into the still wind. Shadows spiraled down from the sky, taking hold of my limbs and pulling them in opposite directions. Power pulsed around me. My shoulders and hips cracked as the darkness tried to rip me apart.

The flames snapped and moved up my forearms, splitting the skin and blistering the muscles beneath. I coughed again, a hint of air sucking into my lungs before I ejected another mouthful of water.

My body spun higher into the air, shadows yanking on my limbs, and Darius watched with a grim smile from below.

When he dropped his hand, the shadows released me and my body fell. Wind rushed past me, but I was paralyzed. Darius' power was wrapped around me, refusing to let me brace for the impact. Instead, I remained still and plummeted to the earth.

I crashed into the ground and darkness swallowed me. I blacked out and a rush of magic snapped me awake. Darius' fingers were on my head, using his power to keep me conscious.

The cuts on my chest shot pain through my body and I screamed. The agony of the impact exploded through my head and core like a sledgehammer. The pain went deep and stuck inside me, forcing more water to discharge from my lungs.

"I think you get the point." Darius snapped his fingers and freed my body.

I tried to move, but there was too much pain. The adrenaline was gone, washed away by fear. I lay face down in the grass, my body trembling. My hands were so burnt they looked like they'd gone through a meat grinder. I couldn't feel my fingers and the muscles were too damaged to move them. Water drained from my mouth like a never ending flood and my lungs hurt as the cold air touched them. The black dots faded as the oxygen rushed through my body, but each breath hurt more than the last.

The grass crunched and folded as Darius' black combat boots stepped in front of my face. He crouched down, the thick leather trench coat drifting around him. "I don't want to do this again." His accent was smooth, each word gentle and soft as he spoke. "This is your final warning. I'd hate to steal another loved one from you, but I will do whatever is necessary. It matters not how many elements you get; it will not be enough. Be wise. Cherish your life. Do what's best for your friends."

I tried to speak, but the words wouldn't come. My body ached and I felt the warmth of blood seeping from me.

"Do try and enjoy the rest of your vacation; it is beautiful here. I must admit, Serephina does nice work." Darius's magic vanished and darkness pulled itself over me. The dream world faded, leaving me alone and floating in the shadows.

Chapter 21

My heart pounded in my chest. Blood moved down my sides and panicked breaths sparked pain deep in my lungs.

"Don't move." A voice shot through my head.

The sound caused a million needles to shoot through my brain. Foreign hands pushed against my body. They were hot and soft against my skin.

Rayna sat in the chair by the window, hugging her knees to her chest. Her green eyes watched with fear, but desperation for sleep tugged at them. What little color her skin held was gone, leaving it a grayish tone.

Garrett, Karissa, and Chief stood over me. Karissa and Chief cared for the wounds on my chest, dabbing the wide cuts with blood soaked cloths, while Garrett mixed something with a mortar in a small wooden bowl. The white blankets beneath me were stained red with blood and sweat ran down my face, dripping onto the covers.

"Stop," I said, but it came out in a hoarse and cracked whisper. "I can fix this." I closed my eyes and reached deep inside. I focused on the healing power of water and drew it to the surface. Magic poured off me and both Chief and Karissa's eyes opened wide.

The rain came down like a waterfall in my mind, washing away the warlock's wounds. I visualized the large gashes closing, but as I imagined the skin folding over itself, the magic faded. I tried to bring it back, but it wouldn't budge. What energy I had left, I'd used calling it forward. I didn't have it in me to heal this. The world around me faded in and out, getting fuzzier with each attempt to bring my magic to the surface.

"Rest, my boy." Chief leaned over me, dabbing my forehead with a cool cloth.

"I can't...they're...coming," I whispered.

"Who is?"

I tried to open my mouth, but I'd lost all control. Black dots swarmed me and the more I fought, the faster they came, until darkness swallowed me.

****

Cloudy voices echoed around me and the sound hurt my head. My eyes were hard to open and I reached up and wiped the sleep away. The room went in and out of focus before I could finally see clearly.

"He's awake!" Rayna moved from the window and leaned over me. "Chase, can you hear me?"

I pushed myself up and realized my hands were still covered in blood. Thick gauze and bandages were wrapped around my chest and I was lying in fresh, clean sheets.

"Yeah, I'm here," I whispered, but it still hurt to speak. "Water."

Karissa rushed over with a glass. Her hazel eyes sparkled, but she looked worried.

I took a sip and the cool liquid soothed my throat. I drank it all and set the empty glass on the table.

"How are you feeling?" Karissa asked.

I shook my head, trying to push away the thick fog roaming inside my mind. "I'm fine...I think. What happened?"

"You had another dream. Riley, I'm guessing," Rayna said.

"No..." I said. "Darius Sellowind."

"One of the Dark Brothers?" Karissa asked.

"That's what he means." Rayna sounded annoyed. "I'll get Chief."

"God, I'm so glad you're okay." Rayna wrapped her arms around me.

"Whoa!" I winced, my voice starting to come back. "Last time I saw you, you wanted nothing to do with me."

"That doesn't matter now. All that matters is that you're okay."

She pulled away and I slid my legs over the bed. My chest stung as I moved, but I gritted my teeth and pushed through the pain.

"How long have I been out?"

"A day and a little bit."

"That long?" I sighed, rubbing my fingers against my temples. A migraine throbbed in my mind and I needed any relief I could get. "Were you able to shift?"

Rayna looked disappointed. "Not yet, but you can't worry about that right now."

"I remember waking up, but my magic wouldn't work..."

"Your powers are getting stronger, but until you can fully control it, it takes too much energy. Energy you don't have right now," she said with a tone and a glare.

The door opened and Chief and Karissa came into the room.

"How are you feeling?" Chief crouched in front of me.

"My chest hurts and my head is pounding, but otherwise I think I'm okay."

"Here, take these." He dropped two aspirin in my hand and gave me another glass of water. I swallowed both pills with a gulp.

"Let's have a look at these." Chief crouched down and peeled back one of the gauze wraps. "Wow. You heal fast. That's impressive, even to a shifter."

The wide gashes were now thin strips of scabs, starting below my shoulder and moving down across my stomach. The edges of them were bright red and raw to the touch.

"You gave us quite the scare. You sure you're okay?" Chief asked.

"I'll be fine," I said, rubbing my temples. "Has Jonathan been around again? Last night, or whenever it was..."

"I heard, and I'm sorry. I've never seen him like this. Obviously my warnings have not been acknowledged, so I've sent him back to Stonewall."

"Is he okay? I didn't mean to hurt him."

"He'll be fine. Nothing more than a bruised ego." Chief smiled. "Best thing for you now is some fresh air. Can you walk?"

I pushed myself off the bed and tried to stand. It hurt at first, but once my feet were on the floor, it felt good to stretch. I washed off all the blood I could, but there were still spots of blood I'd have to get later. I threw a gray hoodie on, careful not to tear the bandaging, and I met Chief on the porch.

"Sorry ladies, I'd like this to be just Chase and I. And Rayna, you need to rest."

Rayna nodded and tried for a smile.

"Ready?" Chief asked.

"Yeah, but can we keep the bush whacking to a minimum?"

Chief laughed and began walking, leading me into the forest with a trail to navigate.

The air was crisp, giving us another sign of fall. Water dripped from the leaves and moisture rolled on the air, leaving the smell of what I thought was a coming storm to fill my senses. Judging by the muddy trail and wet grass, however, I'd already missed it.

"Hell of a night you had," Chief said.

"You're telling me."

"From what I understand, it's been your father entering your dreams?"

"That was the first time. This time it was Darius Sellowind."

"The Dark Brothers are a powerful duo, feared by most of the Underworld. You should tread lightly. They are not a power to be tested."

"So I've heard, and now seen, but I don't understand it. Marcus fought them and made it out in one piece."

"Marcus is a powerful hunter but don't be fooled. The Dark Brothers only let you see what they want you to. They are masters of their craft."

"What's their deal anyways? Until a few weeks ago, I'd never even heard of them."

"The brothers keep to themselves and people don't talk about them. They fear it will bring unwanted attention."

"Who are they? How did they get to be so powerful?"

"Everyone has a different story. Some believe they practice blood magic, stealing life force from others to give themselves immortality. The reality is, nobody knows. I fear for you having them as an enemy."

"I'll take the brothers over Riley, especially if he completes the ritual. A jacked up hunter with the power of a god is not something I want to see."

"Do not underestimate the Brothers. The fact that they're hurting you physically while in your dreams speaks volumes about their power."

"Everyone that's after me is powerful," I said.

"Perhaps I can help."

"How?"

"I can't change what is already done, but I can help in the matter of your dreams being invaded."

"I'm listening."

"It's a matter of having control, even when you're asleep. It may be their magic that harms you in the dream world, but that isn't what allows them to enter it. They have control of their minds in such a way that allows them to leave their dreamscape and enter yours. If you learn to take control of it, you can prevent unwanted visitors."

"So...like I can shield a vampire from entering my mind while awake, you can teach me to shield while asleep?"

"Exactly."

"Why do I feel like there's a *but* coming?"

"I wish to offer my services to your cause. The Hollowlights are willing to help you in any way we can, but before I can make such an offer, I need to know where your devotion lies."

"I'm not sure I follow."

"The Hollowlights pride themselves on being loyal. When we make an allegiance, we live by it. We will stand beside you, no matter who your enemy may be, but we expect the same in return."

"We could definitely use the help, and if there's some way I can return the favor, I'm happy to."

"We have an allegiance then?"

"Are you sure you want to make one? You said yourself the Dark Brothers are not a power to be rivaled."

"I have faith that together we can conquer many things."
Chief extended his hand to me.

"Then we have a deal."

"Excellent." He smiled and shook my hand.

We walked in silence for a few minutes. The aches in my
body began to fade. My muscles loosened up and the pain in my
head receded. The cuts on my chest hurt more, but the rest of me
had started to feel better.

We followed the dirt path deep into the forest, and after an
hour, the gray clouds faded letting the sun break through. The
warmth brought the forest back to life, drying the wet leaves and
waking the birds who sang from the treetops. A mild breeze rode
the air and brought with it the scent of the revitalized woods.

Chief and I stepped through an opening in the trees. It was a
smaller, more private version of the gathering area back at camp.
There were three stumps that sat on the wet earth and the small
fire pit in the middle was filled with old, wet ash.

"Here we are." Chief reached into his jacket and pulled out a
matchbook. He went through several matches trying to light the
moist wood, but each burned out before he could get a spark.
"Care to help?"

I smirked and reached down into my soul, pulling at the fire
magic inside. I channeled the energy down my arm and into my
hand, and the flame came to life with ease. I pushed it forward,
and a stream of heat smoldered towards the wood.

The bark smoked, but the wet, soggy wood resisted the
flame. I turned my focus to the flames' heat, and the temperature
spiked. Small flickers of bright ash shot up into the air, but still the
fire didn't catch. I gave the magic one last push, the flame turning
into a bright white scorch of heat and the wet logs lit up with a
crackle.

The magic pulled back with ease, cooling and then
disappearing. The heat filled me as it moved back down my arm
and through my chest, coming to rest at that invisible place in the
middle. I picked a stump to sit on and let the heat wash over me. I
couldn't help but smile as the flames crackled against the wood. I
was finally gaining some control.

"That magic never ceases to impress me," Chief said. "Now as for those dreams you've been having, let's see if we can put some of that power to good use."

Chief adjusted himself on his stump. He slipped his shoes off, revealing hairy bare feet, and twisted his legs overtop of one another, placing a foot on each of them in a meditative position.

"Before we start, I must warn you. If you damage your psyche or you die in the other plane, it is possible for you to be stuck there, unable to return to the physical world."

"Great."

"I'm very serious. Take caution before you attempt this on your own."

"Okay...I got it," I said impatiently.

"When your enemy enters your mind, you have the advantage. It's *your* psyche, so you are in control. Before you can control this, however, you must first understand it. There is no better way to do this than to step outside of your body. We will try together, but do not be discouraged; very few are able to do this on the first attempt. All you need to worry about now is getting into the meditative state; the rest will come with practice."

I slipped my shoes off, taking the same position as Chief. It was uncomfortable at first, but the feeling faded as I closed my eyes and focused on his voice.

"When you lose your sight, your other senses come to life. They can distinguish things without seeing them. They can touch them without the use of your hands. To step out of yourself, you must enter the meditative mindset. I want you to quiet your mind, hush your soul, and focus only on the life surrounding you."

I kept my eyes closed and reached out with my other senses. The forest changed, coming to life in a new way. It reminded me of the first time I entered the sanctuary with Rayna. Magic pounded inside me, and I pushed it aside. I wasn't playing that game today. Instead of the magic, I focused on the birds, the trees, and the wet earth around me.

"First, reach outside yourself and feel the forest. Hear it, smell it, taste it, and feel it with more than your body."

The birds' chirping became louder, wet leaves rustled, and the sun's warmth covered my skin. I could hear the trees swaying in the breeze and smell the moisture fading from the air. A warm tingle moved over my chest and the senses flew around me. Faster and faster they swallowed me until there was nothing else. The woods existed in a new way—the forest didn't surround me anymore; it was inside me.

Everything sounded and felt different. I could no longer feel the stump beneath me. I could hear the fire snapping against the wood, but it gave off no heat. The forest air drifted around me, but there was no breeze.

I tried to keep my focus and ignore how foreign everything seemed, but I couldn't. I opened my eyes, and to my surprise, I was no longer sitting at all. I was standing in front of the fire. Everything was different. Things were foggy, yet clearer than ever.

I turned around and a swell of fear filled me. I could see myself sitting on the stump. Legs crossed, eyes closed, and an intense focus written over my face.

"Do not panic." I heard the voice in my head.

I tried to talk but no sound came out. *"What the hell is happening?"*

"You've succeeded." The voice chuckled, and I recognized it as Chief's.

I turned to Chief but he was still on the stump. His eyes were closed and he was motionless, looking peaceful in front of the forest's backdrop. I turned, trying to follow his voice, but there was nothing to follow; it was inside my head.

"I am here." The voice came again.

I turned to the cracking of branches behind me and a large white tiger stepped out of the forest. Huge white paws moved the dirt and leaves as it crept towards me. Thick black swirls and stripes covered its furry body and it moved with such power; you wouldn't think it could have grace, but it carried that strength as though it were weightless.

I stepped back and my legs tingled like they had fallen asleep. They moved, but they didn't touch the wet earth beneath me.

"Do not fear me. It is I, Chief." The large cat stared at me and bright purple eyes watched with a gentle ferocity. *"We've achieved what we set out to do. I admit I'm surprised, but we've stepped out of ourselves."*

"How can I hear you?"

"When we astral project, we are not physically here. Voices are a thing that exists solely in the physical world. When you step out of it, you move to a higher plane: one that exists only for our minds and souls. This is a level of consciousness between awake and dreaming."

"Then why are you a tiger?"

"On this plane, we appear as we truly see ourselves. Your projection is the same as your physical form. You see yourself exactly as you are. Interesting."

Everything around me looked the same, but different. The colors were brighter, the smells were more distinct; the world was more alive. *"What now?"*

"You're in a dream state. You can do things here that you cannot do in the physical world. This is all controlled by your mind. This is your astral projection. I have entered it with ease, but in order to protect yourself, you must create a wall to block outsiders. Before you can build a wall, you must first be able to alter your world. Try and take us somewhere else."

I turned and walked into the forest, but the Chief's voice rang through my head again. *"Do not walk somewhere else, simply go there."*

"How?"

"Just go."

I looked at the forest around me and imagined the old apartment. I pictured the old tube television that weighed a ton, the cracked ceiling, and the stained foam mattress that lay beneath it. I could hear the neighbors smashing things against my wall and it startled me as the sound rang through my head.

The forest didn't fade. It morphed around me, becoming something different. The trees merged together, the color fading to become yellow walls. The fresh air that filled my nostrils vanished and turned stale. Old stained carpet covered the forest floor and I was no longer in the forest; I was standing in the middle of my old bedroom.

The old foam mattress I had once called a bed lay on the floor, my blankets thrown aside. The scarred and faded brown dresser was still missing its handles, and the ceiling had the same cracks I remembered. I stared at the nicotine stained walls and sadness came over me. It was my home...but it was missing the most important piece.

"We make homes out of what we're given, but they do not define who we are." Chief's thought came through my head. The huge tiger sat in my doorway, his thick face and bright purple eyes watching me with wisdom I knew an animal couldn't have.

"You're still here..."

"I go where you go, until either I choose to leave, or you make me. This is your plane; try to push me out of it."

I tried the same technique as before. I pictured the apartment without Chief. I imagined pushing him out the door and into the hall, but nothing happened.

"I can't."

"You can. Pushing me out is more difficult than keeping me out, but if you take control of this, you're one step closer to protecting yourself. You must find me in this world."

I changed my approach and reached out with my mind. I felt with my psyche, trying to follow his magic, his aura, anything. The same magic I used to break down glamour reached out and pawed at the air. I could feel his energy lingering around me and I followed it back to his spirit form. It hung in the air and I pushed at it with my mind. I pulled energy from inside myself, but it wasn't my element; it was a mental ability I didn't recognize. I pushed that energy against him and he started to push back.

"Good."

I put all my focus into that power and pushed until I felt his energy break.

"Wait—" his voice came, but it was too late.

The tiger blurred and faded from the doorway. I stood alone in the apartment with nothing but the sound of the neighbor's screams. I felt oddly strange and unwanted, even though there was no one else here. Thick silence wrapped itself around me and I didn't like how out of place I felt. This wasn't the home I remembered.

I pushed the bedroom away and imagined the forest again. The ceiling cracked in half, each piece pulling away from the other. It peeled back like wallpaper and became the bright blue sky I'd left. The walls shook before shattering to dust, and thick branches and trunks burst from the floor. The thin stained carpet disappeared beneath dirt, sticks, and rocks.

Chief still sat on his stump, but the tiger was nowhere to be seen. My physical body sat in its same position, a smile pulling at the corners of my mouth. I looked at peace.

It was strange looking at myself without a mirror. I recognized myself, but I looked different. Nothing I could place. Just...different.

I shook the feeling away and closed my eyes, willing myself back into my body. When I opened them again, I still stood in front of myself. I tried again, imagining the walls of the forest collapsing around me and pushing myself back into my body. Nothing.

I took a few steps back and ran towards my body. I leapt forward and felt a strange vibration as I slid through my physical form. I passed through it and rolled along the earth without touching the ground, a barrier of air carrying my body.

I watched myself sitting peacefully on the stump and cursed in my head. I was stuck. I started to panic, and as nervousness clutched me, the trees began to shake. The sound of thunder boomed in the air and echoed through my head. The trees collapsed and my heart raced. The world became foggy and this reality crumbled.

My astral projection was lifted from the ground and I struggled against an unseen power. The ground disappeared, becoming black, empty space. I tried to bring my focus back but it was too late. My body tore through the air, soaring towards my physical form.

My eyes opened and my body flew back off the stump. Chief's laughter filled my ears as I hit the wet earth and pain shot through my chest. I reached up and touched my face. To my relief, I felt skin. I was back.

"One must be careful not to panic."

"Would've been nice to know what to expect," I said.

"I'm sorry. I didn't think you'd actually project. Very few people succeed on a first attempt. I tried to warn you, but you pushed me out before I could."

"It didn't feel the same this time. Not like it was when Riley and the Brothers were in my dreams."

"That's because you weren't in the dream world. You were somewhere in between. They were entering your dreamscape directly and making it their own. They decided where you went, how you moved and felt, and what you were able to do. You are lucky to be here and not stuck in the other world after what Darius did."

"So if they come back into my dream and kill me, I'll die here?"

"There is a chance of that. If that happened, you would be reborn in the dream world, stuck until your physical body died. Then you'd become a spirit."

"A ghost? You're kidding right?"

"I'm afraid not, but think more poltergeist than ghost. After being trapped in that plane for any length of time, you'd surely go mad."

"I think I've had enough astral...whatever for one day."

We came back through the clearing to the sound of Rayna screaming. Chief and I looked at each other and made a break for the cabin.

He burst through the door first and I expected to see Rayna rolling on the floor in pain, but she wasn't. She stood wrapped in a small towel, trying to keep herself covered. Jonathan Winter stood in the living room. He had one hand in front of him, and the other covering his eyes.

"I'm sorry. I didn't mean to...I mean, I just want to talk. A chance to explain."

"Get out!" she screamed.

I lunged towards Jonathan and tackled him to the floor. Pain seared through my chest and I did my best to ignore it, but before I could do more, Chief's hands pulled me.

Chief grabbed Jonathan by the neck and dragged him outside, throwing him off the porch as easily as he'd throw a stone. Jonathan hit the ground rolling and Chief stormed towards him.

"What did I tell you?" Chief's voice was loud and angry, but his beast didn't rise. He remained in complete control.

"I have a right to explain myself to my own daughter," Jonathan stammered, trying to stand.

"You have the right to nothing. If and when she's ready, she'll let you know. I gave you a direct order to stay away, and you disobeyed me. Again!"

"I thought the Hollowlights were about democracy and equality, not about orders."

"We are also about *respect*, something you are showing none of to me, or Rayna."

Shifters made their way out of the woods and cabins, gathering together and whispering amongst themselves. Rayna stepped out onto the porch with her arms crossed. She'd dressed in a loose pair of sweats, and her body was swimming in one of my zip-up hoodies.

Jonathan's blue eyes looked past Chief as she came out. "Please, Rayna, all I'm asking is for a chance to explain. If you want nothing more from me afterwards, I'll go. I just want a chance..."

"No," Chief said. "You will leave. Now."

"It's fine," Rayna answered.

"What?" I asked.

"If that's what it takes to get him to leave me alone, then let's get this over with. Nothing else seems to be working." Rayna was calm, her face composed and her emotions in check. Her eyes locked with Jonathan's. "You've got ten minutes." Rayna shook her head and walked back into the cabin.

Jonathan pushed himself to his feet and brushed the wet grass off his pants and jacket.

Chief grabbed him by the shirt and pulled him forward. "If you *ever* pull a stunt like that again, you and I are going to have a problem."

"Careful, Charlie, I'm not a cub." Jonathan said with a growl, and his blue eyes shifted to their cat form.

"Is that a challenge?" Chief's eyes were still human, but the beast lurked beneath the surface, power rolling off of him.

Jonathan froze and let his eyes shift back to their human counterpart. He sighed and shook his head. "No..."

"Then watch your tongue."

"I'm sorry...it won't happen again."

Chief released him and Jonathan walked towards the cabin.

"Chase, get in here," Rayna commanded.

Rayna was on the couch. Jonathan sat in a chair opposite her, leaning forward with eagerness.

"I thought we could talk, just you and me," Jonathan pleaded.

"No. Whatever you have to say, you can say in front of Chase and Chief. Your time starts now."

"Oh, where to start..."

"You've barged in on me multiple times and attacked Chase to have this conversation. You've had eighteen years to figure it out and here I am, so start talking."

"Okay..." Jonathan's eyes moved from Rayna, to me, to Chief, and he sighed. "I'd been in love with your mother for nearly a year. We were planning on eloping so I could escape the Circle and we could be together. A few weeks before we were set to leave, the elders sent me on a mission to investigate some missing kids. Turned out it was a problem with shifters, but not like you'd think."

Jonathan adjusted himself in his seat, trying to read Rayna's response. Her eyes locked with his and her expression was unmoving. Jonathan cleared his throat and continued.

"The children had been adopted, but what no one knew was they were born shifters. Their parents were killed by none other than the Circle. When cubs start to shift, they have a natural instinct to join their pack, so naturally, the kids followed the scent. When I found them and tried to take them back, they'd already started to change. One of the younger kids bit me and transferred the virus." Jonathan fidgeted with his hands, his eyes dropping to the floor. "I tried fighting the infection, but I could feel it taking hold. I didn't tell anyone; the Circle would've had me killed. I knew I was going to die, but I wouldn't let it be at their hands, so I decided to run. I knew it wouldn't be long before the Circle found out I was missing, so I went to Sarah...your mother. I'd planned to say goodbye, but we ended up..." Jonathan looked up sheepishly and quickly pulled his eyes away from Rayna.

"Having sex?" Rayna asked.

Jonathan nodded. "I had planned on telling her. I knew she'd understand, but our night together had been perfect; I didn't want to spoil it."

"Please." Rayna rolled her eyes.

"I did! I loved her. She was everything to me." He took a breath to calm himself. "But the virus became active in the middle of the night and I panicked. I didn't want her to watch me die, so I ran as fast and as far as I could before the shift took hold. If Charlie hadn't shown up...I never would have survived."

Rayna looked to Chief, who watched her with a keen eye and he nodded.

"Charlie pushed my beast back and over the next few weeks helped me through the shift. He eased it out, piece by piece, until I fully changed."

"This is all great, but if all you have to tell me is how Chief saved your life, I'm not interested."

"That's only the beginning," he said. "Once I'd garnered control of the beast, I came back to your mother, but the Circle had discovered our affair and she'd fled. I didn't know she was pregnant then, but I still searched for her. I spent over a year following her trail, but I was always two steps behind. When her scent finally vanished, I couldn't wander aimlessly anymore, so I came back to Stonewall. Chief had taken over the Hollowlights by then and I was welcomed into the pride. It wasn't until nine years later that I'd heard she'd returned, but when I finally found out where she was, it was too late..."

Jonathan started pacing the room and looked at Rayna, his blue eyes clouded as they began to well up.

"I didn't even know she'd had a child...not until I got this." Jonathan pulled a crumpled and worn white envelope out of his back pocket.

"What's that?" Rayna's calm and even emotions were wavering on nervous anticipation.

"It's a letter, sent to me anonymously, a few months after she died. Sarah knew about me all along, but didn't contact me in fear it would jeopardize your safety. When I discovered I was a father, I tried to find you, but I didn't know your scent. I didn't know anything about you. I had nowhere to start."

"Can I...read it?" Rayna's voice was quiet.

Jonathan stared at the letter a moment before handing it to Rayna. She pulled a few weathered sheets out of the envelope and began reading.

The silence that filled the room over the next few minutes went from sad to awkward. Tears that Rayna refused to wipe fell from her eyes. Her hands trembled, and as she finished the last few words, she turned to Chief.

"Is this true?" she asked, holding back a sob.

Chief nodded and lowered his eyes.

"I'm sorry." Jonathan said.

Rayna clutched the letter in her hand and moved into the bedroom. The door slammed behind her and silence wrapped around us.

"I need some air," Jonathan said.

"I'll check on Rayna," Chief added.

I followed Jonathan out to the porch. With Chief confirming his story, I couldn't help feeling bad for him.

"I'm sorry," he said. "For the other night, I just..."

"I get it. You just wanted a chance to set things straight. I never realized...I mean, it's a lot easier to believe you're a deadbeat than a man who tried everything to set things right."

Jonathan let out a half-laugh. "I guess it is."

The sun made its descent behind the tree line and darkness crept into the sky. You could see the moon and stars shining through the partly lit sky while the cool air moved in with the eve.

"What's she like?" Jonathan asked. "Rayna..."

"She's amazing. She's beautiful, strong, intelligent, and a stubborn ass." I smirked.

"Sounds just like her mother. She looks like her, too. Gods, she was beautiful." A smile crossed his lips. "Sarah always had this look in her eyes: determination. She wouldn't take crap from anyone, especially me. She was one hell of a witch, too."

"She sounds really great."

"Oh, she was." Jonathan's blue eyes turned to me, practically glowing as he raved about his lost love. "She was more than that. She was..."

"Incredible," Rayna said from behind us. She leaned in the doorway, eyes red with sadness.

"Yes, incredible."

"I remember when–" Rayna stopped, her eyes opened wide with panic, and power crashed over us. She dropped onto all fours and let out a fierce growl.

Chief came through the doorway and he and Jonathan both dropped to their knees.

"Calm yourself, Rayna. You shift on your terms."

Rayna unleashed a ferocious sound through snarling lips. The skin on her arms split and clear fluid dripped out as the fur broke through. Her bones cracked, and although she whimpered, they shifted quickly into the thick black paws of a wildcat.

"Yes!" Chief cheered.

"I'm here, Rayna," Jonathan said, and her beast stared into his eyes. She growled and let out a screech as her fangs dropped and thick white claws shot out of her paws.

Another power entered the scene. Jonathan's beast came to life, his eyes shifting, and a deep screech escaped his lips.

"Jonathan, don't," Chief commanded.

Fear filled Jonathan's eyes as his fangs began to drop. "I...can't...stop." His words were slurred by the large fangs. Blood poured from his mouth and hands as he shifted, a tail ripping itself through his jeans.

"Control yourself!" Chief ordered, pushing his beast over Jonathan, but it was no use.

"I'm trying. It's...her–" Jonathan grunted as his bones snapped, and in moments, he was gone. A waist high panther sat on a pile of torn clothes. It growled at Rayna as her bones moved. Her back arched and her spine snapped as it changed shape. She collapsed to the ground and started panting heavily.

"You're nearly there, Rayna." Chief turned his attention away from Jonathan, bringing his beast to the surface and pushing it against Rayna.

Rayna jumped onto all fours and growled again, a new determination filling her. Green cat eyes watched me as the rest of her body began to move. Her pink tank top ripped, and baggy sweats fell off her hips as black fur pushed through a wave of blood and fluid. She grunted and her skin rippled across her face. Her cheekbones collapsed and her skin stretched as her face reformed. Her jaw snapped and dislocated, taking on a new shape as the last few bones shifted into place. Now there wasn't one, but two black panthers standing in front of us.

Jonathan stared at Rayna, but Rayna watched me. She crept towards me, her body swaying with each step. I took a few steps back until the porch railing stopped me. My pulse sped as she neared and I called my water element, partly to calm myself, and partly just in case.

Rayna stopped and growled.

"Don't," Chief said.

I held the magic inside me for a moment, staring into Rayna's eyes. I could see the beast, but she was in there too, looking out at me. They were one.

She growled again, fiercer this time, and I let the magic recede. She stepped closer and sweat gathered on my palms. My pulse leapt but the nervousness buckled as she pushed her head into my hand. Long whiskers tickled my skin and I moved my fingertips over her head. A deep rumble moved from her throat, but instead of a roar, she purred. She arched her back and rubbed up against my leg, coming up just below my hip.

Rayna stepped away from me and Jonathan moved forward, pushing his head into her neck. She continued to purr and watch me as he nuzzled her.

"She needs to hunt to complete the shift." Chief's eyes focused on me.

I looked down at Rayna, who watched me with an intensity I'd never seen before. I nodded and she growled, taking a few steps and leaping off the porch in unspoken grace. Jonathan walked softly after her, his large feet padding against the earth. He was a few inches taller than her, but they looked nearly identical. Glossy, black fur covered their bodies; the only difference was in their eyes.

Rayna nudged into his neck and the crowd of shifters that had gathered separated as the pair bounded through the clearing. With only a few long leaps, they dove into the underbrush and vanished in a spill of colorful leaves.

"She did it..." I said.

Chief came to stand beside me. "The kinship her and Jonathan's beasts shared was the final piece."

"But he said he couldn't control it. He couldn't stop."

"Probably just the power of a shifter's first change. They're family. Just as with born shifters, the bond completed the act." Chief tried to smile, but he didn't look or sound confident.

"Probably?"

"Rayna is safe. Their beasts have a different, unbiased relationship. They are meant to be together," he said, avoiding my question.

A few men and women pushed through the crowd below and stormed towards us. Garrett and Karissa were among them, and Chief stepped down to meet them.

"What is it?"

"It's time we spoke to *him*," one of the men said. His brown hair hung down to his shoulders and his eyes watched me with an anger I didn't understand.

"Now is not the time."

"Now *is* the time. You said he was a hunter; you never told us who. I had to find out through Karissa."

"Jesse, I didn't mean to–" Karissa started.

"Silence," Jesse commanded.

"I was under the impression everyone knew," Chief replied.

"What's going on?" I asked.

"Tell him, Chief. It's time we learned where his true allegiance lies."

"We know where it lies," Garrett said. "Chief has already spoken to him."

"I want to hear it from him. I'm not losing anyone else!"

"Jesse, come on, he's the one who saved me and Garrett," Karissa pleaded.

"I don't care. I want to hear it from his mouth. I want to see it in his eyes when he tells me. Tell him, or I will."

"What the hell's going on?" I asked.

Chief sighed and turned to me. "There's something you should know, Chase. It's about your father."

"Okay…" The air slipped out of my lungs and I couldn't help holding my breath.

"A few weeks ago, Riley and the Dark Brothers approached us with an offer."

"What kind of offer?"

"To join them…"

"It wasn't an offer, it was an ultimatum," Jesse added.

My pulse leapt and I gripped the porch railing.

"We have not accepted, but he was…unsatisfied with that answer. He killed two pride members in response."

"Two cubs!" Jesse growled.

Chief lowered his gaze. "He said he'd be back, and he hoped we'd change our minds…otherwise we'd suffer Ithreal's wrath."

"And you didn't feel the need to mention this?"

"Rayna was my prime concern. Her shifting took priority; her life depended on it."

"Are you sure about that? Are you sure you didn't offer your help just to get to me?" My power beat beneath the surface, anger swelling in my veins.

"That isn't what happened."

"You should've said something!" I could feel my pulse throbbing in my throat and the fire burning inside me. "I trusted you and you've lied to me this entire time."

"Forget what Chief did. What about you hunter? Are you with your father too, scouting out his enemies?" Jesse snapped.

I leapt off the porch and stood eye to eye with him. "I'm the only one trying to stop him!"

Jesse pushed his beast to the surface and I let the fire rise. We pushed our powers against one another, never breaking eye contact.

"Enough!" Chief commanded, but we didn't stop.

I pushed harder and I could feel fire pulsing in my eyes. Jesse winced as the magic poured off of me.

"I said, enough!"

Jesse flinched at Chief's voice and stepped back as he stormed towards him.

"What is it with you people today? Your arrogance is insulting."

"You're right, I'm sorry. I should've never questioned your judgment." Jesse lowered his gaze. "But I didn't realize we were bringing the spawn of a murderer into our home."

"You people keep all this from me, and I'm untrustworthy? That's bullshit!" I said.

"He killed my kids!" Jesse shouted, but the anger wasn't there anymore. "I won't lose anyone else."

I resisted the urge to unleash my magic, clenching my fist as anger beat through me. I stared at Jesse and he looked weakened. His anger faded and all that was left were the pieces of a broken man.

I tried to feel sorry for him, but the thought that this was all a setup infuriated me. I turned my back on the group and stormed into the cabin, slamming the door shut. The fire raged like a power storm and I took deep breaths, trying to push it away.

"Chase, I'm sorry," Chief said, following me in. "I promise you our primary goal was to help Rayna. We'd been watching her for some time, but I will not deny that Riley's visit sped up our approach. Do not be angry with my pride. They are only looking out for each other."

"You shouldn't have kept this from me."

"Perhaps not, but I stand by my decision to keep my focus on Rayna. Just as I stand by my decision to help you. My pride simply wants reassurance. Everyone fears the Dark Brothers, but the thought of Ithreal entering our world is far worse."

"You want reassurance? Fine," I said, walking back outside to the group. It had grown larger and dozens of shifters swarmed around, whispering amongst themselves. All eyes were on me as I stepped onto the porch and I stared at them, trying to put my anger away and understand their position.

"I want nothing to do with my father's cause," I said, and the crowd's whispers went silent. "His choices are his own. Yes, I'm a hunter, but I don't fight with him, or the Circle. I fight on my own side." I paced the porch. Cold air whipped off the trees and through the clearing, pushing heavy black clouds towards us. "Riley thinks invoking Ithreal's power will seal the divide between the hunters and the demons. By taking this power, he believes he'll bring lost magic back to the hunters. He thinks once he does this, he can rule the Underworld and all the Underworlders in it."

The crowd grew restless, their eyes falling off of me as they conversed with one another.

"I believe we deserve the right to choose. Underworlder or not, everyone deserves their freedom. They have a right to choose. You've already made your choice by declining Riley's offer. Will he be true to his word and come after you? Yes. But I'm with you and when he comes, we'll be ready."

"Yeah!" Karissa yelled. The crowed all turned to her and she fell silent, stepping back awkwardly. The silence was thick and the crowd stared at me.

Chief stepped up beside me, gentle eyes looking over them. "For the first time, the Hollowlights will fight, not *against* a hunter, but *with* one," he said. "You're witnessing history tonight and together, we'll make more of it!"

Applause came in a rush and cheers followed. The cheers turned to roars and the power of the shifters united, crashing over us in suffocating wave. Clothes fell to the ground and the beasts came out.

A huge group of mismatched shifters appeared, their human shells fading and reforming in front of me. The sound of breaking bones echoed and before long, there were no people, only animals.

Chief sat beside me, bright purple cat eyes staring up at me. His wide shoulders were covered in black and white swirls that turned to stripes as they moved down his body. He sat on a pile of torn clothing and gazed out over the crowd. He let out the fiercest of roars and the cats responded.

The sounds of hundreds of feet padding against the grass came in a thundering stampede and a flood of cats leapt into the forest. Rustling leaves and broken sticks exploded into the air and through the darkening woods until there was nothing.

The moon hung overhead and the night made its final push into the world. Bright pinholes in the midnight sky shone as the stars made themselves known, and I sighed in relief. Rayna had survived the shift. We'd made allies with the werecats, which could only help in our fight against Riley, and I was learning to protect myself on more than one level. Things had started to come together. We still had a couple of days to rest before we had to go home and I, for one, planned on enjoying them. In a few days, we'd be back in Stonewall, and dealing with our real problem: Riley.

Chapter 22

I sat on the porch and watched the sun rise. With the exception of the birds, the camp was silent, and I soaked up every moment of it. Rays of pink, orange, and red stretched over the clear sky. The air was cool, and thick dew made the grass shine. Rai had soared over the tree line and found her way to the porch. She looked happier here. Free to go when and where she wanted. I thought about her home in Drakar and realized even then she was constantly cooped up in the goblin's barn. This was the first taste of freedom she'd ever had. The lightning that crackled in her eyes was vibrant, and her feathered coat was fuller and thicker than usual.

I stayed on the porch, watching for hours as the sun moved higher into the sky. The camp had stayed silent as they all slept off the shift, but as afternoon approached, the cabin door creaked and Rayna stepped onto the porch. Her hair was tattered about, strands of red and black mixed together over a baggy gray sweater. Black pajama pants hung low on her hips and the green of her eyes had an unusual glow.

"Morning." I smiled.

"Hey…" Her voice trailed off. Rayna sat next to me and the bench swung as she settled in. She stayed silent and stared out over the clearing, a look on her face I couldn't read.

"How was your night?"

Rayna shrugged.

"That's all I get? Rayna, you did it, you shifted!" I tried to convey how proud I was, but she seemed unimpressed.

"It's no big deal."

I glared at her. "Are you kidding? This is a huge deal."

"I just don't want you to think…"

"We've been through this. I'm proud of you."

"Really?"

"Yes!" I said. "Now tell me about it."

Rayna's lips curled into a smile and she pulled a knee to her chest, a new excitement filling her eyes. "It was amazing," she said. "Once the shift was done, all the pain disappeared. I was this entirely new...thing, and the world was different."

"Different?"

"I don't know how to explain it. It was like, senses I didn't know came to life. I saw the world through something else's eyes, but I was still there. Everything looked brighter, smelled better, tasted amazing."

"That's so great!"

"You mean it? You're not freaked out?"

"No. I mean, at first when I thought you were going to bite me I was a little tense, but after that I was cool." I smirked.

Rayna punched me in the arm and laughed.

"How was it with Jonathan?" I asked.

"Once I shifted and the panther came out, I didn't care anymore. He was just family."

"And now?"

Rayna shrugged. "I don't know. I feel closer to him in a way I can't explain, but it's not like it was when we were shifted. He's still a stranger to me."

"It'll take time."

"I know. It's just weird." Rayna started fidgeting with her fingers. "I'm glad you're not freaked out."

"I told you; I wanted you to shift. I wanted you to be safe and I didn't want to see you go through that pain anymore. This doesn't change anything between us, except now I don't have to worry."

Rayna smiled, but as soon as it came it vanished, and her eyes darted to the clearing. "Someone's coming."

I looked around but I didn't see anyone. "Are you sure?"

"It's Chief."

"How..."

"I can smell him." Rayna gave a sheepish grin.

"You can smell him?"

"Some of the senses from the shift haven't gone away."

"And they won't." Chief came around the corner of the cabin.

"What?" Rayna asked.

"It's different for everyone, but after the first shift you'll notice changes. Your hearing is better, your sense of smell; everything improves."

"I thought it was only temporary. This is going to take some getting used to."

"Soon you won't even notice it." Chief laughed. "I came to tell you how proud we all are of you, Rayna. You should be proud too."

"Thanks." Rayna smiled, lowering her gaze.

"Look you two, we're going to be heading back in a few days, but I still have some work I want to do with both of you. Rayna, I want you to shift once more before we leave, and Chase, I want another session with you."

"Session for what?" Rayna asked.

"Chief's teaching me how to shield in my sleep to keep Riley and the Dark Brothers out of my head."

"You can do that?"

"It's not easy, but yes. Chase has picked it up quickly, and with some practice he shouldn't be receiving any more unexpected visitors. At least not in his dreams."

"Yeah, now it's just the real world I have to worry about."

Chapter 23

Driving home, I was relaxed and confident I could face whatever was coming, but as we pulled up to the condo, all those feelings died. We were back to reality. Back where Riley and the Dark Brothers could pop up at any minute, and deceiving vampires lurked at your neighborhood demon pub. Yup, we were home.

"Be safe. We'll talk soon." Chief smiled at Rayna.

I smirked, and one by one shook his, Jonathan's, and Garrett's hands before I turned around to find Karissa. Hazel eyes gleamed up at me and she smiled, reaching up and wrapping her arms around me.

"It was really great having you there this weekend."

"Yeah, it was...nice," I said, patting her on the back awkwardly.

"We should hang out sometime."

I raised both eyebrows and nodded. "Umm...sure. That'd be great."

"Ready?" Rayna walked up beside me, arching a single brow at Karissa.

"Yeah, I guess."

Rayna's eyes locked on Karissa, and she looked fierce.

"Everything okay?" I asked, looking back and forth between the girls.

Nobody responded, and Chief's voice broke up the awkward moment.

"Karissa, let's go."

"I'm coming." Karissa tore her eyes away from Rayna's. "Bye, Chase." She smiled.

"Bye," I said, trying not to sound confused.

The black SUV pulled away from the sidewalk and I turned to Rayna. "What was that about?"

Rayna shrugged and picked up one of her suitcases, throwing it over her shoulder. "Can you bring these up for me?" She smiled.

"Do I look like a bellboy?" I asked, scooping up her massive suitcases and waddling towards the door.

"Do you really want me to answer that?"

I dragged the suitcases the last few feet down the hallway and tossed them onto the floor. Rayna moved up the stairs silently as Marcus paced the kitchen with a phone in one hand, nodding, as if whoever he spoke to could see him. Rai flew throughout the room, chirping wildly and disappearing up the stairs with Rayna.

"I'm certain he won't go for that." Marcus eyed me and half-smiled as I came into the room. "Well, we'll see. Either way, I will be there and we can discuss things."

I leaned against the wall, watching Marcus as he paced the room.

"Okay, see you soon." Marcus set the phone on the counter and smiled. "Welcome back."

"It's good to be back. Tiki here? I thought he'd be waiting by the front door," I said.

"He's looking into something for me at Revelations."

Marcus stopped his pacing and watched me with an eager expression.

"So..."

"So, what?"

Marcus' head canted to the side and he didn't look amused. "She did it!"

Marcus' thick lips curled up and revealed perfect white teeth. "That's fantastic. I needed some good news."

"Why, what's going on?"

"You were right; Riley's here. He paid a visit to the Circle last night."

I rolled my eyes. "Screw the Circle. They don't want to work with us, so they can deal with him their way, and we'll deal with it ours."

Marcus' gaze dropped to the floor. "Actually…"

"Don't tell me we're getting involved with them again."

"Well…now that they've seen what he's capable of, they've had somewhat of a change of heart."

"I don't care. I'm not working with them."

"I told them you'd say that."

"Good. We'll get our help elsewhere. We don't need them."

"Where exactly do you expect us to find the kind of help the Circle can provide? They're the greatest ally we could have against Riley."

"The werecats."

Marcus shook his head. "I doubt they'll want to be a part of this fight. The Dark Brothers are greatly feared among the Underworld, and once they learn what Riley's capable of, they'll be even more hesitant."

"What if I said they already agreed to help?"

"What do you mean?"

"I spoke with Chief. The Hollowlights are in."

"You what?" Marcus raised his voice.

"I thought you'd be happy."

"Chase, the werecats and werewolves have been at odds for years and the tension between them is rising. If they go to war, you'll have to choose between them."

All the excitement I had vanished and the thought of having to fight against Willy made my stomach tighten. I'd already tried to convince him to leave the Shadowpack once and he wouldn't even consider it. Rayna was right. Willy was proud to belong to something; he wasn't about to give that up.

Marcus sighed. "No need to worry about it yet, I suppose. As long as you didn't make a pact with them, you're not entirely committed."

I turned away from Marcus.

"Tell me you didn't…"

"What was I supposed to do? He put me on the spot and offered his help. Was I supposed to say no, I'd rather fight this battle alone?"

"We're not alone. After we meet with the Circle—"

"I'm not going back there," I said. "I don't want their support or anything they have to offer. I'm done with them."

"Then I'll go alone."

"Why would you do that?"

"Because we need them."

"No, we don't. They need *us*. Not the other way around. I won't have anything to do with them." I scooped up my duffle bag and started for the stairs.

"Yes, we do. Nobody saw this intrusion on the Circle coming. Riley raided the elders' libraries and took out several high-powered hunters. Riley's getting stronger and those books contain rituals going back as far as the original hunters. The Circle and I have seen every move Riley's made so far, but this..."

"What did you say?" The duffle bag fell from my shoulder and hit the ground.

Marcus tore his eyes from me immediately. "Nothing. Forget I mentioned it. I'll go to the Circle alone and you don't have to be involved."

"No, back it up. What do you mean you and the Circle have seen everything coming?"

"It's not a big deal."

"Don't play games with me. I can't take that right now. Not from you, Marcus." A nervous tension gripped my chest and my stomach scrunched into a tight ball of pain. I was frozen, my legs refusing to move.

"I'm an air elemental. Sometimes...I get visions."

"Sometimes?"

"Often...I get them often."

"And when you said you've seen *every* move Riley's made so far, what exactly did you mean by that?"

"He's acted as I expected him to, that's all."

"Don't lie to me. Did you see what would happen to Rayna? Is that how you knew we were in danger when you called? What about Mom?"

Marcus brought both his hands up and began massaging his temples. "It's not that simple, Chase. You need to understand–"

"No! Don't tell me that. For once in your life, answer the damn question!"

"Yes, but I couldn't—"

"I can't believe this." I paced the floor; anger, fear, and sadness all tugged me in different directions. I felt like the world had been torn out from under me and everything I knew had changed. Again. "You knew Rayna was the key. You knew Mom would die and you never told me?" The fire stirred inside me. The flame burned red hot and coursed through my veins.

"I couldn't. Chase—"

"We could've saved her. It didn't have to happen like that!" My anger was a freight train tearing through my insides.

"Let me explain." Marcus stepped forward, hands extended toward me. "Just calm down."

"I won't!"

The smell of burning fabric was thick and smoke billowed out from my shirt. Red embers began to glow around the sleeves until they caught fire. Flames rode up my arms, blue and silver crackling over my skin.

"All you had to do was tell me. She didn't have to die!"

"What the hell's going on?" Rayna rushed down the stairs and stood between Marcus and me.

"Ask *him*," I said, pointing a single finger, alit in flames, towards Marcus.

"First, you need to calm down. You're going to hurt yourself...and us." Rayna walked towards me and her gaze was firm. I felt her element come to life and push towards me in a wave of calm.

My anger fought against her magic, and for once, the elements didn't mingle. My power pushed against hers, trying to keep the calm away.

"Get out of the way, Rayna," I said through gritted teeth. The flame stopped moving up my arms but the fire continued to burn my shirt.

"Marcus?" Rayna sounded nervous.

"He let Mom die." I spat the words at him.

"She knew, Chase," Marcus said.

"That's a lie."

"It's not. I wanted to tell you, but she made me swear an oath that I wouldn't. We were trying to find another way to handle Riley. When I had the vision about Rayna, I tried to call, but it was too late."

"You knew what was going to happen?" Rayna asked. "I knew you got visions, but you never said anything..."

"I was trying to prevent it."

"Did you know about me?"

Marcus sighed. "It's not that simple."

"What about Jonathan, did you know he was alive?"

"Rayna, please."

Marcus took a step towards us.

"Don't," I commanded. The heat of my flame rose and snapped at the air around me.

"Chase, please calm down." He took another step.

"No!" My voice was low and serious. Power swirled around me. Sweat formed on my brow as the temperature spiked and the flames grew.

Marcus brought his element to the surface and sucked some of the air from the room. My chest constricted, struggling to conserve what air it had. The flames nipped at the air, shrinking to nothing as the oxygen faded.

Anger rode me like a storm. I called my own air element, battling against Marcus'. The air didn't come back to the room, but I'd stopped him from taking any more.

Marcus' eyes opened wide as shock took over his features. "Chase..." he took another step forward and I unleashed the next power in line.

Water built in my palms. Ice blue liquid swirled in a beam of dark light before a stream of magic raged towards him. It hit his chest and blew him back. The force pinned him against the wall. Gushes of water crashed against him and the wall cracked.

Marcus' power struck out and pushed my element back. The water moved through me and coursed through the air, but stopped at Marcus' hand. The air made a force field in front of him and the water slapped against the glowing, white barrier of power.

"Chase, stop this." Marcus held his calm exterior together, but sadness pulled at his eyes.

I saw a flash of my mother's face in my mind. Her lips pursed, but a smile pulled at them and grew as Marcus walked into the vision. The sight of it pulled my anger back and I let my elements disappear inside me.

"Screw you, Marcus."

As my magic faded, so did Marcus', but he looked defeated.

"I—"

"Don't. Save your lies for someone else. I don't want to hear them anymore."

I turned away and the look on Rayna's face was distraught. Sadness, anger, fear, and confusion warped her features one after another.

Marcus sighed. "I have a meeting with the Circle. We'll discuss this when I get back."

"You do whatever you have to. When you get back, I won't be here."

"Please don't do anything out of anger. I'll be back late tonight or sometime tomorrow. Please give me the chance to explain."

Marcus' eyes pleaded with me, but I didn't give in. I let him see the betrayal and anger I felt.

He hung his head and walked out of the condo, closing the door gently behind him. Anger seared through me. Mom was dead because of him. All he had had to do was tell me and we could've changed everything.

"Chase, take a breath. Let's talk about this." Rayna regained her composure, trying to be the calm one.

I saw Mom's face again. Her smile grew when she looked up at Marcus, but as she turned away, Marcus plunged a knife deep in her back. Mom turned and fear covered her face, quickly vanishing as a demonic black filled her eyes. Cracks rushed across her skin, and she lit up in a flare of orange and red until her body crumbled to ash.

226

I unleashed a scream and power rushed through me. Fire
scorched the air and the kitchen table exploded. Shards of wood
flew across the room, igniting in a blast of heat. The wood
cracked, and the veneer surface melted as fire sizzled over it.

"Chase!" Rayna yelled.

Flames seared the wood and smoke billowed up, sending the
smoke detector into a frenzy of sound.

"Chase, stop. You're scaring me!"

Fear covered Rayna's face and I pulled the fire back. The last
of my shirt had burned and the thick stench filled my senses.
Pieces of fabric had melted into a tough plastic that stuck in
patches against my body.

"I..." I started, but couldn't finish.

Rayna ran into the kitchen and started filling jugs with water.
She splashed it on the table, but the flame was too far gone. The
fire hissed as the water hit it, turning it to steam upon contact.

"Can you help me out here?"

I fell into a daze as I watched her struggle with a few more
jugs of water, tossing them effortlessly over the flames, but
yielding no results. The white ceiling turned black with soot and
the smoke changed from a light gray to a thick black.

"Chase!" Rayna yelled.

I snapped out of my stupor and shook my head. I pushed the
water element through me, and the ball of power built in my
hands, but I couldn't maintain my focus. Thoughts of Marcus and
my mom flashed before my eyes and the anger swelled again.

Water exploded from my palm in every direction and it
wasn't the cool rush I was used to. Boiling water splashed against
the walls and Rayna ducked behind the cupboards.

"Chase, stop!" Rayna yelled, but I couldn't draw the power
back. A free flow of magic poured from my body and the condo
started to shake.

The ancient picture that hung on the wall crashed to the
ground. The frame snapped, and the painted canvas collapsed
from the wooden border, falling to the floor. Coils of fire lashed
out from the steaming water, reaching towards the walls and

marring them black. All the lights exploded and rained shards of glass over us.

"Get a hold of yourself!"

A burning sensation trickled down my spine and I winced in pain. A wind came from nowhere and charged through the condo, throwing debris across the room. Stuffing from the couch ripped itself from the tears and swirled in a tornado of fluff.

The sensation bit at my back again, a million needles plunging through me at once. The floor began to shake and more glass smashed as plates fell from the cupboards. I pulled back with all the effort I could manage, and the magic sucked itself back inside me. I dropped to my knees. Heavy breaths ran through my lips as steaming water dripped off the walls. The flames of the table had been smothered by the water, leaving a thick haze to fill the condo. Glass, fluff, and wreckage littered the floor and my body trembled, fighting back the tears. Flashes of my mother's face moved through my mind, quickly turning into my recurring nightmare: her unusually tan flesh cracking to pieces, black blood dripping from the wounds before her body stilled and exploded in fire, reducing her to ashes.

Anger and sadness tore through my veins. I clenched my jaw, held back the tears, and tried to contain the powers, but they were rising to the surface again.

"Chase..." Rayna moved towards me, her hand gliding around my body and pulling me against her.

The smell of fruit wafted through my senses and a warm breath blew against the back of my spine. A calm I recognized, but couldn't place filled my body. At first I thought it was Rayna's earth element, but as I looked up at her, I knew it wasn't. She wasn't pushing magic into me. She was staring down at me with sadness in her eyes.

Water dripped down the walls and sparks shot out from some of the outlets where light bulbs had exploded. We both ducked in shock and the building's alarm sounded.

My body throbbed with pain, the elements having nearly torn me apart. I grabbed my duffle bag and Rayna wrapped my arm around her, pulling me to my feet.

We coughed as black smoke filled the condo. I begged for fresh air as we moved to the hallway, but it wasn't there. It was hazy with smoke, and we followed it to the stairwell through a small group of people.

We followed the crowd and descended the stairs until we found the first exit. We pushed through the door that opened into an alleyway. The rush of people ran for the front of the building, and Rayna and I broke away from the group, moving in the opposite direction. We coughed and gagged as we were exposed to the clean air, slowing our pace as we neared the end of the alley.

Cars rushed by on the oncoming street and I dropped to the ground, leaning against the building. I took deep breaths to calm myself, but a storm of emotions still crashed through me. The scent of apples and something more still lingered on the air, and with each breath, the smell grounded me.

"Chase—"

"Don't," I said. "Don't tell me everything's okay."

"I wasn't going to. Everything is far from okay."

"What then?" I snapped.

"I was going to say you're right. He was wrong to keep that from us."

My pulse slowed and my breathing steadied. "You don't think I was out of line?"

"You were completely out of line. You tried to hurt Marcus...maybe worse. I'm saying you have a right to be angry, not to destroy our home."

I let my head fall back against the brick wall as sirens sounded in the distance.

"You said something about a spell."

"What?"

"At the cabin. You said you found a spell that could make the ring work."

"Oh, now that you're mad at Marcus you want to hear about it?"

"My first priority was helping you shift. You've done that. Next is figuring out how to stop Riley. Marcus forfeited his opportunity to be part of that plan."

"Don't be so hard on him. Give him a chance to explain."

"Either you're in or you're out. Either way, I'm moving forward without him."

Rayna stared blankly at me.

"Well?"

She sighed and shook her head. "Well, someone's got to be there to make sure you don't blow yourself up."

Ambulance, police, and fire trucks all roared up to the building, lights flashing and sirens blaring.

I unzipped my duffle bag and pulled on a clean shirt. "We need to get out of here."

Chapter 24

Rayna and I ran onto the next street. When we'd gained a few blocks between us and the condo, we slowed our pace.

"Where are we going?" I asked, as Rayna took a turn down a street I didn't recognize.

"The Ouija Board."

"The what?"

"It's a magic store. We can't do a spell without supplies or the spell book, can we?"

"I thought Marcus had it."

"No, I only found reference to it in one of his books. Not that it matters. Everything we have is in that condo, which is currently filled with firemen and police. How are we going to explain all that?"

I kept walking and didn't respond. I didn't have an answer for her.

"I need the actual book to find the spell, and the store closes in an hour so we need to hurry. Unless you have a better idea?"

"You're the witch with the plan."

The Ouija Board was a new age shop that sat in the corner of a mostly abandoned strip mall. The front door was made entirely of glass and had iron bars across it. A bell clanged against the bars and we pushed through the beads that hung in the entry.

The smell of incense was thick, but there were too many aromas burning at once to distinguish one from the other. Shelves and candles lined the walls: crystal balls, healing stones, and an entire shelf dedicated to Ouija boards.

A short lady in her mid to late fifties approached us. She walked in quick, short strides and a small hunch forced her shoulders to slouch. Her hair was frizzy and gray with stripes of white running through it, and the afro-like hair was thick, bobbing as she moved.

"How can I help you?" She spoke in a shrill, uneven voice. Her green eyes didn't look at us; instead, they looked everywhere around us, the size of them magnified by huge lenses on black-rimmed glasses.

"We're here to pick up a new book and some supplies." Rayna smiled.

"Well, over here we have something new that's very special." The lady walked over to a small brown chest. The box was open and filled with different types of rocks like quartz, tiger-eye, and amethyst. "These just came in. They've already been sunlight charged and they're ready for whatever incantation or meditation you might need." The lady smiled, her thick lenses making her eyes cross as she tried to focus on us. "The books that go with them are just on the shelf below, dear."

I rolled my eyes and Rayna elbowed me. "Debbie, it's Rayna. We're here for an actual spell book and I need some very specific material."

"Rayna!" The piercing voice made me wince. "Why didn't you say so?" Debbie locked the front door and led us through the store, passing row upon row of cheap trinkets. "Where have you been, my girl? It's been ages since you've been in these parts."

"Life's been busy."

"Oh, tell me about it." She moved past the *Employees Only* sign and through another beaded doorway, walking down a narrow, unfinished hallway. She stopped in front of a small white door and smiled. She pulled off her glasses and a wave of magic fell over us. With a snap of her fingers, Debbie changed.

Frazzled gray hair turned into long, thick chocolate locks. Her aged skin smoothed itself and her hunch straightened, making her inches taller. Small and wrinkled hands faded, and a more youthful counterpart appeared with long fingernails painted a shiny red. Her untamed eyebrows thinned into finely manicured arches above almond shaped eyes. She was pretty, and appeared now to be only in her early thirties.

"Goddess, it feels good to be free. Let me tell you—nowadays, I get more mundane coming here looking for something *supernatural*, than I do real witches. What is the world coming to?" The shrill voice was gone, replaced by one that was smooth and even. She pushed the small door open and walked through.

I had to duck to avoid hitting my head on the frame, but the door led into a large room filled with shelves. On one side, there were jars filled with animals and pieces of strange creatures, more crystal balls, and colorful jars full of powder and liquid. Across the room were book-lined shelves filled with aged, creased spines, and the room smelled of old pages. Weapons, cloaks, and armor were closed off in a thick steel cage.

Debbie walked behind a long glass counter and waved her hands over the transparent case, filled with wands, stone ruins, and tarot cards. "Do you have anything specific in mind?"

"I do. I need The Eleventh Dimension."

Debbie laughed and stared at us a moment. "Oh, you're serious?"

"Yes. I was told you had a copy. Is it still here?"

Debbie's eyes flickered back and forth between us. "Are you sure you want that one? It's a rare and very expensive book. I usually don't sell those types to begin with, and when I have them, I reserve those for the more...experienced witches."

"It's not for me. I'm picking it up for Marcus. You know...research stuff."

Debbie idly tapped her nails against the glass counter. "Marcus isn't a witch, dear. He may be able to do a trick or two, but this book requires a real witch's power."

"Like I said, it's for research."

After a long moment, Debbie sighed and disappeared through an opening behind the counter. She came back with a large, dusty brown book. It had a thick, leather bound cover, and its spine was wrinkled with creases. The leather on the front had a few small tears, and a single black strap bound it closed with a brass latch.

"I have to warn you; the spells inside here are very advanced. Research or not, you're not ready for this caliber of magic."

"Thank you for your concern, Debbie, but we'll be fine."

Debbie tapped her nails over the book once more and nodded. "If you're sure. Anything else?"

"I need one tongue of giraffe, three boar claws, a leaf from a Titan Arum plant, one powdered bat wing, and a cup of cinnamon."

"Cinnamon?" I asked.

"Hush," Rayna replied.

"Quite the grocery list," Debbie said. "What's on your agenda?"

"Uh-uh. You know better."

"Can't blame a gal for trying." Debbie moved back and forth behind the counter. She returned with a large straw bag and tied it closed with a strand of black ribbon.

"This one's not going to be cheap. The Titan Arum alone is well over two hundred."

"Just put it on our account."

"If you say so, but please be careful."

"Promise."

We walked towards the small door again when Debbie called out. "Just use the back door, hun. I can't go back out there. If I sell another Ouija board to a lady having a mid-life crisis, I'm going to curse someone."

Rayna guided me to the far end of the shop to a steel door. It had been painted red, but flakes of rust and chipped paint covered it. We slipped out the door and into an alleyway behind the shop.

"Are you sure you can handle this?" I asked.

"Don't start. We just need to make one more stop at Revelations."

"Why there?"

"Debbie wasn't kidding. These spells take a lot of power. I need another person to draw energy from for this to work."

"I told you; I'm not working with that blood sucker again."

Rayna rolled her eyes. "I was thinking more along the lines of Tiki."

****

The club was packed as we sifted through the crowd, but we couldn't find Tiki. Instead, we found everyone in the club eyeing us suspiciously. It wasn't uncommon for me to get unfriendly looks, but it seemed like everyone was staring.

After the third Underworlder rammed their shoulder into me, I was happier than ever to see Willy, even if he was surrounded by a half dozen werewolves. One was Jax, and the other I'd learned was Jason. He was the ring leader I'd stopped from picking on Willy, but I didn't recognize any of the others.

As we approached the pack, I realized being a werewolf hadn't improved Willy's ability to dress himself. An unbuttoned blue flannel shirt had its front pocket hanging by a thread, and the faded red t-shirt beneath it had been washed so many times it was almost pink. His gray cords had been bleached, with splotches of creams and whites decorating them, and both pant legs were frayed at the bottom.

When we neared their table, the pack all turned at once. They rose from their seats and sniffed the air, low growls rumbling past their lips. I reacted and pulled at my elements, but I'd forgotten where we were. Revelations was enchanted with spells, preventing violence and magic. The moment my magic sparked, a shockwave blasted through my core. I stumbled and winced from the energy, catching myself on an empty stool. I took a breath to compose myself and continued forward.

"What are you gu–, guys doing here?" Willy met us halfway and sounded panicked.

"What, is this a werewolves only bar now?" I asked.

Willy glanced over his shoulder at the glaring pack. "That's no–, not what I meant. Please don't cause anymore trou–, trouble for me."

"We're not here to cause trouble; we're looking for Tiki."

"He le–, left about an hour ago."

"Damn," I said.

"He probably went back to what's left of the condo. I guess we'll check there first." Rayna added.

"What's left of the condo?"

"Don't worry about it. Have a good night with your pals," I said, making my way back towards the door.

"Bye..." Willy's voice trailed off.

I turned around and saw the sad look on Willy's face. I stopped and tried to give him a reassuring smile. "You could always come with us...if you want. We could really use you right now."

"I..." he turned to look at the pack, watching his every move.

"Can't. Right. I get it. I'll see you later then." I turned back around to find Vincent's golden eyes looking up at me, and a chill ran through my body.

"I'm not in the mood tonight."

"Now is that any way to greet a friend?"

"You're not my friend. Now move."

"Chase, relax," Rayna warned.

"I simply came to say hello and deliver a friendly piece of advice." Vincent's seductive smirk turned into a creepy smile.

"If you came over here just to threaten me, I promise you, it'll be your last."

Vincent released a warm and deep laugh. "Please, Mr. Williams, when I make a threat you'll know it." He let the smile play over his pink lips as he stared up at me.

"Then what do you want?"

Vincent placed a single hand on my shoulder, leaned in, and pushed his mouth up next to my ear. I tried to pull away, but his grip tightened, pulling me against him. The smell of blood and death was thick on his breath. "The Underworld knows your secret. This may be the last chance you have to accept my offer," he whispered.

Anger thrust through me and I grabbed Vincent by the collar. The moment I touched him, the shock tore into my body again. I grunted through gritted teeth and released him uncontrollably. I made a fist and winced as the last of it left my body.

"You're lucky we're in here right now."

"That anger is an inconvenience, Mr. Williams. You should try and control yourself better."

I clenched my fists and turned as the giant bouncer stepped up beside me. He glared down at me with empty black eyes. "That's twice. It happens a third time tonight and you get a lifetime ban. I think you should leave before you lose your last chance."

I turned back and Vincent was gone. He was back across the room in his regular booth. He let his fangs drop from his gums and flashed me an arrogant smile.

"Let's just go." Rayna ushered me forward.

I tore my eyes away from Vincent and glared up at the bouncer. He followed behind me as I moved for the exit, handing over our weapons as we walked outside. He slammed the steel door and I ran up the stairs into the alley.

"I can't wait until the day I get to kill him," I said, kicking loose gravel down the alley. The night was in full bloom and shadows littered the streets, the red and blue light of Revelation's signs flickering behind us.

"What did he say?"

"He said the Underworld knows about the ring, and this was my last chance to accept his offer."

"He's just being Vincent, trying to get under your skin."

"Well, he succeeded."

"Don't worry about him. Besides, how would the Underworld even find out?"

"I wouldn't put it past him to tell them all."

I jumped as the metal door behind us opened and music pounded into the alley. I turned, but didn't see anyone come out. The door slammed shut, cutting the music off again and leaving goose bumps riding up my arms.

"It's getting late. Let's go home for the night. If Tiki's not there, we'll find him tomorrow."

"Forget it. I'm not going back there. Not if Marcus will be there."

"First of all, it's his house. Second, he said he wasn't sure if he'd be back tonight or sometime tomorrow. And third, don't be so childish. Yes, Marcus may have made a mistake, but are you so perfect?"

"*May have*? He did make a mistake. A big one. And this is different."

"How is this different? He made an oath to your mom. You of all people know how important that is to him, and you should respect that."

"Whatever. You can go on without me." I walked down the alley and onto the street.

"Don't walk away from me, Chase!"

I turned around and faced Rayna as she came up behind me.

"What do you want me to do?"

"I want you to come home."

"What home? I don't have a home."

"Yes, you do. You know that."

I sighed and looked away from her. The condo wasn't my home. It was a vacation. A temporary leave from wherever I was supposed to be.

"Where else are you going to go?"

"I don't–" The shuffling of footsteps cut me off. Brock stepped out of the shadows with a few hunters I didn't recognize following behind him. His bright red hair was freshly trimmed into a square buzz cut, making the green of his eyes stand out. A single scar covered his left eye and ran down his freckled cheek, scrunching as he smirked.

"Long time, no see, brother," he said. His muscles bulged and his shirt was so tight it barely covered the belt holding up his pants.

I shook my head. I couldn't deal with this. Not tonight. I turned to walk the other way, but Lena walked through the shadows and closed off the other side of the street. A chill ran down my spine as a handful of Underworlders stepped into the light behind her.

Lena's platinum blonde hair was tied into a high ponytail and still managed to reach down past her hips. She had intense blue eyes, and her cool, lethal gaze was aimed at me. A tight black tank top hugged her toned body and dark blue jeans wrapped her legs like a second skin.

"I've been dying to see you again." Lena smiled.

The clacking of high heels echoed off the pavement as she walked towards me, hips swaying with each step. She folded her hands together and bent her fingers back, cracking each knuckle. The light shone over her arms, revealing perfect, unmarred flesh.

The last time I saw her, I'd cut her wrist open and every muscle in it, but now it looked perfect.

"I know what you're thinking. How did a little old air elemental like me heal a wound like that?"

"It crossed my mind."

"I had help...from a god of sorts." She giggled and each word rolled off her tongue in a seductive wave.

"Riley did that?"

Lena's pink tongue slipped out between slightly parted red lips. She ran the tip of it along the top edge of her mouth and nodded.

"I hate to break it to you, but he's not a god. He's a disgrace."

"Careful what you say, love. We don't want that tongue of yours getting you into any more trouble, now do we?"

"What? Are you going to cut it out?"

Lena stopped and brought a slender hand to her lips. "I always knew there was a reason I liked you. That's not a bad idea." She let long red nails tap against her chin and smiled. "Actually, I quite like that."

"You would," Rayna said.

"Shut your mouth, bitch." Lena jerked her head to Rayna. "All I want to hear from you are screams."

Rayna stepped forward and I cringed as magic filled the air. In a single motion, Rayna's body left the ground in a violent rush. Lena unleashed her element and Rayna crashed against a building. Her body cracked the brick wall and she fell to the ground. Rayna jumped to her feet and her lips parted, releasing an ear shattering roar as her beast rose to the surface.

Lena giggled. "Oooh, bad kitty."

Rayna pulled her beast back, letting her earth element move around her body to calm it.

"Wait." Brock stepped forward. "You have a chance to save yourself, brother."

"I'm not your brother, and you're not getting the ring. It's time for you to walk away. I'm not playing anymore."

Brock laughed and pulled a lighter out of his pocket. He stood fearlessly with his arms crossed, gripping it. As the hunters behind him stepped forward, I pulled my element to the surface.

The demons on the other side moved and closed in behind us, while Lena and Rayna took up the middle, creeping towards each other. Everyone drew their weapons, but we all turned as a growl roared through the street.

The scrape of gravel echoed and Willy ran towards us, the other werewolves walking casually behind him.

"Wh–, what's going on?"

"Go back inside," I said.

"No, I ca–, can help."

"Now!" We were outnumbered by a lot; I didn't need Willy's death on my conscience.

"No!" Willy pushed out his chest and tried for confidence.

"Oh, Chase, let the puppy play," Lena grinned. "He looks delicious."

"Hell, no. I'm not fighting with *him*." Jason stood defiantly on the sidewalk. "He kills our kind."

"No–, nobody asked you to fight." Willy locked eyes with Jason and there was a ferocity I'd never seen inside him.

"Are you talking back to me, mutt?" Jason stepped forward.

Jax moved in front of him, and although he stood inches below Jason, he looked up with a commanding presence. "If one of us fights, we all fight."

"The more the merrier." Lena laughed. She wrapped her power around the shifters and raised them into the air. Growls shot out from the sky and clear fluid rained down as they began to shift. Willy stepped away as his pack was engulfed by the magic, and there was power coming off of him.

Rayna and I brought our magic up together and unleashed it on Lena. The ground shook as Rayna's earth element came to life, and a thick wall of rock formed behind Lena. I pushed my element out in a fierce wrath of water and it slammed into her, smashing her against the newly made wall.

Lena's power collapsed and the shifters dropped, landing hard on the pavement. There were a few yelps, but in moments they were on their feet. Solid black, gray, and white wolves crept forward, some standing six feet high on all four legs. Their lips peeled back and they bared white teeth.

Willy's human body hit the broken asphalt and swelled. Sweat dripped off his face and he grunted. Skin broke around his hands and arms, leaving gray, white, black, and red fur exploding from the wounds. He muffled a scream as his body convulsed and long fangs dropped from his gums. His face moved and deformed as bones snapped, morphing into a full wolf. He looked at me, and the brown of his eyes was gone. Colorless orbs stared at me, a single black pupil in the center of a sea of white. His body cracked as it made a few final adjustments and he completed the shift.

He was smaller than the other wolves, only coming up to my stomach. His long, chameleon fur changed color as he moved in and out of the shadows. It started as a mess of colors, quickly changing to black, then gray, and finally fading to white with spots of brown, but his face remained entirely red, making his colorless eyes look fierce.

Willy lowered himself to the ground, and a low rumble started in his throat. He lunged towards me with open jaws, baring long, violent fangs.

My eyes opened wide and I ducked, the bottom of his paws skimming over my head. Willy crashed into a hunter that crept up behind me, jaws clamping around him. The hunter screamed as teeth closed around his neck. He brought his element to life, but before it could be released, Willy jumped back, tearing out his throat and silencing both him and his magic.

Blood burst into the air and Willy shook, flinging the loose flesh from his mouth. The bloodied skin hit the pavement with a wet slap, and Willy howled into the midnight sky, his fur changing to match the solid red of his face.

I froze in surprise. I'd never known Willy to hurt anything, and he'd just killed someone to save my life. I was caught up in disbelief and didn't see Brock move in behind me. I heard the click of his lighter and the onslaught of heat warmed my back, but it was too late for anything but defense. I ripped my element up and turned to face him. A shield of blue water exploded in front of me, meeting his orange flame. His magic had gained enough momentum that it hit my shield and blew me backwards.

My power dissipated and I tumbled through the air. Brock pushed his magic over me again and I pulled my element back up. Power surged over my body, and as I hit the pavement rolling, water drew itself around me. A wave of heat pushed against me, but it couldn't penetrate the orb of water that engulfed me.

I stayed hunched down, trying to keep my focus while in amazement of the cool liquid that drifted over my body. When the heat vanished, I let the magic break and the orb collapsed, soaking me from head to toe.

Rayna and Lena's magic had receded and they were taking turns in hand to hand combat.

The werewolves fought against the Underworlders, who had changed from their human shape and unleashed their demons. Gladiator demons stalked the streets, although among the slowest of the Underworlders, they were the strongest and most brutal warriors. Shoulders broader than two grown men supported muscles that a human body couldn't carry. Thick red veins pushed against orange skin, and a second set of massive arms exploded beneath their first set. Two pairs of large hands carried small, bone-lined spikes over them, turning their fists into razor sharp blades. Beady, red eyes shone from beneath thick brows as they moved in an unorganized group of power.

They caught the wolves and tore them from the ground, driving sharp fists into their sides. Another Gladiator grabbed two of the shifters and tossed them left and right along the pavement, leaving their furry bodies to slide across the road. The pack was struggling, but I didn't have time to help them. Willy was fending off three different hunters and Brock had focused his attention on him.

I moved with a hunter's speed and drove my shoulder into Brock as he tried to bring a blade down on Willy's back. His ribs cracked as I tackled him to the ground, and his blade skidded across the road.

Anger rushed through me and I felt the fire riding my veins as I unleashed a fury of punches. Heat pushed itself from my knuckles, scalding Brock's skin with each connection. I used that power to hit harder and I kept swinging until he lost consciousness. His chest moved up and down, but his face was a mess of burns, bruises, and blood. I pulled my dagger from its sheath and brought it up above my head, but I couldn't drive it into him. I grew up with Brock, and as much as he was a jerk, I couldn't take his life.

Rayna ducked as Lena's leg swung over her, and with a burst of magic, Rayna struck out with the force of solid earth. Green energy formed around her fist while rocks and pieces of asphalt broke from the street and wrapped around her. Rayna launched a fist of stone forward, and as it slammed into Lena's jaw, her head snapped to the side and her eyes rolled back in her head. Lena's shoulders drooped and her knees buckled, her body collapsing to the ground.

"Don't ever call me a bitch again," Rayna said, towering over her. Her power vanished and the rocks crumbled, falling off her hand.

The wolves had taken control and cornered the last Gladiator demon. They moved as a single unit stalking their prey. Willy had joined them, and they all pounced at once, jaws snapping and latching around the demon's limbs. The sound of tearing flesh rode the air, and moments later, bright red and orange lights exploded as the demon caught fire and burnt to ash.

The wolves turned and Rayna moved beside me as they crept forward. My stomach clenched and I kept my magic just beneath the surface. As they closed the gap between us, the fur began to shed. Bones cracked and parts that shouldn't have been able to, moved. Their bodies moved and shifted until they had regained their human form.

Jax stepped towards me and extended his hand. I looked at it for a moment before I shook it. Considering he was naked, it should've been awkward, but the surge of battle overrode the strangeness. At least it did for me.

"Oh, gods." Rayna diverted her eyes.

243

"Among our people, Willy is nothing but a coward," Jax said.

Willy dropped his head in shame, and disappointment and anger filled me.

"But..." Jax continued. "He took a stand tonight. Willy doesn't stand up for himself. Not ever. Yet he risked his life for you. That speaks volumes about how you treat your people. Hunter or not, your pack respects you, and I respect that."

I nodded.

"Willy." Jax turned to face him. Willy brought his eyes up hesitantly, as if he was about to be beaten. "You hang your head in shame. You stutter because you have no confidence, and normally you let others determine who you will be. Tonight, *you* decided. You chose not to take a coward's road. Even when you thought we didn't stand behind you, you stood for your friend. Hang your head no more. That is honor, my brother. You should carry it proudly."

Warmth filled me as I watched a new light shine in Willy's eyes. His chin rose a little bit higher, and he stood taller than he ever had before.

"Thank you," he said clearly.

"Tonight, we celebrate. A cub has become a wolf, and a boy has become a man. Tonight, my brothers, we hunt!" Jax yelled and the others howled.

Energy merged around us, and in moments, the men standing before us were no longer men. Their animal forms took over and Willy's wolf stepped forward, colorless eyes staring up at me with pride. His fur cycled through the colors, finally settling on a mismatch of red, black, and white.

"Thank you, Willy. I owe you. Again."

Willy howled, and the other wolves followed suit before they turned and trampled down the road, disappearing among the shadows.

"Wow," Rayna said. "Shifter or not, I'd never have guessed Willy had that in him."

I stared down the dark street and nodded. The smile that hung on my lips was unmovable in that moment. "Neither did I."

Chapter 25

Tiki was asleep when we got back to the condo. He wasn't going to be of any use if he was exhausted, so we gave him the night to rest. Rayna spent the evening prepping the spell, and I spent the night awake, staring at the ceiling in my bedroom.

The authorities had left, but the condo's main floor was a mess. Splinters of wood and fluff littered the floor, black soot clung to the walls and ceiling, and a layer of water covered the kitchen and living room. I should've spent my time trying to clean up, but my mind was elsewhere.

Marcus hadn't come back yet and I couldn't stop running through the details in my mind. Part of me was angry and hated him for what he did, but a small part of me knew Rayna was right. Marcus always kept his word, and knowing my mom, she wouldn't have given him a choice. It didn't take the anger away, but it did make the hatred fade.

First thing in the morning, when Rayna was ready, she ushered Tiki and me into the library. Tiki came up the stairs behind me, his black hair standing in every direction and ruffled from sleep. He was still shirtless and wearing his white pants. He wouldn't even use the belts we bought him, so the frayed rope still hung around his waist.

"What happened to the house?" Tiki asked, but neither of us answered. "And where's Marcus? I have not seen him." Rayna and I ignored him again and Tiki's orange eyes flickered between us, looking worried. "The house is destroyed, Marcus is missing, and neither of you are talking. What did you do with Marcus?"

"He's had a meeting at the Circle. I'm sure he'll be back soon," Rayna said.

"I hope not," I muttered, and instantly regretted what I'd said. Marcus had taken me in and done so much for me. As angry as I was, he didn't deserve that. He deserved a chance to explain.

Rayna sighed and glared at me. "Let's just get started."

"What do I do?" I asked.

"Nothing. Focus on the ring and be quiet. I need to concentrate." Rayna opened the book in her hand and magic sprinkled over the room as she began to chant in a foreign tongue. She added ingredients to a wooden bowl, mixing them together with a small stirring stick. A melody of sweet aromas filled the room as it came to a boil without the assistance of heat. The magic thickened, tingling along my skin and filling the room, but it wasn't her elemental powers at work.

As Rayna crafted the spell, her slit pupils expanded until there wasn't a spot of color. The witch inside her came out, and her solid black eyes filled with magic. Her witch rose to the surface, and as her eyes changed, so did the power.

Wisps of magic moved around her and she extended a hand to Tiki. Tiki stepped forward, and the moment they touched, his orange eyes were engulfed with black and the magic came with a crushing force.

Raging through the air, the spell came to life, moving around me in a whirlwind of energy. Rayna reached towards me and the magic took aim. She repeated the incantation, her voice growing louder as the words came faster. The wooden bowl steamed, bubbles of liquid spilling over the edge. The bowl shook like the table was having an earthquake all on its own. Tremors moved through the condo, the floor shaking and leather bound books flying off the shelves. Thinking it was part of the spell, I didn't move, but as a minute passed, the magic grew, building towards me in a torrent of witchcraft.

Bright sparkles of light began to shine on the air, flickering in and out of transparency. I could see the power forming around Rayna. Her black eyes were locked with mine. The magic pushed closer towards me, but as the colorful crescendo moved over my skin, it exploded. Colorful light flashed between us and the power shot backwards, blowing Rayna and Tiki to the floor. The spell disintegrated on the air and the sparkles of color faded. The crushing force of magic vanished, leaving only silence.

"Rayna?" I asked. I wasn't sure if I should move, but as they both lay motionless, I stepped closer. "Tiki?" There was no response. They were both unconscious.

Rai fluttered into the room, chirping madly. Her feathers were ruffled and small, but powerful wings fluttered around my head. "Not now." I shooed her away.

The aroma from the spell was gone. The bowl was turned over and liquid ran off the table. I moved towards them and the stench of cigarettes took over.

Tiki stirred and Rayna squirmed along the floor. Their eyes opened in unison and they both looked confused.

"What happened?" Rayna asked.

"You were doing the spell and then...you both were on the floor."

Rayna's eyes fell with disappointment. "Dammit!"

"What is it?"

She shook her head and jumped to her feet. She picked up the book, flipping back and forth through the pages. "I did *everything* right."

"I smell smoke," Tiki said, rubbing his eyes. "Did it work? Did you meet the gods?" His voice was innocent and full of hope.

"Not exactly," I said, turning to Rayna. "Are you sure you did everything right? Maybe you pronounced something wrong."

"I didn't."

"How can you be sure?"

"She didn't do it wrong." Grams' voice made me jump. "First, she's nowhere near strong enough for a spell like that. Second, she's doing the wrong spell. And third, what the hell were you thinking?" Grams snapped, standing at the top of the stairs. A half-burnt cigarette smoked from her mouth and she took a drag, the tip of it lighting up in a glow of orange and red embers.

"Do you *ever* knock?" I asked.

"Shut up," Grams snarled, and I did as she said. I didn't need a pissed off witch being...pissed off at me.

She walked into the room in a green dress that wrapped around her frail frame and showed off veiny, wrinkled ankles. Shiny yellow heels tapped along the floor and she flicked her cigarette, sending ashes to the floor as she walked.

"How do you know this is the wrong spell?" Rayna asked. "If I can channel the spirit that powers the ring–"

"Because a witch can't do a spell to use The Ring of Contact, and even if they could, that spell is for *channeling* a god's spirit, not summoning it. There's a difference."

"How do we get the spirit to come out then?"

Grams laughed and smoke slipped through tight lips. "Naïve girl. There is no spirit in that ring."

"Yes there is," Rayna challenged. "I was there when she gave it to us."

Grams chuckled and more smoke spilled out of her nostrils. "This is what happens when untrained witches practice magic," she grumbled. "The spirit you speak of is a piece of the Goddess, bound to her soul piece. That's The Ring of Contact, not the soul piece."

"Then what's the soul piece?" Rayna spat the words.

"How the hell should I know?"

Rayna rolled her eyes. "So you just came to save us from killing ourselves? How thoughtful."

"Of course not." Grams waddled towards her and tore the book from her hands. "I went to buy this book today, only to find some punk and his girlfriend had already picked it up. Now that I've remedied that, you can go back to playing sorceress and whatever he's supposed to be." She pointed at me.

"Hey, that's mine!" Rayna reached for the book, but Grams slapped her hand away with surprising speed.

"You're not ready for this."

"How do you know? I'm getting stronger all the time. I can handle it."

"Is that how you explain that pathetic excuse for a spell? That much magic entering a trained witch all at once is a challenge. You handled it pitifully. You're lucky the backfire didn't kill you."

"If you know so much about all of this, how does the ring work?"

"You need to channel the air element into the ring. Whoever is the wearer at that time receives the effects."

"Marcus isn't here; we don't have one," Rayna started.

"Of course you do." Grams began coughing and slapping her hand against her chest until a disgusting sound broke in her throat. She turned the bowl back over and spit a thick ball of brown and green mucus into it. "He's that arrogant shit, right there." Her crinkled finger pointed at me.

"Chase isn't an air elemental; he only has fire and water."

"Shows what you know, silly girl. Looks like your boyfriend is keeping secrets."

"How do you know that?" I asked. "How do you know any of this?"

"I've been around a while, hunter." Grams made her way back to the stairwell.

"Wait. Since when are you an air elemental?" Rayna's hands were on her hips and she looked unhappy.

"I'm not. I mean, I might be. I don't know. It comes and goes."

"You mean to tell me you nearly burnt down our house because Marcus kept a promise to your mother, and you're the one hiding things?"

"That's not how it is."

"That's exactly how it is. You're a hypocrite and a liar!" Rayna stormed past Grams and out of the library.

"Ladies man." Grams grinned, revealing brown nicotine stained teeth. "Well, I got what I came for." She laughed and started down the stairs.

"Are you sure channeling my element will work?"

"Of course I'm sure, but good luck getting anything out of those assholes." Grams pointed to the roof.

I looked at Tiki, who was still half asleep and not bothering to get up from the floor. He smiled and gave his usual shrug. I was really starting to miss Willy.

"It's worth a try, I guess," I said mostly to myself.

I closed my eyes and reached for the air within me. The image of trees swaying against the strong wind filled my head. The magic swirled, lifting my feet off the ground. The element was a strong and uncontrollable force, like I'd unleashed a tornado inside me. I focused on moving that tornado, directing it where I wanted it to go. The air moved through my veins and I pushed it all down one arm. I pictured the air as a visible force moving through me and into the ring.

Air broke through the surface and books flew off the shelves. Tiki winced as the wind cut past him, blowing his ruffled black hair over his face. He brought an arm up to cover his eyes as papers flew and the furniture began sliding across the floor.

The magic vibrated through my hand and the red gem came to life. The ring sucked more magic from my body and white power swirled inside the ruby. That energy grew until the gem was no longer red, but a solid white square. The light brightened, emanating from the ring until it burst through the room in a blinding wave.

Rai's chirps rang out in a panic and she fluttered towards me, but wind rushed around the room and she was pushed back. More books flew off the shelves and Tiki jumped to his feet, nervousness clutching his features.

Grams stood halfway down the stairs, veiny arms wrapped around her newly acquired book. Thick locks of white hair flailed around her and she winced as the rush of wind and light flowed out of the ring.

Air tingled along my face and ran through my hair. It smelled fresh, like it had just rolled off a mountain and the cold would burn my skin. I closed my eyes as the light grew, swallowing the room and leaving a vibrating sensation strumming along my skin.

The ring pulled more magic from my body and the light exploded around me as my feet finally settled back onto something solid.

The light faded and revealed white marble columns rising endlessly into a cloudy sky. The matching floors reflected a blue light that hung on the air. It surrounded me, but came from nowhere, existing on its own, just like at the sanctuary. Air rushed through the spaces between the pillars, but it was warm and fresh, not the cold wind that bit at my skin. I looked over the edge between two pillars, but all I could see was light. It was bright, yet it didn't hurt my eyes.

"I wondered when you'd arrive." A soft voice moved around me.

A woman appeared in the middle of the room. Her hair was half pinned up with pearl tipped pins while the rest of the platinum strands hung near her lower back. Vibrant purple eyes carried both innocence and wisdom. Her skin was flawless, lightly tanned, and decorated in a purple dress, a single white ribbon tying it together in the back.

"Serephina?"

She smiled, showing perfect white teeth, and the sight of it filled me with warmth. It made me feel something I hadn't felt in what seemed like an eternity: happiness. A soft white glow hung over her skin and her bare feet moved without touching the ground. She glided towards me, drapes of purple and white fabric drifting behind her and caressing the marble floor.

"I thought you'd come sooner."

"I did the best I could. I wasn't given much direction."

"Such is our way." Her voice was warm and comforting.

"I need your help."

"I know, but I cannot help in the way you want me to."

"You're the goddess; you have to. My world...*your* world, it's in danger."

"I cannot alter that course."

"But it's your world."

"My soul piece still powers it, yes. But it hasn't been my world for some time." Serephina shook her head.

"What does that mean?"

"After Ithreal's Great War, the other gods and I made an oath never to return to the worlds of our own will. I could not come, even if I wished it. It belongs to the humans now."

"So Ithreal gets to break free of his prison and you'll just stand by and watch?"

"I've not stood by and watched yet, why should I start now?"

"I don't understand."

"I blessed your kind with the abilities to defeat him, but it's up to you to use them. Why do you think I created the Mark?"

"But what *is* the Mark? What does it do?"

"The Mark was created for the Protector. The one who bears the Mark is the chosen one."

"Chosen for what? Am I supposed to put Ithreal back in his cage?"

"Ithreal, in his true form, is not so easily released. He is trapped by the combined powers of the gods. Until that power is broken, he cannot be truly freed." She spoke, and although her lips moved, her voice came from everywhere.

"So Riley can't take his power?"

"Riley will be a vessel for Ithreal's essence: a part of his soul, but Riley has much to do before he can complete the ritual. He's completed the first step: he has the blood of the creature from both worlds."

"What else does he need?"

"He must retrieve the ring that guided you here. That ring allows its wearer to communicate with any of the gods. Ithreal will lead Riley to the last part. He needs to obtain each of Ithreal's soul pieces. I only know of one: Ithreal's dagger, in the dimension of Theral."

"So if I stop any of those things, he can't finish it?"

Serephina didn't reply. She lowered her head in a gentle nod, beautiful purple eyes watching me with a curiosity I didn't understand.

"I can hide the ring," I said.

"Hiding it will not be enough. With the Brothers beside him, they will find it. You must destroy it."

"But that will kill Elyas and weaken you."

Serephina smiled and shook her head. "I'm not so foolish as to put a piece of myself into a small trinket so easily destroyed. The ring is not the soul piece. The soul piece is safe; that I assure you. You must destroy the ring with a godly item."

"Ithreal's Dagger."

Serephina nodded, her lips curling into a gentle smile. "I've requested help from the other gods in hopes to find you an easier method, but they will not comply."

"Where in Theral is it?"

"When you get there, you will know."

I sighed and paced the white marble floor.

Serephina's laughter echoed around me. "You are tense, Chase. You must relax." Her power moved over me and warmth filled me. The energy calmed my nerves, making all my worries vanish. Her warm assurance told me everything would be fine, and I basked in the positive energy.

Serephina drifted around me. Even gliding, she held an indescribable grace. She moved in front of me and stared into my eyes. Her power overwhelmed me and the smell of sweet fruit encircled me. I pushed myself back and stepped away from her. Her power faded and I had to force myself to remember why I was here.

I stepped away and my thoughts rushed back to me. "I realize you're *the* goddess, but how can you sit here and put all your faith in a single person? The Great War happened because of Ithreal, and Riley's working overtime to bring him back. Aren't you worried?"

"Before the war, Ithreal wanted to merge with me and bind my power. He knew he could not overcome me in a duel, and so he sought to steal it."

"Merge? Like sex?"

"In a sense. To merge is to come together as one. This can be done by choice, and the more powerful god absorbs the other, or, the other god can overpower the other in a duel, in which case the winner absorbs the power."

"So he tried to destroy Earth to weaken you?"

"It's more complicated than that." Serephina drifted back away from me, and a white lounger appeared on the air. She draped herself over it, the purple gown flowing over the white fabric as she settled in. "There are seven gods. We've existed this way for more time than you have a word for, but once, there were many of us. We created worlds, we made life, and lived among our people. Only seven gods remain now because the rest have merged with us, or their essence has been stolen. We keep it this way to ensure no one god gains too much power."

"To keep the balance."

"Yes." Serephina smiled. "Once this law was put in place, it was not unlike us to merge with our creations, but because they could not bear witness to our true essence, we were forced to take on their forms. Over time, however, we grew tired of the restrictions those bodies forced upon us. We could not be at full power while in such a frail shell."

Serephina tapped the spot next to her, but I ignored the motion. Her essence was pure seduction, power, and life. I felt like I couldn't get enough. I was drowning in her perfection, even from a distance. I knew if I went closer, I might never leave. Her bright eyes locked with mine and their warmth filled me. A smile I couldn't control came over my face and I turned away.

"This body you see before you is one I created just for you. Do you like it?"

"Of course I do. I love it. I just can't focus when I'm close to it."

"Such is our way as gods." She smiled, pulling herself off the lounger and gliding towards me. "You are handsome. I regret having sworn my oath in this moment." She lifted her hand and slid a finger down the side of my neck. Her touch was softer than anything I'd ever felt. "You remind me of the men I had when I lived among the humans. If that time was now, you would be chosen to lie beside me."

I tried to pull away, but her touch filled me with warmth and passion. She rubbed her hands over my chest and the faint smell of fruit grew stronger. I never wanted to leave.

That realization startled me. I shook my head, trying to push the feeling away, but it wouldn't fade. I reached up and tried to pull her hands off of me, but the moment my skin touched hers, my body grew weak.

Serephina giggled and pulled herself away. She broke the connection between us and glided back towards her lounger, glancing over a perfectly tanned shoulder as the distance separated us. "Your willpower is impressive. Most men would crumble, if not under my gaze, than by my touch. You are the perfect bearer for the Mark."

I cleared my throat and ran a hand through my hair, watching her fall back into her chair. "Back to Ithreal…"

"As you wish."

"Why did he invade earth?"

"Ithreal did not wish to destroy earth because of the men that inhabited it. He wanted to destroy Elyas. She is a piece of my soul. If a soul piece is destroyed, the world dies and that part of the god's power is gone forever."

"So, Ithreal wanted to weaken you?"

"Any god who has ever refused to merge with him has had their essence taken. Ithreal spent many thousands of years trying to match my power, and because I would not succumb to him, he wished to do the same with me. But he knew he could not defeat me so easily."

"But you were more powerful, so why didn't you just stop the war?"

"Because of the oath, I was forbidden to interfere. It is against our laws to harm a fellow god's creations."

"But Ithreal was killing your people and trying to harm you. He broke your laws."

"Ithreal did not attack my people. He commanded his creatures to do so."

"How is that any different?"

Serephina smiled. "There are ways around even the strictest rules. I did not harm Ithreal's creatures directly either. I used my power and created the Circle of Light: the hunters, as you call them today. It was they who defeated Ithreal's armies. It was they who cast Ithreal's demons from their world. The Circle set up the barrier to keep the other worlds out. I simply gave them the power to do it."

"Then what happened to Ithreal? Why isn't he free?"

"When the Circle locked him out of their world, Ithreal was angry and tried to break the seal himself. Because he was directly trying to interfere, he had broken our laws. The other gods joined me and we banished him to his own dimension."

"But now Riley's going to summon him, and Ithreal will be here."

"And just as before, the hunters' army will defeat him." Her perfect smile made her figure glow, and she spoke with such confidence.

"But I don't have an army. I can't do this alone."

"There are more of you than you think."

"Who?"

Serephina lowered her gaze and a look of frustration crossed flawless features. "I cannot...the other gods are calling me back."

"Tell me what to do, please?"

"I've told you what I am permitted. Use the Mark, Chase. Let it guide you."

"But I don't know how."

Serephina's smile filled me with an assurance I knew I shouldn't have, and her body began to fade. It grew transparent at first, allowing me to see through it, and then she was a mist that vanished on the air.

The dark red gem on the ring exploded with bright light and blinded my vision. Air rushed around me, lifting me from the marble floor and cold air rushed over my skin. My body began to spin at incredible speeds before the light swallowed me.

Pressure surrounded my body as I soared through the ice cold air, but in seconds, the air was gone and I was thrown to the library floor. I hit the ground hard and shocks shot through my wrists, forcing the rest of my body to the floor.

Tiki and Rayna jumped from their chairs and rushed towards me.

"Are you okay?" Tiki asked.

"I think so." I got to my feet and turned to Rayna, but I didn't know what to say.

Rayna's eyes were angry and she stormed towards me, slapping her hand across my face. My head jerked to the side and all the warm seduction of Serephina vanished.

"Okay, I may have deserved that."

"You're damn right, you did."

"I'm sorry, okay? I didn't know what was happening to me, and we were busy trying to get you to shift. "

"That one wasn't for lying to me. This one is." She slapped me again and my head jerked the same way, leaving a stinging sensation over my face.

"What the hell was the first one for?" I rubbed my cheek.

"Because we've been sitting here worried sick about you!"

"Why?"

"You've been gone all day!"

My eyes opened wide. "No...it was just a few minutes."

"Not here, it wasn't."

"Time works differently in each dimension," Tiki said. "Wherever you were, time moves much slower than here. Where exactly did you go?"

"I've no idea; it felt like I was on a cloud."

"Sounds like the Overworld." Tiki nodded.

"What's that?"

"It's what my people call the plane the gods live on."

"Did you talk to Serephina?" Rayna asked.

"Yeah." I moved to a chair and sat down. My legs were tingling and I couldn't stand any longer."She said Riley needs the ring; it's the only way he can communicate with Ithreal."

"So we use a spell to hide it."

"No, she said the Dark Brothers would find it."

"And what happens if he gets the ring?"

"He can speak to Ithreal and find out where all his soul pieces are. Once he has them, he can finish the ritual. But Riley isn't taking Ithreal's powers. Riley's body will be his vessel. Ithreal can't leave his world in his pure form; the gods' powers hold him there, but once the ritual is complete, his essence—a part of his soul—will take over Riley's body."

"Did she say anything else?"

"She said to destroy the ring. If we do, his link to Ithreal is cut off and he's flying blind, but we need a god's weapon to do it."

"I'm guessing she didn't give you one?"

"No, but she told me where to find one. One of Ithreal's soul pieces is a dagger, in a dimension called Theral. If we get it, we can destroy the ring and we'll have one of the pieces Riley needs."

Tiki's eyes widened and fear filled them. "Theral is a dark dimension, full of the purest, most evil Underworlders. They never leave their world, and no one goes there. Ever. You need to find another way."

"We don't have a choice. We need to do this and we need you to take us."

"We will all die. I will not do it."

"You said when we needed you, you'd be there," Rayna said. "We need you now."

Tiki shook his head. "It's too dangerous."

"If Riley manages to get this ring, he's that much closer to bringing Ithreal into our world. If you're this worried about something Ithreal made, think about what the god himself will be able to do. You want to talk dangerous now?"

Tiki's orange eyes flickered between both of us and he sighed. "I need to think," he said, and walked out of the room, his bare feet silent along the wood floor.

"Still mad?" I turned to Rayna with a sheepish grin.

Rayna glared at me and rolled her eyes before walking towards the stairwell.

"I said I'm sorry."

Rayna turned and didn't hold back the anger in her voice. "You know, the more I think about it, the more you sound just like Marcus. You hate that he keeps his secrets, but that's exactly what you're doing. We're supposed to be on even ground, working together, but instead, you're off on your own trying to be everyone's hero. If you think an apology is enough, you're wrong."

"You're right."

"What?" Rayna's anger turned straight to surprise.

"I didn't know what was happening to me, so I kept it from you. It started when Riley invaded my dream, but I ignored it. I refused to believe it was more than a dream. Then we were at the werecat's camp when it came again, but I didn't want to tell you. I didn't want anything to distract you from shifting."

"Don't act like you did this for my sake." Rayna crossed her arms, but as much as she tried to hold onto it, the anger faded.

"I didn't know what was happening to me. Since I couldn't explain it, I thought it best to keep it to myself."

Rayna shook her head, the remaining anger evaporating around her. She came forward and stood in front of me, reaching out pale, slender hands on either side of my face.

"I don't know how many times you need to hear it before it gets through your thick skull, but I'm with you. Together, we can do this, but we need to trust each other. With everything that's happening, I need that trust, now more than ever. I don't need secrets, Chase. I need you."

Rayna's eyes moved back and forth over my face, and for the first time, I realized how beautiful she was. There was something new in her eyes: a sparkle of power that had nothing to do with magic. She stepped closer and pushed up on her tiptoes. Her breath was warm as it rolled across my skin and the sensation sent a chill down my spine. I leaned towards her, and the scent of her perfume forced me to close my eyes and revel in its fragrance. Her breath grew warmer as she neared, and my hands found her hips. Her warm, soft hands slid over my neck, forcing goose bumps to scurry down my arms.

"If I do this..." Tiki interrupted.

Rayna and I immediately pulled away. We turned to face Tiki and he watched us intently from the doorway. We were silent and I felt awkward with his eyes glaring at me. His head tilted to the side, as if he was trying to understand what he saw. He shook his head and walked into the room. "If I do this, you need to understand what you're getting yourselves into."

"We're listening," I said, and cleared my throat.

"Theral is not like Drakar. It is not pretty and full of life. It's a world full of darkness and death, lit only by moonlight. It reeks of corpses, and the creatures that inhabit it are ferocious. You think Vincent is bad? Wait until you see his ancestors."

"Pureblood vampires?" Rayna asked.

"Yes, and they aren't the worst thing that lives there."

"Just tell me how to kill them and we're good," I said.

"It's not like it is here. There is no sunlight to burn them. You must use fire, or cut off their heads. Your stakes will not hurt them."

"Well, I've got fire covered."

"It's not that simple." Tiki moved to the bookshelves. He pulled a book out and skimmed through it, opening it out on the table. "This is an understatement of what you're up against, but it has similarities."

The book showed a black and white sketch of a demon. It looked like a dwarfed human with a hunch and apelike arms. Its head was bald and the body scrawny. Claws hung from long, gangly hands and its mouth was filled with violent looking teeth. Small, jagged bones lined its jaw and forehead, and its eyes were huge.

"It doesn't look *that* bad," I said.

"This picture does not do the beasts justice. They are fully resistant to spells and their mental power is unparalleled. Their entire body is covered in a protective film no blade can pierce, and fire won't harm them until that armor is gone. They are faster and stronger than anything you have ever faced."

"Great," Rayna said.

"How do you get through the armor?" I asked.

"There is a single bare spot on the front of their throat. If you cut deep enough, it hits a vital vein and they'll bleed out."

"But loss of blood doesn't kill vampires," Rayna said.

"That's why you need to be fast. The blood is acidic. It will burn away the protective coating, but if it touches you, it'll do a lot worse to you than it will to them."

"An opening on their throat is all we get?"

"There are two other things that can pierce the armor: another vampire's claws or the bite from a changeling."

"What's a changeling?" Rayna asked.

"In your world, it's a shifter, but in the Underworld, pureblood changelings are not restricted to one shape; they take on many. Changelings, however, are among the rarest of creatures."

"Vincent's got vampire claws, think he would come?" Rayna smirked.

I laughed. "And put himself in harm's way? Not a chance."

"I'm not sure he would be of any help, or you for that matter. You are a shifter and Vincent is a vampire, but you are both half-breeds. Typically, our abilities do not affect purebloods."

"This just keeps getting better," Rayna said.

"So, you see my concern?"

"I get it. It's dangerous, but it doesn't change what needs to be done."

Footsteps came from the stairwell and we all turned to find Marcus standing there. He carried his huge form up the last few steps and cleared his throat. Awkward didn't begin to explain the silence. Everyone's eyes were on the floor, except Marcus'. I could feel his eyes burning into me.

"I'd like a few moments with Chase. Alone," Marcus said, his deep voice didn't sound angry. It was quiet, and I wasn't sure what to expect.

"I don't want to talk. I'll find a way to pay for the damages," I said, and Tiki and Rayna vanished from the room.

"Well, I do. I don't care about the damage, but as long as you are under this roof—"

"That can change."

"Chase, what would you have me do? I made a promise to your mother that we wouldn't say anything until we knew what our options were."

"That doesn't make it okay."

"You need to realize you weren't the only one who lost someone, Chase. We're all hurting."

"You lost a friend. I lost a mother," I snapped.

"I lost the woman I love!" Marcus shouted, and his words silenced me.

My pulse was a hammer, smashing against my inside. "What?"

261

Marcus' eyes were full of anger, then fear, and finally, sadness. "I...loved her. I always had. I could never break a promise to her. Not ever." He dropped his gaze.

I didn't know what to say. Marcus had finally broken down and shown me a piece of what hid behind his neutral expression, and it stole all the anger burning inside me.

"I...didn't know."

Marcus stood across from me, his massive form seemingly indestructible, but the sadness in his eyes was greater than any emotion I'd ever seen from him.

"I understand why you did it," I said.

"You do?"

"I'm not angry with *you*." I sighed. "I mean, I am, but...you weren't the only one keeping secrets. She's just as guilty." I didn't realize who I was truly angry with until I said it, and I instantly felt horrible for even thinking it.

"She was your mother; her first instinct was to protect her child."

"Well, she shouldn't have. If you two would've told us, Rayna might not have been discovered. We might never have been in Drakar, and Mom...might still be alive."

"That's a lot of *ifs*. It was a decision your mother and I made together, and although I regret the results, I stand by my choice."

"Well, when your decisions affect my life, I should be included. You don't get to decide what I know and what I don't."

"What would you like to know?"

"Right now, I want to know how to get to Ithreal's dagger. That's all that matters."

"You can't go hopping around from dimension to dimension. It's a risk I'm not willing to let you take."

"This time it's not up to you. Unless you've had some vision you'd like to share."

Marcus ran a large hand over his smooth scalp and shook his head. "I haven't."

"Then we're going."

"Rayna is not ready for that, and neither are you."

"Excuse me?" Rayna's voice came from the stairwell.

Marcus sighed. "You two are listening anyway, so why don't you join us?"

Rayna and Tiki came back up the stairs. Tiki looked slightly ashamed, but Rayna was angry.

"I'm going," Rayna said.

"You're not," Marcus commanded. "I won't lose anyone else."

"We can't let Chase go alone. Not with those...*things*."

"What things?"

"Pureblood vampires," Tiki said.

"Purebloods? Okay, none of you are going."

"Riley's out there right now, trying to get everything together to invoke Ithreal. If he succeeds, we all die," I said.

"We'll find another way."

"There is no other way; don't you see?"

"Chase, I promised your mother I wouldn't let anything happen to you. I'm in charge of this, and until that changes—"

"Then maybe it's time for a change." I felt guilty immediately, but using my mother as leverage wasn't going to work. Someone had to stop Riley, and that someone was me.

"Chase, we can find another option. I can't let you continue to throw yourself in harm's way. I won't."

"Nobody is trying to get themselves killed here. Serephina said if we don't destroy the ring, Riley *will* get it. Once he has it, he can start gathering the soul pieces. I have no choice but to destroy it, and I need all the help I can get. I need your help."

Marcus stared at me with his empty expression. His dark eyes moved over each of our faces before he uncrossed his arms and sighed. "Start by telling me about Serephina, then show me what we're dealing with."

Once we'd given Marcus the rundown, we went to the training room and the arsenal of weapons it carried. I always had my daggers, but I loaded up on throwing knives and a sword. If Tiki was even half right about the purebloods, I wasn't going in light.

"Everyone have what they need?" I asked.

"Yes," they all said at once.

"Good. Tiki, you're up."

Tiki shook his head. "I cannot do it here."

"Why not?"

"I've been trying to focus my power, but it's not working."

"Why are you telling me this now?"

"You never asked." Tiki shrugged.

"So, what now?"

"We need to get away from the city. There is too much interference here. It's preventing me from teleporting. I need an open place, away from everything. Preferably a place of magic."

"The sanctuary?" Rayna offered.

"Before we get ahead of ourselves, do you know where the temple is, Tiki?" Marcus asked.

"I don't know of its location, and even if I did, I couldn't take us directly there. It is hard enough to transport this many people. If I can get us all to Theral, where we end up is not in my control."

The buzzer sounded through the condo and we all jumped.

"Also..." Tiki trailed off looking guilty.

"Also what?" I asked.

"I may have told Willy what was happening."

"You, what?"

"He is a shifter. If there is a small chance his abilities will work against the vampires, I thought we could use more than one."

I shook my head. "Willy isn't designed for things like this."

"Tiki might be right," Marcus said. "It can't hurt to have more than just Rayna with us."

"Why don't we just call all the shifters and see if they want to tag along then?" I asked sarcastically.

The buzzer rang again; this time Willy pushed it repeatedly.

"Fine. But you invited him, so he's your responsibility."

Chapter 26

We pushed past the last line of undergrowth and stepped into the clearing. The sun had set and the moon was high. Rai disappeared off my shoulder, flying into the bluish light that hung on the air.

"This place is incredible." Tiki's voice reveled in amazement, gliding his fingers over the bark of the tree.

"We don't have time for appreciating the scenery; every second we waste is another second Riley could be getting closer," I said.

Tiki looked up at the colorful flowers that always seemed to be in bloom and smiled. "Gather 'round."

We all stood in a circle around him, and as his power started to wrap around us, a white light flashed, washing his magic away. Elyas stood in the middle of the clearing, her long blonde hair flying up in wisps around her body. A white glow encircled her form and vibrant blue eyes stared at me. She was beautiful and perfect, yet plain all at once.

"Your adventure begins," Elyas said. Her lips moved, but no sound came from them. Her voice moved around me in every direction. It made me feel warm, confident, and unstoppable.

"Nice of you to show up. I've been trying to contact you."

"I am quite aware, but I am not a magic eight ball. You cannot summon me as you wish. I appear only when directed."

"Serephina sent you?"

"Who sent me is not of your concern, Protector. I am here to aid you in your travels to Theral."

"But we have Tiki."

"He is not a pureblood, so he cannot take you all. If he does this alone, you will be scattered throughout the dimension. I shall aid him, and with my help, I can get you closer to the temple."

"He's taken this many of us before."

"Yes, but you need more help. The wolf and cat will not be enough."

"We don't have anyone else. This has to be enough."

"Don't be so sure," she said, and her figure started to fade. "When you are ready, I will assist."

"Wait!" But it was too late; she was gone. "We don't have anyone else..." I whispered.

The snapping of branches sounded and Vincent stepped out of the woods with a small group of vampires behind him. His pants and dress shirt were torn, with dirt and leaves stuck to them.

Rayna stepped forward. "What are you doing here?"

"We came to assist you of course." His cool gaze watched me and a destructive smile pulled at his lips.

"He's not here to help." I put my hand on Rayna's shoulder and pulled her back. "He's here for the ring."

"Nothing gets past you, does it, hunter?"

"Why are you doing this?" Rayna asked. "We were friends."

"We were never friends, my sweet, and to question me shows just how little you know about me. I've offered you an opportunity to join me. I thought you'd eventually come to your senses, but now I see you will not. I can show no more charity. I have a name to uphold."

"And upholding your name means coming after us?"

"You are a naïve little girl. And self-centered too, it would seem. Not everything is about you." Vincent walked towards us, colored leaves rolling at his feet. "At first, I wanted the ring for the power. To have an item crafted by the gods on my finger would do wonders for my family. Then when the Underworld came calling, I realized I could sell it to the highest bidder and make a nice little profit. But now I realize I can have it all. I can keep the ring for myself, and rent it to Underworlders, a single use at a time."

Vincent tilted his head up and basked in the moonlight, his pale flesh illuminated in the glow.

"That's not going to happen," I said.

266

"And the barbarian speaks. Don't kid yourself, Mr. Williams; your macho act is tiresome. You've seen but a glimpse of what I can do. Don't think I won't kill you if necessary."

"You talk about that a lot, and to be honest, I've had enough of you and your games. If you're going to kill me, stop talking about it and do it." I didn't wait for him to respond. I pulled my magic to the surface and let the power crush him. Vincent's body flailed into the air and surprise tore across his features. I pushed my magic into him until his body disappeared into the forest. The sound of branches breaking and leaves rustling echoed through the clearing. Birds and bats scattered from the shadows and then there was silence.

The vampires surged forward in response and Rai fluttered into the clearing. Like nails on a chalkboard, she rubbed her talons together. After a few sparks, a bolt of lightning came down and blew one of the vampires into pieces that quickly turned to ash.

The vampires' pale skin faded and transparent counterparts came to life. The color left their skin and black veins pushed against the clear flesh, revealing their muscles and inner workings of their face. Long bonelike claws shot out of their fingertips and ivory fangs dropped from their gums. The color of their eyes receded until all that was left were shiny black orbs. They all roared unanimously and the battle began.

Blurs swirled around us and I brought more power to the surface. Fire shot from my hand and screams barreled through the air. Blue and silver flames engulfed a vampire and his screams stopped when his body exploded in a blaze.

Each demon chose its target and was quickly swept away. Rayna's magic plunged forward. She swung her fist out, and a stream of earth shot from the ground, smashing into the demon. A rapid assault of dirt and rocks blasted him back and Rayna brought her dagger down into his chest. The transparent skin bubbled, steam rolled off his flesh as it cracked, and bright light exploded out of him.

Marcus unleashed his power like an invisible hand, wrapping it around the neck of the nearest vampire. His head jerked painfully to the side and the sound of his spine breaking was bone chilling.

Willy backed away as Tiki picked up the last two. Black filled his eyes and he released only a portion of his demon. Claws so fierce they made a vampire's look gentle shot from his hands. With a single swipe, their heads rolled off their shoulders. Ashes littered the moist grass around the tree and the clearing went silent.

"That was too easy," Rayna said.

Marcus nodded. "Vincent wouldn't plan an assault like this with only a few soldiers."

I felt more magic stirring within me, but this time it had a strange familiarity to it. The forest came alive around me. The leaves rustled and rolled over the earth. The smell of the woods was stronger than ever, and the hundreds of footsteps that were trying to be silent trampled in the distance.

"Chase..." Rayna said.

"There are more," I said. "Vincent's brought an army."

"Chase, I know that magic. It's earth magic...and it isn't mine."

"It's his." Elyas appeared behind us. "Look at the Mark."

I didn't fight Rayna as she lifted up the back of my shirt.

"There are more glyphs," Rayna said. "Earth, Air, Fire, and Water."

"What?" I tried to look over my shoulder.

"Does this mean he's getting all of them?" Rayna asked.

"You have many enemies approaching; I suggest we get you to Theral."

"But you said we didn't have enough peo–"

Rayna was silenced by Elyas' hand.

"She's right," I said. "There are five of us and an army of them. We need to leave." I pulled the magic back inside me. "Tiki, are you ready?"

"I am," he said, the black of his eyes fading and the orange returning, white triangular pupils spinning in the middle.

We circled around Tiki and each placed a hand on him. His power shook around us, stronger than before. Elyas was adding her own magic to the mix. The air wrapped around us when hands grabbed my shoulders and tore me from the huddle. Vincent held me down, his yellow eyes gone and swallowed by black.

"Don't stop!" I yelled.

"We cannot leave without you," Tiki replied.

I struggled against Vincent as dozens of vampires pooled out of the trees.

"You won't, just keep going," I said through gritted teeth.

I pulled both the earth and air magic up at once. The demons ran towards us and the ground rumbled in a violent quake. Earth exploded and towers of thick rocks jutted from the ground. One by one, square pillars of solid earth shot up around us, blocking the vampire army out, and locking Vincent in. Dirt rained down and I pushed Vincent away. Air wrapped around him and pulled him from my body, breaking his grip. My magic paralyzed him and held him at an arm's length away.

Tiki's magic came in a wave and a black hole opened beneath the group.

"Let...go." Vincent struggled against my magic, his eyes wide with panic.

"No," I said, "you're coming too." The ground below vanished, and I jumped towards the group as they fell into a pit of darkness.

Chapter 27

Darkness swallowed us and I pawed desperately through the shadows. When I felt Tiki's warm flesh, I squeezed my hand around it. I could feel my nails digging into his shoulder and it took all I had to keep my grasp on Vincent. Keeping my magic focused was hard enough on a good day, doing it while mid-teleport was a different story.

Weight shifted around me, compressing my body as though it might implode. I fought to keep my breath, my magic wavering as my body writhed in pain. I had to keep my hold on Vincent; he'd be no good to me if he showed up lost somewhere in Theral.

I gritted my teeth as the power tightened its grip around us, building up and crushing my lungs and skull. The darkness broke and a faint glow shone beneath us. It grew brighter, turning into a rainbow of colors that became a kaleidoscope of power. The pressure grew, squeezing the air from my body as the rainbow faded and a gray surface came into view. As the portal expanded, the gray turned to blue and black stone. It went on endlessly in every direction, spikes of stone jutting from the earth. Cold air hammered against my skin as I neared the opening, but I was losing my elemental grip on Vincent.

The portal ripped open, letting the blue glow flood the darkness before the last push of magic spat us out. I hit the ground hard and tried to land on my feet, but the force made my legs buckle and my body rolled against the ground, breaking my focus. My element disappeared, sucking itself back inside of me.

With the exception of Tiki, everyone gasped for air and groaned from the impact. Tiki stood on his feet, strong and unaffected, but he looked weathered. Transporting this many people, even with Elyas' help was hard on him.

The black hole above had opened into a dark sky, floating on the air. I scanned the litter of bodies around me, but the vampire wasn't here. Panic filled me, and then the pale figure of Vincent came rushing out of the portal, followed by his scream before he smashed into the ground. Once it released him, the portal began to consume itself. Shrinking smaller it folded into itself until it was gone, leaving a starless navy sky above.

I clambered to my feet and struggled with the first few steps, my legs aching from the rough landing. Rai's feathers were ruffled, but still they glistened in the light as she spread her four wings and leapt into the cold air.

There was a huge blue moon shining to one side of us, and a green moon on the other. They seemed so low in the sky I felt as though if I walked far enough I could touch them. The bright glow lit the world in an eerie light. Tiki was right; this was nothing like Drakar.

We sat in the valley of a cold, rocky wasteland. Arches of stone were so black they gave off a reflection of everything around them, like a polished onyx. Blue rock walls grew up around us, with high cliffs on either side. Loose boulders and crumbling pillars made up the rest of the landscape, no hint of life anywhere to be seen.

"You imbecile, what have you done?" Vincent stormed towards me.

"You got exactly what you deserved. You're a deceiving little cockroach and now you're right where you belong: in the Underworld."

"You forced me into another dimension?" In a blur, his hand was on my throat. His breath came in angry waves and the smell of coppery death poured from his lips. I channeled the fire element through my body and into my neck, picturing my skin to be scalding to the touch. Vincent tore his hand away, his pale skin marred and steaming.

"That's right, and you're going to help us or you're going to die, whether at my hand, or your ancestors."

"What ancestors?" He waved his hand in the air, watching the pale skin fold over and repair itself at a rate that alarmed me.

"Vampires, just like you. Only pureblood, making them older and more powerful," Rayna said.

"Such things are a fallacy."

"They are not," Tiki said. "They are very real and very dangerous. The pureblood vampires are no laughing matter."

"This is ridiculous," Vincent muttered.

"Maybe next time, you'll think twice before you cross me," I said.

Vincent mumbled something under his breath in a language I couldn't understand.

"Any ideas where the temple might be?" Rayna asked.

Everyone shrugged.

There was nothing but high walls surrounding us. The air was cold enough that I could see my breath, and I wondered how Tiki wasn't freezing. He'd refused to come to Theral wearing the clothes we'd bought him, but even with his baggy pants and shirtless body, he seemed unaffected.

"Follow the moon." A voice echoed around me.

"What?" I asked.

Everyone turned to me with a strange look.

"Who said that?"

Rayna shook her head. "Nobody said anything."

"It is I, Elyas. Follow the blue moon and it will take you to where you need to go." Elyas' voice echoed through my head. I turned in a circle trying to find her, but she wasn't here.

"You must hurry."

"Should we just pick a direction?" Willy asked.

"No," I said. I shook my head as the feeling of Elyas faded. "We need to walk towards the blue moon."

"How do you know?" Rayna asked.

"I don't..." I started, but as bright green eyes looked at me, I started again. "It's Elyas; she told me."

Rayna arched a brow.

"It's like she's in my head."

"Wonderful. Our fearless leader hears voices," Vincent said.

"Let's go. You're up front," I commanded.

I could see the hate in Vincent's eyes. He wanted to respond. He wanted to kill me, but we both knew I was his only ticket home. Until he got there, he was going to do whatever I told him. Vincent's first priority was Vincent. I could count on that.

We walked for hours in silence. My senses were alive and straining to pick up a hint that something lived here. We knew there were pureblood vampires, but there were other creatures here, too. We just didn't know what.

The fact we hadn't seen an inkling of life made my stomach clench. Tiki had been here only once before. He knew the power the vampires held, but still, he came. He knew I had to do this and he felt obligated to come. I glanced at him as he walked behind me. He was focused and ready for battle, but I found myself doubting him. I didn't understand why he was helping me. Without him, I never would've been able to save Rayna and I'd be trapped in Drakar. But we only met by chance and once he found out who I was, he'd sworn some silent oath to me. He'd been loyal so far, but he was still a demon: untrustworthy to the end.

Tiki's orange eyes were wide, scanning the world around us. Two short swords sat in a sheath on his back, moving with each step. Marcus trailed behind him. His brown gaze moved out over the endless rocks, looking for signs of life. His midnight skin reflected the moon and the look on his face was fierce. In this moment, he wasn't the Marcus I knew; he was a soldier.

"You okay?" Rayna asked.

"Yeah, I'm fine. I just want to find the dagger," I said. I'd promised to be honest with her, to tell her everything, but this wasn't the time or the place. Besides, I wasn't even sure that what I had to say was worth sharing. I was questioning someone I had no reason to question. I shook the feeling away and gave Rayna a smile I knew she'd believe.

"Okay," she replied.

The scuff of rocks constantly made my pulse jump. My hand moved to my blade and my eyes shot to each and every face, watching the people I trusted stand guard around me. My gaze fell on Marcus again and all I could feel was hatred. His dark brown eyes never told you anything, even when you knew he had something to say. He was all about secrets. He was the reason my mother was dead. If it hadn't been for him, none of this would've happened.

My eyes opened wide and I couldn't believe what I was thinking. I knew better than that. I'd forgiven Marcus. It wasn't his fault my mother asked him to keep it a secret. He was honoring the request of a lifelong friend. Someone he loved with all his heart. After all he'd done for me, I owed him some respect.

I brought my water element up and let it calm me, pushing the anger aside. The cool river of magic flowed through my veins until it washed the emotions away.

"You sure you're okay?" Rayna asked. "You look...weird."

"I'm sure," I said, trying to look genuine. "It's just what happened back there...with the earth element. Suddenly, I have another power and I don't understand it. I'm starting to be able to control the two I have, adding two more to the mix isn't helping. It's strange, that's all."

"We'll figure it out. Don't worry." Rayna gave a reassuring smile.

I smiled, but it was insincere. I wasn't worried. I was happy to have more power. More power meant I was getting stronger. I would be harder to defeat. Soon, Riley would be begging for my mercy. Power meant respect. Power meant it'd be easier to take out the traitors surrounding me.

We walked for more miles than I could keep track of. I didn't doubt Elyas' words, but I could feel everyone else doubting me, even in their silence. I shuddered, and I wasn't sure if it was because I knew what they all thought about me, my power, or if it was the filthy demons surrounding me.

I checked in on everyone, watching what they watched and keeping an eye on their weapons. They all paid close attention to the columns of black rock that jutted from the earth, each pretending to be there for me, but I knew they were only here for their chance to get the dagger. They wanted to steal the power that was rightfully mine.

The eerie feeling that someone was watching me moved through my body. I looked out to the rocky hills and tried to distinguish something, anything that might be there, but it was useless. This was a wasteland of stone and moonlight.

When I looked back at the group, I found Rayna staring at me. She scowled, and even though her lips weren't moving, I could hear her words in my head. *"You think I don't know? I do. I know exactly what you think of her, and me for that matter. You're a liar. I'd love to beat that smug look off your face. Gods, it would feel good to hurt you."* Rayna shook her head and her eyes changed from angry to confused. She turned away and watched the path ahead.

"Weird," I whispered to myself.

"What was that?" Willy's voice snapped at me. His brown eyes were angry and his beast was staring out from behind them. His forehead was creased and his eyebrows furrowed.

"Nothing."

I could feel his angry gaze even after I'd turned away. It was burning through me and I wanted to keep an eye on him. I knew he'd stab me in the back the first chance he got. He was a shallow demon; a cheap shot was just up his alley. Wolf or no wolf, he knew he couldn't take me face to face. He'd be the first to try and get to me.

I shook the thoughts away. I didn't really feel that way...did I? No. Willy would never do something like that. Besides, Willy was a coward on a good day. I didn't even know why he was here; he was as useful as a knife with no blade. He wouldn't fight back if I threatened to kill his Grams. Come to think of it, that wasn't a half bad idea. I hated that old broad.

"If that's really what you think, why don't you say so?" Willy asked.

"What?" I turned around and anger filled me. Surely this small, lost, little demon wasn't talking back to me.

"You heard me. If you think I'm so useless, why keep me around? In fact, why don't you just kill me yourself? You're supposed to be a big bad demon hunter, but given the company you're in, I'd say your daddy issues have you confused."

Anger raged inside me, and with it, the air element came. I turned around and my magic blew Willy's body off the ground, throwing him back into a black column of rock. The pillar's base broke and crumbled with the impact, and we all jumped back as it fell.

"I'll kill you, you stupid mutt!"

A deep, earth shaking sound echoed through the valley as the pillar hit the ground, and Willy growled in pain and anger. He jumped to his feet and his wolf took over. His eyes shifted and thick claws jutted from his hands.

"Hey! What's the matter with you two?" Marcus stepped between us.

"Don't stop them; let them have a go." Vincent's yellow eyes were gone, replaced by solid black. "Let the little wolf bite him and see what happens. Once he's out of the way, I'll make a nice snack out of you." His pale skin vanished and his demon broke through. Long, bonelike talons sprouted from his hands, and I could see the black blood pumping through his veins, pushing against his glassy skin.

"Something's not right." Rayna sounded confused, but I didn't take my eyes off Willy. A deep growl rumbled from his lips and I slid a silver blade from its sheath.

I whistled. "Here, doggy, doggy."

Rayna's magic fell over us. Her element moved through my body and sparked the same element inside me. The power pumped through my veins and it brought a calm over me. All the hatred I felt faded, and the horrible thoughts vanished, replaced by guilt. Rayna's magic amplified my own element, and our powers merged, pooling together and spreading out around the others.

"She's right. Something isn't right here." I rubbed my temples, trying to rid the feeling of someone poking around in my brain. The grainy feeling inside my skull reminded me of the night at the Circle with Riddley's magic.

"There's something here," Rayna said. "I can feel its power. It's trying to get inside our heads."

"A spell?" Marcus suggested.

"I'm sorry," Willy said. His brown eyes returned and they stared at me with sadness. "I didn't mean it."

"Neither did I...none of us knew what we were saying."

"I did." Vincent smiled. His demon was gone, but long fangs still hung from his mouth.

"Of course *you* did, but something else is here. It has the rest of us thinking these thoughts. It wants us to fight amongst ourselves," Rayna said.

"She's right. I can feel it pushing against our magic. It's trying to break through," I said.

Rayna's eyes darted carefully around the valley. She reached down and unlatched her whip, gripping the handle and letting it unravel to the ground. "Everyone, get behind me."

We all stepped back at once while Rayna snapped her whip to the ground. The silver claws hit the rocky earth and sparks shot around her. She continued pushing her element together with mine and it swirled around us, shielding everyone from whatever was out there.

Foreign magic splintered our shields and I could feel its anger. Outside our circle of protection, they were fighting back, smashing our power away, one layer at a time.

"It's breaking through," I said.

"I know!" Rayna scowled.

The shield shattered and the foreign magic swarmed in. I could feel it around my throat and it made it difficult to breathe. It moved through my head, like sandpaper against my brain, and I winced. Angry thoughts filled my mind and I squeezed the dagger in my hand, turning angry eyes on Willy.

Rayna brought her beast to the surface and managed to keep it in control. She didn't struggle against its force, but it was the beast looking out of her bright green eyes. She snapped the whip again and smiled. "Gotcha." She threw the whip forward and the silver tip soared through the air. The claws moved towards a towering rock and when she snapped her wrist back, the whip coiled around what seemed like nothing. The air around the whip blurred for a moment and Rayna pulled back, but there was resistance on the other end. She tugged again with force and power exploded over us. The whip snapped back towards her, and a figure appeared, soaring towards us with Rayna's whip twisted around its neck.

The demonic magic broke, and the angry thoughts vanished. The creature hit the ground and dust shot up around it. Rayna dragged the beast towards her, and it struggled to pull the coil from its neck, but Rayna kept the whip tight, not giving any slack.

We crowded around as the dust settled and the body became visible. White scars decorated slate gray skin. Breasts sagged off its chest and from the waist down was the body of a snake: thick and slimy scales with a rattle flickering at the end of its tail. Red eyes were wide with black veins running through them. Scarred flesh dangled where its eyelids had been chewed off. Pieces of dried skin still hung over one eye and tiny jagged teeth filled its lipless mouth.

"Filthy creaturessss," it hissed. "Ithreal will have your soulsssss!" Its voice was demonic, with a white snake tongue slipping out over its face.

"Wh–, what... is it?" Willy asked, stepping back from the squirming serpent.

"It's a Visceratti," Tiki said.

"What the hell's a Visceratti?"

"They are snake women. They can put the most horrible thoughts into your mind, and as you've seen, make themselves invisible. They force their prey to turn on one another and when there are only a few left, the entire nest swarms and eviscerates them."

"Charming," Vincent stated.

"That's not the worst of it. If they get inside your head, you become their puppet. They gain full control over you and your magic."

"Did you say an entire nest?" Marcus asked.

"That's right. They travel–" Tiki's feet flew up into the air and his head smashed against the ground. Everyone drew their weapons, and the sound of swords sliding from their sheaths ricocheted off the stone walls around us.

"Shit. They're here. All of them," Rayna said, her beast prowling behind her eyes.

Hissing came from every direction, followed by the rattle of a snake about to strike, but they were unseen.

"I can't see them!" I yelled.

"I can." Rayna tugged the whip tight against the demon's throat and pulled out her dagger.

"How do we kill them?" I asked.

"Hurt them to break the invisibility. Cut off the head to kill," Tiki said.

"Put your shields up; don't let them in your head," Marcus shouted.

"Give us our Missssha back," one hissed.

I turned in a circle, following the voice, but there were only rocks.

Willy yelped as his body was blown back by a solid force, and he crashed against a rock wall. He crumpled to the ground and released a growl. Rolling onto all fours, he pushed his beast to the surface. Brown eyes shifted and became colorless with a single black pupil.

"I can see them." He spoke with a lisp as his fangs came down from his mouth.

"Where?" I yelled.

"Two, right behind you."

I turned with all the speed I had and swung my sword through the air. Orange blood exploded from nowhere and splattered against the blue and black stones. The demon hissed and her body came into view; a deep gash across her chest had bright orange liquid trickling down her body.

"Marcus, right in front of you!" Rayna yelled.

He sliced the short sword through the air and fire exploded in front of him. A headless body revealed itself as it burst into flames and crumbled to a pile of glowing embers.

"To your left, Chase!" Willy yelled.

I ripped my blade through the air. I felt it hit something but the blade stopped. I pushed harder and turned my whole body with the blade until I heard a snap. The demon's body exploded in flames and more hissing surrounded us.

"Kill them all," the voices said unanimously. They chanted the words repeatedly, and I followed the voices to my next victim, thrusting my sword into her stomach.

Tiki slashed his claws sporadically, trying to hit anything he could. His body jerked into the air and then smashed into the ground. He tried to get to his feet, but something was holding him down. Claws tore across one of his arms and blood spurted from the wound. He swung his claws forward, trying to break the demon's hold, but his arm was pushed away and pinned to the ground.

Vincent lunged over Tiki, shifting into his demon form in mid-air. He tackled the transparent creature and tore into her with razor talons. The creature's magic faded and her tail slapped against the ground as Vincent tore at her throat.

I called my element to life and pulled it around us. A wall of blue flames shot up and a ring of fire encircled us. Hisses followed as the flames caught several Visceratti. As soon as they were visible, I pushed the power over them. The demons caught fire with ease, immersed in blue and silver, and everyone moved towards the ones we could see.

Willy finished his transformation and pounced, bringing two down with his massive claws. His fangs ripped into each of them savagely, leaving smoldering ash behind him as he stalked his next victim.

Rai released a thunderous scream from her tiny beak. Feathers exploded into the air like someone had torn open a pillow. Bright light flickered around her, and in moments, she was a massive version of herself. Four huge wings cut through the air, pushing her higher into the sky. She struck her talons together and lightning flashed, exploding over the ground. Rocks burst into the sky and rained over us. Among the falling rocks was a trio of Visceratti, a hissing song coming from their lips as they hit the ground. Rai dive-bombed to the earth, her huge claws grabbing a handful of demons and pulling them into the navy sky. A blood curdling screech came from her beak, and she tore them to pieces, leaving white and gray ash to snow down from above.

I leapt over the fire and brought my sword down to kill a flaming Visceratti. I cursed as unseen claws ripped through my shirt, catching my shoulder. I swung the sword behind me and hit nothing but air. Claws sliced into my stomach, tearing away strips of flesh. I grunted and arched the blade above my head, bringing it down and stabbing the air in front of me. Orange blood spilled from the snake's back and I drove the blade through her. Her cries were masked with a hiss and she slithered away, vanishing again with the sword stuck in her gut.

I watched the air closely, as though if I focused I could see her. Her body reappeared, red eyes thick with hunger. She reached down and snapped the blade jutting from her gut and the rest of the sword slipped out her back and clanked against the ground. She was bigger than the other demons, a tarnished silver tiara sitting over matted black hair.

"You dirty half-breedsss. You think Ithreal'sss dagger can sssave you, but you're no match for his power!" Her body weaved from side to side as she slithered towards me, leaving a thick, viscous fluid behind her. She lunged forward, her tail rattling in the air. Her lipless mouth opened wide and long fangs came towards me. I pulled a dagger from my back and ducked. Her mouth snapped as I slipped away and brought the blade back around, cutting into her tail. Orange blood pooled beneath her as her rattle fell limp to the ground. The demon turned to face me and I jumped towards her, plunging my dagger into her throat. The muscles snapped as the blade sliced through. They rolled under her skin and she screamed. I tore the dagger out and she brought slate gray hands up to cover her throat, trying to hold in the steady flow of blood. I moved behind her and gripped thick, matted hair with my fist, pulling her head back and opening the gash. Her screams turned to gurgles as the blood flooded her throat. I pulled again, using every ounce of strength I had, and her body bent back with me. Her skin tore as I stretched the wound and brought my blade down in a single, swift motion. Her head separated from her body and she lit up in a glow of orange and yellow before all I was holding was a handful of ashes.

"The princesss! She'ssss dead," one demon shouted.

"You will pay, half-breedsss!" The hisses came from everywhere and the remaining demons slithered away. "Our queen will not be pleasssed." Some of the demons disappeared into the shadows while others dove under rocks and burrowed into the ground, leaving us with the faint sound of rattles.

"Are they gone?" Tiki asked.

Willy ran towards us, orange blood covering him. A growl rumbled between his black wolf lips and colorless wolf eyes looked up at me.

"They're gone," Rayna said, gasping for air.

"Strange. I've never heard of a creature that could see a Visceratti," Tiki said. "Their bodies are frail, but their magic is strong."

"Thanks for the heads up on those." I slipped the dagger back into its sheath and picked up my sword. The blade was split in half and what was left was bent and mangled.

"They are not supposed to be here. They are not from this world and they would not have come by choice. Nobody comes here by choice. Someone knew we were coming. I fear we may be unequipped to handle this."

"I second that." Vincent raised a once pale hand, now stained with dried orange blood. "We should leave."

"We're not stopping. We need to destroy the ring."

"Tiki makes a good point." Marcus slid his blade into its sheath. "We got lucky, but there are still vampires and who knows what else out there. We aren't prepared for this."

"Did I mention I agree?" Vincent chimed in.

I glared at Vincent and turned to Marcus. "Let me rephrase this. *I* need to destroy the ring, so *I'm* not leaving. If you need to go, I understand, but I can't stop."

"Don't be foolish," Marcus said.

I looked around until I found the blue moon and started walking. I threw my broken sword into a pile of shattered rocks and footsteps trampled up beside me. Rayna watched me with intensity as she coiled her whip and latched it to her hip. Orange blood had stained her shirt, and there was a single tear in the fabric near the bottom, drying blood coloring the open gash around the wound.

"Are you–"

"I'm fine," she said.

More footsteps came and Tiki's sandaled feet walked over the rocks with ease. Willy ran up beside us. His shirt was gone, revealing an overly hairy upper body. His pants were on, but completely torn along both sides.

Marcus sighed. "Let's go."

"So, on we go then. Wonderful," Vincent said.

Chapter 28

Thankfully, Willy's torn pants were salvaged enough to cover the necessities. We'd come to a rocky wall that had forced us to climb, and the last thing I wanted was Willy's naked butt above me. Rai soared over us, her voice screeching into the sky. The sound made me wince, but as I pulled myself to the top of the wall, I saw what she was excited about.

The large blue moon was partially masked behind a massive stone pyramid only a few miles away. We were nearly there.

I helped the others as they reached the top and everyone was happy to know we didn't have to climb down the other side. We were on level ground now, and the landscape had changed.

Massive slate rocks still jutted from the earth, but now they had flowerless vines wrapped around them. Green, blue, and yellow plant life wrapped itself around the stones and spread out over the cold ground. Patches of brown grass and pools of black, frozen liquid littered the cracked earth as we started our final stretch towards the temple.

Now that we were out of the valley, it was even colder. The wind was harsh, like tiny beads of ice cutting into my skin. A thick fog rolled off the pyramid's stones in the wake of the cold air and I shivered. I had to pull my fire up to keep my teeth from chattering, but no amount of heat could keep this chill from my bones.

The moon rose up above the pyramid, silhouetting it in an eerie beauty. With the exception of the rocks crunching under our feet, there wasn't a sound, and the saying *it's a little too quiet* flashed through my mind.

"Anyone else find it strange we haven't run into any other demons?" I asked.

"They are here," Tiki said. "I can feel them. They're waiting on orders from their master."

A chill ran down my spine, but it wasn't from the cold air.

As we approached the pyramid, it looked out of place, reminding me of something from ancient Egypt. It was built out of small brown rectangular stones that rose into the sky in a triangle of power. Each set of stones was set further into the pyramid, like a giant staircase leading to the peak, but as I came to the base, I realized there was no doorway.

"Fascinating." Vincent was in awe as he gazed upon the structure. "I can feel Ithreal's power beating like a pulse." He took in a deep breath through his nose and smiled. "Pure, godly energy calling me forth."

"Interesting." Marcus rubbed his hand along the stone and pulled it away quickly. "They're burning."

Energy poured from the temple and heat rolled off in waves, revealing that it was not a fog, but steam coming off the rocks. I reached out and touched the stones, pulling my hand back just as Marcus had. "Dammit." I waved my hand in the air. "How are we supposed to get in?"

"In the Underworld, only true darkness allows one to see."

I reached for my dagger as the voice echoed around me.

"What is it?" Rayna asked.

"Elyas says we need true darkness to open it."

"What does that mean?"

"It means we need to cover the moon and stars in shadows," Marcus answered.

"I'm not powerful enough to do this alone," I said, my eyes meeting Marcus'.

Marcus nodded and stepped forward. "But together, we are."

Marcus and I drew our air to the surface and shadows leaked from the darkness. I'd never merged power with anyone but Rayna, and feeling Marcus' was strange. It was profusely powerful and he had intense control.

Pools of black slid over the ground like liquid. Our magic linked together and pulled shadows from every direction. Thick black arms reached out from the cracks in the earth and into the sky until a blanket of darkness covered us. The blue and green moons vanished behind a wall of shadows, and each pinhole of light a star created was filled with an inky blackness.

My vision vanished as shadows covered the area and I felt lost in space. The darkness was thick, physically weighing me down. Heat filled the air and power throbbed from the pyramid. The clatter of stones sounded in front of me as each brick began to vibrate. They lit up in a glow of red, chattering together and sliding over one another. The pyramid became a tower of inflamed bricks, glowing in the solid night we'd created.

A rumble came from the earth and the pyramid moved. The top few bricks vanished first. Then the next level followed, dropping down inside the pyramid. Steam rolled off of the steps, growing hotter as each layer fell into the next, until there was a four-sided staircase leading into the earth.

The staircase shook and continued to change. Scalding bricks slid over top of each other until they created a small entrance at the bottom. When the stones finally settled, a fire ignited from the base and crawled up each step. Smoke billowed from the bottom, and as the flames grew higher, they reached into the black sky with ember arms. Marcus and I pulled our magic back and the shadows withdrew. The darkness collapsed and the moons and stars exploded in light above us.

"Great, how the hell are we supposed to get in now?" Rayna asked.

"We'll send Vincent; he loves fire." I smirked.

Vincent's cool and unfriendly gaze met mine. "I think this is more your area of expertise."

I turned my focus to the flames and cast my own element over them. Water exploded from my hands and showered the heat in a wash of cool liquid. The sizzle of boiling water was loud as it hit the stones, but the flames didn't react. I pushed harder and a single wave of ice blue power rushed over the fire. The flames hissed and the steam thickened, but the fire crackled higher, responding to the water like an accelerant. I tried a different approach and channeled the fire element. Magic reached into the flames, trying to extinguish them. They wavered against the magic but didn't recede. They only swayed like a soft breeze had blown through.

"Magnificent. Our brave hero is sterile." Vincent rolled his eyes.

I wanted to unleash my fire on him, but I didn't lose focus. I kept a hold of my element and let it retreat just beneath the surface. I reached my hand into the flames. I couldn't control this fire, but just as I could survive my own, this flame didn't burn me.

"I have to go alone."

"Absolutely not," Marcus responded.

"Do you have another way?"

"Yes, we return home. Together we can keep the ring safe."

"No, we can't. Deep down inside you know that. Riley gets stronger every day and we haven't seen a sliver of his true power. Don't you see? Destroying the ring is the only way and the weapon to do it is down there."

Marcus sighed.

"I'll be back as soon as I can," I said, and I stepped towards the staircase.

"Wait," Rayna said. "Maybe Marcus is right. We could try and keep the ring safe. If all of us—"

"Rayna, stop. We need to destroy it. If we don't, sooner or later, Riley will find a way to get it. We've come this far; we can't turn back now."

"But the dagger might not even be down there. It could just be a trap."

"It could be, but I have to try."

Rayna watched me and sadness shone in her eyes. "Just come back in one piece."

I turned back to the staircase and faced the flames. They danced and rolled inside themselves, and I called my element to the surface before taking the first step.

The smell of burning rubber was instant as my shoes hit the steps. They stuck to each stone as I walked down the staircase. I descended quickly as the flames nipped at my clothes, jumping down two at a time.

When I reached the bottom, I patted the ankles of my pants and parts of my shirt to extinguish the embers that crawled up them. The soles of my shoes were soft, and with each step, the bottoms became more uneven.

I stepped through the entranceway into a corridor. The passageway was a long, stone hallway, twisting and turning as I moved. The further I went in, the darker it became as I left the burning staircase behind. The air was cold and damp with the smell of rotting flesh lingering around me. The light from the flames faded as I made a second turn, and darkness took over the hall. The sound of my footsteps echoed off the walls and I ran my hand over the cool stone as a guide. I'd only made it a few steps around the corner when screams sounded behind me. Hissing followed and panic set it. My body moved back towards the staircase, but the bricks began shifting again. I pushed myself faster and the stale death that rode the air whipped past me.

I summoned my element to protect me and jumped out of the corridor and into the flames. The bricks moved and folded back up into the air. The stairs vanished and I could hear screaming and fighting as I tried to scale the wall.

"Marcus!" I screamed, but there was no answer. "Rayna!"

"Chase!" Rayna's voice sounded distant.

I scaled up the wall and the bricks were hot, but I kept my element just beneath the surface, trying to protect my skin. The stones continued to move, making each inch more difficult to climb than the last. As I neared the top, I was hanging at an angle, only holding on by the tips of my fingers. Bricks began sliding as the top of the pyramid formed, and at the angle they were at, I could no longer climb. I strained to listen for any hint of my friends, but there was nothing. The last level began sliding into place and the bricks pushed my fingers, breaking my grip.

I flailed back and a hand grabbed me from what was left of the opening. Relief washed through me, but as I looked up to see a hissing Visceratti, that feeling vanished.

"I told you you'd pay hunter. Ithreal will give us many blessings for our sssacrifice." The Visceratti lashed out at me and grinned, revealing a mouthful of jagged little teeth.

I tried to pull myself free of its grasp, but I didn't have anything to use as a foundation. I was hanging above a pit of shadows by the hand of a demon.

"Your friendsss will pay for your choicesss and you will watch them die!" She hissed, and sharp nails dug into my wrist before she let go.

I fell through the darkness, my limbs flailing, trying to grasp onto anything that could slow my fall. Nothing but shadows hung around me and the last flicker of light that the night sky provided vanished as the final bricks closed into place. I screamed through the shadows, waiting for my body to hit bottom. I tried to focus my power and bring my air element to life. I wanted the shadows to reach out and grab me, to save me from the impact.

The power surged and the air became thick. I thought I felt my body slow, the shadows ready to break my fall, but it wasn't enough. I hit rock bottom. Literally.

My body crashed into the bottom of the pit and my head smacked the ground. A flash of light exploded, and the pain was sharp, shooting through me like a bullet before the darkness claimed me.

Chapter 29

My eyes opened and panic filled me. My entire body felt broken. I tried to sit up, but even in pure darkness the world felt fuzzy. I reached inside and the water came with ease. It soaked my body from the inside out, sliding through me as it closed my wounds.

A tingle moved at the back of my head, and as the pain receded, my stomach tensed. I pushed myself to my feet, carefully feeling around me. Blue flame filled my hand as I called the element, allowing myself to observe my surroundings.

I sat at the bottom of a pit, the smell of rotting corpses alive on the air. I turned in a circle until I found the corridor and I walked along it, using my hand to brace myself. Objects jutted from the wall; a long metal rod was embedded in the stone, and as I brought my flame up to it, it caught fire and flickered to life. Torches that lined both sides of the corridor ignited one by one.

Light and shadow danced in the cool tunnel air. They were still far enough apart that I had to walk in darkness every few feet until I reached the next blue flame. I followed the winding path, my nerves rattling inside me each time I entered a section of shadows. My senses strained in the eerie silence, begging to hear anything, but all there was, was my own breathing.

I stopped in the next segment of light and leaned up against the wall. My body ached. Adrenaline and fear tore through my veins. The sounds of Rayna screaming echoed in my mind and guilt cut through me. Images of my friends' dead bodies played through my head, blood and flesh hanging from the lips of the Visceratti that stood over them. I shuddered and shook the images away.

The rotting smell that lived in the air was briefly lifted as a sweet scent passed by me. It was foreign and familiar and filled me with a new wave of hope. I pushed off the wall and continued, quickening my pace. I didn't know if they were dead and I couldn't assume. The sooner I got out of here, the faster I could find them. There might still be time to save them.

I moved down the corridor until I was running, row after row of torches blew past me and I followed the winding walls until they came to an end. A set of three short staircases stood before me, each leading to a single door with a knocker on it.

The first was black with soot, and the knocker's ring was held in the mouth of a dragon. Red jewels sat where its eyes should've been and they gleamed as if freshly polished.

The second door was the largest, covered in flakes of brown rust. The knocker was gold– although tarnished with dirt–and made to look like a creature I didn't recognize. It had a horse's body, a wolf's legs, the wings of a bat, the tail of a tiger, and the head of a snake. Blue sapphires occupied its eyes and the knocker weaved through its legs.

The last door was plain. The steel was cold and dark, and in the center, the warped imprint of a hand reached through. The fingers pushed out of the steel and gripped a round black knocker.

My gaze flickered between the three doors. Which was the right door? Where did they each lead? The thoughts reminded me of Elyas' words. "In the Underworld, only true darkness allows one to see," I whispered.

I turned back to the corridor and extended my hand, pulling at the flames that lit the way. The fire wavered as I reached out with an invisible hand of magic. The torches flickered and the flames bit at the air, leaning towards me. I pushed my power down the hall and closed my fist. One by one, each flame vanished and the scent of smoke surrounded me.

Surrounded by silent darkness, I slowed my breathing and stepped forward until I found the first door. My hand slid up the smooth, metal surface to the knocker. The cold steel vibrated along my skin and I pulled it back in my hand. I opened my mind, reaching out past the door with my senses, and an assault of images raged through my mind.

I was surrounded by bright red flames. Black and blue scales towered in front of me, leading up to the massive form of an incredible dragon. Even with its mouth closed, long black teeth jutted from its lips. The dark green eyes glowed beneath a rough and jagged brow. Its neck snapped to the side and the ground rumbled as it lowered its head. The dragon looked straight at me, clouds of smoke shooting from its gaping nostrils. Its mouth opened and an earth shattering roar shot through my body.

I closed off my mind and the images vanished. I took a long, deep breath. My head throbbed with the resonating sound of the dragon's roar and I stepped back, feeling through the shadows until I found the second door.

The rust was rough beneath my fingers and I followed it up to the handle. I wrapped my fingers around it and hesitated before opening my mind and reaching forward. Instead of images filling my mind, something tore through me and pulled me into another reality.

I was walking deep in a cave. Moist air rolled over my skin and it amplified the scent of decaying bodies. Everywhere I looked there was death. The corpses of animals and people scattered around me. Some were bare skeletons while the others were fresh kills. I walked further into the cave, and the creature I'd seen on the knocker was there. Blue blood surrounded it and its eyes stared at me, filled with a lifeless gloss. I stepped back as the blood trickled towards me; whatever this was had died only moments ago.

The cave shook and a growl unlike any I'd ever heard came from the shadows. It was deep like a wolf, but managed to have the hiss of a snake. I reached for my daggers but the sheath was empty. My stomach clenched and my pulse sped. I tried to close off my mind but nothing happened. This was different.

I searched the cave, looking for an escape, when an odd feeling moved through me. A shiver ran down my spine and the world around me wavered. The reality shifted and the roars faded. This wasn't real.

"Sorry to interrupt." A voice said. It was a man's voice: deep and masculine.

My eyes followed it through the shadows until I found the glowing red eyes of a wolf staring at me.

"Who are you?" I asked, trying not to let the fear that pounded through my body come out in my voice.

The wolf's eyes shifted, morphing into the eyes of a snake. "I'm a friend of your father's here to deliver a warning; forget the dagger."

"Get out of my head!" I yelled.

The eyes shifted again, this time into bright yellow cat eyes. The man laughed. "Get out? I just got here." The creature paced in the darkness, following me with its eyes.

"Well, you're not staying," I said. I reached out with my other senses, touching the world around me and searching for his energy.

"Your father is very disappointed in you, Chase. You should have taken his offer and joined our cause."

I didn't reply. I kept my focus on finding the invader, straining my senses through the cave.

"Isn't it ironic that your father has enlisted the help of a demon to gain your cooperation?"

I stopped searching and stared into the beast's eyes. "Nothing will make me help him."

"I wouldn't be so sure. As a master...I can be very convincing."

"What does that mean?"

"Whether you like it or not, you're a part of this now. Take this offering."

The reality wavered and a door appeared. It was an old wooden door. It creaked open, and the world on the other side kept changing. First it was a dark and empty desert. Then it was a beautiful world, full of the greenest water and the lushest plants. A warm breeze pushed through the door and wrapped around me, enticing me to follow it.

"This is your way out, Chase. I'm doing you a favor. Forget the dagger. This door is a gift, from us to you. It will take you wherever you wish to go. All you have to do is walk through it."

I stared through the doorway as the world inside it changed, and I was tempted. I was tempted to leave and forget it all, but the moment I thought it, frustration filled me. I had to save them. I refocused my mind and reached out through the cave. My senses strained until I found his energy. His aura was dark, foreign, and filled with rage. I pushed at it and it wavered.

"Don't do that," he growled.

"Stay out of my head," I said again, and this time I put all my focus into pushing him out.

His aura broke and the cat eyes faded. I stood alone in the cave and the cold air sent goose bumps down my arm. I shut my eyes and focused on closing my mind. The reality shook and vanished, and when I opened them, I was back in the corridor, surrounded by darkness. Sweat was running down the inside of my arms and dripping off my hands. I slid my fingers out of the knocker and let the water element soothe me, clearing my head before I reached for the last door.

I didn't need to open my mind this time. I could feel power coming off the surface and drawing me closer. I reached forward and the dark steel was warm to the touch. I found the metal handprint and locked my fingers around the knocker. My knuckles rubbed the steel fingers that jutted from the door, and I shuddered as a pulse of magic moved through me. I pulled back on the silver ring and slammed it into the door. The knock boomed through the other side and the temple started to shake.

Dust and small bits of rock shook from the ceiling before the door unlatched and squeaked inward. I pushed through the opening and into a room where the smell of death was thicker than before. Skeletons were scattered over the floor, their legs broken and no longer attached to the bodies that lay across the room. Swords and battle axes lay rusted and forgotten along the floor, and an archer's bow that once wrapped around his chest was now broken, splinters of wood sticking between his skinless ribs. The walls were painted red with dried blood and the torches were alight with flames, reflecting gold flakes embedded in the walls. Tall columns ran along each side of the room, and massive stalactites hung from the ceiling like giant icicles waiting to fall on an unsuspecting victim. In the center, the dagger floated on the air, bathed in a ray of golden light that came from everywhere and nowhere all at once. It shone from the solid ground and into the ceiling, existing completely on its own. The dagger had a blade on either side of its black leather handle. Both blades curled at malicious angles with small, jagged teeth chiseled from the base, an ideal feature for gutting its victims.

"And the hero arrives." A man's voice swirled around me. It came from the dead bodies, echoed off the walls, and it rode the stale air that lived in the cave. I searched the cavern with my eyes but couldn't see anything.

"Who's there?" My voice bounced off the cave walls and came back to me, as though I'd asked the question to myself.

"Come now, do you really need to ask?" Thick black smoke swirled through the room and into the golden light. As the black tornado slowed, a man appeared.

His gray skin sparkled in the light and it made his dark eyes unforgettable. Long dark hair fell against his back, matching the black cloak that covered his body. The cloak dragged along the floor behind him with blood red thread lining the edges. He crossed his arms in front of him, his hands disappearing into the opposite sleeve as he moved towards me, unaccompanied by the sound of footsteps. The intensity of his gaze made me want to turn away, but I couldn't. His face and body looked young, but his eyes were full of horror.

"You're the soul piece," I said.

"Correction: the dagger is the soul piece. I am Salvatore, the portion of Ithreal's soul that is bound to the blade." He floated around me and I couldn't resist following his eyes. "You hunters are an interesting breed. Sad to think it was this pitiful creature that defeated my master's army. I can feel your magic; it is weak by comparison."

"It was strong enough to win the war."

"Silence!" Salvatore screamed from every direction. His voice was dark, laced with the deep rumble of ancient magic that vibrated along my skin. "You are not in your pretty dimension, hunter. In Ithreal's world, you show the master respect. Your insolence will not be tolerated. This is your only warning."

"I'm not here to pay my respects. I'm here for the dagger."

"I'm quite aware as to *why* you are here. You think destroying the ring will stop the second coming, but it won't. My master has followers everywhere. They will not cease until he has been freed."

"I won't let that happen."

Salvatore laughed, and it was pure evil, cackling around me. "I love your ambition, but let us be realistic. Ithreal commands an army larger than all the gods combined. Not to mention, the very sight of his true form would reduce even you, a hunter of the Circle, to a pile of ash. I've been forced into this pitiful shell for you. Your weak eyes cannot handle even my purity!"

"We did it once. We can do it again."

Salvatore frowned and floated towards the dagger. "I've spoken to no one in hundreds of years, and somehow, you manage to bore me. On with the trials."

"What trials?"

"Surely, you don't expect to just *take* the dagger. You must first complete the trials of Ithreal." Salvatore grabbed the double-sided blade and spun it in his hand. "For thousands of years, the most powerful of creatures have come in search of this. Those who were lucky enough to find it are dead, which brings us to you."

"What do you want me to do?"

"You ask as though you have a choice. You have made it this far, and as such, you're options are limited. You do the trials and die. Or you refuse, and I kill you." Salvatore chuckled and placed his hand back in the light, releasing the blade to float in the golden rays. "This temple, with its winding halls and mysterious doors, is unique for each who enters it, as are the trials. Let's take a look at what's in store for you, shall we?"

His cloaked form glided towards me and power latched onto me. I tried to step away, but I was paralyzed. Salvatore's hands slipped from the cloak, his skin vanishing and turning into streams of black smoke. He reached towards me and the tendrils shot into my body. My back arched as pain rippled through my insides like someone took a chainsaw to my soul. His hands twisted and my elements came to life; all four pushed through my body, trying to balance the pain with magic.

Salvatore shredded through my insides and pulled himself from my chest, the slate gray color coming back and reforming his hands and fingers. He smiled, wiping his hand down the front of his cloak. "You are lucky. Your trials are quite simple. For you, there are only two."

Salvatore snapped his fingers, and a tornado of black smoke swirled into the room. The stench of decaying flesh was thick as the wind picked up, spinning with the smoke until it hit the floor. A pureblood demon with jet black eyes stared at me and I recognized it immediately: vampire.

Its hair was ratty and gray with patches of bald spots throughout its scabby scalp. A clear, slimy armor covered its dark gray skin, except for a small white spot on the front of its throat that looked like a scar. Different sizes of fangs filled its mouth, and long, scrawny arms hung down around its knees. The gangly claws that jutted from its fingers dragged along the ground leaving white scratches on the stone floor, and small teeth-like bones stuck from its jaw and forehead.

I grimaced as the beast slapped its lips together and a thin black tongue slipped between them. It roared the most horrific sound and charged towards me, moving faster than I could follow.

Talons tore into my back and launched me across the cave. My body spun and I felt the wall break beneath me as I hit it. Pain ripped through my body at the force, leaving rocks and dust to shower me. The vampire grunted from across the cave, and I pulled a throwing knife from my sheath.

I jumped to my feet and the demon roared its primordial sound, standing patiently while I charged him. I snapped my wrist, sending the dagger flying, but the vampire's claws cut through the air, deflecting it to the floor. The demon grunted and swung towards me. I tried to block, but talons tore through my shirt and split the skin, splattering blood across the floor. The burning sensation was instant and so was the pain.

I leapt towards the vampire, tackling him to the ground. His hands slammed against me from one side to the other as I fought to pin him down. His skin was cold and slimy, forcing my hands to slip off. A knee came up and hit me from behind with strength I'd never felt and I flipped over his body. Dust wafted around me as I hit the floor, and I tried to roll to my feet, but the demon was too fast.

His claws rained down on me, one swipe after another. Blood spilled from my arm, then my chest, and finally my face. Black dots filled my vision and adrenaline exploded through me. The air element came to the surface and blasted him back, sending him to the ground. I knew I couldn't kill him with my power, but maybe I could hold him back.

I brought fire up next and cast a small circle around the demon. Blue flames crackled against the ground and the demon's roar resonated off the walls. He swiped at the fire and the strangest of looks crossed his distorted features, one I imagined was a smile. He walked slowly and stepped through the flame, unaffected by the power.

I reached for the throwing knives and grabbed a handful, snapping them all towards him. Blades bounced off his armor and *tinked* against the floor unsuccessfully. I dodged his next strike and jumped back, pulling the last remaining throwing knife from my leg sheath. I arched back and thrust it forward. The silver glinted as it turned end over end, cutting through the air. It made its last rotation and the tip began to pierce the soft spot in his neck before the vampire's hand shot out and stopped it. He gave me a toothy snarl and threw it to the ground.

The vampire stalked towards me and I ducked his onslaught of talons. Blood dripped from my arms, back, chest, and face. I couldn't afford to get hit again. I leaned back from his next strike and the claws barely missed my throat. I swung my arm forward and cracked my fist off his slimy face. His head snapped to the side, but with unnatural reflexes he came back, striking me with the back of his hand. The force was incredible and my body spun in the air before I hit the floor. Black and white dots swarmed my vision, and the sound of wet, slimy feet slapped against the floor before powerful hands grabbed me. Each hand wrapped around my body and lifted it with ease. Air whipped over my face and body when his arms snapped and threw me across the cave. Blue and gray rocks swirled around me while my body spun, stopping against the rock wall. I felt my daggers slide from their sheath and heard a soft *tink* before I hit the floor.

The demon stood above me before I could react. He crawled over my body, letting scrawny, yet powerful legs straddle me. He lowered himself, pushing his face against mine and rubbing his slime over me. A black tongue slipped from his lips and it slid from my neck to my jaw. I tried to pull away, but there was nowhere to go. His hot breath rolled over my flesh and a wheezing sound escaped his throat. The death on his breath rolled over my face and saliva ran down my neck. He pulled his head back and locked his eyes with mine. The lifeless orbs were filled with death and his power crashed into me.

Visions of my friends filled my mind, their bodies torn apart piece by piece and remade as vampires. Each of them stalked towards me, a part of the undead. Long fangs hung in each of their mouths and they all exploded in unison with a primal roar. Saliva poured from their lips as long claws reached out for me. Fear exploded inside me when Salvatore's voice shattered the vision.

"Finish him!" Salvatore commanded.

The demon tore his power out of my mind. He slapped his lips together and opened his mouth, letting all his teeth descend. They were covered with green and black spots as the fangs extended and drool trickled from his mouth. I pulled the air element up and tried to push him back, but he was too strong and I was exhausted. He fought the magic, making his way closer to me. His eyes filled with satisfaction at the meal he was about to receive and he broke my power down inch by inch.

I stretched my arms out, feeling along the ground. I searched for anything I could use. My pulse sped as scarred fingers wrapped around the base of my dagger lying amongst the rubble. I gripped it tight in my hand and used all the energy I had left. The last of my magic snapped and the vampire's fangs dropped to my throat, but I was already there.

Long teeth hit my neck and broke the skin. Blood ran over my skin, but the fangs didn't go further. His body stopped against mine, hot breath panting in waves, but the wheezing was gone, replaced by a gurgle.

He pulled his head up, feeling around his throat. My blade had gone through, piercing the only weak spot on his body. The demon stopped and looked confused. His long fingers wrapped around the leather grip and adrenaline surged through me. My blade was the only thing preventing me from getting covered in his blood. I didn't want to be beneath him when he pulled it out.

My arms felt heavy, but I pulled them off the floor and pushed the demon to the side in a panic. He reached up and drew the dagger from his throat and dropped it on the ground. Bright blue blood followed the blade and the demon's skin steamed as the armor melted away.

I struggled to my feet and fed the adrenaline into my soul. I unleashed my fire and blue flames coursed through the air. The demon screamed as fire washed over him and his slimy skin ignited.

The flames snapped against the vampire's skin and he roared, making a final attempt towards me. He lunged through the air, but as the last few flames swallowed him, his body exploded in an array of orange and yellow embers.

I stared at the pile of ash, breath catching in my throat. My heart beat so loud it vibrated inside me, and pain covered my body. Black smoke swirled through the air and Salvatore appeared; both arms were clasped behind his back.

"Well, that was discouraging."

"Sorry to disappoint," I said through heavy gasps.

"No bother, I'd hoped you'd make it past the first trial anyway. I'm very excited for the next one."

I pulled the water element up from within and tried to close the gaping wounds on my body. The power whirled inside me and as the water touched the wounds, a burning pain shot through them. I muffled a scream between gritted teeth and tried to push past it, but there was only more pain. Not only were my powers useless against the vampire's armor, they couldn't fix the damage it inflicted either. If it was possible, I think it was making things worse.

Exhaustion tugged at me. I didn't have enough control over my elements to be using them like this. If there was another fight ahead of me, I was already a few cards short of a full deck.

"What's the next trial?" My words were slurred as blood crept into my mouth and I spit it to the floor. I leaned against the wall, using it to hold myself up. My legs were weak and pain burned across my body.

Salvatore watched me spit up the blood, and disgust covered his face. "You've dedicated your life to hunting demons. Recently you've changed your path and now, you only hunt the *bad* ones." He laughed. "Since you killed one of those wonderful little creatures in your first trial, it only makes sense that you sacrifice something for your second." The smile from Salvatore's thin pink lips widened and a truly evil look crossed his face. "Are you ready for this? I thought this one up all on my own," he said proudly.

The pulse quickened in my throat and pain shot through my stomach, like someone beating me with a mallet from the inside. "What?"

Salvatore's magic filled the room with a thundering force and the cave shook. Rocks and dust fell around us, and the floor at one end of the cave collapsed. One wall moved up into the ceiling, revealing a dark hallway, and the hisses that followed stole all the hope I had for succeeding.

Six Visceratti entered the cave. One at a time their thick gray bodies slithered out, leaving a glossy trail behind. Each of them pulled a rope, dragging one of my friends across the cave floor. As the last demon slid from the darkness, it had no rope. Instead, it clutched a small wire cage with Rai inside. I could see the magic surrounding the cage, black and red streams of power keeping the bird contained.

"I told you you'd pay for our princessss," the first snake hissed. "The queen is very angry."

Marcus, Rayna, Tiki, Vincent, Willy, and Rai were all inside the cave now. The Visceratti pulled them to their feet and broke the ropes with ease. They each chanted a strange passage and dark magic seeped into the room. The same black and red power that surrounded Rai formed around them, lingering on the air like a waft of smoke that wouldn't fade.

My friends' eyes darted from wall to wall, panic and fear marring their faces.

"I'm so sorry," I said, letting my eyes move from face to face. "I'm sorry I got you all into this."

"They cannot answer you. I have silenced them. We don't want anyone trying to be the hero, now do we?" Salvatore smiled. "Take me, no take me!" he mimicked their voices. "You should feel lucky. If not for me, the Visceratti would be having their way with your friends already. You should be thanking me."

My eyes found Salvatore and anger filled my body.

A deep chuckle rushed from his lips, taunting me with his power. "Now, there are some rules. First, you must look them in the eye when you take their life. There will be no cowardly murders here. Secondly—"

"I choose Vincent."

Salvatore sighed. "*Secondly*, you cannot kill the vampire; he's just here for show."

"Why not?"

"You've dedicated your life to killing creatures you hate. If you wish to lay claim to Ithreal's blade, you will sacrifice someone. Killing the vampire is hardly that."

"I've already sacrificed someone." I spat the words at him.

"Oh, yes, dear mummy. You didn't sacrifice her yourself though, did you? No, you let someone else kill her while you ran away."

Anger swelled inside me and I pushed myself off the wall, leaping toward Salvatore. His power wrapped around me, stopping me in mid-air and pushing me to the ground.

"You're merely a peasant. You're no match for even a piece of Ithreal." Salvatore floated around me, amusement in his eyes. "Now, where was I?" he asked, turning back to the Visceratti.

SHIFT

"Oh, yes! The sacrifice." Spotlights flashed above Marcus, Rayna, Tiki, and Willy. "These are the ones you care for the most. You will choose from them."

I struggled to my feet and glared at him. "And if I refuse?"

The smile faded from Salvatore's face. "Do you really need to ask?" He vanished and reappeared in front of Marcus, black wisps of smoke moving around his body. He moved back and forth in front of the quartet and smiled. "Pick one. You take their life in exchange for the dagger."

"I won't do it. I will not choose."

"You *will* cooperate, or I will kill them all in the slowest, most painful manner I can fathom. I've been doing this a long time; you'd be surprised where my imagination can wander." He smiled. "Once they are all dead, I'll release the half vampire. If he agrees to kill you, I'll grant him his freedom and send him home. Wouldn't that be a way to go? Knowing that in refusing to sacrifice one, you killed them all?" Salvatore chuckled. "I really need to give myself a pat on the back. This is definitely one of my more clever trials." He reached over his shoulder and patted himself on the back, his hollow black eyes watching me. "Now choose."

I looked over at my friends. They each watched me and they all looked nervous.

"Do it!" Salvatore screamed. The walls of the cave rattled as power enveloped the room. "All you have to do is sacrifice one and you can stop this."

I looked over their faces and caught myself weighing the value of their lives. The thought made my chest tighten, and acid rose from my stomach, burning in my throat.

"Do it now, or so help me Ithreal, I will." He disappeared in a mist of shadows and reappeared behind Rayna. He grabbed both sides of her head and twisted it at an awkward angle. The black and red power holding her receded enough to let her cry slip through.

"Fine!" I pulled the dagger from my sheath and stepped forward.

Anger and hate filled me. I was tired of games, tired of trials, and tired of looking over my shoulder. I needed that dagger. I was ending this the only way I knew how.

Salvatore looked surprised and released Rayna's head. Wisps of smoke floated around him as he glided towards me.

I looked back over each of my friends. Marcus' expression was still, neutral, and told me with his eyes to take him. Tiki stood strong, caramel flesh gleaming in the golden light. His stomach was tight, revealing each row of abs, and he lifted his chin proudly. Rayna's eyes watched me, filled with fear, and I could see her beast throbbing beneath the surface. Willy's skin changed, cycling through every color around him. Sweat dripped down his face and his body trembled.

"I must admit, I'm impressed," he said. "To watch the life slowly drain from the eyes of someone you care for is a rare talent. I didn't think you had it in you."

Anger burned in my eyes and expanded through my body. I grinded my teeth as I clutched the dagger, my knuckles turning white as though they might burst from their sockets.

"I don't."

Salvatore looked confused and I summoned every ounce of energy I could find. Letting anger propel me forward, I stuck the dagger deep in his chest, turning the blade and tearing open the wound. Thick red blood poured out of the hole with streams of black swirling throughout it. I conjured air and pushed it over his body. Salvatore's eyes opened in surprise, and as he rose from the ground, I moved him with my mind and slammed him against the wall. Chunks of the cave collapsed with the impact and I continued the assault. His body broke the wall repeatedly before I released the magic and he dropped to the ground.

Salvatore grunted in anger and I summoned fire. Anger thundered inside me and I poured white heat over his body, but this time he responded with his own power.

"Insolent creature!" he screamed.

Magic flooded the cave and my elements died, sucking themselves back into my soul. Salvatore pushed himself to his feet, his face a mess of wide gashes and stained with blood. A rhythm of power filled the room and all his wounds closed. He ripped the blade from his chest and stared at the silver weapon, now coated with red and black blood. He shook his head and screamed, but the sound didn't belong to a human; it belonged to a beast.

He threw the knife back towards me and he was too fast. It cut through the air and slid into my shoulder. I screamed as the metal tore through flesh and cut into my muscles. The blade stopped as the handle hit my body and the tip of it poked out the other side.

"Your brazen disrespect for our lord is deplorable. I will end you!"

Swirls of black filled the cave, and the tornados of power hit the ground, raging towards us. Salvatore raised his hand and the smoke dissipated, revealing a dozen pureblood vampires. More hissing came as a swarm of Visceratti slipped into the room. They slithered throughout the cave until we were surrounded. The only thing stopping them from ripping me apart was Salvatore's magic.

"Not yet, my children." He glided towards me, leaving the demons roaring in frustration. "After I kill each of your friends, I'm going to unleash my children, but you will not die. No, I have a fate much worse for you. The vampires will turn you. You shall become one of my children." Salvatore smiled. "I have the power to grant you that curse, and so shall it be." He enunciated each word perfectly. "Once you're turned, you'll spend eternity as the Visceratti's plaything, and my personal servant. But first, you will suffer."

His energy plowed through me and something moved inside my body. Salvatore poured his magic into my soul and a beast roared from within. Blades of power cut me internally and I keeled over on my hands and knees. I could feel my stomach expanding as it filled with blood, and more claws tore apart my innards.

I tried to scream, but I gagged, coughing furiously and holding my stomach as though that could ease my pain. A gush of fluid filled my throat and I dry heaved until a torrent of blood and black fluid flowed from my mouth. Panic surged as my lungs begged for air. Another claw tore through my chest and I collapsed to my hands and knees. A second wave came up my throat, and this time there was no blood, only the thick black fluid that spilled onto the ground.

My mouth burned as the liquid dripped from my lips. I could feel the skin around my mouth blistering as though I'd just ejected acid. My back arched as another set of claws ripped through my insides, this time tearing through my body and splitting the skin. I tried to get to my feet as black spots dotted my vision. I was going to pass out. I tried to fight it, but it was too strong. Darkness clutched me and pulled me down, but just as everything faded around me, the power stopped.

My chest wheezed as I sucked in waves of oxygen. Dust from the floor flooded into my lungs, and I coughed and choked, gasping for clean air. I rolled onto my back and coughed out grains of dirt and sand. Tears filled my eyes as the grains scratched my throat, but it only forced me into another fit of coughing.

Salvatore stood above me, his hand out and power coursing through his veins. I could see the anger in his eyes, but he wasn't moving. He was frozen in time, magic stuck roaring inside him unable to be released.

The tapping of shoes against the stone floor resonated off the walls around me. I rolled onto my side to find shiny black shoes with silver buckles.

I gasped for air, the burning in my throat searing with agony, as though I'd just torn open a battery and poured it into my mouth. My eyes followed the boots upwards, past dark pants, a waist length leather coat, and a tight white t-shirt. I looked into the black eyes of Drake Sellowind, the other half of the Dark Brothers, and all the air I'd just inhaled escaped me in a single gasp.

"You do find yourself in the strangest predicaments, don't you? Challenging the power of Ithreal's soul piece, really? I thought even you'd be smarter than that." His voice was higher than Darius', but the tone was cool and even. He sounded both surprised and amused. "Get up."

I struggled to push myself up and the motion forced me to cough up thick, bloody mucus, lined with streams of black. I grimaced and came to my knees, using them to push myself the rest of the way. They wobbled and I fell back against the wall for support. Blood ran in a steady flow down my body. My entire torso was covered in gashes that seared with pain.

"You've gone to so much trouble for a single blade. You wouldn't be trying to destroy the ring, now would you? Because that would be foolish."

I didn't respond. I was using all my energy to keep myself from collapsing.

Drake watched me and a smile crossed his lips. "Salvatore and that vampire did a number on you. Let's see what we can do about that." He extended his hand and I wanted to move. I wanted to fight back, but I didn't have the energy. I flinched as his magic poured over me, and in moments, my pain was gone. The black dots that threatened to swallow me disappeared, and the wounds on my body vanished. I didn't feel the cuts close or the pain fade, it was just...gone.

"Why are you doing this?"

Drake laughed. "Haven't you figured it out yet? I need you alive, Chase. You're part of this now; you made sure of that. I can't have you dying and ruining my plan."

"What do I have to do with you raising Ithreal?"

Drake's eyes watched me. He stared at me a moment before shaking his head. "All in good time, child."

I pushed off the wall and looked around the cave. "Where are Riley and Darius?"

"They are preoccupied."

"First you guys attack me, now you're saving me? What is it that you want?"

"The same thing we've wanted this entire time. The ring."

"Darius told me that unless I gave it to you, you couldn't take it. You know I won't give it up, so if you can't kill me, you don't get it," I said, and I tried to sound confident, but I was exhausted. My wounds had been healed, but my energy hadn't been restored. I'd overused my elements again.

"I'm very different from my brother. Darius lacks certain, finesse, if you will. Had he come, he would have made you watch as he killed all your friends. Then he'd throw you back to your dimension with a force you could not begin to fathom."

"He sounds like Salvatore," I said.

"He should; they have the same father. As do I, I suppose."

"Isn't Ithreal the father of all the demons?"

"My, you are not as bright as I'd hoped." He sighed. "Every creature was created by a god. There are only seven gods left, but there were many who contributed to life on these worlds. The fact that you lump so many of those creatures under Ithreal's banner is...distasteful."

"I'm not exactly educated in the history of the dimensions," I said spitefully.

"You are ill informed of our past. I cannot hold that against you. Drake and I have been around for all of it, and as such, we've been privy to the...evolution of the dimensions."

"How old are you?"

Drake smiled but otherwise ignored the question. "I'm going to make you an offer, Chase. It will come only once, so think hard on your decision." He walked towards Rayna and ran a single pale hand over her cheek. "Beautiful thing, isn't she?"

"What's the deal?" I asked impatiently.

"You will give me the ring and I will take the dagger," he said plainly.

"That doesn't sound like much of a deal."

"Well, if you consider what I'm offering in return, I'd say it's quite fair." Drake's dark eyes turned back to me. "In exchange, I'll return you and each of your friends back to your dimension. Safely, I might add."

"And if I refuse?"

"Look at your friends, Chase." Drake moved in front of Marcus and looked up at his massive form. "This one projects an image of strength, but he is terrified and angry. The woman he loves is dead, and you blame him for it. Tessa Williams was the love of his life, and because you tried to be the hero, she died." He walked up to Tiki and Willy. "These two are pathetic excuses for Underworlders. Filthy half-breeds at best, but they are willing to die for you. And they probably will. A most admirable loyalty." Drake took a few more steps and stopped in front of Rayna. "And this one. She's the key that started it all. She loves you unconditionally. That emotion is your kind's downfall. It has become your greatest weakness." Drake ran another finger over her face. "But how do you feel?" he asked. "That is the question." Drake turned back and walked towards me. "Do you care so little for your friends? For Rayna? Can you truly refuse me and leave their fate in Salvatore's hands? That's what will happen to them. I'll release them to Salvatore and he can do what he wishes to them. Give them to the Visceratti, make them vampires, whatever he chooses. You can stop all their pain before it starts, Chase. You have the power to grant them that."

I looked over at my friends. They were frozen in their struggle against the Visceratti's magic. Guilt tugged at me as I met each of their faces. I wasn't losing anyone else.

"Okay," I said.

"It is agreed, then?" Drake extended a single white hand.

"How do I know you'll hold up your end of the deal?"

"I could tell you I'm a man of honor and although I may seem brutal, I follow certain...codes of ethics, but you wouldn't believe that. I could give you my word, but that too, means very little to you. To be honest, Chase, you don't know I'll hold up my end, but when you consider the alternative, I think you'll see I'm doing you a small courtesy in exchange for your cooperation."

I stared at him for a long moment before grabbing his hand and giving it a firm shake. "You have a deal."

Drake released my hand and turned his up, opening his palm.

I stared into the pale, smooth flesh, turning the ring on my finger in hesitation.

"Come now, child," he said.

I slid the ring off and dropped it in his palm.

"Thank you for making this easy."

He reached towards the dagger and his magic tore it from the golden light. The double-edged blade floated towards him until his fingers wrapped around the leather grip.

"Now my friends," I said.

Drake's dark gaze met mine and he smiled. "You are an impatient one," he said. "I always keep my word, Chase. Always." He snapped his fingers and the cave vanished.

Darkness swallowed me and I spun out of control. The force of teleporting from one world to the next crushed my body. Bright colors swirled around me and I was forced to close my eyes. Searing pain covered me as the portal squeezed the air from my lungs. I tried to scream, but there was no air to let it out. The swirling colors faded as the portal opened beneath me, growing wider until the condo appeared below. I moved at an incredible speed as the wood floor of the library came into view, and there wasn't time to brace myself.

Chapter 30

The collision winded me and I coughed, rolling over and trying to catch my breath. The air tasted sweet as I pulled it into my lungs, and my body relaxed against the floor. The black portal above me swirled and spit out body after body. Once everyone had hit the floor, the black mass wavered and consumed itself. Moans and groans came from everyone as they struggled to their feet.

"Chase!" Rayna ran towards me. She leaned down and wrapped her arms around me before I could stand, and it felt amazing. Everyone had made it home in one piece. This time.

"Brilliant plan. You nearly got us all killed." Vincent scowled and came to his feet. "And you were going to kill *me* for that dagger!" He stormed towards me, but Marcus' massive form stepped in front of him.

"Don't test me, hunter." Vincent's gaze crucified Marcus.

"I think we've had enough fighting for one day."

Vincent and Marcus locked eyes for a moment before Vincent backed away. "You better watch yourself, Mr. Williams. The Dark Brothers are going to be the least of your worries now." Vincent turned, and in a blur, vanished from the room. The condo door slammed shut and the walls rattled from the impact.

Everyone gathered in front of me looking tattered and defeated.

"I'm sorry...I lost the ring," I said, dropping my eyes to the floor. "I didn't know what else to do."

"Don't worry about it," Willy said.

"We tried, Chase Williams. That is what is important," Tiki added.

I looked up to Marcus and still he held a neutral expression. "We never should've gone there. We're lucky nobody got killed."

"I know."

A loud beeping burst through the library and Willy looked to the black box vibrating the table. "Uh-oh. I need to go."

I nodded and extended a hand to Willy. "Thanks for your help. You did really great."

He smiled and a new wave of confidence beamed from his eyes. "Glad to be part of the team." He gave my hand a shake and I realized I couldn't remember the last time I'd heard him stutter.

Willy said his goodbyes to everyone and left. Tiki followed after him and went to his room, leaving just the three of us in the library.

"Chase—"

"Please don't, Marcus. I don't need a lecture right now."

"Rayna, can you give us a minute?"

"Sure." She looked at me and slipped out of the library.

"I don't want to lecture you, but we never should've been there. You should have listened to Tiki and me."

I wanted to argue. To defend my decision, but I knew he was right.

"But I understand why you did it," Marcus added.

I looked up and met his gaze. "You do?"

"You've got a great deal on your shoulders, son. It wasn't long ago you lost the person most dear to you. Your father's trying to force an apocalypse, and you're fighting an uphill battle against me and everyone else to stop it. The only person that's supported you entirely is Rayna, a girl whom you've only known a few months."

"You're not making me feel better."

Marcus smiled. "What I'm saying is, I'm proud of you. When everything and everyone is against you, you stay strong and push forward until you succeed."

"Is this what you call success? I'm covered in blood and scars, I nearly got everyone killed, and I lost the only advantage we had."

"We are our own harshest critics, but there's more to it than what you see. You stood by Rayna while she relived a nightmare.

And you went after her, alone, into a foreign world to save her. She's alive because of you."

I shook my head and turned away. Marcus was trying to point out the silver lining, but there wasn't one. Not right now.

"You're the one who convinced Rayna to go see Chief and learn to shift, saving her life again. Today you made a choice to destroy the ring, and when everyone told you it was too dangerous, you accepted that. You were willing to go alone."

"But everyone came with me and we all nearly died."

"But we didn't. You did whatever you had to in order to keep everyone safe," Marcus said. "I thought I was the one leading this crew and making the decisions, but today I learned that wasn't the case. I found myself falling in line behind *you*. Following *you* into another world, not because I had to, or because I felt obligated, but because even if I don't agree with your methods, I believe in you, just like they do."

I was at a loss for words. I nearly got everyone killed and he was proud of me? I knew I wanted to thank him, but part of me couldn't believe I was hearing this.

"You could've completed the trial in Theral and had the dagger. There's a chance you might've even destroyed the ring before Drake arrived. All you had to do was sacrifice one person and this could've all been over."

"I would never hurt any of you!"

"I know. For you, it wasn't even a decision. Had anyone else been in your shoes—myself included—the outcome might've been very different." Marcus stepped forward and extended his large midnight hand. "I'm proud of you, Chase, and I promise from this point forward, no more secrets. I want you to know that no matter what, I stand behind you. You can take my word on that."

A warm feeling filled me in that moment. I looked to Marcus not as a boy, or some kind of mentor, but as an equal. I took his hand in mine. "That means a lot to me. Thank you. And I'm sorry about earlier...I didn't mean the things I said. I know you had a promise to keep."

"I appreciate your understanding," Marcus said. "Had I not had a promise to uphold, I would never have let things happen like they did. But your mother was very..." Marcus trailed off.

"Important to you," I whispered. "I know."

Marcus nodded.

"What about the Circle? You never told us what happened at the meeting."

"I'm not sure we've accomplished anything yet. Riddley Peterson has disappeared. Nobody has seen him since shortly after our meeting there. The elders suspect he is working with Riley, but I'm not convinced. As it stands right now, I'm still not sure who we can trust, but if I'm certain about anything, it's that the council is feeling vulnerable right now."

"Let them. They deserve it. I'm still not working with them," I snapped.

"I know..."

I sighed. "Sorry. It's just not easy for me to put my trust in them."

"I understand, and I'm not asking you to. Right now we don't know who we can trust. For right now, why don't we try and get some rest? We've got a lot of work ahead of us. Starting with the condo."

"Yeah...sorry about that, too."

Marcus smiled. "Goodnight, son," he said, his massive form moving for the stairwell.

"Night," I said.

I looked at the mess around me and guilt tugged at my insides. Books littered the floor, the table and desk had been turned upside down, and black soot still covered the walls. Marcus was right; we had a lot of work to do.

My body ached as I came down the stairs. I was exhausted, but I needed a hot shower. We could deal with our next move in the morning. I took the last few steps and tried to quietly walk past everyone's room, but as I passed Rayna's, her door creaked open.

"Sorry," I said, wincing as my feet made the floorboards screech.

Rayna had washed the blood and dirt from her face and tied her hair back in a ponytail. She stepped out of her room and came towards me, but before I could say anything, her hands slid around my neck and she pulled me down against her lips.

Adrenaline surged through my body, forcing my heart to pound in my chest. I closed my eyes as our lips pressed together and slid my hands around her waist, pulling her against me. Her touch was soft and I could feel her magic simmering on the surface. It vibrated against me and brought my elements to life. All of them rose to the surface at once and intertwined with hers. Together, they danced as one, coursing from one body to the next.

Rayna's lips were soft, and as they parted, they filled me with warmth I'd never experienced. When she pulled away, I opened my eyes. Beautiful green cat eyes stared up at me, and I couldn't control the smile that came over my face.

"What was that for?"

"Just because," she whispered. Rayna smiled and walked away, disappearing into her room. I saw the last of her smile as she closed the door and I was left standing alone in the dark.

On second thought, I was going to need a cold shower.

Chapter 31

Voices moved through the floorboards and I opened my eyes. I lay in bed and listened as the conversation seemed to get heated. I recognized the first voice as Marcus, but the other two, although familiar, I couldn't place.

I made my way downstairs before I recognized the other voices as Chief, and one of his werecats, Jesse. They were sitting in the living room, which was still destroyed. The talking stopped as I entered the room and they all turned to me.

"Chase is the one who made the arrangement," Marcus said. "He is the one you need to speak with."

"What's going on?" I asked.

"Sorry to barge in on you. Marcus told us you just got back." Chief stood from the leather couch.

"What is it?" I asked.

"The tension between the Shadowpack and the Hollowlights is growing. In the past week, they've attacked twice, interrogating my cats for information about Rayna and the whereabouts of their new wolf."

"Willy?"

Chief nodded.

"It seems," Marcus said. "What was a day in Theral, was nearly two weeks here."

Both my eyebrows rose. "I'm not sure why that surprises me, but it does." I sighed. "Willy went back to the wolves yesterday; I'm sure he'll clear everything up."

"Chase, the werecats were not the only Underworlders Riley approached. Since we refused his offer, naturally, he's moved on to the wolves."

"Are you backing out of our agreement?"

"Quite the opposite, actually."

"Some of us are still concerned where your loyalties lie." Jesse interrupted.

"Jesse," Chief warned.

"We've been through this already," I said.

"Yeah, but that was before we learned you had friends in the pack." Jesse spat the words at me.

"Quiet yourself." Chief eyed Jesse and he sat back down. "If the wolves accept your father's offer, he'll force the war to start again. I don't want to lose any of my family to another war, but we made a pact and we intend to stand by it. We just want to be sure that if push comes to shove, you'll be fighting with *us*."

I stayed silent. The thought of having to go against Willy made me sick to my stomach.

"Well?" Jesse asked.

"I'm with you," I said. I didn't have a solution, but if the Shadowpack and Hollowlights went to war, I'd find a way to keep Willy safe.

"Really? Because if the wolves go to war with us, your friend will fight. He'll fight, or they'll kill him. You're going to choose us over him?"

"I said I'm with you, so I'm with you." I let Jesse feel the heat of my gaze.

"Chase?" Rayna came down the stairs, her hair ruffled from sleep.

"Forgive him," Chief said. "The Underworld is growing restless. With Riley and the Dark Brothers throwing their weight around, there's no telling who may be on his side. We aren't the only breed to decline their offer and it won't be long before an example is made out of someone."

"What's going on?" Rayna asked.

"I'll explain later. Chief and his pet were just leaving," I said.

Jesse let a growl slip through his lips and Chief silenced him. "We don't want to intrude, so we'll be on our way. Thank you for your time. I'm sorry if we imposed." Chief grabbed Jesse by the arm and pushed him down the hall and out the door.

"What was that about?" Rayna asked.

I shook my head. "Marcus can explain. I'm suddenly exhausted again."

"Chase, wait," Marcus said. "You made a pact with the werecats and you need to understand how serious that is."

"You did what?" Rayna stammered.

"Yes, I did. And I'd do it again. We need all the help we can get to stop Riley. The werecats are on board, which means they'll be there for us when we need it."

"But are you prepared to be there for them?" Marcus asked.

"I can't stop Riley without more people on my side. I had a decision to make, and I made it," I said. "If the cats and dogs want to fight, we'll cross that bridge when we get there."

****

I tossed and turned, fighting to get back to sleep. The sun shone through the window and I couldn't stop thinking about Riley and the Brothers. I felt lucky to be alive and even luckier to have everyone back with me, but we'd lost the only advantage we had. It was time to find another way to stop them.

I spent the afternoon working with my arch nemesis: the library. I went through book after book. I didn't have any direction, but I was determined to find *something* that could help. When the phone rang through the condo, I waited for someone else to pick it up. I'd been living here for over two months, but I still wasn't comfortable answering the phone. On the third ring, I sighed and picked up the blinking line on Marcus' desk.

"Hello?" I asked.

"Ch–, Chase..." Willy gasped, his stutter as thick as ever.

"Willy, what's going on? Did you get everything sorted out with the pack? Chief was here earlier and said–"

"We're in trouble."

"What's wrong?"

"Riley and the Bro–, Brothers are here." Willy panted and I could practically hear him wincing through the phone. He was hurt.

"Where are you? Are you okay?"

"At the ca–, camp. Radek ref–, refused an alliance with Riley and now he's attacking." Willy coughed into the phone. "I've managed to sneak away, but you've got to come. They brought purebloods. They're killing everyone."

"Stay safe and hidden. I'm on my way." I dropped the receiver and raced down the hallway. "Come on, Tiki. We've got to go!" I yelled as I ran past his door. I jumped down the stairs from the second to the main floor in a single leap with Tiki right behind me. Rayna and Marcus were training together and they both jumped as I came through the door.

"What's going on?" Marcus asked.

I pulled Marcus' short sword off the wall and threw it to him. He caught it with ease and looked confused.

"Chief wasn't kidding when he said Riley would make an example out of someone. He's attacking the Shadowpack. Willy's in trouble. We need to go."

Rayna reacted with haste and pulled her usual weapons off the wall. Tiki strapped the sheath across his bare chest and slid two short swords into them.

"We can't possibly fight them right now. Let me call the other rogue hunters," Marcus said.

"There isn't time; the wolves are getting slaughtered now."

"And we'll be among the dead if we go," Marcus reasoned.

"But Willy's there..."

"Marcus is right," Rayna said. "I don't want anything to happen to Willy, but there aren't enough of us."

"Maybe right now there isn't, but there will be."

Chapter 32

The Jeep's tires squealed as Marcus slammed the gas pedal down. With a jerk forward, we flew from the underground garage. Sparks fell around us as the jacked up SUV bumped into the concrete overhang and out into the street. We swung into traffic, forcing other cars to slam on their brakes. The screeching of tires, the sound of horns, and angry drivers surrounded us. Marcus ignored the rules and dropped down a gear, making the engine roar to life.

"I need a phone," I said.

Marcus reached into his pocket and handed me a small black flip phone. I gripped the dashboard as he weaved in and out of traffic, rushing through yellow lights. At this rate, we were going to be arrested before we had a chance to save anyone.

We tore through downtown with Marcus taking a hard right onto 4th Street, giving us a straight shot to the freeway. Rayna called the phone number out to me and the cell phone beeped as I pressed each button. I had to redial twice before I got it right, the sweat and trembling of my hands getting in the way. The phone rang and I told it to hurry, as if that could help. When the fourth rang came, I cursed into the phone, praying for someone to pick up.

"Hello?" A woman answered.

"I need to speak with Chief, right away."

"Chase? It's Karissa, how have you been?" I could hear the smile in her voice.

"I don't have time for this. I need Chief," I demanded.

"What's the matter?"

"Just put him on the damn phone!" I yelled.

"Whoa! Relax, I'll have to find him."

The phone echoed loud in my ear as she set it down. I heard her talking to other people in the background and I silently urged her to hurry.

Marcus pulled the Jeep off the main street and hit the off ramp at an incredible speed. The Jeep left the ground briefly and as it hit the road again. I dropped the phone and it snapped shut.

"Dammit!"

I picked it up and dialed again. The phone rang busy.

"What is it?" Rayna asked.

I dialed again. Still busy.

My knuckles turned white as I gripped the dash and I felt the phone might shatter in my grip. I dialed again. The line was silent for a long moment. I looked down at the screen and it still showed *calling*.

"Come on," I demanded.

Relief washed over me as the phone rang. Static crackled from the other end as it got picked up, and I was relieved to hear Chief's voice.

"Hello?" He sounded confused.

"Chief!" I said.

"Chase, I didn't think I'd hear from—"

"Just listen. I need you to get everyone together. The Shadowpack is under attack by Riley, the Brothers, and a whole bunch of purebloods."

"I knew it wouldn't be long before he made an example out of someone."

"Well, it's happening right now so I'm calling in this so-called alliance."

"It doesn't work that like, Chase. The wolves are sworn enemies and as much as I'd like to remedy that, we can't help them."

"You were just in my house this morning to make sure if you went to war with them, I'd still fight with you. I said yes, even though one of my closest friends belongs to that pack, and now you're telling *me* no?"

"You need to understand—"

321

"Look, I swore an oath to you and you did the same to me, so I don't give a shit what you think I should understand. We're on our way to the Shadowpack's camp, so pack up your pride and get your ass there. If you don't, and I survive, this alliance is off and I'm coming for the Hollowlights next. That's a promise."

I flipped the phone shut and stared down at it.

"Chase?" Rayna asked.

I didn't answer. My pulse throbbed in my neck and my veins were on fire.

"Chase?" Rayna repeated.

I threw the phone against the window and it shattered into two pieces, cracking the glass.

"They're not coming..." Rayna's voice was empty and hollow.

"It doesn't look that way," I said. "Dammit!" I slammed my fist into the dashboard.

"We will be okay, Chase Williams," Tiki said.

"Stop with the Williams already! Chase is fine," I yelled. Uncomfortable silence filled the car and I closed my eyes, taking a long, deep breath. "Tiki, I'm sorry. It's just..."

"I know. There is no need to apologize."

The Jeep jerked off the highway and moved onto a gravel covered side lane. Dust clouded the road and the sound of rocks hitting the vehicle rang through the cab until the camp came into sight.

Smoke rolled in thick waves from the top of the forest. We were a mile away and the smell of fire already burned my nostrils. Marcus was focused on the road ahead, the look of a warrior in his eyes, but I knew he was right; we didn't have enough people.

"Marcus I..."

"What is it?" he asked.

"The Hollowlights aren't coming. I'll understand if you turn around."

Marcus was silent, his eyes not moving off the road.

"I don't want to be responsible for any one of you getting hurt," I said. "Just drop me off at the edge of the forest."

"No. We'll go together."

"I don't—"

SHIFT

"You were right. It doesn't matter what we're up against. Willy's in trouble and he's part of this family. I said I'd stand behind you and I will. No matter what."

"Me too," said Rayna.

"You know I will be there," Tiki added.

I nodded and tried for a smile. The engine roared, spewing gravel behind us as Marcus floored it for the final stretch. He dipped off of the road and into a ditch. We bounced around inside as the Jeep shook from left to right and I gripped the handle to steady myself.

"Where are you going?" I yelled over the engine. The shocks squeaked and struggled, absorbing as much as they could.

"Trust me." Marcus' voice was empty. His dark skin was motionless but I could see the anger in his eyes. He was a soldier jumping headfirst into battle. He didn't care that we were outnumbered now, or that the werecats weren't coming; he was ready.

The Jeep screamed down the path and the sun vanished beneath clouds of dark smoke. Shadows littered the ground and the forest grew up on either side of us. The SUV burst through a layer of bushes and into an opening on the other side. The grass was painted red and waves of heat washed over us from patches of hot flames.

Rows of cabins lined the far side of the field, all of them ablaze in thick, black smoke. Human and wolf bodies lay everywhere. Ash floated around us as the bodies of demons burst up into flames, and wolves jumped out of the forest, growls filling the air as they fought an army.

There were Cyclops everywhere, and they beat down waves of attacking wolves with thick wooden clubs. The hunters that worked under Riley had unleashed their elements. They pushed the wolves back with magic and let silver weapons slice through them. It sent them into an epileptic-like seizure, forcing their bodies back to their human form, covered in wounds they couldn't heal.

Half-demons that had agreed to bow to Riley fought against the shifters. Some of them were vampires who'd come out as the sun faded. Others were witches, casting spells and forcing their enemies to crumple. Gladiator demons worked through the crowds, snapping wolves' necks and tossing their bodies to the side before they could turn to ash.

Riley and the brothers stood on the top of a high cliff, overlooking the battle and commanding their army, but there was a strange man that stood with them. Long black hair flowed down his back that looked vibrant against his dark, tanned skin.

The Jeep didn't slow as it entered the clearing and Marcus put both hands on the wheel. "Hold on," he said, and the engine screamed.

The SUV jerked forward and drove straight for a pair of Cyclops. I gripped the dash and prepared for the impact. My body jerked against the seat belt as we crashed into them, and the front of the jeep folded from the force. The Jeep rocked back and forth as it plowed overtop of their bodies. Marcus shifted it into park, unclipped his belt, and we all jumped out.

I hit the ground and pulled my sword from its sheath. Marcus and I moved around the vehicle and brought our blades down on the demons he'd run over. The Cyclops screamed as the blade bit through their skin. Bright orange ash lit up their bodies as our swords sunk into the earth beneath them.

Rayna's magic exploded around us and the ground shook. Dirt exploded as rocks shot into the air and plowed through an onslaught of charging Underworlders. Bodies flew back as the rocks hammered against them and Rayna went to work. Her whip cut through the air and the silver claws tore out the throats of the fallen demons, forcing them into piles of smoking ash that the wind swirled around us.

My spine tingled as Tiki bellowed through a fanged mouth. His claws came out and for the first time, he fully unleashed his demon. His eyes went black and razor bones pushed themselves out of his body. White bones covered his forearms, shins, and fists, making each of his limbs a deadly blade. His body grew larger, his skin stretching as new muscles formed. He wasn't as large as the Cyclops or Gladiator demons, but he was a force to be reckoned with. He roared as a trio of Cyclops charged, and his body vanished. The Cyclops stopped, looking around confused, and Tiki reappeared on the air behind them, tearing them to bits with a demon's speed.

As they burst into flame, he turned to the next group, ripping apart a small gang of half-breed vampires, sending them into the air in an explosion of red and orange. Blood burst as his claws tore off a witch's head and he stalked the ground as a different creature.

Rai dove into the clearing, scooping up groups of demons and tearing them apart, letting their remains rain down over the forest.

Marcus' sword cut through the air as he battled a group of hunters. His element came to life through the blade and as he sliced the air, a ray of power blew them back. He thrust his magic into the next horde and their skin paled as he stole the air from their lungs. He walked over them as they collapsed, moving to fight alongside a small pack of wolves.

Brock and Lena worked together, slashing wolves in half with silver blades. They channeled their elements through their weapons and cast waves of flames and bursts of wind over their opponents.

I ran towards them, summoning water. It tore through me and power shone from my hands as it built between them. A large wave of water tore over the ground, growing higher with each inch that it moved. By the time it reached Brock and Lena, there was a massive tidal wave that crashed over them. They hit the earth and the water drenched the ground, receding until it vanished into the dirt.

They both choked, gagging as they cleared their lungs. Brock jumped to his feet, opened the zippo and flicked the lighter beneath his sword. The silver blade lit up in a burst of fire and he unleashed a stream of it. The green flames crackled on the air as they came towards me and I took control of his element. I sent the green flames flying back towards him like a flame thrower and the magic blew him back into the woods.

Lena ran towards me, her daggers pulled back and ready to strike. I gripped my sword and prepared for her to attack, but the sharp silver claw of Rayna's whip snapped around her neck and pulled her down. Lena's eyes lit up in surprise as her body jerked back and hit the ground. Rayna didn't bother with dragging her. She ran towards her and came down through her chest with her blade. Lena cried out and Rayna twisted the dagger. She slammed her foot against Lena's throat, shattering her esophagus and leaving her choking through whimpers of pain.

Lena coughed and struggled to her feet, but Rayna was ready, slicing her dagger across her face. Lena screamed. Her hands came up to feel the wound and anger filled her eyes. Her flawless skin was marred and blood poured from her jaw. She jumped to her feet and swung out towards Rayna.

Rayna dodged her fist and came back with a dagger, plunging the blade deep into Lena's chest. Rayna pulled Lena's blonde hair back and she whimpered against the force. Anger filled Rayna's eyes and I expected her to bring the blade across her throat, but instead she bought her knee up and smashed it into Lena's face. Lena's body went limp and fell to the ground, blood still running down her cheeks and pouring from her chest.

Green fire soared out of the woods and hit Rayna in the back, forcing her to the ground in a wave of heat. Brock stepped out of the forest and magic poured from his hands. I charged towards him, but thick gray hands picked me up with ease. The Cyclops' hands were rough, and my skin rubbed raw at his grip. He heaved me above his head and slammed me into the ground.

I hit the earth hard and rolled away just as his foot smashed down. The demon grunted and his other foot swung into my side. I felt a snap with the impact and a sharp pain moved through my torso. I tried to roll away, but huge fists were already pounding against my body. The demon's strength came in droves and hammered at my shoulders and arms, trying to break the cover I'd created. When he realized he couldn't, he picked me up again and threw me across the field.

I hit the ground, and more pain shot through my side. I could feel broken ribs poking at my skin, trying to free itself from its fleshy shell. The pain was piercing when I tried to breathe, and from where I was laying, I could see the fight was not going well.

Tiki had been pushed down to his knees, a group of vampires tearing at his body with razor talons. He did his best to protect himself, but each time he tried to teleport to safety, sharp talons ripped into his flesh.

Marcus stood against a group of witches who had stolen his blade and silenced his magic. They chanted in a circle around him, holding him to the ground. I could see the midnight skin that covered his body growing sick with illness as the spell poured over him. Sweat dripped off his face and he chanted his own counter incantation, but he wasn't strong enough. His body jerked at a painful angle and thick waves of black fluid spilled from his lips and nose.

Rayna was standing, but struggling to stay on her feet against a vampire and a Cyclops. She was doing no offensive work, but had so far managed to dodge everything they threw at her.

Rai was pinned to the ground by a group of witches. She screamed as hunters tore into her wings with silver blades, and bright red blood burst from her body, staining perfect white feathers.

I could feel the anger building inside me. The four elements stirred in my soul, begging to be released in an angry thrust, but there was something else weighing me down and this time it wasn't magic; it was defeat. We were losing.

Injured shifters covered the grassy field, which held no color but red. Ashes of werewolves were thick on the air and fires raged through the woods, leaving dark smoke to billow into the sunless sky. Riley, the Dark Brothers, and their new companion were gleaming at the top of the cliff, untouched from battle.

The bright blue eyes of my father were evil, and even at this distance, I could see his satisfaction. He looked down at his hand and the glint of the red gem on his finger made my stomach sink. He smiled, spun it on his finger, and although I couldn't hear him, I saw him laugh. He was ecstatic, watching the battle from the safety of his high peak, smiling at the death he'd created. He had made his point. You either joined him, or you died.

Footsteps approached and I moved for my dagger, but I wasn't fast enough. Brock's magic was already there. Green flames swallowed me and searing pain covered me. I could feel my skin singe as his flames snapped at my body. Panic sparked through me and my magic came to life on its own.

A wall of dirt shot up from the ground, suffocating Brock's flames. It stopped his flow of magic but Brock didn't let up. He moved closer and flames began crackling through the dirt. I pushed the magic harder, but it was my earth element and I had yet to discover its true potential. Flames broke through the shield and the heat scalded me again, causing blisters to bubble on my skin. I screamed and called my water element, but before it came forward, a white tiger with thick black stripes leapt over me.

Chief's beast pounced on Brock and the weight of the tiger crushed him to the ground. Green flames vanished, leaving me with such pain I wasn't sure I could move. Brock screamed as claws dug into his chest and Chief brought a paw across his face. Brock's head shot to the side. The unsettling sound of his neck snapping sent a shiver through my body. Chief turned to face me, bright purple eyes meeting mine before he unleashed a ferocious roar.

In response to his call, a wave of werecats burst through the forest. An army of panthers, tigers, leopards, cheetahs, lions, and lynx flew from the woods in a stampede of thunder. Chief's claws tore up the dirt as he led his pride into the battle, leaving Brock's dead body behind.

The sight of the werecats brought a surge of adrenaline through my veins. With them here, we had a fighting chance.

I finished calling my element, and water coursed through my veins and began repairing my body. The open wounds closed, new skin folded and knitted itself over the raw burns, and I heard a *click* in my chest, making the pain disappear and allowing me to breath with ease.

More beasts jumped from the forest and I pulled both daggers in fear. Bears, foxes, coyotes, and unnaturally large birds broke through from the other side of the field. Eagles soared and cried above us with massive and prehistoric size. Falcons the size of small cars tore through the air, and my nerves faded as their beaks tore into unsuspecting demons.

Riley's satisfied smile faded, and for the first time, doubt covered his face. The Dark Brothers remained emotionless, but slowly they stepped back from the hill and vanished into the woods. Riley yelled in anger, storming into the thick forest behind them. The newcomer stayed on the edge of the cliff, his dark eyes locking with mine before he followed in line behind them.

I moved after them with unparalleled speed. I wasn't letting them get away. If I couldn't kill them, I could at least try and get the ring back.

I weaved through cats and ducked under eagles, moving as fast as ever. There was no way I could climb the face of the rocky cliff and catch up to them in time, but as I neared it, power beat through me and something told me what to do.

I jumped near the base and let the air element explode beneath me. My body soared upward at a speed I never thought I'd be able to travel. Air whipped around me and I came down, planting my feet onto the edge of the grassy cliff top.

I broke into a run and leapt through the brush. I moved with no direction, and I'd run nearly two miles when I felt the magic and realized I was chasing shadows. The power of a recently opened portal was thick on the air. I was too late.

I kicked at the dirt and rocks around me, and screams echoed from the battle I'd left. I turned around, moving back towards the fight, but I'd only taken a few steps when the voice sounded. I recognized it, but before now I'd never had a face to go with it. The strange man who had stood with my father was watching me, amusement dancing in his eyes.

"So you're the infamous Chase Williams," he said, his voice gruff and gravelly.

A set of three claw marks scarred his face, from one corner to the other. His skin was so tanned it looked olive and long black hair hung down to his waist. Thick, muscular arms were covered and black eyes stared out under furry, unkempt eyebrows.

"And you are?"

The man smiled and stepped towards me, extending his hand. "I'm a good friend of your dad's. The name's Arian."

I stepped back and reached for my daggers.

"So, you've heard of me," he chuckled. "That's good. Then you know what I'm capable of."

"I know you're a disloyal predator whose own pride celebrated your dethroning."

The smile faded from his face and he took another step towards me. "Now, you watch how you speak to your future master. I'm the one granting you this gift."

"Master?" I laughed. "What gift could you possibly give me?"

"Your father has decided since you like demons so much, you might as well be one. I'm going to be the one to give you that gift."

I stepped back and didn't take my eyes off of him as he circled me.

"It didn't have to come to this. If you would have cooperated, you could have avoided this fate."

"And what makes you think making me a shifter is going to change that?"

"You won't become just any shifter. You'll become like me. You see, I'm not your everyday animal. Unlike those other half-breeds, I'm immortal now. Once I bite you, you'll be compelled by my beast. Your loyalty will be forever mine."

"Is that why your pack was so happy to be rid of you?"

His expression turned serious and he muffled a growl. "They were weak. They knew me as only a werecat. Your father has given me a gift that brings a whole new meaning to the race of shifters. Soon, they'll all bow to us."

I laughed. "Us? If you think for a second that Riley will share any power with you, you're delusional." I pulled my water element to the surface and channeled it into my blades.

Arian laughed. "He already has. Allow me to show you." His beast rose to the surface in a collage of strange power, and his shift was seamless. Bones cracked and moved without the hint of blood or fluid. Dark fur pushed itself out of his skin, and his entire form changed shape at once. In seconds, the man who stood in front of me became not just a cat, but a hybrid. His legs had become agile like a cheetah, his body thick like a tiger, and his head was massive like a lion's. He gave a quiet growl and circled me, his thick paws crushing the forest beneath his feet. Bright red eyes stalked around me and I didn't wait for him to attack.

I sliced my blade through the air, creating a wave of power. It turned to ice and he tried to leap out of its path, but the range was too much. Ice cut through his body and threw him back in a blast of white light.

Arian rolled and came up on his feet, shaking the leaves and dirt off his body. I stepped back, giving myself more room to work, but then something unexpected happened. Power moved on the air and his body shifted again. Thick paws vanished and his body hit the ground with a thud. Fur sucked itself into his body, and a clear, slimy film covered him. His head snapped left and then right, his furry mane and sharp teeth disappearing as the diamond shaped head of a cobra formed. Two long fangs hung from his mouth and the color of his skin changed to a dark green, blending in with the forest floor.

"Which animal sssshall I make you to be?" he hissed, slithering towards me.

I threw my power towards him again, but he ducked low, sliding along the earth.

"Not thisss time."

His body was massive, with thick scales pulling him along the ground. He coiled himself around the trunk of a tree, and with demonic speed, he slithered to the top, disappearing among the canopy of green leaves.

I squinted, scanning the treetops for his huge form, but somehow he remained hidden. I turned at the rustling of leaves and the snake's tail snapped above me. It smashed against my face and knocked me to the ground. I moved with the momentum and came to my feet, straining to hear another sound. I pushed out with my earth element and the forest came to life. I felt the trees, their branches stretching up into the sky, and I could hear blood curdling screams from the battle below, but there was no sign of Arian.

The flutter of wings shuddered above me and I jumped back, waiting for Arian to strike, but there was only silence. I moved towards the edge of the forest when the snake lunged from the undergrowth, his massive body twisting around me.

"Ssssurprisssse," he hissed, and his muscles contracted, crushing my body.

He wrapped himself around me from my ankles to my shoulders, leaving only my head exposed. He brought his diamond shaped head before me and bright red snake eyes stared into mine. His pink tongue slipped between long fangs and flickered across my face. His body coiled around and tightened its grasp, squeezing the air from my lungs.

I fought the lack of oxygen and called the hottest fire I could manage, letting the magic tear itself out of me in a wave of authority. Arian hissed, pulling his head back and aiming to strike. His tongue flickered out again and he snapped his head towards me, but I pushed the magic harder in an adrenaline-charged panic.

Fire blasted around me and the air came to life, an unseen force lashing out, and it connected with his face. His head snapped back and his fanged mouth smashed into a tree. I pressed the magic against him, pinning him against the bark as his body released its hold on me.

Arian hissed as I broke through the last of his grip and I squeezed the daggers in my hands. My air element crushed his body and flakes of bark fell to the ground as he struggled against it. I brought my blade above my head, preparing to cut into his body, when his tail flipped off the ground and smashed itself into me. I flailed through the air and fell into a thorn covered bush. Wooden spikes carved my skin and I tried to push through, but it only allowed the wooden stems to do more damage. I struggled to my feet to see the last of Arian slithering into the brush. I stalked towards him, waiting for him to strike.

"Now isss not your time. We will meet again sssoon." Arian slid from the bushes and shifted until a red and white wolf stood in front of me. He growled and Arian's red eyes stared into mine. His lips curled back into a fierce snarl before he broke into a run. The creature weaved around trees, racing away from me before he vanished deep into the forest.

My pulse pounded and I didn't lighten the grip on my daggers. Tiny cuts burned along my body as I stared at the trees, waiting for him to lunge back out, but he never came.

A tingle moved through me and the smell of something sweet moved on the air. More screams cut through the air and I sprinted toward the cliff, pushing myself faster than I knew I should be able to go. I jumped out of the woods and didn't stop for the drop in front of me. I pulled the air element around me and leapt off the edge.

The wind cut past me, and as I hit the ground feet first, the earth exploded in a circle around me. Dirt flew into the air and before I could gain my footing, a vampire came forward with long talons. The claws tore into my arm and I blocked his next attack. I stepped into him and grabbed his throat. I lifted his body with incredible strength and slammed him into the ground. I pushed magic into him and his body exploded in a strange burst of flame.

I turned, waiting for the next attacker, but the fighting had stopped. There were cries of injured warriors, and fire crackled over the forest, but the battle was over. The werecats roared, the wolves howled, and the other animals screeched in victory. The clearing was full of bodies, but there was nothing but us and the shifters standing now.

Blue Cyclops' blood hung on the green plants and over the red field. Black and white ash rained from the sky, and any of Riley's Underworlders that hadn't been killed had retreated.

Marcus, Tiki, and Rayna were bloodied but alive, and they each looked proud as they walked towards me. Rayna ran ahead of the others and jumped into my arms. She pulled back and I could see the blood and cuts that covered her skin. She tilted her head and pushed her lips against mine and a new kind of adrenaline filled me. Her magic vibrated in a wave of relief and ecstasy. Our lips parted and closed in a long embrace, our tongues meeting softly for only a moment.

She pulled away at the sound of footsteps and Marcus cleared his throat. His neutral expression was gone, surprise covered his face, and both his eyebrows rose. "I think you two have some serious explaining to do."

Rayna gave a sheepish grin, and before I could respond, Chief came up beside us. His white tiger was gone and he stood in a pair of torn pants that covered only the necessities. His brown gaze stared into mine and he, too, was covered in blood, but the wounds you'd expect were nowhere to be seen.

"Thank you," I said.

Chief nodded. "I'm sorry we weren't here sooner. It took time to gather everyone."

Gagging and coughing came from behind us and we all turned to see the naked body of Radek Lawson lying on the ground. A large gash bled heavily from his shoulder, all the way across his body. He tried to turn on his side as blood ran from his mouth, but he winced and choked again.

I dropped beside him and carefully turned his body towards me. He screamed in pain, but it forced the blood out of his mouth and gave him air to breathe.

"I've...killed them. My own arrogance has...destroyed this pack." He coughed again.

"Don't you dare think that. Riley will not win this," I said. "We'll find a way to stop him."

Radek tried to laugh but it caused him to cough. "You can't stop him. He's a god and he has gods on either side of him."

"Let me help you," I said, pulling my magic to the surface.

"No. I don't want your filthy magic inside me." He tried to push me away, but he was too weak.

I brushed his arm to the side and continued. I pulled it up and brought a calm wave of healing power around us. I pushed it into Radek, placing both hands over his marred body and filling him with power. The element swirled around him, pulsating from my hands and into his body. His muscles relaxed and his eyes rolled back in his head. The bleeding slowed and his skin began repairing itself. The wounds took more time than usual to close, but once they had, all that remained were thin white scars that looked like any other wound he'd healed over the years. He fell onto his back, breathing heavily, and light blue eyes stared up at me, looking haunted and angry.

"I said no!" He pushed himself to his feet and released a growl.

"If Chase hadn't healed you, you could've died," Rayna said.

"Stay out of this you filthy cat. Arian will never get the best of me!"

"Arian?" Chief said.

"That's right. The big guy's back and it just so happens, he's fighting with gods."

"We will find a way to stop them," Marcus said.

"You can't stop them. You think your magic can save you? You can't compete with a god," Radek said.

The uninjured wolves began gathering behind Radek and none of them looked pleased.

"We just saved your pack from extermination. I think a *thank you* would be fine," I said.

"Our pack doesn't need the likes of you anywhere near us." Radek spat the words at me.

"You just said yourself your arrogance was to blame. How can you say you don't need our help?" Rayna asked.

"That's right, my arrogance of thinking we could fight them. I won't make that mistake again."

"You're going to join with him?"

"You're damn right I am. If I'm going to war, I want to make sure I'm on the winning side."

I shook my head. "You don't deserve to lead this pack. You're a disgrace."

Radek stepped forward and his eyes shifted as he released his beast. His power pushed on the air in a suffocating force and everyone drew their weapons.

"Enough!" Chief yelled, and it caused even Radek to flinch. "Your war was with Arian, not us, and now you want to align yourself with him? If we put the past behind us and join together, we can stop him."

"I won't endanger my people again. If it keeps me and my people safe, it doesn't matter. And as far as I'm concerned, your people and mine will forever be at war."

"Then so be it, but for now, we have a common enemy who has more power and resources at his disposal than any of us on our own. Helping him destroy the Underworld isn't the answer. Your concern shouldn't be the history between your pack and my pride, but our future as a race. We, as shifters, need to unite against this enemy."

Radek's wolf eyes stared out at Chief and a low rumble vibrated through his lips.

"He's right." Willy's voice came. He limped out of the woods using a stick as a crutch, covered in cuts and bruises. His one shoulder had been dislocated and his leg was broken, the white of his bone sticking out of the flesh. He limped with the stick under his good arm, keeping his broken leg from touching the ground.

"Get in line," Radek commanded.

"No."

"I said, get in line." Radek grabbed Willy by the scruff of his neck and pulled him towards him. Willy cried out in pain as he dropped the stick and hobbled on one foot.

Fire tore through my veins and I stepped forward.

"No, Chase," Willy said. He fought through the pain and looked Radek in the eye. "Ri–, Riley's going to kill us all, and if I'm going to die, it'll be fighting for my freedom, not because you're too cowardly to."

"How dare you disrespect me!" Radek threw Willy to the ground.

Willy cried out and I stepped forward again, but he put his hand up to stop me. Willy grimaced and a tear rolled down his face as he pushed himself up on one elbow. He took in a deep breath and met Radek's gaze. "You can call it disrespect, but I'll die before I bow down to that son of a bitch!" Willy spat the words at him and although glossy with pain, his brown eyes were strong, steady, and unmoving.

Radek stepped forward and the sounds of bones crunching came. He raised a thick, clawed hand and Willy tried to shield his face. The claws cut through the air in an angry strike, and the smack of a hand on skin stopped Radek's hand inches from Willy's face.

Radek glared at the hand and Jax stood strong and confident, holding him back.

"Release me," Radek commanded, but Jax didn't react. "That's an order."

"You will not harm him again." Jax's deep voice was quiet and serious.

"You've been a good soldier. You've earned your place and moved up the ranks. Don't mess that up now. Stand down."

"I said no more."

Radek sighed and turned to Jax. "Are you challenging me?"

"If that's what it takes. I won't let you destroy this pack, and I won't fight for that disgrace. He has no honor."

Radek growled and pushed his forehead against Jax's, grabbing either side of his face with now human hands. His bright blue wolf eyes broke through and Jax returned the action, his brown eyes fading and dark red wolf taking over.

"I *will* kill you," Radek said as a snout pushed from his face.

Jax pushed Radek back and his long fangs dropped into view. "Maybe, but I will not stand by and watch you hurt this pack."

Radek unleashed his beast and shifted into a solid black wolf. His fur was long and slick, hanging off a massive body that stood nearly six feet high.

Jax changed with ease and everyone stepped back as power filled the air. A circle formed around the pair, and a few shifters crept in to drag Willy away from the duel.

Radek's eyes gleamed as he bared his fangs and shook his black fur coat. Jax's gray and white fur was thick and his eyes were blood red, looking demonic against his pale coat. He snarled and Radek lunged in a leap of strength and power. Jax met him in the air and they snapped, clawed, and bit at one another. Blood spilled from both of their bodies and they backed away, circling each other.

Radek attacked again, pinning him to the ground. Jax yelped as white and gray fur flew into the air and Radek pulled his teeth from his neck. Fur hung from his jaws and both paws straddled either side of him. Jax lay on his back, bare spots on his neck showing open wounds against hairless gray skin. He whimpered on the ground, bleeding from his neck in a steady stream. Radek lifted his head and howled into the air, and Jax used the opportunity to get away. He squirmed beneath him until he'd gained enough traction to free himself.

Radek snapped at the air and chased after him, colliding into Jax as he skidded on the dirt. His jaws nipped at his ankles and Jax's body arched and turned, catching Radek off guard. Wide, angry jaws opened and wrapped around Radek's throat. He yelped, but Jax didn't let up. He closed his vicious fangs around him and tore his head back. Black fur and skin ripped off his chest and Jax shook his head, opening his jaws and throwing it to the ground. His dark red eyes stared at Radek, awaiting his reaction.

Radek lashed out, but Jax was ready. He knew Radek wouldn't submit. Not ever. Jax snapped at the open wound, grabbing a mouthful of flesh and pulling it away, tearing the black wolf open. Blood spilled from the wound, and with it came a burst of clear fluid. Jax pounced back as power filled the air and both wolves shifted into human form.

"This is no longer your pack," Jax said. He was covered in blood and panting for air. The large gash in his throat began to close, but blood still ran down his body.

Radek's neck and chest were full of bite marks. Blood ran over his body, but still he didn't stop. He made a final attempt and leapt forward, but Jax dodged and grabbed both his arms, pulling them back behind him.

"Do you concede?" Jax offered.

Radek fought against his grip and Jax pushed his arms together until both shoulders popped and snapped out of place. Radek growled in pain and crumpled to the ground, his skin covered in blood and dirt. He stared at Jax with hatred and jerked his arms until they both snapped back into place. The sound made me shudder and Radek pushed himself up.

"This will never be your pack. They'll never follow you." He spit blood at Jax's feet.

Silence filled the air before one shifter finally stepped forward. "I will," he said.

"So will I," said another voice.

"And me," said a third, and soon they were all moving to stand behind Jax.

Radek watched his pack changing sides and he growled, charging towards them. Jax caught his head under his arm and Radek thrashed against him, slamming enraged fists into his body, but Jax didn't even flinch.

"Just know I never wanted it to come to this," he said.

"I'll kill you!" Radek screamed.

Jax's expression was calm, and with a firm twist, Radek's neck snapped and his body went limp. His body crumpled to the ground and empty blue eyes stared up into the dark sky. His tanned skin began to smoke. Cracks formed over his body and bright red embers shot into the air before he was consumed by flames. Orange, yellow, and red danced over him, and as it faded, he became nothing but a pile of ash.

All the wolves lowered themselves, getting down on one knee and bowing their heads to their new leader. Jax howled and the pack joined in after him, a single tone of wolves now free from an enraged leader.

The howls faded and Jax walked towards me. "It would be my honor to fight by your side."

"And the werecats?" I asked.

Jax turned his neutral gaze to Chief and nodded. "You were right. Our war was with Arian, not you. Please accept my offer of peace."

Chief smiled and they had a firm handshake. "May our races unite and fight as one."

"We shall." He nodded. "But if you'll excuse me, as you can see, I have many injured to tend to." He turned his back and began walking towards the wolves that struggled for life throughout the clearing.

"We," I said.

"What?" Jax turned to me.

"*We* have many injured to tend to."

Jax's blank expression watched me closely before he nodded. "We."

Epilogue

I used my water element to help speed the recovery of the injured wolves. I didn't have the energy to heal them fully, but I did what I could, and Willy called Grams to help with the rest. As much as Grams acted like she disliked us, she was on our side. She knew if we wanted a chance at stopping Riley, everyone needed to bring their best. She came and fed the wounded some of her healing slop, and I was grateful, but I was happy it wasn't me who had to drink it this time.

When we returned to the condo, Rayna and I had an extremely awkward conversation with Marcus. I'm not sure what we accomplished, but it was the most uncomfortable hour of my life.

Marcus spent the next few weeks contacting hunters and anyone we thought might join us. If there was a rogue or exiled hunter around, we wanted them on our side. We needed as many people fighting with us as we could get.

Riley had put together a small army and we had defeated them, but nobody expected that to be the end. He would come back with more powerful purebloods, and our numbers wouldn't suffice. Riley was building an army, and it was time we did the same.

Rai hadn't strayed far from me since we had returned. She was badly hurt, and two of her four wings were broken. She was healing, but it was a slow process that my magic hadn't been able to help with.

I spent any time I had researching the Mark. Something was happening to me and I was tired of being surprised. Hunters didn't get more than two elements and I had four. The only one missing was lightning, and that element had been dead for centuries. If the Mark had something to do with Riley, or if it could help me in beating him, I needed to know how.

We knew the Dark Brothers were Ithreal's descendants, but we didn't know anything else about them. They were older than anything we knew and they were something greater than mere Warlocks. Nobody could understand why they were taking orders from a hunter. There were too many missing pieces to this puzzle, and the one piece we had, I lost.

I didn't have the ring, which meant I couldn't contact Serephina. Not that I thought she'd help, but it would've been worth a try. Riley wasn't an air elemental and Lena was dead, but Riddley Peterson was still missing. Whether or not he was working with Riley, I didn't know. I did know that one way or another, Riley would find a way to use the ring, and when he did, he'd know where the rest of Ithreal's soul pieces were. He already had one. Now it was a race to find the rest.

Riley already had a part of Ithreal's essence inside him, and his power was growing. I had to find a way to stop him. I needed to destroy the other soul pieces. If Ithreal was released, no book or spell in the world could help us. Even if his true form was still contained inside his hellish prison, we were no match for him. He'd overwhelmed and merged with every god he'd ever challenged, and it took the combined power of the six that remained just to trap him in his own dimension. I wasn't a god. I was just a hunter. I could search for answers and fight forever—and I would—but at the end of the day, I was left with the same question: how was I supposed to kill a god?

########

About the Author

M.R. Merrick is a Canadian writer, and author of The Protector Series. Having never travelled, he adventures to far off lands through his imagination and in between cups of coffee. As a music lover and proud breakfast enthusiast, he's usually found at the computer, between a pair of headphones and in front of a large bowl of cereal.

Connect With M.R. Merrick

Website: http://matthew-merrick.blogspot.com/

Made in the USA
Charleston, SC
27 April 2012